KT-564-942

ALAFAIR BURKE

City of Fear

AVON

AVON

A division of HarperCollins*Publishers*
77–85 Fulham Palace Road,
London W6 8JB

www.harpercollins.co.uk

This production 2011

First published in the U.S.A. by HarperCollins*Publishers*
New York, NY, 2008

Copyright © Alafair Burke 2008

Alafair Burke asserts the moral right to
be identified as the author of this work

A catalogue record for this book is
available from the British Library

ISBN 978-0-00789-969-2

Set in Minion by Palimpsest Book Production Limited,
Grangemouth, Stirlingshire

Printed and bound in Great Britain by
Clays Ltd, St Ives plc

CITY OF FEAR

A former deputy district attorney, Alafair Burke now teaches criminal law at Hofstra Law School and lives in New York City.

For further information about Alafair please go to www.alafairburke.com.

For James Parker, Emma Marie,
Jack Owen and James Lee.
From your favorite aunt.

Part I

The Best Night Ever

Chapter One

The man leaned forward on his stool to make room for a big-boned redhead who was reaching for the two glasses of Pinot Grigio she'd ordered. He asked for another Heineken while the bartender was down his way, figuring he could enjoy a second beer before anyone in the restaurant bothered to take note of him.

He was good at blending into the background in even the most generic settings, but he certainly wasn't going to stand out here, given the commotion at the other end of the bar. Four men in suits and loosened ties were throwing back limoncello shots, their second round with the group of girls that had brought the man to the restaurant in the first place. Actually, his interest was not in all three – just the tall blond one.

He was used to taking more time with his selections, but he needed to find a girl tonight. This would be his first time on a schedule, let alone a tight one. NoLIta had seemed as good a starting point as any. Lots of bars. Lots of booze. Lots of beautiful young people trying so hard to have fun that they paid little attention to someone like him.

3

He had been wandering the neighborhood for about half an hour when he'd spotted the trio crossing Prince Street, the blonde the obvious leader. The other two were nothing special: one average-looking brunette in average-looking clothes; the other, petite one slightly more interesting with her close-cropped black hair and bright yellow dress.

But it was the tall blonde who was a head-turner, and she knew it. She wore tight black pants and a low-cut red satin tank over a gravity-defying push-up bra. Topping off the ensemble was a well-placed V-shaped choker necklace – the equivalent of a vertical arrow sign hanging from her clavicle, instructing, 'Direct Gaze Here.' And her hair was perfect – long, shiny, white-blond waves.

He'd ducked into Lord Willy's on Mott and perused the dress shirts while they'd passed, then continued his pace about forty feet behind them until they'd parked themselves next to the bar at Luna. Fortunately, the girls had been kept waiting for their eight o'clock table, so he'd had plenty of time to study the blonde up close before making a final decision.

He liked what he saw. He even had a chance to speak to her briefly when she split off from her friends to go to the restroom. That had been risky on his part. But her two gal pals were so smitten with the limoncello boys that they hadn't noticed the exchange.

He felt a twinge of disappointment as the hostess notified the girls their table was ready. Then he heard a male voice. 'Stay for one more shot.' Apparently the

4

men in suits believed that plying the girls with drinks was going to get them somewhere.

Instead, the short girl in the yellow dress handed one of the men her cell phone and asked him to take a picture of the three friends. Mission accomplished, the brunettes followed the hostess to their table with barely a thank-you to their liquor-pouring benefactors. At least the blonde gave them each a hug before she trailed along.

The decibel level in the bar area fell noticeably in the wake of the girls' departure. The other patrons seemed relieved, but he took it as a signal to leave.

On Mott, he walked north toward Houston, forcing himself to adopt a leisurely pace. His car was parked only ten blocks away, and the girls would need at least an hour for dinner.

He had plenty of time.

Chapter Two

Somehow Stefanie Hyder always knew that her friendship with Chelsea Hart would lead to a night like this.

Since the day Stefanie had been introduced to her second-grade class at Fort Wayne Elementary as the new girl from Miami, the two had been inseparable. By the end of Stefanie's third week, she had earned her first-ever detention after the girls were caught reading Judy Blume's *Wifey* on the playground. As planned, the girls insisted they'd mistaken the book for the sequel to *Blubber*, but Chelsea had already earned her reputation with the teacher.

Over the course of the intervening years, Stefanie had survived her fair share of Chelsea-induced drama. Chelsea tapping at her window, well after curfew, cajoling her to sneak out for a forbidden cigarette. The R-rated games of truth or dare that Chelsea invariably initiated at middle-school parties. Rocking a sobbing Chelsea to sleep after Duncan Gere snubbed her in the ninth grade, despite the previous weekend's activities in the backseat of his father's SUV. Hitchhiking home from a frat party in Ann Arbor their junior year.

Chelsea was trouble, no question. Stefanie's mom lovingly called her the Notorious B.I.C., short for Bad Influence Chelsea. But she had a spark that made her recklessness endearing and infectious, and she was unfailingly loyal, and so over the course of the past ten years, she and Stefanie had remained fast friends.

They even chose the same college, where they were now suite mates. Stefanie's parents had warned her not to be surprised if she and Chelsea went their separate ways at Indiana University, but here they were in New York City, spring break of their freshman year, as tight as ever.

Until this final night of the trip, Chelsea had more or less kept her most impulsive ways in check. At Stefanie's insistence, they had hit the Metropolitan Museum of Art, MoMA, and the Guggenheim. Jordan, who lived down the hall from them at school, hung on to all of the admission buttons for the scrapbook she promised she'd be assembling back home. They also made a point of seeing a different neighborhood every day: Upper East Side, Upper West Side, Midtown, the Village, SoHo, even Chinatown. By the third day of their trip, they were relying on subways instead of taxis, and by the fifth, a stranger stopped them on the street for directions.

But on this night – their last in Manhattan – Stefanie sensed that Chelsea's inner wild child was determined to come out and play. It started with the slutty outfit, then continued at the dive Italian restaurant. All the attention from the guys at the bar hadn't stopped Chelsea from flirting with some other men on her way to their table, fabricating a farcical autobiography the way she always did in these situations.

If it had been up to Stefanie, they would have turned in early after dinner, happily sated with pasta and gelato, but Jordan agreed with Chelsea that their last hours in Manhattan should not be squandered. They wound their way through Little Italy into NoLIta, across SoHo, and up the West Village into the Meatpacking District. Jordan insisted they hit a club called Pulse because, according to *US Weekly*, Jared Leto had celebrated his birthday there three weeks earlier.

Thanks once again to their fake Indiana driver's licenses and Chelsea's megawatt smile, they had made it past the red velvet rope and through the club's heavy wooden double doors. Stefanie had to admit they had entered fifty thousand square feet of nightlife paradise. The DJ worked from an elevated booth surrounded by stagelike platforms. Cameras projected the dancers' images throughout the club in staccato sync with the music. The centerpiece of the club was the twenty-five-foot pink-lit runway protruding from the bar.

Even on a Sunday night, the place was filled to capacity. With Jordan leading the way, the girls nestled into a pocket of space adjacent to the dance floor. Stefanie had taken only one sip of the club's signature martini – a toxic concoction that tasted like Robitussen-infused lemonade – before she noticed Chelsea talking to a guy with blond floppy hair. Catching her eye, Chelsea pointed excitedly to the white curtains that set off a VIP lounge from the rest of the club, then disappeared through the curtains behind the blond.

Stefanie hesitated. She hated the way her friend was so open with strangers. Chelsea, despite her occasional lapses in judgment, was a good and decent person at heart, and so she automatically – and carelessly – assumed the same of others. Still, as usual, Stefanie and Jordan followed Chelsea where she wanted to go.

Stefanie began to sense what was coming around one o'clock, when she noticed both the time and Chelsea's glassy-eyed wobble. She pointed to her watch, but the gesture proved too subtle. Forty-five minutes later, she went so far as to follow Chelsea onto the catwalk to tell her it was time to go home. The only reward for her efforts was two songs' worth of swaying her hips with her hands undulating stupidly above her head.

Finally, at two-thirty, even Jordan was done. She joined Stefanie in the backward time calculations. Seven a.m. flight. At the airport by six. In a cab by five thirty. Wake-up call at five – five fifteen at the very latest – if they packed tonight and skipped showers. They'd get little better than a two-hour nap if they left right now. It was definitely time to call it a night.

Stefanie found Chelsea dancing on a banquette, her floppy-haired companion replaced by a tall, skinny guy with an angular face. He was passing Chelsea another highball glass. Chelsea grabbed Stefanie's hand and tried to coax her onto the banquette, but Stefanie matched the gentle force of the tug until Chelsea simply pulled her hand away.

'Come on, Chels,' Stefanie yelled over the music. 'We still need to pack. Let's go.'

Chelsea looked at her watch, then grimaced and shrugged. 'No point in sleeping now. Looks like we better make it an all-nighter.'

'Two against one.' Stefanie used her index finger to pull back the curtain closing off the private room so Chelsea could see Jordan slumped over her black patent leather clutch purse on an ottoman. 'You're the weak link. Time to go, babe.'

She pulled again at Chelsea's hand, and once again, Chelsea jerked away. Stefanie heard a male voice ask, 'Why do you have to be such a drag?'

She turned to take a closer look at Chelsea's most recent dance partner. He was about six feet tall, probably in his mid-twenties. His brown hair was gelled into a fauxhawk. He wore straight black pants, pointy black shoes, and a white shirt with a thin black tie. Stefanie shot him her best death stare, then returned her attention to Chelsea.

'Seriously? You're costing us precious minutes of REM sleep for Duran Duran here?'

'You mean Jake? He looks like Jake Gyllenhaal, don't you think?'

Stefanie didn't waste another second on the guy. 'We've had a good run, Chels. But really, we're leaving.'

'Go ahead,' Chelsea yelled. 'I'll be fine.'

Stefanie stole another look at Jordan, who was on the verge of sleep despite the thumping bass notes vibrating through the glossy white wood floors.

'Don't be ridiculous. We're not leaving without you.'

'I'm fine. I'll be back in time for the flight. I promise.' Chelsea downed the last of her drink, gave her a Girl

Scout's pledge sign, then brought her hand down for a mock booty slap.

Stefanie couldn't help but smile at Chelsea's goofy moves. 'Please tell me you're not leaving with New Wave Boy.'

Chelsea laughed. 'Of course not. I'll take a taxi. I just want to dance a little longer. This is like, the best night ever.'

Stefanie looked around the club and realized she had no hope of persuading Chelsea to leave with them.

'You've got cash?'

Chelsea jumped off the banquette and gave Stefanie a quick hug. 'Yes, Mom. And credit cards.'

'We can't miss our flight,' Stefanie warned.

'Obviously not. I'll come straight back, closing time at the very latest, right?'

Following Jordan out the double doors of Pulse, Stefanie tried to settle the uneasy feeling she still carried. Last call was in an hour. What was the worst that could happen?

She did not notice the blue Ford Taurus parked half a block down. Nor could she know how happy the car's driver was to see the two brunettes leave in a cab together, without their friend.

11

Chapter Three

They say New York is the city that never sleeps, but Ellie Hatcher knew it got pretty drowsy around five in the morning. So did she.

'Wake up.'

Ellie felt her sticky eyelids flutter open, then immediately fall shut, shielding her from the sliver of brightness peeking into her bedroom through the unwelcome crack in the door. The crack widened into a flood of white light, and she pulled her comforter over her head.

'Unngh,' she groaned under the safety of the navy-blue down.

She felt something hit her right hip, then heard her brother's voice. 'Get up, El.'

Jess sounded annoyingly chipper, so Ellie did what any sane person would do in the face of such early-morning cheer. She ignored him.

Another quick thump, this time dangerously close to her head.

Ellie threw the comforter aside, tossing the source of the two thumps – a pair of Saucony running shoes

– to the parquet floor. 'Go away,' she muttered, burrowing back into the covers.

'This is your own fault,' Jess said, tugging at the socked foot she'd managed to leave unprotected. 'I believe you threatened to charge me rent if I didn't wake you up today. This was *your* pact: skip no more than twice a week, and never two days in a row. Sound familiar? You slept in yesterday.'

The worst part of having your own words thrown back at you, Ellie decided, was that you couldn't argue with them.

They ran in silence for the first two and a half miles.

They had struck this deal three weeks earlier. For Ellie, the 5:00 a.m. runs were the start of an early morning; for Jess, the end of a late night at work. And for both, the exercise was a means of counteracting the cigarettes and alcohol for which they seemed to reach so frequently these days. And because Ellie was best at sticking to rituals that were clearly defined, there were rules: they could skip up to twice a week, but never twice in a row.

Jess had come to learn another, less explicit rule: these runs were not a time to discuss her recent trip back to their hometown of Wichita, which they both knew – but never acknowledged – was the true reason Ellie needed this solitary routine to mark each new day.

This particular morning, however, they were not the only ones in East River Park.

'So what do you think's going on over there?' Jess asked.

Ellie followed her brother's gaze to a group of three men gathered at the fencing that surrounded a small construction site next to the FDR Drive. The men wore T-shirts and running shorts and had the long, lean frames typical of serious runners. One of the guys also wore a fanny pack and was speaking into a cell phone. Ellie couldn't make out the man's words from this distance, but she could see that his two companions – peering through the honeycomb mesh – were shouting information to him.

She also detected the high-pitched jingling of an electronic gadget. Something about the melody was familiar.

'Don't know, don't care.' Ellie just wanted to get home, catch her breath, and give her legs a rest. The construction site had been there on the west side of the park since they had begun their routine. For Ellie, the only significance of the location was its proximity to the Williamsburg Bridge, the official turnaround point on their established route. Her sole focus remained on the path in front of her – the tennis courts were a few yards ahead, followed by the bridge, then it was time to head back.

'Come on, where's your sense of adventure?' Jess began to jog toward the fence.

Ellie still couldn't figure out how her brother – with his lifestyle – managed these runs, at this pace, with such apparent ease. She stayed in good shape with kick-boxing and weight training, but serious running like this had always winded her. Anyone looking to resolve the nature-versus-nurture debate need only look to Ellie and Jess. Their lung capacities were just two of the many differences between them.

'If I stop, you may very well have to carry me home,' she panted.

'You weigh too much for that,' Jess called out, sticking out his tongue as he ran backward. 'Come on. What could be good enough to get the attention of a group of New Yorkers?'

As they approached the three runners, she could see that the men's expressions were anxious. The one with the fanny pack flipped his phone shut.

'They're on the way,' he announced.

A wave of relief washed over the runners' faces. Ellie had seen the phenomenon countless times when she'd arrived in uniform to a crime scene, NYPD badge in hand.

Jess had wondered what could distract New Yorkers from their routine, and she had a bad feeling about the answer. She tried to tell herself it might only be vandalism, maybe a bum seeking a temporary camping zone.

'Something worth seeing here?' she asked.

'You might not want to look,' one of the men said.

Ellie readied herself for the worst, but she could not have anticipated the scene she encountered as the runners stepped aside. A section of wire had fallen slack between two metal braces that had been knocked to the ground, leaving a substantial gap in the perimeter around the construction site.

The woman – she was just a girl, really – was propped like a rag doll against a pile of white PVC pipes, arms at her sides, legs splayed in front of her. Her sleeveless red top had been unbuttoned, exposing a black satin push-up bra and matching panties. Her legs were bare. High-heeled gold sandals dangled from her feet, but whatever other clothes had covered the lower half of her body were gone.

It was the rage behind the violence that struck Ellie immediately. She had seen her fair share of murder scenes, but had never come across this kind of brutality. The girl's wavy hair had been hacked off in handfuls, leaving large portions of her scalp exposed. Her body and face had been crosshatched with short, deep stab wounds resembling the outlines of a tic-tac-toe game. Ellie winced as she imagined the terror that must have come at the first sight of the blade.

She heard one of the men say that they had been unable to find a pulse, but Ellie had already concluded there was no point in checking. She forced herself to focus on the clinical facts she would need for her report.

A chain of ligature marks blossomed around the girl's neck like purple delphinium. Her eyes were bulging, and her swollen tongue extended between lips caked with dried saliva and bile. Rigor mortis had not yet set in, but the girl's skin – no doubt vibrant and pearly just a few hours earlier – was now gray and entering a deeper stage of lividity, particularly in the body's lower extremities. Lumps of red blood cells had formed boxcars in her retinas.

As gruesome as the mutilation had been, it had also been gratuitous. It was the strangling that most likely claimed her life.

The jingling that Ellie had noted earlier was louder now. It was coming from somewhere near the body.

She was startled by a retching sound behind her. She turned to see Jess doubled over next to a black tarp draped across a fence post, just as she became aware of sirens sounding in the distance.

'May I?' she asked the jogger, reaching for his cell phone. Punching in a number she had memorized surprisingly quickly, she led the joggers away from what would soon be marked as a crime scene.

By the time she hung up, the first car of uniform officers had arrived.

Chapter Four

The jingling turned out to be a Gwen Stefani ring tone on the dead girl's cell phone. The alarm had been set to go off at 5:32 a.m. Thirty-two minutes after Ellie woke up. One hour and twenty-eight minutes before she was due at the Thirteenth Precinct.

What had been the significance of that specific moment to this unnamed girl? It could have been her preferred time to get up on a Monday morning. Or maybe it was a reminder to go home on Sunday night. Time to take her medications, or walk her dog. Whatever the alarm's original purpose, by 5:32 a.m., the girl was dead, and the sound's only effect had been to draw the attention of three passing joggers to her corpse.

It would take Ellie's partner at least twenty minutes to reach the scene from his apartment in Brooklyn Heights. For now, she had to make sure his trip would not be wasted.

The uniform officer riding in the passenger seat exited the sector car first. He looked like a lot of new cops. Fit. Baby-faced. Enthusiastic. Short haired. Maybe in a different decade, he would have enlisted in the army. These days, he probably had a mother who stopped him. Now he was law enforcement.

He directed a flashlight at the dead girl. Ellie could tell from his reaction that this was his first body.

'Oh, Jesus.' He reached for his stomach on reflex.

'All upchuckers, over there.' Ellie directed the officer's attention to Jess, who, as instructed, was standing well east of the crime scene, looking out at the river, taking deep breaths. 'Detective Hatcher, Manhattan South homicide. I need your radio.'

Ellie had wrapped up one week in the homicide bureau, and so far all she'd done was help her new partner tie together loose ends on his old cases and play support for other teams while she supposedly 'learned the ropes'. Now she'd practically stumbled over this poor girl's body inside the Manhattan South borough. She was the first cop on the scene, and she was a homicide detective. If she couldn't weasel her way onto this case, she didn't deserve her new assignment.

The uniform looked at her, blinking rapidly. First a disfigured body, now a sweaty woman in a Pretenders T-shirt and sweatpants, demanding his radio.

'But –'

The young officer's partner found the words he'd apparently been searching for once she'd stepped from the driver's side of the car. 'I'll confirm it,' she said, reaching for the Vertex radio microphone clipped to the shoulder of her navy blue uniform. 'And no one's taking our radios. Sorry, ma'am.'

Ellie nodded. The woman was a good cop. Depending

on what precincts she'd been working, this could easily be her first body as well, but she was cool. Cooler than her partner. Just a quick glance at the body, then a more careful monitoring of everyone at the scene. Three runners, pacing. The sweaty woman who wanted their radio. The tall guy, looking out of place by the water.

'Make sure that guy's not going anywhere,' she said to her partner. She was definitely good. Of the people at the scene, Jess was the one who should have registered on a cop's radar. And asking her partner to keep Jess company gave the obviously nervous young cop some distance from the body.

'You're right,' Ellie said, holding up her palms. 'Call it in. But tell them homicide's already here. Shield 27990. Hatcher. They'll have me down as Elsa.'

She listened as the officer radioed in the essentials. They were at East River Park, south of Houston, north of the tennis courts. They had a 10–29–1.

It was standard 10 code. A 10–29–1: 29 for a past crime, 1 for a homicide. Across the country, 10-codes were dying out in favor of so-called plain language. The Department of Homeland Security had gone so far as to force the NYPD to train its officers in the kind of plain English that was supposed to assist interagency communications in an emergency. Instead, the entire notion of an eight-hour training session on plain talk became just another opportunity for the NYPD to mock the feds.

'We still need EMTs,' the officer said. Emergency Medical Technicians would have been dispatched with the original 911 call, but these days ambulances were in higher demand and correspondingly slower to respond than law enforcement. The homicide call-out would now bring technicians from the crime scene unit and the medical examiner's office. So much for solitude along the East River.

Ellie motioned the woman to speed it along. The officer confirmed Ellie's badge number and notified the dispatcher that a homicide detective was already at the scene.

'And tell them J. J. Rogan's on the way too,' Ellie added. 'Jeffrey James Rogan, my partner. Tell them to put us in the system. No need to do a separate homicide call-out.'

Ellie nodded as the woman repeated the information. Then she went to check on Jess. 'I see you met my brother,' she said to the young male officer. 'He's not as dangerous as he looks.'

Jess cocked his thumb and forefinger toward the cop. 'Turns out your compadre here is a certified Dog Park fan.'

Dog Park was Jess's rock band. Their biggest gigs were at ten-table taverns in Williamsburg and the occasional open mic nights in Manhattan. To say that Dog Park was an up-and-coming band would be a serious demotion to those groups that were actually on the ladder to stardom.

'I knew someone out there had to love them as much I do,' Ellie said.

'Yeah. Small world.' The officer smiled with considerable enthusiasm. Jess was eating it up, but Ellie suspected that at least some of the officer's excitement was attributable to his relief at having a subject of conversation other than the dead body he'd just seen.

She turned at the sound of an engine and saw a second blue-and-white arrive at the scene.

'Would you mind giving my brother a ride home, uh, Officer Capra?' Ellie asked, squinting at the officer's name tag. 'I think his heart's had enough of a workout for the morning.'

'Sure. No problem.'

'He'll give you my gear and a suitable change of clothes for you to bring back here, if that's all right.'

'Uh, yeah.' Capra glanced at his partner, as if worried about her reaction. First he'd almost vomited on the body. Now he was being sent away on an errand.

'I really need my gear,' Ellie said, following his gaze. 'I'll make sure she knows I told you to go.'

She touched Jess's shoulder. 'Get some sleep. I'll call you later.'

Ellie looked at her watch. Five forty-five. Forty-five minutes since Jess threw shoes at her head. Thirty-four minutes since she made a mental note of her start time outside the apartment. Thirteen minutes since the first jingle of the Gwen Stefani ring tone.

She looked at the girl, abandoned and exposed against a pile of construction debris. If Ellie had kept on jogging, this would be someone else's case. Someone else could deliver the news to the family. Someone else could offer their anemic reassurances that they were doing all they could to find out who'd done this to their daughter. But she had stopped. She had made the patrol

22

officer use her name on the radio. This was her case now. This girl was her responsibility.

It was time to find out who she was.

Two hundred feet away, on the other side of East River Drive, a blue Ford Taurus was parked outside an apartment building on Mangin Street. The man at the wheel watched as a second patrol car arrived, followed by an ambulance with lights and sirens. Two patrol cars carrying four uniform officers had all arrived before the ambulance. He found that ironic. Good thing the girl was beyond saving.

The first of the patrol cars to have arrived left the park and turned north on the FDR. One cop up front. Civilian male in back, no cuffs. Everyone else remained at the scene for now. He wanted to stay and watch, but knew they'd be canvassing the neighborhood soon.

He turned the key in the ignition. The digital clock on his dash read 5:46. He adjusted the channel on his satellite radio. Fourteen minutes until Howard Stern.

At 5:48 a.m., twenty-two miles east in Mineola, Long Island, Bill Harrington's eyes shot open when his newspaper carrier missed the porch once again, thumping the shutter outside his bedroom window. His body felt clammy. He kicked the quilt away to the side of the bed and welcomed the slight chill on his bare legs.

He had been dreaming of Robbie.

The dream began at the Alcoa plant outside Pittsburgh, a place he hadn't set foot in since Penny insisted that they retire to Long Island five years ago. But he had worked in that plant five days a week for twenty-five years of his life – the majority of them happy – melting and pouring steel castings. In his dream, when he walked into the familiar employees' break room, he found himself instead at the Harrington family's old kitchen table.

It was Robbie's sixth birthday. Jenna was only twelve at the time, but she'd insisted on baking the cake with only minimal assistance from her mother. The cake was lopsided, lumpy, and topped with a bizarre shade of green frosting, but Robbie hadn't seemed to notice.

There she was, propped up on her knees on the vinyl padding of the kitchen chair, elbows on the table, her blond hair held back by a pink paper birthday-girl tiara, eagerly staring at the six burning candles while Bill, Penny, and Jenna drew out the final line of the birthday song to prolong Robbie's excitement. Bill had smiled in his sleep when Robbie clenched her eyes shut, took that enormous breath, and whispered it cautiously across the tips of each candle. *I did it, Daddy. I got every one of them, just like you told me. Will I really get my wish?*

You'll have to wait to find out, Robbie. But, remember, don't tell anyone.

In Bill's dream, Robbie had crawled down from her chair and walked out of the kitchen into what had moments earlier been, in his mind, the Alcoa plant. Bill followed her, longing for more time, but it was too late. He found her as he'd last seen her nearly eight years ago – naked on a stainless steel gurney, draped with a white sheet.

All these years later, Bill still found himself thinking about his younger daughter. How often, he'd never bothered counting; at least once a day, certainly; usually more. And, just as he had in the very beginning, when Penny was still with him and Jenna still lived nearby, Bill occasionally woke from dreams that gave way to nightmares.

But it had been a long time since Bill Harrington had been visited by such vivid memories of Robbie.

Chapter Five

Ellie was still in her T-shirt and sweatpants when J. J. Rogan pulled up in a white Crown Vic, hopped the curb off the FDR, and claimed a patch of dirt as his parking spot.

As she walked toward her partner, she cursed the young Officer Capra for not yet having returned from what should have been a quick errand. Her mind flashed to an image of her brother showing off a guitar riff to his newest fan while she worked a crime scene in her dirty running gear.

Her self-consciousness only heightened as Rogan stepped out of the car. As usual, he was dressed to the nines. Today's ensemble consisted of a three-button black suit, well-starched steel gray shirt, and a purple tie with small white dots. Two days earlier, she'd seen the label on a jacket he'd thrown on the back of his chair. Canali. About two grand. She assumed this one ran about the same.

Ellie hadn't figured out how her new partner could afford the wardrobe – or whatever other, less obvious indulgences he might have – but she wouldn't have been surprised to learn that he worked off-duty as a model. He was average height, but with a solid frame, probably just shy of six feet and at least two hundred pounds. Dark mocha skin. Smooth bald head. Really good smile.

In short, J. J. Rogan was at the top of the bell curve for looks.

And apparently that fact wasn't lost on the almost entirely male squad of homicide detectives at the Thirteenth Precinct. Nor had it escaped their attention that Ellie wasn't half bad herself. Ellie had already overheard another detective referring to them by a team nickname: Hotchick and Tubbs. She assumed that with time they'd conjure up something more clever, but the general theme had been established.

'Barely six a.m., Hatcher. You know this shit should have been someone else's call-out.'

'You're telling me that if you were first at a scene, you'd wait for someone else to catch the case?'

She couldn't tell whether Rogan was satisfied with her response or was simply moving on to the business at hand, but he made a beeline to the construction site. A crime scene analyst was still cordoning off the area with yellow police tape.

Rogan winced at the sight of the body. 'I guess someone meant business. Where are we?'

'No official word from the ME, but based on the swelling in her face and eyes, my guess is she died from the strangling.'

Rogan nodded his agreement and shone a flashlight across the body. 'And the cuts were just for fun. Most of them look postmortem.' Without a beating heart to move the body's blood, stab wounds inflicted after death were dry and bloodless. The hatch marks in the victim's skin had the telltale look of sliced Styrofoam. 'Have you found ID yet?'

'We found a purse, probably tossed over the fence, but no wallet, and no ID.'

'What about her hair?'

'Nothing yet. He either chopped it off before he brought her here, or carried it off with him – maybe kept it as a souvenir.'

Rogan was still taking in the full visual of the body. 'Too healthy for a working girl. No track marks. Fresh pedicure. Matching lingerie.'

Ellie had made the same observations.

'How old, do you think? You know that's not my strong suit,' Rogan said with a small smile. When he'd first met Ellie last week, he had volunteered that she looked a mere twenty years old, but then added that he could never tell with white people.

'Early twenties, tops. She could even be a teenager.'

Rogan clicked his tongue against his teeth.

'We pulled a cell phone from behind the body,' Ellie said. 'It must have fallen out when the guy dumped her, before he tossed her purse.'

'So start dialing all her contacts. Let's find out who this girl is.'

'Easier said than done. There's something wrong with the screen. The display kept cutting in and out when I was turning off the alarm. Now I can't get any image at all. Nothing but black lines.'

Rogan took a look at the broken phone. 'The same thing happened to me when I dropped my Motorola at the gym. That thing's shot.'

'I did, however, find this in her purse.' Ellie held up a ziplock bag containing a white plastic card not much larger than a business card.

He smiled, registering the significance of the bag's contents. 'Now that narrows it down. You plan on staying in your sweaty clothes all day?'

As if on command, a marked car pulled up next to Rogan's Crown Vic. Officer Capra stepped out, carrying a familiar blue backpack. She hoped Jess had remembered to pack her shield, Glock, and the necessary undergarments.

'I'm ready when you are.'

The white plastic card was a hotel key emblazoned with a blue capital *H* surrounded by a curly *Q*.

'We got three Hiltons in Manhattan,' Rogan said. 'Times Square, Rockefeller Center, and the Financial District. Try your luck.'

Ellie was wriggling out of her running clothes in the footwell of the backseat, trying not to think about the various forms of mucus that had been hurled and smeared against the upholstery since the car's last disinfection.

'Girls that age don't stay near Wall Street.'

'Unless they're hookers,' Rogan interjected.

'And we don't think she was. So between the other two, I'll go with Times Square. Who doesn't love Times Square these days?'

By the time Rogan pulled up to the giant copper clock outside the hotel's Forty-second Street entrance, Ellie had just finished snapping on her holster. As she stepped from the backseat, she waved off a uniformed valet. Rogan flashed his shield as he followed behind her. 'We'll be quick, man. Thanks.'

To their surprise, the hotel lobby was on the twenty-first floor. They bypassed whatever businesses occupied the tower's bottom half with an express ride in the Art Deco elevator. At the front desk, they cut to the head of a long line of guests who were presumably waiting to check out.

The woman who greeted them had pale skin, red hair knotted into a bun, and glasses dangling from a chain around her neck. 'How may I help you?'

Rogan produced the hotel key and explained in a hushed voice what they needed and why.

'Oh, my.' The clerk lowered her voice as well. 'Unfortunately, that key isn't ours.'

'Are you sure?'

'I'm certain.' She produced a white card that looked identical to the one they'd found in the victim's purse, but with the addition of the words *Times Square* below the corporate logo. 'This here's one of our keys. People like the Times Square thing, you know. And we're considered "boutique style". People like that, too. You should try our hotel at Rockefeller Center. They've got over two thousand rooms.'

'And the one in the Financial District?' Ellie asked.

'Five hundred and sixty-five.'

'So, if you're playing your odds –'

'Our Rockefeller Center location is on Fifty-third Street and Sixth Avenue.'

As the two detectives rode the elevator back to the ground floor, Ellie watched as Rogan checked out his freshly shaven scalp in the mirror. She snuck a look at herself, then quickly thought better of it. She knew from experience that messy strands of her shoulder-length blond hair would be flipped in every direction, thanks to dried sweat and the ponytail holder she'd worn during her run. At some point she'd try to find a hairbrush and at least wash her face.

'How come between the two of us we didn't figure out to hit the monster-sized hotel first?' Ellie asked, keeping her eyes on the elevator's digital display as it counted down each passing floor.

'I guess the first twenty floors are misleading. Makes it look larger than it really is.'

'That's what *she* said.' Ellie hadn't meant to slip into a Michael Scott impersonation in front of her new partner, but the response to his comment had been automatic.

So was Rogan's. He laughed. It was a good laugh. Loud. From the gut. 'Careful, Hatcher. If word gets out you've got a sense of humor, the guys at the house will really be chasing after you, and I won't be able to protect you. That is, assuming you ever get around to taking a shower.'

The Monday-morning traffic was already starting to pour from the Lincoln Tunnel into Midtown. Rogan hit the wigwag flashers on the headlights of the Crown

31

Vic and made it to the circular driveway at the Sixth Avenue entrance of the Hilton in four minutes flat. Leaving the car pulled up behind a large Trailways bus, he badged the valet as they headed for the lobby, working their way through a large group of teenagers wearing John Marshall High School band T-shirts and dragging backpacks and instrument cases. Most of them were using cell phones to snap their final photographs of Manhattan as they milled around, waiting to board the jumbo bus.

Ellie knew they'd found the right place when she spotted two girls huddled next to the bell stand on the opposite side of the lobby. She couldn't make out their words, but she could tell from the pitch of their raised voices that the girls were distressed. They appeared to be arguing, but then one of the girls burst into tears, and her friend placed an arm around her shoulder. A bellhop in a red uniform and captain's hat stared at the girls awkwardly, clearly wishing to extract himself from the situation.

J. J. started toward the reception desk, but Ellie grabbed his elbow and cocked her head toward the agitated girls.

'You go check that out,' he said. 'I'll take the key to the front desk and see if they can get us any information on it.'

As she approached the bell stand, she was able to catch the tail end of the girls' conversation.

'We can't leave without Chelsea.' The crying girl had dark brown hair pulled back in a low ponytail, topped off with a black headband. She wore a pink hoodie sweatsuit and Puma tennis shoes.

32

The girl's friend was rubbing her shoulder soothingly. 'I didn't say we should leave without her. I just said we should go to the airport. Chelsea's probably there.'

The comforting girl was petite with a black pixie haircut. Ellie spotted the top of some kind of tattoo peeking out from the back of the waistband of her jeans. The girl looked at her watch with a furrowed brow. 'We're missing our flight anyway. It's almost seven o'clock.'

'They said it was delayed,' the girl in the ponytail reminded her. She was starting to get control over her tears. 'Chelsea would never leave us hanging like this.'

Another bellhop hurried past the duo and grabbed a set of car keys from the counter beside them. 'Andale,' he shouted, hurrying along the perplexed bellhop who was trapped with the girls.

'Chewanna cab or not?'

The question sent the crying girl into sobs again, and the bellhop finally gave up, grabbed a set of keys from the counter, and fled to the hotel entrance.

'Do you two need some help with anything?' Ellie asked.

The pixie threw her an impatient look, as if the attention of strangers was yet another piece of unwarranted drama.

'We're fine, ma'am. We didn't mean to make a scene.'

'No need to apologize.' Ellie flipped up the badge that was clipped to the waistband of her pants. 'You're looking for one of your friends?'

'She's just running late. It's fine –'

'Stop saying it's going to be fine, Jordan.' The crying

33

girl pushed her friend's hand off her shoulder. 'She's missing. She should be here, and she's not here. She knew what time we were leaving, and she's not here. She's . . . she's *missing*.'

Ellie heard the girl's pain in the way she spoke that single word. She said it with the knowledge that to be missing meant so much more than to be in an unknown location.

The petite girl with the pixie haircut and tattoo, the one whose name was apparently Jordan, said they just needed to get to the airport. If they could get to the airport, they could make it onto a later flight and wait for Chelsea.

'I told you, I'm not leaving.'

Jordan muttered something under her breath. Ellie heard it but hoped the crying girl hadn't.

But she had, and she responded as predicted. 'Seriously? Chelsea's missing, and you decide to say you're going to kill her? Do you have any *idea* how disgusting that is?'

'All right. Just try to calm down, both of you. Your name's Jordan?' She spoke directly to the tattoo girl, who nodded in response. 'No one's killing anyone, Jordan.'

'Yeah, I'm sorry. Sorry, Stef.'

'And you're Stef?' Ellie asked the crying girl.

'Yeah, Stefanie. Stefanie Hyder.'

'Okay. So you're obviously upset, but I need one of you – only one,' she said, holding up a finger, 'to tell me what's going on. Can you do that, Stefanie?'

The girl sniffed a couple of times and tugged on her ponytail nervously. 'We're on spring break. Our flight leaves this morning – like, basically now. And our friend Chelsea isn't here.'

'But –'

Ellie held up her hand. 'You'll get your turn.'

Stefanie continued without prodding. 'We went out last night. It was time to come home, and she wouldn't leave. Chelsea wouldn't leave. I should have stayed, but it was time to go home. And she promised.'

Jordan placed her arm around Stefanie's shoulder once more, and this time Stefanie didn't push away. Her tears brought on sobs as she spoke.

'She looked me in the eye, and she promised she'd be back by now. She promised she'd be here. She promised. And she's not. Something happened to her. Something's wrong.'

Rogan had snapped a digital photograph of the girl from East River Park, but she didn't want to do the ID that way. Not in a crowded Midtown hotel lobby. Not now.

'Do you have a picture of your friend?'

The girls both shook their heads.

'You sure?' Ellie recalled the band students outside snapping shots with their phones. 'Not in your cell phone or something?'

'Yeah, right. No, of course.' The one called Jordan stepped over to a tangle of bags that were piled in the corner next to the bell stand counter. She rifled through a large white tote, pulled a patent leather clutch from the larger bag, and then began sifting through its tightly packed contents. 'Sorry. You have to put everything in two bags for the airlines.'

She finally slid out an iPhone and pushed a few buttons before holding it out toward Ellie. 'That's her, just last night at dinner. In the middle.'

Ellie took the device from her and peered closely at the picture. The three friends were huddled together, posing for the camera with open-mouth smiles, as if they'd been laughing. A bystander in the background didn't look too happy with them. The girls had probably been too rowdy for the restaurant. At least their last night together had been a happy one.

It was a small screen, but she could make out three faces. The girl on the right was Stefanie Hyder, with her hair down and her eyes bright, not bloodshot as they were now. The one on the left was pixie-haired Jordan.

And Ellie recognized the girl in the middle as well. She recognized the long shiny blond hair before it had been hacked off. She recognized the red sleeveless shirt, chosen no doubt to match the crimson bead chandelier earrings that peeked out from behind the beautiful blond hair. And she recognized the smiling face before someone had used it as a carving board.

Chapter Six

When Ellie was seven years old, her father had come home with a bandage on his temple.

Jerry Hatcher had been working a missing child case for more than a month. For more than thirty nights, the family had known their daughter was missing. The family had known for more than a month that their girl was last seen leaving Cypress Park with an adult male whose description was wholly unfamiliar.

Ellie's father focused on a suspect who had a pattern of arrests for indecent exposure to children in Cypress Park. The guy had missed work the day of the abduction. The next day, too. The evidence was thin, but the case was high-profile. Ellie's dad managed to get a warrant. He found the missing girl's body in an oil drum that was buried beneath the suspect's brand-new hot tub.

Three days after delivering the news to the girl's parents, Detective Jerry Hatcher had used the past tense. He hadn't known how to fill the silence as the parents sat side by side on the sofa, staring at the framed picture of their daughter's second-grade portrait. *Everyone tells me your daughter had a smile that lit up the room.*

It was a sentiment offered in kindness. Trite, maybe, but well intended. The victim's father had upended the coffee table and shoved Jerry Hatcher into the fireplace mantel. Why? Because he'd used the past tense too soon.

Ellie's memories of her father were filled with stories like that one. Other kids' fathers talked about client meetings when they got home from work. Or a real piece of work on the delivery route. Or a tough cross-examination of a trial witness. Ellie's father explained why he had a bandage on his head, and if the telling of the story happened to involve an eight-year-old girl buried in an oil drum, so be it.

And, although she didn't realize it at the time, she'd learned from those stories. On that particular day, she'd learned never to use the past tense. Even after delivering the news to the family. Even after the official ID. Even after the body's in the ground. Until the family starts using the past tense, everyone else must remain in the present.

Of course Chelsea's friends still spoke of her in the present. They didn't know her body was on a stainless steel table at the medical examiner's office.

Rogan led the way through the Thirteenth Precinct, past the front desk officers, the precinct briefing room, and two wire holding cages, up the narrow staircase to the third-floor homicide squad. Their head start on the day was over. Detectives bustled throughout the squad room, crowded to capacity with desks, chairs, file cabinets, and random boxes of evidence waiting to be cataloged. Jack Chen, one of the younger civilian aides, sat perched at the front desk.

Rogan asked Chen to get two coffees and Danishes, then handed him a twenty-dollar bill from his wallet. Ellie flashed three fingers over Rogan's shoulder and threw Chen a wink.

Detouring around their desks, Rogan headed for the back corner of the squad room, then down a hallway leading to three interrogation rooms. He skipped the first two doors and held the final one open for Stefanie, Jordan, and Ellie. Because it was at the end of the hall, interview room 3 was the least used, and therefore the most presentable, of their interrogation rooms.

There were only three chairs surrounding the small laminate table in the center of the room. Two on the left. A single on the right. Two detectives. One suspect. That's how the room was arranged.

The girls stood awkwardly until Ellie gestured toward the chairs. Jordan and Stefanie sat together, side by side.

They started with names and dates of birth. Stefanie Hyder was the worried brunette with the ponytail and headband. Jordan McLaughlin was the girl with the dark pixie hair and a tattoo on her lower back. And Chelsea Hart was their missing friend.

Ellie jotted down all three names, in that order, in a spiral reporter's notebook. She circled the last one. All the girls were nineteen years old.

Rogan let her take the lead on questioning. 'I heard you mention at the hotel that you're here in New York on spring break?'

'Right,' Stefanie said. 'We got here Tuesday. We were

supposed to fly out this morning. Chelsea didn't come back to the hotel last night, and she wasn't there when we were ready to leave for the airport.'

Jordan shifted in her seat. She was clearly still fixated on that flight home.

'When was the last time you saw Chelsea?' Ellie asked.

'Last night. Or I guess this morning. We were out late.'

'Doing what?'

The girls stared at the table. Stefanie studied her pearly red fingernails. Jordan chewed her lower lip.

'You can't find your friend. I think we can look past a little barhopping.'

'We went clubbing. We left around two thirty.' Stefanie paused and dropped her head. 'Chelsea stayed.'

Ellie scribbled '2:30 a.m.' in her notebook.

'Stayed where? Was she at a specific club?'

'Yeah. It's called Pulse.'

Ellie was pretty sure she'd heard of the place, one of the newest, hippest Manhattan hot spots among the many new, hip Manhattan hot spots that were several notches too cool for her to frequent. 'In the Meatpacking District, right?'

The girls nodded.

'What other clubs did you hit?'

'None.' Stefanie shook her head. 'That's it.'

'You sure? No quick pop-ins somewhere you might have forgotten about?'

The girls shook their heads. It was just the one club.

'You went straight from your hotel to the club?' she asked.

40

The girls started to speak at once, then Jordan deferred again to Stefanie.

'No, we went to dinner first. Some place in Little Italy. Wait. I've got the name.' Stefanie slipped her fingers inside a small black purse and pulled out a wrinkled piece of yellow carbon paper. She smoothed it out. 'Luna.'

Ellie wanted to nail down a basic timeline while the girls were still relatively calm, before she had to deliver the news. She walked them through the activities of the previous day. Brunch at Norma's at 10:30 a.m. At the Museum of Modern Art by twelve thirty. One drink at the hotel bar at five o'clock. Back to their rooms at six to get ready. Taxi to SoHo at seven fifteen. At the Luna bar by eight. Seated at eight thirty. Ate between nine and ten. Left around eleven and walked to Pulse. Two of the girls left at 2:30 a.m. Chelsea stayed.

Into the notebook it all went. Somewhere in that timeline Chelsea's killer had found her.

'And it was just the three of you the entire day?'

Two nods for *yes*.

'No guys?'

Two shaking heads said *no*. Ellie didn't buy it.

'So tell me about the restaurant. Luna. You didn't speak to anyone while you were there?'

'No,' Stefanie said. 'We ate by ourselves. Well, we had a couple shots with these lawyers at the bar, but we didn't see them again once we were seated.'

'No chance Chelsea gave one of them her number and hooked up with him later in the night?'

41

Stefanie shook her head. 'No way. Those guys were probably, like, thirty. Way too old for us.'

'You sure about that?' Rogan asked. 'You said you had two drinks with them.'

'It's not like we were bonding or anything. Chelsea gave them fake names and told them we were models in town for a car show. They knew we were messing with them.'

Ellie had always assumed that the New York City dating scene was kinder to men than women, but these girls were painting a different picture.

'What about the club? Did you meet any guys there?'

Two sets of shrugged shoulders and nervous eyes until Stefanie spoke up. 'She started talking to some guys in one of the VIP rooms. We were all hanging out in there.'

'Did you get any names?' Ellie asked.

'No.'

She looked to Jordan, who shook her head.

'Nothing? First names? A nickname?'

'It's really loud in those places. You just say things like, "Hey, cool place, have you been here before?" that kind of thing, unless you take it outside to actually talk.'

'And you didn't see Chelsea go outside?'

Two shaking heads.

'Okay, well, was Chelsea with anyone in particular in the VIP room? Or just a big group?'

'Mostly just the whole group,' Stefanie said. 'But she was talking to this one guy when we first got there, and he was the one who brought us all into the VIP room.'

'Can you describe him?'

'He was tall, probably a little over six feet. Sort of shaggy, sandy blond hair. Cute.'

'Oh, I remember him,' Jordan said. 'Chelsea was with him for, like, a couple of hours, I think. They were dancing. Looked pretty hot and heavy.'

'It was flirting,' Stefanie admonished.

'I know. I'm just saying, I noticed.'

'So you got a good look at him, too?' Ellie asked.

Jordan nodded. 'He kind of looked like an older Zac Efron. You know, cute more than good looking.'

'And I would know him from where?'

'*High School Musical*? *Hairspray*? Like, every single tabloid magazine known to man?'

Feeling slightly older than she had a minute earlier, Ellie tried not to think about how much easier this would be if the people who met at Manhattan clubs bothered to exchange names like normal people. She was going to have to sit these girls down with a sketch artist in the small hope of finding someone who apparently looked like an overage teen hunk and probably had absolutely nothing to do with Chelsea's death.

'Now, Jordan, you said Chelsea was with this guy for a couple of hours. Did you see her with anyone else?'

Jordan shook her head, but Stefanie spoke up. 'Yeah, she was dancing with some other guy when I told her we were leaving. I didn't really pay any attention to him, though. He was giving me a hard time for trying to get Chelsea to leave. Jesus, I let it get to me, and I shouldn't have. I should have made her come home with us.'

Jordan told Stefanie it wasn't her fault. Ellie got the impression she'd spoken those words many times that morning.

'Can you remember anything about him?'

Stefanie chuckled to herself. 'Yeah, I called him Duran Duran. He had that poser fauxhawk hairdo.'

'Kind of gelled into the middle?' Ellie said.

'Exactly,' Stefanie said. 'And he was dressed like some retro eighties MTV video star. Skinny pants. Skinny tie. Really stupid.'

'What about the basics? Height, weight, age?'

'Also kind of tall. Not as tall as the first guy. Probably right around six feet. A little older than us, maybe mid-twenties? Dark brown hair. Kind of thin, I guess. I really didn't pay any attention, but I might recognize him if I saw him again.'

'Well, I can understand how the outfit might have distracted you.' Ellie was hoping a little humor might deter Stefanie from another guilt-induced digression.

'Oh, and Chelsea was calling him Jake.'

'His name was Jake?' Ellie clarified.

'No, like for Jake Gyllenhaal. It's this thing Chelsea does. If someone looks like a celebrity, she'll just call them that. So, I didn't get a great look at the guy, but according to Chelsea, he looked like Jake Gyllenhaal.'

Ellie could certainly see how a guy who looked like that – regardless of the outfit – might get the attention of a nineteen-year-old girl from Indiana.

'Okay, so we've got the shaggy-haired guy who brought you into the VIP room and Jake the bad dresser,' she said. 'Anyone else from last night you can remember?'

'No.'

'What about back home? Does Chelsea have a boyfriend?'

'Her boyfriend's not here,' Stefanie said.

'Where is he?' Ellie asked.

'Indiana. He went to Cancún for break, but he came back yesterday so he wouldn't miss any classes. Oh, my God. He's totally going to flip out when we're not on the plane.'

'Worry about that later. What's his name?'

'Mark. Mark Linton.'

Two more words for the notebook. She didn't care whether the boyfriend was supposedly hiking in the Amazon rain forest. Until she verified his whereabouts, the boyfriend was always a suspect.

'Who else?' Ellie asked.

Stefanie cocked her head, clearly put off by the question. Jordan gave her an annoyed look.

'Who else other than Mark Linton?' Ellie asked again. 'I mean, it's not like they're married, right?'

'Not married,' Stefanie said defensively, 'but dating. And for like nine months. He's her boyfriend, okay? She was dancing with some guys last night, but so were the rest of us.'

'No problem. Sorry if I offended you. I figured in college most people would still be dating around. You girls all right? Need to take a bathroom break or anything?'

Jordan raised her hand chin-high.

'Detective Rogan will show you the way.'

Jordan scooted past her friend and followed Rogan

out, while Ellie continued to walk Stefanie through the basics. Chelsea had no enemies. No one was watching them. No one was following them. No tawdry affairs or illicit drug deals over spring break. The guys at Pulse seemed harmless enough, and Chelsea wouldn't have left with any of them anyway.

It was just a fun night in the city. In fact, Chelsea had told Stefanie, just before they left her alone at the club, that it was the best night ever.

When Rogan returned to the room with Jordan, he gave Ellie the look she was expecting.

'This has been good, you guys. Very helpful. We're going to make a few calls, and we'll be right back.' Ellie waited for the door to close behind them to talk to her partner in the hallway. 'So?'

'Miss All-American Innocent, my black ass.'

Ellie feigned a judgmental *tsk*. 'My goodness, Jeffrey James. You are so cynical.'

Facts. Reality. The truth. A timeline. It all sounds objective. Absolute. Black and white.

It never was. Sometimes a story changed because a witness lied. But more often, it was simply because there was another side to the story.

According to Rogan, it hadn't taken much to get Jordan to come clean.

'I caught her on the way out of the ladies' room,' Rogan said. 'I told her I noticed her expression when Stefanie insisted Chelsea had only the one boyfriend. She gave me the usual "I don't want to say anything about my friend".'

46

'And then you said we need the truth if we're going to help.'

Rogan nodded. 'Chelsea was getting her party on last night. Hard. All these girls were polluted by the time they left, and Chelsea was probably the worst. And she's got a wild streak. She's got the one boyfriend, Mark Linton, but that doesn't stop her from flirting with other dudes behind his back, or even in front of his face.'

'Just flirting, or following up on the flirting?'

'That's where the girl was less certain. She's personally witnessed Chelsea make out with guys at bars – not last night, but in the past. I think she suspects things have gone further from time to time, but doesn't know for sure and didn't want to be too catty under the circumstances.'

'We don't have long before this one breaks.' The local crime reporters always had a way of learning about cases involving photogenic young women whose pictures made good front-page coverage. Add in a tourist at a trendy nightclub in Manhattan's premier party district, and Chelsea Hart's story became irresistible.

'And we need to get to the parents before that poor chump of a boyfriend goes to the airport and sees that his girl's not on the plane,' Rogan added. 'And we *definitely* need to get the Lou on board.'

The idea of Lieutenant Dan Eckels being on board with anything having to do with Ellie was a long shot. To say that Ellie wasn't her lieutenant's favorite detective was like saying the Hatfields and McCoys weren't the friendliest of neighbors.

'At least you can fuel up before you face your maker.'

Jack Chen turned the hallway corner, juggling a pastry bag and a cardboard tray filled with three Styrofoam cups of coffee. Ellie recognized both as coming from a deli on Third Avenue. She took one of the cups and removed a cherry Danish from the bag, along with a napkin, while Chen handed five dollars and some coins back to Rogan. Rogan waved him off, and Chen thanked him before heading off to deliver the rest to the girls down the hall.

Ellie took a much-needed first sip of the black coffee.

'I'll meet you back out here in ten?' Rogan said.

'Are you going somewhere?'

'I'm going in there to prepare these girls to sit down with a sketch artist,' he said, hitching a thumb over his shoulder. 'You, however, are going to tell Eckels about your morning jog.'

Chapter Seven

Ellie studied her lieutenant for ten full seconds through the open slats of the blinds covering the window between his office and the squad room. Dan Eckels's short, chunky frame rested in his black leather armchair, and as far as she could tell, he was staring into space, doing absolutely nothing. She tapped her knuckles three times against his closed door.

'Enter.'

Eckels's square face darkened when he looked up to find Ellie in the threshold of his office.

'Morning, Lou. I come bearing pastry.' She extended the napkin-wrapped Danish in his direction.

'Is that powdered sugar on there, Hatcher, or did you get carried away this morning with a little arsenic?'

'They always say you've got a wicked sense of humor.' They didn't. No one. Ever. Ellie suppressed a stomach growl and tried not to think about how much she would have enjoyed that cherry pastry.

Eckels met her fake smile with his. It wasn't a look that worked for him. With his salt-and-pepper hair, block-shaped head, and low forehead, the grin created an unfortunate Frankenstein effect.

'Let me guess. You and this heart-attack-inducing breakfast ball are here to explain why you and Rogan were already well into a call-out when I arrived here at seven o'clock.'

'Something like that.' She explained how she came upon the crime scene that morning before the first blue-and-white had even arrived. 'I was already there, Lou. What was I supposed to do? Miss the opportunity for us to get a head start on the investigation just so I could finish my run?' She said it as if she'd really been looking forward to that last mile.

'You know what your problem is, Hatcher? You're a smart-ass, just like Flann McIlroy.'

Ellie dropped the sunny smile. The last time she saw Detective Flann McIlroy, he was dying in her arms on a cabin cruiser at City Island, gunshots in his stomach and throat. 'McIlroy was a great cop.'

'He was a good investigator. He knew how to follow his gut. Problem was, his instincts could be back-assward, and he wouldn't listen. He didn't listen to anyone. He thought he was smarter than everyone else.' Eckels pointed to imaginary people standing around his office. 'Thought he could go his own way as long as he shined on all the stupid people around him.'

'I'm not like that, sir, and I'm not shining you on.'

'But you do think I'm stupid,' Eckels said, rocking back in his chair.

'Of course not, sir.' Ellie hadn't realized until that moment the kind of insecurity Dan Eckels must live with.

Eckels locked eyes with her, sucking his teeth. Ellie held up both palms. 'No bullshit, Lieutenant. I'm here to pull my weight. And I won't bring you breakfast anymore. For the sake of your heart. And, well, I really can't stand being a kiss-ass.'

'Jesus H.,' Eckels grunted, letting his weight drop forward. 'Just go ahead and tell me what you've got.'

She drew him the bare-bones picture they'd gathered so far.

'A college student killed on spring break in Manhattan? Please tell me the girl's a bow-wow.'

Ellie shook her head. 'She was very pretty. And blond. I hear the public likes crime stories about midwestern blondes.'

The self-deprecating crack about her own personal brushes with the media was enough to get another creepy smile out of him.

'I was tempted to reassign this case to another team, Hatcher, the way you grabbed it. But you know something? You want to be in the middle of the shit storm? Then go for it. You weaseled your way into this squad after only five years on the job? We'll see how much the brass loves you when your clusterfuck's on the front page of every paper in the country.' He unfurled the imaginary headline with outstretched hands: '*Murder in the Big Apple.*'

'I won't say I wasn't warned.'

'Keep me in the loop, Hollywood. McIlroy never did.'

'Not a problem, sir.'

She turned to leave his office, but Eckels wasn't finished. 'How are things with Rogan?'

'Good. Real good so far. Thanks.'

'Just so you know, you'd be paired with that lazy fuck Winslow if Rogan hadn't saved you. Don't be a pain in his ass.'

Ellie let the door fall closed behind her.

She found Rogan on his cell phone at his gray metal desk.

There were at least eight different varieties of desks among the twenty that were scattered throughout the squad room. From the looks of things, someone with a borderline case of obsessive-compulsive disorder had at some point attempted to pair them into matching sets for partners. Eight variations. Twenty desks. The math did not work. She took a seat at her own wood-veneer setup.

Rogan lowered his voice to a whisper and swung his chair away from her. She heard him mutter something about 'three thousand.' She wondered if the call had something to do with his wardrobe. Maybe the price of a new suit. Or maybe a bet to help pay for the next one.

To avoid any appearance of eavesdropping, she picked up her phone to make a call of her own.

'Peter Morse.'

'Hey there.'

'Hey, yourself. I'm glad you called. I was worried maybe you met some other guy last night when I wasn't on watch.'

'Nah, maybe back in my old skanky days. I kicked it at home alone last night.' Ellie had only known Peter

52

Morse for two months, and she'd been in Kansas for half of that time. But since she'd been home, they'd spent more nights together than apart. 'Did you get a lot of work done?'

Peter was a crime beat reporter at the *Daily Post* by day, aspiring author by night. After spending all weekend together, Ellie had insisted that they have two nights on their own so he could have some time to write.

'Oh, tons. Forty pages, at least. A book contract is just around the corner, complete with an all-expenses-paid tour and a straight shot to the top of the best-seller list.' Peter tended to understate just how important his writing was to him, and sarcasm often proved handy on that front.

'If you're really on a roll, maybe we should take tomorrow night off, too.'

'Don't even joke. I was sort of hoping I could come over tonight.'

'Nope. Two nights. Those are the rules.'

'Damn you and your stinking rules.'

'You were the one who told me it always takes you a day to get up to speed after a long break.'

'Damn me and my big mouth.'

'Tonight you'll be in the zone,' Ellie said.

The grumble on the other end of the line suggested he had doubts. 'And tomorrow?'

'And tomorrow, we'll make up for lost time.'

'Now I like the sound of that.'

Rogan flipped his phone shut at the desk across from her.

'Hey, I've got to run. I'll call you tomorrow.'

'Promise?'

'I always mean what I say,' she said before hanging up.

'Sorry about that,' Rogan said, holding up his cell. 'With you dragging my ass out of bed so early this morning, I didn't get a chance to take care of some personal business.'

'No need to explain.'

'So, turns out our girls from Indiana are a little tougher than you'd think. I told them we found a body this morning. Said you and I both saw her. That she resembles the picture they showed us of their friend.'

'You didn't tell them the rest, did you?'

Rogan shook his head. 'I made it clear there still needs to be an official ID, but they know we're pretty confident this is Chelsea. For a couple of kids, they're handling it all right. A whole lot of crying, of course, but I persuaded them to give me their phones until we've had a chance to call the family.' He opened his desk drawer to reveal two cell phones.

'And we've got a sketch artist on the way?'

'Done,' he said. 'It sounds like they got a decent enough look at the shaggy-haired guy that we might have a shot with him. On the one they called Jake, their descriptions are so vague, it might be a lost cause. Anyway, that's for the doodler to figure out. We can have a victim's advocate get them back into the Hilton once they're done here.'

'So what's next?'

'I call the parents. You call CSU and the ME. See if they're ready for us.' Breaking the news of a daughter's death compared to checking on the status of the crime scene unit and medical examiner's office? Definitely not equal billing. The call to Indiana was something she had signed on for when she took responsibility for the girl she'd found during her run.

To a cop, it was one call at the beginning of yet another case. One call to deliver the news before the real investigative work started. But to the people at the other end of the line, that one phone call would mark the indelible moment that changed everything they thought they knew to be true. One minute, they're living their lives – worried about the costs of remodeling the kitchen, trying to lose a few pounds before the upcoming reunion, wondering what to eat for dinner. The next, the phone rings, and nothing else matters.

Ellie's father used to say that was the worst part of the job – the knowledge that good people would forever remember your voice, your words, that one phone call, as the moment that changed everything. Ellie wasn't looking forward to making her first call to a family, but she knew she had to do it eventually.

'Not exactly a fair trade,' she said.

'That first call to a family is enough to rework your brain for the next twenty-four hours. I'd rather make the call than be stuck with a brain-dead partner all day.'

Rogan was offering to carry the load for her on this one. He had been a detective in NYPD's homicide squad for a little more than eight years. That was a little more than eight years longer than Ellie. With some amount of guilt, she gratefully accepted.

*　*　*

Her calls took less than three minutes. CSU would be ready for an initial briefing from the crime scene in an hour. The ME needed two.

Rogan was still on the phone. He had his head down, eyes closed – right hand on the handset, the other massaging his left temple. It was as if he were picturing himself outside this room, away from New York City, standing on a front porch with two parents in Fort Wayne, Indiana. Ellie could almost imagine Rogan looking Mr. and Mrs. Hart in the eye and breaking the news: *Your daughter was supposed to take a cab back to the hotel, but she never arrived.*

The image gave her an idea. She opened Internet Explorer on her computer, Googled the New York City Taxi and Limousine Commission, and dialed the telephone number listed on the commission's Web site.

For decades, drivers of New York City's taxis had maintained their trip sheets by hand, using pen and paper to log the location and amount of each fare. Trying to track down a cab driver on the basis of paper trip sheets was like searching for the proverbial needle in a haystack of thirteen thousand yellow cabs.

The tide in the sea of paper had shifted just last year, however, when the city's new high-tech requirements for all medallioned cars had gone into effect. Although a few drivers remained at war with the commission over the expensive technology, a critical mass of taxis was now equipped with computers that not only accepted credit card payments but also used GPS technology to automate the ancient trip sheet practices. Obtaining a list of the cabdrivers within a one-block radius of Pulse around the time of last call would have once been impossible; now it was just a matter of a few keystrokes on a computer.

Ten minutes later, they had finished their calls. Rogan had learned that Chelsea's parents would be coming to New York City on the next available flight. Ellie had faxed a photograph of Chelsea Hart to be circulated among cabdrivers who'd picked up early-morning fares in the Meatpacking District. And the lives of Paul and Miriam Hart were forever changed.

Chapter Eight

The processing of the East River Park crime scene was in full swing. NYPD vans lined the park, backing up traffic on the FDR in both directions as drivers slowed to rubberneck. Yellow police tape, fortified by rows of uniform officers, closed the park from Sixth Street down to Cherry.

They badged an officer standing guard north of the tennis courts, ducked beneath the yellow tape, and made their way to the construction site. Ellie had never been here in full daylight. Torn up and cluttered with piles of dislodged dirt, backhoes, and other heavy equipment she couldn't name, this area of the park would have been almost as desolate as it had been during her early-morning runs, were it not for the chaos of the ongoing police investigation.

Four officers were working the scene inside the fence. Rogan headed directly for a tall female officer with long red hair pulled into a braid that ran down her back. She was crouched in a squat, using tweezers to place something in a ziplock baggie.

'Is that Florkoski?'

The woman sealed the evidence collection bag and eased herself back to standing. She had a broad face that broke into a friendly smile at the sight of Rogan.

'Hey there, Double J. Good to see you.' She snapped a latex glove off of her right hand and extended it for a shake, first to Rogan and then to Ellie. 'Mariah Florkoski.'

'Ellie Hatcher,' Ellie said, returning both the smile and the handshake.

'New partner,' Rogan said.

'Oh, sure.' Florkoski nodded. 'I recognize the name.'

Ellie had no doubt that the recognition was due to her one and only previous homicide case two months earlier, when she had been recruited to help investigate a series of murders tied to an Internet dating company. By the time the case was solved, a serial killer was arrested, a Russian identity-theft ring was busted, and one of the best cops Ellie would ever know was dead. And apparently other cops knew her name as a result.

'What happened to Casey?' Mariah asked.

'Retired. Last month.'

'Don't tell me. He's finally going to Scottsdale.'

'The movers are coming next week.' Rogan turned to Ellie and explained. 'My last partner. Jim Casey. He'd tell anyone who'd listen he was retiring to Arizona.'

'That his only wish was to die on a Scottsdale golf course,' Mariah said.

'With a gin and tonic in hand,' Rogan added.

'You getting along all right without him?'

'Hatcher here's good peeps.'

Ellie gave a tiny mock bow of gratitude.

'Well, at least you didn't wind up with that lazy slug Winslow.'

Ellie struggled to place the name, then remembered Lieutenant Eckels's remark – that she would have been the one stuck with Winslow if it hadn't been for Rogan.

'I take it this case belongs to the two of you?'

'What have you got so far?' Rogan asked.

'Well, I can tell you the vic wasn't killed here.'

Rogan's lips set into a line of disappointment. All crime scenes were important. Any could yield evidence. But it was the primary crime scene that was most likely to yield blood, saliva, semen, hair, fibers, and fingerprints – all of the physical evidence that jurors increasingly insisted upon, now that the fictional world of the multiple *CSI* shows had become ingrained in the minds of ordinary people.

Mariah pointed to a male officer who was photographing the dirt in front of him. 'We've got a whole bunch of footprints in the area in front of her body – all with treads, consistent with athletic shoes. But fortunately, our runners didn't crowd the body. They gave her some space. Closer in to the corpse, we've got another set of footprints – smooth bottomed, not likely an athletic shoe – pointing into and then away from the body. One guy. He carried her in, dropped her, then walked out.'

'Any chance you're going to tell us the shoe is one of a kind,' Rogan said, 'custom-made at the foot of the Swiss Alps?'

Mariah smiled and shook her head. 'It looks like any footprint you'd see on a Ballroom Dancing 101 instruction chart. Oval toe, square heel. No markings. About as generic as it gets.'

'How do you know she didn't walk over here with him, then he walks out alone?' Rogan asked.

'Chelsea was wearing high heels,' Ellie said.

'Lucky for us.' Mariah walked a few feet to a blue plastic storage bin resting on the ground just beyond the yellow crime tape. She reached in and pulled out a larger baggie containing a pair of high-heeled sandals. Ellie recognized them as the shoes Chelsea had been wearing that morning.

'These bad boys would have left behind an imprint like a big exclamation point.'

'Anything else?' Rogan asked.

'We picked up a bunch of garbage lying around – Coke cans, cigarette butts, that kind of crap. We'll look for prints. Have you guys talked to the ME yet?'

'Next stop,' Rogan said.

'Well, I've got one piece of good news for you. I took the shoes, but the ME took the clothes. But before they carried the vic away to the bus, I dusted her shirt. I pulled one latent off the underside of the top button of her blouse.'

'Chances are, she was the one to leave it behind.'

Mariah nodded. 'Probably, but that's not the best part.' She paused to make sure she had their full attention. 'When I was working on her blouse, I saw a stain that may or may not have been seminal fluid.'

Rogan rubbed his palms together. 'Now that's what I'm talking about.'

'Don't go getting too excited. The girl could've

61

dripped a smoothie on herself, for all I know. I can run the print in a couple of hours, see if there's a match in the database. The stain – I can tell you within a day or so whether it's bodily fluid or Tasti-Delite. But if it's the former, it'll take a good couple of weeks before we get DNA back.'

'But the fingerprint in a couple of hours?'

'End of the day at the latest.'

'Call my cell, all right?' Rogan gave her his card.

'No problem. And congrats on landing Jeffrey James here, Hatcher. He's a good egg.'

More than five miles north, a man exited the 6 train at 103rd Street and Lexington. He kept his head down and his hands in his pockets, focusing on each step as he tried to ignore the steady push of harried subway riders hoping to catch a waiting train.

He hated the proximity to other people that was required by mass transportation. The eye contact. The bumps. The pressing of sweaty bodies against one another in the rush of squeezing onto the train before the doors closed. The name – mass transportation – said it all. The transport of the masses. Moving through narrow turnstiles like cattle moving through the sorting gates. Moo, cow, moo.

His hatred of the subway was part of the reason he paid for a car and two garage parking spots, one near home, one near work. But today his car was on West Eleventh Street for complete interior detailing – rugs vacuumed, mats shampooed, every surface hand-polished. He had worked quickly last night on that desolate Tribeca corner outside the Holland Tunnel, but he'd nevertheless been careful, strangling the girl in the front seat, then moving the body to the carefully draped plastic tarp in his trunk for the cutting. Now, for a mere hundred bucks, any trace of the girl would be gone from his Taurus.

He walked briskly up Lexington Avenue to the familiar brick building at 105th Street. He used his security key to open the front door. No doorman. No elevators, which meant no cameras. No electronic entry system that tracked the residents' comings and goings. Those were the kinds of luxuries that could cost you big-time down the road.

He climbed the stairs to his third-floor apartment. Used one key on the auxiliary mortise dead latch. Heard the metal tumble from the block cylinder. Used another key on the dead bolt. Inserted the same key into the doorknob. Then he was home.

He did a quick protective sweep of the apartment. Living room, kitchen, bedroom, bathroom, two closets. Everything was in place. He checked the light on his answering machine. No calls.

He rolled the brown leather ottoman away from its matching chair and pushed it against the living room wall. Then he took a seat on the floor – back against the ottoman, legs crossed in front of him – and carefully pulled up six wood parquet tiles, stacking them neatly to his left as he went, one through six. He worked his index finger into a crevice in the subfloor. It took three tries before he popped up the rectangular piece of removable particleboard. That was how perfectly he had cut it to fit – like the last piece of a jigsaw puzzle, disappearing into the rest of the world around it.

He propped the particleboard carefully against the sofa, then took a deep breath. He reached in and removed two ziplock bags. He placed both on the floor in front of him. He didn't dare remove the contents of the one on the right – too much of a danger that it wouldn't all make it back in. He allowed himself to open the one on the left and remove a single earring and a small plastic card.

The earring was a chandelier of crystal and red beads dangling from a simple gold hook. The plastic rectangle was an Indiana driver's license. It had been in the girl's teeny-tiny purse, along with a lipstick, a cell phone, a hotel key, and a credit card. Name: Jennifer Green. According to the date of birth, she was twenty-four years old.

The license probably wasn't real. She hadn't said she was from Indiana, and girls like that often had reasons for using fake names and IDs. Not to mention, he realized now, that the photograph was too good – too posed, too pretty – to have originated with any Department of Motor Vehicles.

The girl's credit card had been in yet another name, and the thought had crossed his mind it might have been stolen. He'd tossed it in a garbage can along the FDR, along with the tarp and the girl's pants.

The picture on the license was definitely his Jennifer, though. Those were undeniably the same girl's bright blue eyes, round cheeks, and square jaw. That sexy smile, turned up on one side like she had a secret she might just be willing to share under the right circumstances. And, whether it was real or not, the card had belonged to her. She had carried it, touched it, used it. Those were the things that mattered – not the name or address.

He looked at his watch. He was running on empty but had a meeting at three. He held the ID carefully between his left index finger and thumb. He unbuttoned his pants with his right hand. For the next three minutes, his eyes remained fixed on the other plastic bag – still sealed, its contents still safe and contained. All of that beautiful wavy blond hair worn by Jennifer Green in her fake Indiana driver's license belonged to him now.

Chapter Nine

By Ellie's estimate, the drive from East River Park to the medical examiner's office up by Bellevue would take at least eight minutes, even with the help of police lights on the FDR. Eight minutes wasn't a lot, but it was too long to ride in total silence, and just about the right amount of time to ask Rogan the question that was on her mind.

'So I noticed Mariah Florkoski said you were lucky not to get paired up with Larry Winslow.' She had seen Winslow around the squad room. As far as she could tell, he worked on his own, and only on desk jobs.

'You got Florkoski's name after just one meet? I thought I was good with names.'

'I think the name I was more interested in was Larry Winslow.'

'The guy's the next to retire. And he's lazy. Now Casey, my old partner, he did it right. Everyone knew he wanted to ride out the end in Arizona, but he worked the job a hundred percent every day. Everyone was surprised when he took off right at twenty years. But Winslow's just counting down the hours. No one in the house wants to work with that. Lucky for me you came along.'

'But you never would have gotten partnered with him after you'd just had one partner retire on you. Eckels made it sound like I was the one who was supposed to inherit Winslow. In fact, he said I had you to thank for sparing me.'

Rogan reached for the radio, hit the power button, and began scanning for a song that met his approval. He settled on Hot 97, a mainstream hip-hop station. He turned up the volume on a Kanye West tune, and Ellie reached over and turned it down a notch.

'Sorry, but if we're going to be partners, you need to know now I like dealing with things head-on. If I'm out of line, bringing up something I shouldn't, just tell me. I'll back off. But drowning me out with the radio?'

'Don't read into it. It's just, this is my joint, y'know?' Rogan moved his head back and forth with the beat.

'Yeah, I know. And I also know there's some story behind how you and I became partners. And if everyone else in the house knows about it, I thought maybe I should, too.'

'See? This right here? That's what the issue was.' Rogan turned the radio off.

'What do you mean, "This right here"?'

'This whole dialogue.' Rogan moved his right hand back and forth between them. 'It's like fighting with your girl or something. Like, "C'mon baby, we just need to talk." '

'Uh, except I'm not your girl, and I didn't call you "baby." '

'That's not what I meant. It's just, partners need to *get* each other, you know? And, well, some of the guys weren't so sure you'd ever be able to get them, and vice versa.'

'Because of the whole not-having-boy-parts thing? Because that's not really something I can get past.'

'Honestly? Yeah, that's probably part of it. But it's got a lot more to do with how you got into the unit. It doesn't help that McIlroy brought you over – my moms taught me not to talk smack about the dead, but no one liked that guy. He was a show-off. He had a picture of him and Rudy and Bill Bratton on his desk. Who does that? And then that First Date case exploded all over the place, and suddenly it's your face in all the papers instead of his. Then your cute little self makes second grade in record time, and you're in the squad? You have to see that's a hard pill to swallow. The guys in the squad are all asking who's your rabbi.'

The old Tammany Hall phrase was now standard code for questioning a fellow officer's connections. She had wondered how long it would take for another detective to call her out on the genesis of her new assignment. After four years on patrol, she had spent only one year as a detective before the First Date case had come along. In the aftermath, she found herself holding newfound leverage with the department brass. A gig in the homicide squad was unusual for her level of experience, but not prohibited, and Ellie had cashed in all her chips to get it. She supposed she was her own rabbi.

'Look, I know I got here faster than most, and I know I have to put in my dues, but I made sure to stay out of the papers on the First Date case.'

'That trip to Kansas wasn't exactly secret.'

'That was on my own time. For my family. Anyone who would even *begin* to suggest that I get off talking to the press about my father has no idea what we've been through.'

For more than twenty-five years, the Wichita police had insisted that Jerry Hatcher killed himself. For more than a quarter of a century, Ellie's mother had to live with the consequences of that decision: no insurance money, no pension, no answers. The trip to Wichita had offered a chance to prove that her father had not voluntarily widowed his wife and left his children fatherless. Of course she had to go. And when *Dateline* called her for an interview, she had to give it.

'I'm not saying any of this is fair,' Rogan said. 'I'm just saying how it is. You worked with McIlroy. You're in the news just like McIlroy. That means you've essentially inherited his shit. Plus you're a woman, plus you're all blond and pretty and wholesome looking, and people think you got a leg up from that.'

'And so how did that translate into me almost getting partnered with Winslow?'

Rogan paused before answering. 'Because Lieutenant Eckels told everyone that's what he was planning to do unless someone else volunteered. It was Eckels's way of leading from the top down, making sure we all knew it was all right with him if we gave you the cold shoulder. You should've seen Winslow's face. Ironically, I don't think it had anything to do with you personally. That man just doesn't want to be out in the street anymore.'

'So why aren't I with Winslow? Why am I with you?'

Given the strings she'd pulled, she knew why Eckels never said good morning when he passed her on the way to the locker room. She got why he'd given her nothing but grunt work last week. She would even have understood if Eckels had partnered her up with a loser like Winslow. What she didn't understand is why Rogan would have gone out on a limb for her. Cops who were skeptical of her, she could handle. Old news. She'd eventually win them over. A man who gave her a pass for no obvious reason was another problem altogether.

Rogan kept his eyes on the road.

'Because, you know, I'm not looking to get personal with anyone I work with.'

Rogan's stoic expression changed to a stifled smile, then he broke out into a full laugh. 'In your dreams, woman. I'm very much spoken for. Oh, my lord, look who thinks she's all irresistible and shit.'

'That's not what I meant. It's just – I didn't know why – really, that is *not* what I meant.'

'That's exactly what you meant. Stupid-ass Eckels goes and tells you I stepped up to the plate, and you assume the only reason a man would help you out is if he's looking to hit that. Well, don't think I didn't get the same flack around the house. That, or they figured I was somehow sympatico with you because of the number of times I've heard bullshit behind my back. *Affirmative-action hire. Diversity detective.*'

'And that's not it either?'

'Nope.'

'So this is just going to remain a lifelong mystery?

D. B. Cooper, Jimmy Hoffa, and why J. J. Rogan rescued Ellie Hatcher?'

His smile faded as he turned onto First Avenue. 'I trust my instincts about people. I thought Eckels sticking you with Winslow sucked, and I thought it was going to cost the squad a good cop. And let's just say I haven't always had the easiest time with partners myself.'

It was the closest she was going to get to an answer, at least for now. 'So you saved me,' she said in a fairy-tale voice.

'If you want to think of it that way.'

'I do.'

'All right, then. Can I listen to my radio now?'

'You may.'

He turned up the volume and began moving with the beat again. 'And I'm sorry to break this to you, Hatcher, but I really am spoken for. I was just telling my girl last night you and I were getting on good.'

Ellie looked out the window and bopped her head a little, too.

The Manhattan office of the chief medical examiner was located on First Avenue and Thirtieth Street, just north of the Bellevue Hospital Center. As they rolled past the canopied glass entrance of the hospital's new addition, they caught a glimpse of the original building's historic facade, still standing behind the modern entrance.

Bellevue Hospital is the site of the nation's first ambulance service and maternity ward and the oldest public hospital in the state. But outside of New York, it's known for one thing and one thing only: its crazies. Ellie had lived in the city for ten years now, but it was still hard for her to hear the word *Bellevue* without envisioning a stringy-haired man in a straitjacket screaming like a hyena.

Rogan found a spot on the street in front of the ME's office. When they stepped out of the car, the sun was peeking out through a break in the clouds above them, and the air was still.

They made their way through the building's glass doors and up to the fourth floor. A clerk at the front window checked their shields, buzzed them through to the back, and pointed them in the direction of a stocky man standing at a nearby desk, dictating into a digital voice recorder. He had brown curly hair and a graying beard, and wore a white lab coat over khakis and blue sweater. He held up one finger while he completed his thought, then flipped a button to turn off the recorder.

'J. J. Rogan, right?'

Rogan accepted his handshake. 'You've got a good memory, Doc. This is my partner, Ellie Hatcher.'

'Richard Karr,' the man said, extending his hand. 'We spoke on the phone. First murder case?'

'Second,' Ellie said, 'but close enough.'

'All right, well, our first one all together, then. Let's hope I can help you out. Now when you called, Detective, you said our young Miss Hart was nineteen years old and was last seen alive at a nightclub last night at two thirty a.m., correct?'

'That's right.'

'That's consistent with my best estimation of her time of death. Rigor mortis hadn't set in yet.' Corpses began to stiffen about three hours after death, due to changes in the muscles' biochemistry. 'I found undigested pasta. You said she last ate at ten o'clock?'

'That's when her friends say they finished eating.'

'Again, it's consistent. Digestion was well past the gastric phase, and into the duodenum –'

'She was killed sometime between three and five this morning?' Ellie asked, cutting to the chase. Chelsea's friends last saw her dancing at two thirty; her pallor was gray by the time Ellie saw her at five thirty. It only stood to reason.

'Sorry, some of the detectives are more dazzled by the science than others,' Dr. Karr said. 'Okay, so, on to some other findings, then. You probably already know this too, but Miss Hart appears to have taken full advantage of the libations at said club. She had a blood alcohol content of point-two-six.'

'Drunk times three,' Ellie said.

'Three and a quarter, to be precise. Now, it takes the liver sixty to ninety minutes to metabolize the alcohol in a single serving of liquor, so the body's BAC actually continues to rise during that time before it starts to dissipate. Depending on how long she was drinking –'

'Her friends say she had an early drink before dinner,' Ellie cut in, 'but then the real partying started around ten. She was definitely still drinking at ten thirty, and the club closed at four.'

Karr nodded, looking up to the ceiling as he ran the

numbers. 'Very well, then. Assuming she continued her consumption, I'm probably correct that she was still on the upswing at the time of death. With a body weight of only a hundred and twenty-two pounds, my best guess is she must have consumed nine or ten drinks over the course of the night.'

Ellie shook her head at the stupidity of it all. Attractive girl, scantily clad, underage. Blasted out of her mind. Wandering the streets of Manhattan alone in the middle of the night. A few times a year, a handful of girls were killed after making the identical mistake. And no one seemed to learn.

'Plus we've got the tox screen. Positive for crystal meth.'

That one caught Ellie by surprise. She liked to think she could spot a liar, and none of the usual red flags went up with Chelsea's friends. They'd been clear: no sex, no drugs.

'Can you tell how recent?'

'She used within four hours of her death.'

Add methed up to attractive, scantily clad, underage, and drunk. Ellie couldn't think of a more dangerous combination.

Rogan cut in with a question of his own. 'CSU thought the vic was killed off-site and then moved to the East River scene.'

'Oh, yes. Certainly. As you might know, it's the power of the beating heart that keeps our blood cells and platelets all mixed together in our vessels.' He panto-mimed a mixing gesture with his hands. 'So once the heart stops beating, and the mixer loses its power, the red blood cells begin to settle with gravity. That's what causes the telltale discoloration of lividity – that look of a layer of grape jelly beneath the skin.'

'And the discoloration on Chelsea?' Ellie asked.

'Her body may have been found propped up in a seated position, but the grape jelly was on her back.'

It meant that Chelsea Hart's body was lying faceup after her death and was then moved into the position in which she was found.

'The movement of the body was not the only postmortem activity. Based on the minimal amount of blood on the wounds' edges, my best estimation is that the cuts you saw on her arms, legs, and face were inflicted after death. If you told me she'd been immersed in water – a hot tub or a bath, for example – I might revise my opinion to antemortem cuts, but there's no evidence of that, especially in light of the speed with which the body was discovered.'

'So cause of death is strangulation?'

'I still need to complete the entire autopsy, but yes, I'm confident that's what I will ultimately conclude. Looking at the pattern of bruising on her neck, you can see she was strangled manually, from the front.' He held his hands out, fingers strong and splayed. 'Thumbs at the larynx, palms on the carotid arteries, fingers wrapped all the way around the back of her neck. With her on her back, and him on top of her, it creates a tremendous amount of pressure.'

Manual strangulation was in many ways the most dedicated form of murder. It wasn't an instantaneous decision, like the pulling of a trigger or the slashing of a throat. It wasn't remote, like poison or a contracted kill.

And there was nothing to physically separate the killer from his victim – no rope, no scarf, no belt to do the strangler's job for him. Everything about the act guaranteed that if the killer had any kernel of doubt – any second of hesitation – he could stop. Among murderers, stranglers who used their bare hands were the most committed and least repentant.

And they were almost always motivated by sexual desire.

'Any evidence of sexual assault?' she asked.

'Surprisingly, there was no indication of either vaginal or anal trauma. I did a rape kit anyway, obviously. Sometimes we get a hit on the oral swab. It will take a couple of days for the initial results on the swabs – weeks for any DNA profile, if we do in fact have any fluids to examine. Will there be evidence of voluntary sex within the last few days?'

'Not according to her friends. She has a boyfriend who's supposedly been in Mexico all week.'

'Well, at least we'll know that any DNA we find is for us. That's all I have for you now,' Karr said, switching gears abruptly, 'but I'll be in touch when we get those labs back.'

As they walked back to the car in the sunshine that was warming the cold morning into day, Ellie thought about the last hour of Chelsea Hart's life and the fear and pain she must have experienced. Then she pictured Chelsea two hours earlier, smiling, dancing, and telling her best friend that she was having the best night ever.

Chapter Ten

Chelsea Hart's favorite movies were *Run Lola Run*, *The Notebook*, and *The Princess Bride*. Her favorite books were *Wuthering Heights* and *The Unbearable Lightness of Being*. Her favorite drink was called an Angel's Tip, a mix of dark crème de cacao and heavy cream that she swore prevented hangovers. She wanted to meet Ellen DeGeneres and Johnny Depp.

She had ninety-two friends.

Ellie scrolled through Chelsea's MySpace profile one more time as she snacked on spoonfuls of the Nutella spread she kept in her top desk drawer.

'You sure you don't want any?' she asked, extending the open glass jar in Rogan's direction.

He glared at her. 'Are we going to continue this ritual every afternoon? You offer me that funky stuff you call food, so I can say, No, thank you?'

She pulled the jar back and removed a healthy spoonful. 'Seems rude not to offer.'

'You can offer it to me today, tomorrow, and every day 'til I retire, and I promise I will always decline. So consider yourself excused from all social obligation when it comes to that stuff.'

That was fine with Ellie. No sharing meant more for her.

Chelsea Hart's top MySpace friends were Stefanie, Jordan, and a Mark whom Ellie assumed was her boy-friend, Mark Linton. She listed as her heroes 'my parents, friends, and random-ass people I meet everyday.'

Ellie clicked on the link that read 'My Pictures.' The majority of the photographs depicted groups of teenagers clustered together, arms around each other's shoulders, smiling for the camera. Chelsea was in the middle of most of the clusters. Stefanie was almost always close by.

An entire photo album was devoted to a white-and-brown English bulldog that was apparently named Stacy Keach. Another contained pictures of Chelsea in various high school theater productions – *Godspell*, *A Chorus Line*, *Into the Woods*. Another of Chelsea in a purple-and-gold track uniform. Ellie stared at the intensity in Chelsea's face – a perfect blend of happiness, pride, and pain – as she pressed through the ribbon across a finishing line, and she wondered how a girl like this had wound up drunk, alone, and on crystal meth in New York City.

'We need to get hold of Chelsea's parents,' Ellie said. 'All I did was Google the name Chelsea Hart, and her MySpace page popped right up. Once the news hits, every member of the press will be scouring this for all the details about Chelsea's personal life. They need to pull it down.'

'They've got to be on a plane by now. When I talked

to them this morning, they sounded like they were literally going straight to the airport once we hung up.'

'Knock, knock.' Jack Chen rapped his knuckles against an imaginary door. 'Detectives, there's a couple here to see you. They say they're Chelsea Hart's parents?'

'Talk about *on cue*.' Ellie gave a mock shudder. 'Creepy.'

Rogan's phone rang. He held up an index finger toward her before answering. 'Rogan . . . Correct. That's my case . . . Yes, I believe they just walked into the precinct a second ago . . . That goes without saying . . . Of course . . . I'll be sure to tell them you called.'

He returned the handset to its cradle. 'Amend that to *really fucking creepy*. That was the mayor's deputy chief of staff. Apparently, they want to be certain that we give the Harts our closest attention.'

They were on their way to the front of the squad room when Dan Eckels popped his head out of his office. 'A word with you two?' he said, waving them over.

'The vic's parents are up front, sir.'

'I just got a call from the assistant chief. The Harts have already been in contact with the mayor's office.'

'We know, sir. We don't want to leave them waiting.'

'Right. You're taking them to interview three?'

'Assuming it's empty,' Ellie said, still following Rogan. 'I'll sit in.'

'Of course. Whatever you want.'

Paul Hart had thinning brown hair, ruddy skin, and an extra twenty pounds on his large frame. He wore a light blue crewneck sweater over a collared shirt and navy blue dress slacks. His wife Miriam wore a long black jersey dress that could have been selected either for mourning or simply as a wrinkle-free travel outfit. She had chin-length light gray hair that had probably once been blond, and she seemed unconcerned with her red, puffy eyes or makeup-free face.

They were probably just hitting fifty, married more than twenty years, and walked into interview room 3 holding hands. Even on the most difficult day of their lives together, the Harts carried themselves like good people.

Rogan took care of the introductions and gestured for the couple to be seated next to each other. He took the chair on the other side of the table. Ellie and Eckels stood against the window of the interview room, creating the impression of more privacy.

'Thank you for coming so quickly,' Rogan said. 'We weren't expecting you until later tonight.'

'We made some calls on the way to the airport,' Miriam said. 'A friend is a friend of a friend of the CEO of Centennial Wireless. They had a private jet waiting for us at the Fort Wayne Airport.'

'The people close to us are doing everything they can.' Paul gave his wife's hand a squeeze. 'We're at least fortunate in that respect.'

Were Ellie in their position, she did not think she would be able to find anything to be thankful for. She was constantly amazed by the variation in human responses to misfortune.

'It's as if we had this entire network of people

working the phones for us while we were coming to terms with all this on the plane,' Miriam continued in businesslike fashion. 'It turned out that Paul's brother-in-law was fraternity brothers with someone in your mayor's office. He made some calls, and now we're supposed to speak this afternoon with some volunteers with the Polly Klaas Foundation – you know, just to help us navigate the system and figure out what we need to do.'

'They're an excellent organization,' Ellie said, wondering if her words sounded as hollow as they felt.

'You just let us know how we can assist,' Eckels said.

'You can assist,' Paul said firmly, 'by finding the person who murdered our daughter.'

Ellie intervened before Eckels unwittingly offended the Harts further. 'We're doing everything we can on the investigative front. The crime scene unit and the medical examiner's office have collected some physical evidence that might prove very important. We obtained detailed statements this morning from your daughter's friends. They were extremely helpful. Thanks to Stefanie and Jordan, we have a thorough timeline of their activities yesterday and are following up on every lead.'

'Are the girls here?' Paul asked.

'They just left a few minutes ago,' Rogan said. 'They worked with a sketch artist for a couple of hours –'

'You have a suspect?' Miriam interrupted, sitting up straighter.

Rogan shook his head. 'It's too early to say. Just a man Chelsea was talking to at the club last night. But the sketch artist wants to work with the girls again tomorrow, so we had a victim's advocate take them back to the hotel.'

'We're going to need them to stick around in New York for the time being,' Ellie said. 'Once we have a suspect, it's essential that we get a prompt identification.'

Miriam nodded. 'I'll call their parents and the university this afternoon and make sure they know it's important that the girls stay here. We'll be here, too. However long it takes. Those poor girls,' Miriam said, her voice breaking. 'I promised their parents I'd make sure they were holding up.'

'They're strong girls,' Rogan said. 'They're hanging in there.'

'I do think they're putting some of the blame on themselves,' Ellie added.

'They shouldn't. Do you know how many times I caught Chelsea breaking curfew, just to learn that Stefanie had been there trying to get her to come home?'

'Our daughter wasn't perfect, but she was a remarkable girl,' Paul said.

That single sentence was enough to fully break Miriam's composure. Her shoulders began to shake, and she choked back a sob. 'She was unique and wonderful and remarkable in every way. But she did what she wanted, Paul. I was trying to say it wasn't Stefanie or Jordan's fault. They didn't do this.'

'Shh.' Paul placed an arm around his wife's shoulder. 'What do we need to do next?' he asked quietly.

'Unfortunately, I think you need to prepare yourselves for significant media attention. Reporters are going to call you for quotes, for photographs, for old

82

yearbooks. Your daughter's MySpace profile will have thousands of hits before the end of the day.'

'The Polly Klaas people mentioned that, too,' Paul said, 'right off the bat. They're going to contact the company on our behalf to remove her profile.'

'Good,' Ellie said. 'They can help you juggle the media requests as well. You're also free to refer anyone you want to the NYPD's public information office.'

'What else?' Paul asked.

Rogan cleared his throat. 'When you're ready, we're going to need you to make an official identification of your daughter's body.'

Miriam let out another sob, but Paul nodded stoically. 'We're ready. I'll do it,' he said to his wife. 'You won't need to see.'

'I can take you to the medical examiner's office,' Eckels offered, 'while Detectives Rogan and Hatcher continue the investigation.'

The Harts muttered their thanks as they rose from their seats. As Miriam Hart passed Ellie, she turned and looked at her directly with puffy, bloodshot, pleading eyes. 'Chelsea wasn't just a drunk girl at a club last night. She was my baby.'

'I know,' Ellie said, returning the eye contact. 'She loved *Wuthering Heights* and that bulldog of hers. She lit up a stage and could run like the wind. And she was good to her friends. She was the glue that held them together, and she could make them laugh through anything.'

A tear fell down Miriam's cheek, and she mouthed a silent 'Thank you.'

Part II

Dream Witness

Chapter Eleven

The distance between the Thirteenth Precinct and the Meatpacking District was almost exactly two miles, but culturally, the neighborhoods were a globe apart. The short drive from the east twenty-something blocks of Manhattan to the far west teens unveiled a dramatic transformation from the sterile and generic high rises of Stuyvesant Town to what was currently the city's hottest neighborhood.

The key to the Meatpacking District's current popularity rested in its unique blend of glamor and grit. All of the upscale requirements were here – high-end boutiques, trendy clubs with signature cocktails, expensive restaurants with tiny portions piled into aesthetically pleasing towers. But they existed in loftlike, pared-down spaces that still had the feel – if not the actual structure – of rehabbed warehouses. The streets outside were narrow, many still cobblestone, adding to the sense of an old neighborhood uncovered, dusted off, and polished by its latest visitor.

And, of course, there was the name. Not SoHo. Not Tribeca. Not NoLIta. Nothing cutesy, crisp, or clean.

This was the Meatpacking District, and, lest you forget it, the distinctly bloody odor emanating from the remaining butchers and beef wholesalers was there to remind you: this was a neighborhood with substance, history, and dirt beneath its blue-collar fingernails. Just ask the Appletini-sipping supermodel taking a load off her Manolo Blahniks on the stool next to yours.

Ellie had called Pulse from the car on their way to the west side. There had been no answer at the club where Chelsea was last seen – just a recording over techno music with the club's location and hours – but Rogan figured it was worth a pop-in before trying to track down a manager through business licenses and other paperwork.

The entrance to the club was underwhelming, at least before sundown. No velvet rope. No bass thumping onto the street outside. No well-dressed revelers lined up in front, eager to be selected for admission. No stone-faced body builders clothed in black to pass judgment on who was worthy and who must remain waiting. Just a set of double wooden doors – tall, heavy, and closed, like the sealed entrance to a fortress.

A frosted glass banner ran along the top of the threshold, the word *Pulse* etched discreetly across it. The trendiest establishments always had the least conspicuous signage. Some bars had no signs at all. One hot spot around the corner from here didn't even have a name. If you were cool enough to be welcome, you'd know it was there, and you'd know where it was.

As Ellie pulled open the heavy wooden door on the right, the first thing that struck her about the darkened club was its temperature. In the second week of March, it shouldn't have been colder inside the building than out. 'Geez. They're taking the whole meatpacking concept a bit literally,' she said.

'Don't you get out, Hatcher?'

'Not to places like this.' Ellie wondered again about her partner's off-duty lifestyle. She scanned the lofty space. The club was dark and windowless, but had enough accent lights here and there to provide a general sense of the place. Clean. White. Really white. Swaths of crisp cotton hung from the twenty-foot ceilings to the floor. Ellie's usual haunts were decorated by dartboards, jukeboxes, and dusty black-and-white photographs of pregentrified New York.

'A few hours from now, bodies will be crammed into this place like a full pack of cigarettes. And trust me, no one will be complaining that it's cold.'

'Hey, numbnuts.' A tall, muscular man wearing a fitted black T-shirt and dark blue jeans appeared behind the glass bar. 'We're closed.' His announcement delivered, he continued on with his business of unpacking bottles of Grey Goose vodka from a cardboard box.

Ellie looked at her partner with amusement. 'Which of the numbnuts gets to break the news?'

Rogan flashed a bright white smile, pulled his shield from his waist, and held it beside his face. 'You say you're closed, but your door out front's unlocked. Who's the numbnut?'

The man behind the bar emptied his hands of the two bottles he was holding and brushed his palms off on his jeans pockets. 'Sorry 'bout that. You guys look more like customers than cops.'

He stepped around the counter and met them halfway, next to an elevated runway extending across the dance floor. A trim of hot pink neon light ran along the runway edge.

'I'm expecting a couple deliveries,' he said, nodding toward the entrance. 'But I'm the only one here right now.'

'Not a problem if you're the person who can help us out,' Rogan said. 'And who exactly are you?'

'Oh, sorry.' Two apologies already. That was good. Rogan was establishing his authority over a guy who was used to lording over the minions who felt blessed to enter this sanctuary. 'Scott Bell. I'm the assistant club manager. Is there some kind of problem? We've been keeping our occupancy down since the last time you guys were out.'

'We're not here about fire codes. We're here because of her.' Rogan removed a sheet of paper from his suit pocket and unfolded it. It was the photograph of Chelsea and her friends that had been taken with Jordan's iPhone the previous night at the restaurant before dinner. Ellie had cropped it down to a close-up of Chelsea. They were more likely to find people who recognized her using that picture than one taken today.

Bell the bartender took a two-second glance at the printout. 'I don't know what to tell you. We've got hundreds of girls just like her coming through here every night.'

'Well, this particular girl was here last night,' Rogan said. 'Late.'

'So were a lot of people.'

'Yeah, but my guess is, most of them got home safe and sound and are sleeping it off as we speak.'

'What's the problem? She OD'd, and you want to blame it on my club? I don't know how many times I've told you guys that we do everything we can to keep that shit out of here.'

'You really think two detectives are going to show up in the middle of the day about some drugs going in and out of a Manhattan nightclub? Why don't we go down to Christopher Street and bust some of the flip-flop boys for having wide stances while we're at it?'

'Hey, whatever floats your boat.'

'Take another look, Scott,' Rogan said. As he tapped the paper in front of the bar manager another time, Ellie found herself looking at it as well. Now that the picture was cropped to focus only on Chelsea, something about it was bothering her. She scanned the photograph from top to bottom, left to right, but couldn't place her finger on the problem.

'She was here last night. She was hanging in one of the VIP rooms.' Bell locked resentful eyes with Rogan until the detective dropped the bombshell. 'And she was found strangled a couple hours later.'

Bell's eyes dropped immediately to the printout. 'Oh, fuck.'

'There we go. That's the most authentic response you've given us since we got here. By tomorrow morning, the name of this club is going to be in every

91

newspaper, next to a picture just like this one, while everyone who scans the headline is going to wonder whether this is a safe place to be. So if I were you, I'd drop the attitude and start asking how you can help us.'

Bell swallowed. 'I – I –' He ran the fingertips of both hands through his dark brown hair. 'Fuck. I don't know what I can do to help. I *don't* remember her.'

'You're sure?' Ellie asked.

He shook his head. 'If you're saying she was here, then she was here. But when you spend enough time in clubs, everyone looks the same.'

Ellie had of course never met Chelsea Hart, but she found herself replaying flashes of the conversations she'd had that morning with Chelsea's friends. *Chelsea would never leave us in limbo like this. She was always the one who'd meet other people for us to hang out with. Chelsea's going to freak if she misses the deadline for her Othello paper; she wants to be an English major. Someone has to remember seeing her – she's a really good dancer.* It seemed profoundly sad that Chelsea had spent her last couple of hours in a place where no one was special, where everyone looked the same.

'Her friends said she was in a VIP room,' Ellie said. 'Who were the VIPs?'

'You're kidding, right?'

'Hey, now, I thought we were done with the attitude,' Rogan said.

'Sorry. It's just, I mean, we call them VIP rooms, and sometimes we get some actual celebs in here, but usually because they're C-list and we're paying them. Most nights, it's just some dumb group of nobodies who called with enough notice and slapped down a fat enough deposit for prepaid liquor to create a guest list.'

'See, you're more helpful than you think,' Ellie said. 'We'll take a look at those guest lists.'

Bell's face momentarily brightened before it fell again. 'Shit. They'll be gone by now.' He made his way over to a stainless steel podium near the entrance and fished out a clipboard from a built-in shelf. He skimmed through the top few pages, then flipped to the back. 'This one's for tonight. We got rid of last night's already.'

'It's not in a computer?' Ellie asked.

'All in pencil. Too many last-minute changes to run back and forth to the office.'

'Garbage?'

'Gone,' Bell said, shaking his head. 'We've got to get the place clean right after closing so it doesn't stink like all the spilled booze.'

'We'll take credit card numbers instead,' Ellie said. 'Easy enough for us to get names from there.'

'What credit card numbers?'

'You said people have to leave a deposit for the VIP rooms? I assume that involves credit cards.'

'Yeah, right. Okay, yeah. I can get that for you. Definitely.' It was clear from Bell's eagerly nodding head that he was happy to have finally found a way to be useful.

'A list of employees would be nice, too,' she added.

The nodding continued for a few rounds, but then slowed to a pensive halt. 'Employees. From here?' Bell asked, pointing to the ground in front of him.

'Unless you know of some other club this girl went to before someone tossed her body by the East River.'

'But – but what does that have to do with –'

'Um, hello? Does the name Darryl Littlejohn ring a bell?'

A couple of years earlier, a student from Ellie's alma mater, John Jay College, disappeared after having a final drink at a SoHo bar just before closing time. Her barely recognizable naked body was found the next day on a road outside Spring Creek Park in Brooklyn. It took police a week to conclude that the helpful bouncer who told them he'd seen the victim leave alone was in fact the same man who'd stuffed a sock in the girl's mouth, wrapped her entire head with transparent packing tape, and then brutally raped and strangled her. When she saw the victim's photograph in the newspaper, Ellie thought that she might have met the criminology graduate student during an alumni event at John Jay's Women's Center.

'That's my point,' Bell said. 'That guy had, like, five felony convictions.'

Seven, actually, Ellie thought. And he was on parole. His mere presence in that bar past nine o'clock at night would have been enough to violate him if his PO had known.

'We don't run that kind of club. I do background checks. We do drug testing. We have biannual employment reviews.' Bell ticked off each of his good deeds on his fingers.

'Scott, calm down.' Rogan put his hand on Bell's shoulder and gave it a small squeeze. It was one of the standard moves that Ellie rarely got to use. For Rogan, and about ninety percent of cops, a small touch like that was a sign of brotherhood, a soothing indication that the touch's recipient was viewed as one of the good guys. From thirty-year-old Ellie, with her wavy blond hair and a body that men always seemed to notice no matter how modestly she dressed, that kind of contact was viewed – depending on the confidence of the recipient – as either provocative or emasculating.

'When are you gonna clue in?' Rogan continued. 'We are not code enforcement. We're not vice. We want to find out who murdered this sweet college girl who was visiting New York from Indiana. That's all we're trying to do. There's no problem here.' Rogan moved his hand across the gap between the two men's chests. They were copacetic.

'Yeah, all right. I got it on the computer in back. With the credit cards.'

'Good man, Scott.'

'I gotta call my boss, though, okay? The manager.'

'You wouldn't be doing your job if you didn't. But you'll tell him we're cool, right?'

'Yeah, no problem.'

'Do we need to worry about him back there alone?' Ellie asked, watching Bell walk through an office door at the rear of the club.

'I don't get that feeling,' Rogan said, helping himself to a spot behind the counter to check out the labels on the various liquor bottles. 'Do you?'

'Nope.'

'Just checking?'

'Yep.'

Ellie was grateful to have a few minutes away from Scott Bell so she could refocus her attention on the photograph of Chelsea Hart that had been bothering her.

'Take a look again at this,' she said, laying the now-familiar image before Rogan on the bar. 'Notice anything significant?'

'No, but apparently I'm supposed to. What's up?'

'Earrings. She was wearing earrings last night at dinner, but not this morning when we found her at the park.'

He squinted, mentally pulling up an image of the body he'd seen at the crime scene. 'You're sure?'

'Positive.'

He was silent for a few seconds, and Ellie assumed he was having the same thoughts that ran through her mind when she'd first made the observation. No pawn-shop would buy what was obviously costume jewelry, so there was no point following that avenue. The earrings could have fallen out in a struggle. Or, more interestingly, they could have been removed as a souvenir.

'Any ideas about how we use that information?' Rogan asked.

'Not yet.'

'Well, at least we know what to look for.'

'If only we knew where to look.'

Bell returned from the back office carrying a thin stack of paper just as Rogan's cell phone rang. Rogan flipped open the phone, read the screen, and excused himself to the corner of the bar.

Bell handed Ellie a two-page document, neatly stapled together in the upper left-hand corner. 'This is a list of bills last night for parties with bottle service – amounts with form of payment. A couple of them paid cash, but there's a bunch of credit cards there as well.'

Ellie gave the single-spaced document a quick scan and had to suppress a cough. The two parties who paid with cash had racked up bills of nearly a thousand dollars each. Most of the credit card charges went into the four digits.

'Are these charges just for drinks?' she asked.

Bell folded his arms across his chest, his confidence returning for a subject matter that was familiar territory. 'Depends on what you mean by 'just drinks'. We don't serve food, that's for sure. But people pay big for bottle service.'

'That just means you pay for a bottle of liquor. Even if you use a triple markup, how much can that be?'

'We don't look at it as a markup.' His grin told a different story. 'It's not just a bottle. It's bottle *service*. You get the VIP room. You get a private server assigned to your room to mix and pour the drinks. It's the personal touch that people are paying for.'

'That,' Rogan said, returning from his phone call, 'and not having to wait in a five-man-deep crowd around the bar, just to get a drink.'

Ellie suddenly got the picture. In a world where a $15 martini bought you crummy service, the wealthy were willing to pay for something different.

'So how much is, I don't know, a bottle of Grey Goose, for example?'

'We're at $350.'

Now she did allow herself a cough.

'Bungalow 8's at $400,' Bell continued. 'I hear a few places are about to go even higher.'

'Some of these bills are a few thousand dollars,' Ellie said, thinking of a month's worth of take-home pay. 'A group small enough to fit in one room goes through ten bottles of liquor?'

Bell shook his head. 'No. They *order* ten bottles of liquor. One guy drinks Goose. His girl likes Patrón. His bro prefers Jack.'

'And if they don't finish it all –'

'It's just money.' Bell handed Ellie a second, thicker printout, also neatly stapled. 'I also got you our list of people here.'

Ellie flipped through the document. Six pages. Two columns on each. Names, social security numbers, addresses, phone numbers. Bell's boss must have instructed him to give full cooperation. Probably about sixty employees, all told.

'Now, like I said, on that' – Bell pressed his palms together in a prayer position near his chin – 'we do everything we're supposed to. But we've got a lot of people, you know? And if someone squeaked through –'

'I told you we're not out to sweat you,' Rogan said. 'We didn't even mention the fact that this girl we're talking about was underage.'

'Oh, Jesus. We check ID. I tell the guys every night. And we really check them. Like, no way some kid's getting in here with a Hawaii driver's license that says his name's McLovin, you know?'

Ellie smiled. 'Her friends say she had a fake ID, with a real name and everything. Thanks for this,' she said, holding up the pages Bell had given her. She retrieved a business card from the badge case she kept clipped to her waist and offered it to Bell between her index and middle fingers. 'Give us a call if you remember anything from last night that might be pertinent.'

'Yeah, okay. Thanks.'

They were almost at the exit when Bell called after them.

'Hey, um, I don't suppose there's some way you could leave our name out of the reports or anything, huh? You know, my boss wanted me to ask.'

'Sorry,' Rogan said, as he opened the heavy brown door. They both squinted as they emerged back out into the light. 'That phone call earlier was from Florkoski at CSU. The latent she pulled from the button on Chelsea Hart's shirt didn't belong to the victim.'

Chapter Twelve

They had a latent print. Now all they needed was a suspect.

That left them back at their adjacent desks, divvying up their to-do list. In her one year as a detective, Ellie had gotten used to other cops assuming she would be the one to do this kind of paper-driven legwork, perhaps because she was junior, but most likely because some of the older detectives – at least in the general investigation units – were not yet comfortable with the technological end of modern police work.

She and Rogan, however, were sharing the load. He had the list of the club's credit card charges, while she ran the list of its employees through the department's database of crime reports and through NCIC for criminal records.

Rogan scribbled something on the notes in front of him, and then thanked the person at the other end of the line before hanging up. 'I still can't get over these bar bills. Here's one for three thousand dollars, plus the guy tacked on a five-hundred-dollar tip.'

Ellie shook her head disapprovingly. 'That's barely

fifteen percent. Cheap bastard. I'm never complaining again about paying ten bucks for a drink. And where I usually go, that's with a twenty-five-percent tip.'

'Only in New York,' Rogan said. 'I got a buddy who just moved to the city a year ago from Atlanta. He says, his whole life, he thought he was doing pretty good. Had some money in his pocket. Then he came here and saw what money really is.'

She saw her opening. 'Well, if you don't mind me saying, you at least look like you're doing better than some folks.'

'You must mean my fine 'do,' Rogan said, running one hand across his shiny bald head. 'Thirteen bucks at the Astor Place barber.'

'Nice. I meant the clothes. Sorry, I notice those kinds of things.'

'That's just taste.'

Ellie didn't respond.

'Go ahead,' Rogan said with a toss of his hand. 'Ask.'

'I don't know what you mean.' She typed another name into the computer and hit the enter key.

'I don't blame you. You want to know. You want to know how I can wear the clothes in my closet, smoke a decent cigar every once in a while, drive a decent ride. Even for a detective first-grade, it's a stretch.'

Ellie apparently wasn't as curious as she thought. She'd seen Rogan smoking a cigar outside on Twenty-first Street two days ago, but hadn't thought to wonder about its price. And she'd never even seen Rogan in his own car.

'Sorry,' she said. 'I didn't mean to pry.'

'It only makes sense you'd speculate. Who wants a partner on the take, right?'

'That's not what I meant –'

'Or dealing drugs on the side. Maybe a few too many bets. When a brother's got some extra spending money, he must be up to no good. Is that about right?'

Ellie's eyes were wide, and she was suddenly very aware of the teaspoon full of hazelnut spread in her mouth. Rogan just kept staring at her. Other detectives in the squad were looking at them. She had no idea what to say.

Then Rogan slapped his hands together and began to laugh. At her, not with her. 'Oh, lord, someone take a picture of that.'

Other detectives joined the amusement.

'He pulled that speech on me six months ago.' The voice belonged to John Shannon, the detective who sat with his back to hers, facing his own partner. Shannon might have grunted a hello to Ellie, once, a few days ago. 'He gets everyone with that. Welcome to the club, Hatcher.'

When the hilarity subsided, she leaned over toward Rogan. 'Thanks. I'm in a club now.'

'Sorry. I couldn't resist. Works every time. Look, it's no big deal. A few years ago, my grandmama died. A few years before that, she married the guy who sang "Just Between Us."' Rogan hummed one bar, and Ellie immediately recognized the tune. 'Anyway, she left each of us a little extra money. Not enough to treat the house at a place like Pulse – not like that shit – but, you know, invested in the right places, I can indulge myself once in a while.'

'You don't need to explain.' Even though she hadn't meant to imply any type of accusation against Rogan, she found herself grateful for the information.

'Like I said, it's all relative in New York. Three thousand dollars for a night of partying. That's some crazy shit.'

'Do you have a sense yet who the idiots are who shelled out that kind of money last night?'

'Investment bankers. Commercial developers. And, with at least some of these, apparently shortchanged shareholders and duped clients. So far I've already got three corporate cards.'

'No known pimps? Rapists? Perhaps even a very naughty pornographer?' Ellie asked.

'Not yet. Anyone worth checking out on your end?' Just as Rogan finished asking the question, the last employee on the list popped up clean on NCIC, the National Crime Information Center. 'I gotta hand it to Bell. He wasn't kidding when he said they ran a tight ship. Most of these places are run by lowlifes, but I've got nothing.'

'Nothing? Impossible.'

The arrest of the SoHo bouncer had revealed the flagrant disregard that bar managers showed for the city's hiring regulations. That case had been a wake-up call, but only so much can change over a few years in an industry driven by profit margins.

'That goes without saying, but it's not much. I've got one guy – Jaime Rodriguez – with a six-year-old

Burg II conviction and a couple pops two years ago for suspected drug distribution, but no convictions.'

'How does he get popped twice without charges? How hard is it to make a drug case?'

'Both times, he was picked up on the street in the Bronx,' Ellie said, looking at her notes. 'High-crime neighborhood, late at night. Seen walking between open car windows and a nearby building. No drugs found in the searches incident to arrest.'

It was a standard setup for street-level drug dealing. Rodriguez would've been the negotiator, coming to an agreement on price and quantity with the customers in their cars and then directing them to a nearby location. He'd send a signal to someone – most likely a juvenile – who would run to an area stash house and meet the buyers at the agreed-upon delivery spot. Rodriguez keeps his hands clean.

'I get the picture,' Rogan said. 'I wouldn't call that nothing. The vic had meth in her system, and if it didn't come from her friends, it came from somewhere else.'

'Problem is, Rodriguez wasn't working last night.'

'Damn.'

'We'll get to him, but –'

'Yeah, I know. Anyone else?'

'I got a janitor. Leon Symanski.'

'A Polish janitor? Insert joke here.'

'I don't think you're supposed to say that.' Ellie wagged a finger in Rogan's direction. 'Leon the janitor has a prior conviction for sexual misconduct. But it was twenty years ago.'

'Could you track down any of the facts?'

'I already had the reports faxed over. He admitted having sex with a sixteen-year-old who lived in his building. Apparently the girl was a regular at the Symanski apartment – talking to the wife, helping with the baby, that kind of thing. The dad was snooping around the girl's room and found some records from an abortion clinic. He pulled her out of the Symanskis' apartment and was smacking her around in the hallway. All hell broke loose, and when the cops showed up, Symanski owned up that he was the one who got the girl pregnant. The girl said it was consensual, but at sixteen, of course, that doesn't matter.'

'Twenty years ago?'

'Yeah. Symanski would've been twenty-six at the time. He got a year's probation. No problems since.'

'A year of probation? No time?' Rogan asked.

'Weird, huh?'

'I've got to think that even twenty years ago you got more for sleeping with a teenager than shoplifting.'

'Right. So that's why I don't think we've got anything here. My Spidey senses tell me that whatever prosecutor caught Symanski's case didn't think it was a predator kind of situation.' Although all kids under the age of consent were legally off-limits, those in law enforcement frequently used their discretion to distinguish between men wrapped up in a precocious teenager's March – September experiment and the true sex offenders. 'Twenty years of law-abiding behavior since then suggests they got it right.'

'I'll call Mariah Florkoski at CSU to make sure she compares the latent from the victim's shirt against both

Rodriguez and Symanski. Maybe one of them somehow got left out of NCIC.'

'Can't hurt,' she said. It wasn't likely to help, either. Florkoski had already run the latent in the NCIC database, which should have contained prints for both Rodriguez and Symanski.

'Well, on that uplifting note, I say we get some rest and start anew tomorrow,' Rogan said. 'We'll start with the biggest credit card charge and work our way down until we find the right VIP lounge. We should have a doodle from the sketch artist by then. That will help.'

Ellie was never good at walking away from a case before she at least had a theory. She'd been that way even with her petty fraud cases. But fresh eyes and a rested mind could make up for hours of spinning the same old wheels. As much as she hated to leave, she could feel in her bones they weren't going to break this case today. Starting again tomorrow sounded good.

The man was disappointed to find a woman named Gail in the seldom-used lunchroom. She was one of a few different two-hundred-pound assistants who seemed to roam the building. He found her unpleasant to look at. Her hair dye was so black it was blue. She wore too much blush, too much lipstick, and too colorful an outfit for her amorphous frame.

But he made a point of being pleasant, even to his most disgusting coworkers.

'Hey, Gail.'

Gail glanced up from her fashion magazine, grunted a hello, and removed her second Twix bar from the wrapper. The idea of a woman like Gail using her break to focus on fashion and beauty tips struck him as pathetic. Here's a tip on self-improvement: Walk around the block and stop eating candy bars.

The man fed a dollar into one of two side-by-side vending machines. It took three attempts before the machine registered his credit. He pushed the buttons B and 3 and watched the black metal spiral spin on the second row of the machine, releasing a bag of peanut M&Ms. He retrieved the candy and his quarter of change from the machine.

On the muted television that hung on the wall next to the vending machine, the credits were rolling on *The Oprah Winfrey Show*. The man watched as Oprah peacocked across the set of her talk show in a red turtleneck and black pants, alternately pointing at the guests in their comfortable chairs and pumping her flattened palms robustly above her head. He could imagine her voice, imploring her audience to 'give it up' for the earnest speakers.

'I just love her,' Gail said.

'Doesn't everyone?' the man said in agreement.

He made his way back to his office and sat in his black leather desk chair. Using the remote control on his desk, he turned up the volume on his flat-screen TV. He pulled on the sides of his M&Ms bag to open it, then shook a couple of the colored candies directly into his mouth.

The chipper music on the television changed to a lower, more staccato tune, and Oprah's designer set was replaced by an image of the station's talking-heads duo sitting behind a desk. As seemed to be the case at least twice a week in New York, the top story was a fire, this time at a home in Long Island. Cause? Most likely an electrical problem, although police were investigating reported connections between the homeowner and the Mafia. The flames made good film from the helicopter hovering above. More at eleven.

Up in the Boogie Down Bronx, police exchanged bullets with a car full of teenagers outside the Morris housing projects in a late-night shootout. One suspect was in custody, and police continued the search for four more.

Only two stories, then straight to commercials. A freckle-faced imp fed his oatmeal to the family DVD machine; it was time for a visit to the appliance store. He flipped to another network. A dog rubbed his backside on the carpet; time to buy rug cleaner. Flip. A smiling brunette trying to convince him he needed pore-cleansing facial strips.

Back to ABC.

One more advertisement – another canine, this time selling him on light beer – and then the talking heads returned. The attractive Latina woman on the right side of the screen broke the story:

It was supposed to be the spring break of a lifetime, the trip that a young midwestern woman would always remember. But after the body of an Indiana college student was found early this morning in Manhattan's East River Park, the police are now searching for her killer.

Sources tell WABC that the victim is nineteen-year-old Chelsea Hart, a freshman at Indiana University in Bloomington. She was visiting New York City this week for spring break. Friends who accompanied Hart to a nightclub last night in the Meatpacking District say they tried to persuade her to leave earlier in the evening, but Hart chose to stay behind for one last drink. That decision proved deadly.

The frame cut to the face of a young woman with cropped black hair. The bottom of the television screen read, 'Jordan McLaughlin, friend of victim.' A reporter held a WABC microphone below her chin. The man recognized the girl from the previous night. She'd been wearing a short yellow dress.

'All we heard before we came here was how the city had changed from the old days, how it was good for tourists now. That it was safe for us to come here alone. Now I wish we'd stayed home.'

The clip ended, and the attractive news anchor returned to the screen. 'Police are still investigating. We'll bring you more, right here at WABC, as the story unfolds.'

The gray-haired male anchor on the left side of the screen used the Indiana girl's comment about good ol' safe New York to segue into another crime story, this time a home invasion in Westchester.

The man flipped through the other networks, searching for additional reports about the early morning discovery of the dead body in East River Park. Nothing.

Either the other stations were all finished with their coverage, or only the ABC affiliate had broken the story.

Chelsea Hart. A college student from Indiana. He thought about the driver's license he'd grasped between his fingers only a few hours earlier on his living room floor. Jennifer Green. Date of birth in 1983.

So she had been from Indiana, but the license wasn't real after all. She was only nineteen years old. Her name was not Jennifer Green. And she'd been a college student from Bloomington.

The realization that he'd been ignorant of these basic details about the girl struck him as bizarre. He was the one who'd slid off her tight black pants and seen the purple birthmark on her right hip, peeking out from beneath those silky bikini panties. He was the one who'd run his fingers through those long blond waves before cutting them off to take home with him. He was the one who'd felt the firmness of her veins beneath the soft pale skin around her throat.

A lizard appeared on the screen to push insurance. As he hit the mute button on the television, the man wished he'd had more time last night. He had rushed with Chelsea, formerly known as Jennifer Green. He would take more time with his next project, once he found her. To his surprise, he was already anticipating it.

He still needed to put in another couple of hours of work, but he was rested from the quick catnap he'd caught after his meeting. He would start looking tonight.

Chapter Thirteen

The perspective of the camera continually changed, but the images always came to her in black and white. Sometimes Ellie watched the scenes unfold through the eyes of the victims. On other nights, she was a neutral and omnipotent observer floating overhead.

This time, she was pushing open the unlatched heavy oak door of a prairie-style home. She walked through the living room, passing in front of a fireplace, and then turned into a long hallway that led to the bedrooms.

She found the boy's body first, laid out on his twin bed with a plastic shopping bag over his head, a rope around his throat. His mother was in the master bathroom, blindfolded in the tub with a bandanna. Ellie knew that the woman had been tortured before being drowned – held repeatedly under water to the brink of suffocation, then revived, only to be submerged again.

As she descended the basement stairs, she tried to block the image that she knew would come next. William Summer had saved the twelve-year-old daughter for last.

Just as Ellie caught sight of the soiled rag next to the

girl's body, a rumbling sound pulled her away from the nightmare. She opened her eyes and remembered she was alone in her Murray Hill living room. According to her cable box, it was 9:58. She had dozed off watching a show about Dexter, a wily serial killer who targeted people who truly deserved to die for their own heinous wrongdoings. If only real murderers were so delightfully discriminating.

She grabbed her vibrating cell phone from the coffee table and flipped it open.

'Hatcher.'

'Morse.'

It was Peter. 'Hey. I didn't check the screen first.'

'Guess what I learned today?'

'What?' She smiled at the sight of the plush green frog heads springing from her toes. She had tried to find a way to leave behind the slippers her mother had purchased for her in Kansas, but she had to admit they were actually pretty cute.

'Writing the news all day straight, and then coming home to write some more, totally sucks.'

'Isn't that pretty much what your life was like before you met me?'

'I suppose.'

'And while I was in Kansas?'

'And your point would be?'

'Write one more page and then go to sleep.'

'A *page*? Do you have any idea how long it takes me to write a page?'

'You write fast,' Ellie said. She had seen him hammer out articles as fast as he could type them.

'That's when I'm Peter Morse, crime beat reporter for a tabloid that calls itself a newspaper. It's different with my own stuff.'

'Fine. Write another paragraph and go to sleep.'

'I think I'm fried for the night. It didn't help that I got stuck at work. WABC beat everyone to the punch on a body this morning at East River Park, so I had to stay and bang something out for tomorrow morning's paper. Kittrie must think it's going to be a big story, because he awoke from his deep slumber as an editor and insisted we work on the coverage as a team.'

George Kittrie was Peter's editor, and, at least according to the stories Peter had a tendency to tell, he was about as fond of Peter as Lieutenant Eckels was of Ellie.

'You probably don't want to know, but that's actually my case.'

'So instead of scrambling for two hours at the paper trying to satisfy Kittrie, I could have just called you?'

'Nope.'

'Oh, come on. I could have at least weaseled my way into a little hint.'

'Nothing. Nada. I'm Fort Knox.'

'I know. You sure you don't want company?'

'Two nights on our own. I told you.'

'You are *such* a cop.'

'Good night.'

''Night, Detective.'

She rose from the sofa and cleared away the debris from her dinner, lamb rogan josh and samosas delivered from a neighborhood Indian joint. Her stomach still felt hot from the spicy brown sauce on the lamb dish, and it dawned on Ellie how acclimated she had become during her decade in New York to the consumption of foods whose ingredients were a complete mystery to her.

She flipped to the early round of the late-night news. The local ABC affiliate may have been the first to break the story of Chelsea Hart's murder, but now the department's Public Information Office had released an official statement, and the case was finding its place in every stratum of the media.

Watching a case transform from real-life incident to ubiquitous cultural phenomenon reminded Ellie of the sprouting process in *Gremlins*, a movie she still watched every year on Christmas Day. It all started with a single, manageable creature. But add a little water, and suddenly several new balls of mischief were spawned, brewing until they transformed into separate and independent troublemakers that had to be watched over and cared for, each with the potential to hatch its own havoc-wreaking offspring.

And so it was with crime reporting. It started with a single case, followed by the first story. But that initial media coverage provided the germinating water, and from there, the sprouting began. By the end of the week, she would have a precinct full of Gremlins.

Ellie flipped between the two ten o'clock news programs. Both covered all the bases: Chelsea's name and age; the fact that she was on spring break, alone at night in the Meatpacking District; the discovery of her strangled corpse early this morning by joggers along the East River. No mention of the mutilation of her body or the violent removal of her beautiful hair. Give them time, she thought. Peter had scrambled quickly for the basics, but by tomorrow, reporters would be contacting everyone Chelsea Hart had ever met – at the hotel, at the club, back home in Indiana. Whether they wanted to or not, the public would eventually gain access to all of the ugly and salacious details that boosted ratings and swelled circulation numbers.

And Ellie's job would get that much harder.

She changed the channel to a *Seinfeld* repeat to keep her company while she got ready for bed. She had removed her contact lenses and started to brush her teeth when she heard keys in the front door.

She heard a soft *clank*, followed by her brother's voice. 'Chain!'

Ellie called out an apology through sudsy toothpaste foam, made her way to the front door (it didn't take long in her small one-bedroom), and released the safety chain.

'You've been doing that a lot lately.' Jess set his hard-shell Fender guitar case by the door, shook off his black thrift-store jacket, and tossed it on the nearest piece of furniture, an off-white armchair in the corner. 'Should I take that as a hint that it's time for me to find another couch? I could swing it now that the job's working out all right.'

For two months, Jess had been working as a doorman at Vibrations, an establishment on the Westside Highway that euphemistically billed itself as a 'gentlemen's club'. Jess and Ellie preferred to call it the

Shake Shack. The Shimmy Shed. Booty Barn. The Rubby Cubby. Titty Towers. The T and A Getaway. Even though Ellie hoped a better job was waiting for her brother somewhere down the road, a part of her wanted him to stay at Vibrations forever just so they could continue conjuring up alternative names for his employer.

'Don't be ridiculous,' she said. 'What would I have done this morning without a roommate to put together my backpack?'

'Did I get everything? I was a little creeped out going through your underwear drawer.'

'Perfect.' In truth, he had forgotten about the Kahr K9 that she now carried as a backup gun and the corresponding ankle holster, but she saw no reason to nitpick. 'Seriously, Jess, it's been nice having you here through all this.'

In reality, the stressful events of the last two months had little to do with Jess's presence as her couch-inhabiting roommate. Jess tended to move several times a year, depending on his employment status, dating status, and the tolerance of his friends. In between the various moves, he frequently spent days or weeks in her living room. Given that it was Jess who'd helped Ellie find this rent-stabilized apartment in the first place, it only seemed right. Karma and all.

'You sure?' he asked.

'Mos def.'

'In that case, what the fuck is that shitastic smell?'

'Dinner. Indian.' She patted her full belly. 'You missed out.'

'Jesus, why don't you bury a piece of cheese beneath

116

the sofa cushions while you're at it? This room'll stink for a week. Not to mention the increased risk of another upchuck incident after this morning's festivities.'

Ellie jumped onto the sofa and pulled the window up a few inches.

'Thanks,' Jess said, plopping down next to her. 'So what'd you do tonight? No, wait, let me guess.' He closed his eyes and pressed his fingers to his temples like a mind reader. 'You worked late on your case, came home and called Mom, then ate takeout and watched TV. How did I do?' he asked, opening his eyes.

'You've got the Ellie Hatcher schedule down to a T.'

'How's Mom?' Jess asked.

Ellie shrugged. 'You know.'

Jess knew precisely. That's why he had a tendency not to be around when Ellie made her nightly phone calls to their mother in Wichita. Same reminiscing. Same self-pity about her present life as a bookkeeper and widow whose children didn't visit enough. Same vodka-glazed voice. Somehow Jess managed to distance himself from all of it, but Ellie still felt the need to look after her mother despite the fourteen hundred miles lying between them.

'You're not working tonight?' Ellie asked.

'Nah. I got the guys together for a couple hours of practice instead. I figured finding a dead body with my sister this morning was a pretty good excuse to play hooky.'

'You didn't give them any details, did you?'

'Dead chick in the park was about all they needed to hear. Don't worry. I'm not divulging any secrets of

117

your case. Unless someone offers to pay. Now that would be different.'

She knew for a fact that her brother was only kidding. After the Wichita police charged William Summer with the College Hill Strangler murders, both Jess and Ellie had been hounded by the media for their stories. *How would your father have felt about the arrest? What is it like to know he died without the answers you now have? Why are you so convinced that William Summer killed your father, despite the city's insistence it was a suicide?*

Ellie had played along with the game, hoping the media attention would put pressure on the city. Lord knew her mother could use the pension. But Jess's position had been firm: Not even if they paid me a million dollars. And Ellie had known from the tone of his voice that he meant it. If Jess was going to be in the public spotlight, it was going to be as a rock god, not for anything having to do with policing or dead bodies.

'No Peter tonight?' Jess asked. Ellie arched an eyebrow in his direction. 'Okay, for once, I wasn't trying to be dirty. No Mr. Morse this evening?'

'No. There's no Mr. Morse.'

'Problems in paradise?'

'I just sleep better alone, in my own apartment.'

'Yeah, right, because your bed's so comfortable. I slept on that mattress while you were in Kansas, and it's like lying in a giant taco shell.'

Ellie had never been particularly at ease discussing romantic relationships with her older brother. Jess, of course, seemed to have no problems whatsoever opening up about his various encounters, sometimes going so far as to describe the bizarre things his freakier girlfriends had suggested. Ellie usually tuned out and escaped to a mental happy place to avoid the images.

'We took a couple nights off so he can write,' she said.

'His novel?'

'I didn't ask him for specifics, but I don't think so.'

Peter had told her on their first date that he'd been struggling for years on the same manuscript – a novel about a Manhattan-based journalist living, like Peter, in Hell's Kitchen. Now his writing had been rejuvenated by his idea for a true-crime book based on the First Date case.

'That little bitch would be dead if you hadn't saved his scrawny ass.'

'Well, as he sees it, his ass wouldn't have been thrust into the middle of the case in the first place if it hadn't been for me.'

'So you're supposed to be understanding while he uses this case to become a celebrity journalist?'

She shrugged. 'I get where he's coming from. He lived through it all too, and if he wants to write about it, that's his prerogative. As long as I don't get dragged into it.'

Ellie'd had enough of the spotlight for a lifetime. First it was the flurry of stories a year ago about the College Hill Strangler arrest. Then it was the First Date case. A month ago, when she sat down with *Dateline* for an exclusive interview about the crimes of William Summer, she had sworn she was done being a story.

'Maybe if you're really lucky, the jacket of his book

will be that class picture you love so much.'

'Fuck you twice,' Ellie said, flipping him the bird for good measure.

For some reason, the media covering the College Hill Strangler arrest had all seemed to glom on to the same goofy school photograph of Ellie in fifth grade, with bright shiny eyes and an enormous toothy grin, completely oblivious to her ridiculous bangs and the asymmetrical pigtails jutting from the sides of her head. To the best of Ellie's recollection, she had cut her own bangs the night before, desperate to emulate the look of her most recent pop hero, Debbie Gibson.

After the media had unearthed the photograph, Jess had terrorized her for weeks, e-mailing her links to every online story he could find containing the image and taping copies of the picture in the most innocuous places – the inside of her medicine cabinet, the side of a milk carton, even a wallet-sized version around the grip of her service weapon. The reign of horror had finally ended after Ellie dug out an old picture of Jess in his Wham days. A white tank top emblazoned 'Go Go' in pink neon letters would do nothing for Dog Park's street cred.

'You know what we should do?' Jess said. 'Let's go out.'

'It's already past ten o'clock.'

'No place worth going any earlier. Come on. You're home. I'm home. I'm still totally torqued by what I saw this morning. When was the last time we went out – like *really* went out?'

Ellie hadn't outgrown the stage of occasional late

120

nights, but she was ready to hit the sack. She started to make her excuses, but then realized there was one place she wouldn't mind checking out.

'Ever heard of a club called Pulse?'

Chapter Fourteen

Not only had Jess heard of Pulse, he was pretty sure he knew someone who worked there. He scrolled through his cell phone directory until he came to the name he was looking for.

'Here she is. Vanessa.'

'Vanessa Hutchinson?' Ellie asked.

'I don't do last names. I met her a few weeks ago at a bar in Williamsburg. She's a friend of Kate. You met her once. She came with me to Johnny's about a year ago.'

'The lawyer?'

'No, that was Rose. Kate's in marketing or something. Short brown hair? Really tiny?'

Jess was proving once again the vast reach of his impressive social network, yet another difference between them. Ellie would love to be one of those women with a tight circle of best friends, but a good portion of her life was dominated by a job that made her an outsider to most women, and those same women certainly didn't want her cozying up to their husbands and boyfriends. Between work, serial monogamy, and part-time caregiving to the rest of the Hatcher family, she had enough on her plate anyway.

Her brother, in contrast, had a way of meeting people once and forging lasting friendships with them, even if he didn't run into them again for a year. And, more curiously, many of his social supporters were former girlfriends and past hookups who never seemed to begrudge Jess his refusal to commit to one woman (or one job, for that matter, or one mailing address) for more than a month at a time. Ellie's best guess was that he had a way of attracting women who at least appreciated that, with Jess, what you saw was what you got: a fun guy and a good man who chose to remain in a perpetual state of adolescence.

'Who's the Vanessa Hutchinson you know?' Jess asked.

'A bartender at Pulse. Mid-twenties, as I recall. No priors.'

Jess gave her a perplexed look, and Ellie explained her newfound interest in the club, as well as the list she'd been given of all of the club's current employees.

'I should've known you had an ulterior motive for checking out a Grade A meat market.'

'I figured it wouldn't hurt to get a firsthand glimpse of the scene, see if anyone remembers seeing Chelsea.'

'I guess hanging out with the yuppies one night isn't going to kill me.'

'Now I'm having second thoughts,' she said.

'You're killing me, El. I was just getting my brain into club mode.' He bounced his shoulders and mimicked the ubiquitous and repetitive *uhnn-chk, uhnn-chk* beat of techno music.

'I'm not even sure we could get in.'

'What good is that handy dandy badge for, if not pushing your way past a behemoth of a doorman?'

'That would defeat the whole purpose. I was thinking I'd just go and hang out. Watch people. Talk a little. Be stealthy. But the club manager will recognize me. I was just there this afternoon –'

'Yeah, looking like, well, the way you look when you're working.'

Ellie gave him an insulted look.

'Sorry, but you know you can do better. Get yourself all slutted up, and you'll blend in with the rest of the chicks. Besides, the manager of a club that big and that crowded is *not* going to pay attention to the likes of us.'

She remembered Scott Bell, the club manager, speaking almost identical words that afternoon: *When you spend enough time in clubs, everyone looks the same.*

Fifteen minutes later, Ellie emerged from her bedroom. Clothes? On. Makeup? Slathered. Hair? Fluffed, thanks to some backcombing and a few spritzes of spray.

'Let's get a move on before I change my mind.'

Jess looked up from the black Hefty bag that he was digging around in on the living room floor. She recognized it as the bag of belongings from his last semi-permanent address, which he had snuck behind her television while she was in Kansas.

He took a look at the outfit she had chosen: a black turtleneck sweater, her best jeans, and a pair of short black boots.

'That's what I thought,' he said, continuing his

124

rummaging. 'Aha. I *knew* there was something in here that did not belong to me.'

He pulled out a purple baby doll dress with a halter neckline.

'Seriously?'

Ellie offered to splurge for a cab to the Meatpacking District. With her bare legs popping out of her tiny new dress and her feet covered in nothing but her one pair of high-heeled sandals, a few bucks for a heated car struck her as a bargain.

She made sure to keep her knees together as she swung herself out of the taxi. 'Jesus. I don't know what kind of woman lent you this dress, but I'm having a hard time not pulling a Britney here.'

'Hey, you were the one who said you wanted to blend. Plus, I got news for you. The very attractive woman who left that dress behind is five inches taller than you.'

Ellie was relieved to see fewer than twenty people waiting behind the red velvet rope erected outside the club entrance. She could tolerate a line of that length. Noticing that most of the other patrons were dressed at least somewhat appropriately for an early March night, she punched Jess in the bicep. 'I was fine in what I had on.'

'Those are the people who are waiting outside when it's not even eleven o'clock yet.' Jess grabbed Ellie by the wrist and marched along the velvet rope to the muscled doorman posted at the club's double doors. He was dressed entirely in black, all the way down to the cord spiraling from the earpiece he wore in his right ear.

'Jess Hatcher. I'm on the list.'

The man eyeballed Jess first. With his usual scruffy dark hair, three days' beard, and long sleeved black T-shirt and skinny jeans, he could have been anything from a bicycle messenger to the lead singer of any one of the current postpunk bands that she found so interchangeable. Then the man's gaze turned to Ellie.

The Hatchers apparently passed with enough credibility for him to check the list. A frown started to form on his face as he browsed the clipboard. Then he flipped to a second page.

'You're good,' he said, stamping their hands with a rubber triangle sopped in red ink. When he stepped aside so they could enter, Ellie heard a few exasperated huffs from the dejected souls behind the velvet rope and realized she had never been so appreciative of special treatment. Down with egalitarianism. She was too freezing to care about the masses.

'I called Vanessa while you were changing,' Jess explained. 'And, you were right, her last name is indeed Hutchinson.'

Once they were inside the club, Ellie had to concede that Jess had been right about her wardrobe choice. What had been a dimly lit empty warehouse just a few hours ago was now brimming with activity – primarily of the dancing, drinking, and flirting varieties, and almost entirely by young, fashion-forward, beautiful people. Not a single Gap sweater in the house.

Jess led the way, forging a circuitous path around the dance floor, past the runway, and through the three-person-deep huddle encircling the bar. He raised a hand toward a tall, thin waitress with long blond hair, heavy bangs, and a lot of black mascara. In the middle of a vigorous rattling of a silver martini shaker over her shoulder, the woman caught Jess's eye and flashed him a bright wide smile. Vanessa Hutchinson was beautiful.

She pulled the lid off the shaker and poured something bright blue into a martini glass, then handed the glass and a bottle of beer to a guy across the counter. He handed her forty dollars and told her to keep the change. Ellie wondered if she'd just witnessed a big tip to Vanessa, a big rip-off of the customer, or both.

Vanessa ignored the many patrons who were eagerly competing for her eye contact and instead beelined toward Jess. 'Hey, man. How are you?' She couldn't manage a hug with the bar between them, but she did raise her arm high for some quick hand-squeezing contact.

'Good. Pretty good. Thanks for taking care of us on short notice. This is my sister, Ellie.'

Ellie said hey and thanked Vanessa for setting them up with the doorman.

'Not a problem. Jack Daniels straight up, and what else?' she asked Ellie.

'Johnnie Walker Black.'

'Jack and Johnnie. I guess whisky runs in the family.'

Seconds later, she handed the drinks to Jess and waved off the money Ellie tried to hand her. 'I've got my hands full here, but you guys have fun, all right?'

Jess thanked Vanessa again and asked her to find them if she got a break. She assured them she would.

'Now what?' Jess asked, handing Ellie her drink.

'Now we watch.'

At 11:04 p.m., Bill Harrington sat alone in his living room, watching the evening news from his recliner.

A disturbing discovery to tell you about tonight in Manhattan. In the early hours of the morning, joggers found the partially nude body of nineteen-year-old Chelsea Hart at a construction site along the East River. Police tell us that Hart was a freshman at Indiana University and was in New York City for spring break. Police believe she was last seen alive at a club in the Meatpacking District on the west side of Manhattan. Anyone with information related to the case should call NYPD's tip line at –

Bill Harrington pressed down the footrest of his chair, stood, and made his way to the kitchen for a pen and pad of paper. He did not know anything at all about Chelsea Hart or her trip from Indiana, but he could not help but wonder if her murder had something to do with the dream that had pulled him from his bed so early that same morning, brushing his cheek like the tip of an angel's wing.

Chapter Fifteen

'This detective work's really hard.' Jess used a gap between two customers seated at the bar to drop off his empty glass.

It had taken them only fifteen minutes to circle the entire club. Now they were back where they began, at the bar.

'So tell me what you noticed,' Ellie said.

Jess shrugged. 'Hot girls. Rich guys. A lot of booze and bad dancing.'

'See, here's what I noticed. That girl over there?' She pointed to a petite brunette in a sleeveless turtleneck and skinny black pants. 'She's wearing the turtleneck to cover up marks on her throat, but when she looked in the mirror she didn't see the finger-shaped bruises on the backs of both her arms. That explains the scratch on her boyfriend's face.'

Jess looked at the brunette's male companion, a tall guy with a prominent forehead, five o'clock shadow, and, sure enough, a couple of claw marks near his right eye.

'My guess is it happened last night or this morning,'

Ellie explained over the mind-numbing dance music. 'He's taking her out tonight to make it up to her.'

'Jesus, Ellie. Being you has got to be pretty fuckin' depressing.'

'That girl over there?' Ellie pointed to a younger-looking woman in a clingy wrap dress and high-heeled boots. 'She just handed her ID to a guy who was heading out for a smoking break. He'll be back any minute with some jailbait girl in tow. Oh, and there he is now,' she said, just as a young couple walked through the entrance.

'Ellie Hatcher. Crime-detecting robot.'

'And, finally, my guess is the bouncer – the one posted over there by the side exit – his name's Jaime Rodriguez. Also on the list of Pulse employees. '

Ellie was fairly certain she recognized the man from the booking photos she'd pulled up on her computer earlier in the day, when she ran all of the employees for criminal histories.

If the bouncer was in fact Rodriguez, he'd cleaned up considerably in the last two years. In each of his prior booking photos, he'd carried that rough look found on so many kids who were raised more by the streets than by their parents. He'd worn his hair long and unwashed, his face concealed by sideburns and a goatee, his mouth set in a scowl. Now he was clean shaven with close-cropped hair and looked downright friendly. Had Rodriguez changed, or had he simply upgraded his chosen locale for slinging drugs?

Jess ran off for a second round of drinks, and Ellie continued her people-watching. From what she could

130

tell, Rodriguez's job tonight was to stand near the exit to make sure no patrons used it to sneak their friends in. A false alarm set off by an open door would invoke hysteria, and locking the exit from the inside was the kind of stunt that could get a club's ticket pulled with the city. So there Rodriguez stood, exchanging a few words here and there with passing patrons.

One male customer must have been a regular. He had moppish blond hair and wore black dress pants, a gray sports coat, and a blue collared shirt that matched his eyes. He emerged from behind the long white curtains that separated the VIP rooms from the rest of the club and headed directly for Rodriguez, checking out the surroundings as he walked. After a brief but close-faced exchange, the two men dapped fists, top to bottom, bottom to top, then straight on.

The mop-haired man walked back to the VIP lounge, and a tall, thin woman emerged, with that had-to-be-a-model look about her. Once past the curtains, the woman scanned the club, spotted Rodriguez, and made her way over to him. Ellie noticed the woman's hand touch the bouncer's, then immediately saw Rodriguez's other hand pass over the top of the model's handbag.

Only twenty minutes in the club, and she'd already witnessed the staff involved in a hand-to-hand. If she was going to need leverage over Rodriguez or the club's management, she had some now.

A few minutes later, the same mop-haired guy emerged again from the VIP lounge. Another conversation with Rodriguez, this one a little longer. Rodriguez pulled a couple bills off the roll he'd taken from the model and handed them to the blond. The blond gave the bills a passing glance and pushed them into his front jacket pocket.

Jess was back at Ellie's side now and handed her another drink.

As Ellie took a sip, she watched the man return to his private room and shook her head at his appearance. They were in the middle of Manhattan, and this guy looked like he'd just hopped off a surfboard. Why a grown man would opt for such a teeny-bopper hairstyle was beyond her.

The fuddy-duddy nature of her own thoughts made Ellie feel old. She supposed that if she were a mere decade younger, she'd think the guy was good looking. Hot. Smokin'. Whatever the young people were calling it these days.

Then she realized she'd stumbled onto something better than the kind of small-time hand-to-hand drug transactions that were taking place in every club in the city tonight. The guy in the VIP lounge had blond moppish hair. Cute more than good looking. Like an older Zac Whatever-His-Name-Was.

'Jess, we need to talk to Vanessa. Now.'

Chapter Sixteen

Vanessa met them at the end of the bar, in front of the office door Ellie had seen the club manager use earlier that day.

'Jess. I love you, man, but I gotta work.'

'This'll just take a sec.'

'If someone just walked through that curtain over there' – Ellie pointed to the place where she'd last seen the shaggy-haired blond – 'can you tell which VIP room that is?'

'Yeah, sure.'

'Can you find out what credit card's being used to hold the room?'

A worried look crossed Vanessa's face. 'Look, I don't know what you guys have in mind, but –'

Ellie leaned in closer. 'I'm a cop. I was here today with my partner, talking to your manager, Scott Bell. Is he here?'

Vanessa's expression changed to one of recognition. 'Oh, shit. Is this about that girl?'

'Scott told you?'

'I heard him talking about it on the phone when I

came in tonight. Oh, my God. I thought you were just here with Jess –'

'I am. Do you remember seeing Chelsea Hart here last night? She would've been drinking Angel's Tips.'

'For chicks who want to get wasted off a milkshake. No, I'd remember that one.'

'I really need that credit card information. You can run it past Scott if you have to –'

Vanessa didn't require convincing. She walked directly to the cash register behind the bar. She hit a button to open the drawer, flipped through a few pieces of paper, and returned with an American Express Black Card bearing the name Capital Research Technologies.

Ellie didn't need to check the list of credit card accounts in her purse to be certain, but she made the comparison anyway. Same card. Same club. One night earlier.

J. J. Rogan walked through the front doors of Pulse a mere fifteen minutes later.

'Nice outfit,' Rogan observed. Rogan was sporting the same suit he'd worn to work during the day, and Ellie wondered if he'd been out himself when she'd interrupted. 'Don't you ever sleep, Hatcher?'

'That's what my body double's for.'

'Hold on a sec,' Rogan said, his attention pulled away by something – or someone – behind him. 'I thought you said you were going home.'

An attractive woman in her mid-thirties with caramel-colored curls and alabaster skin flashed a perfect smile. 'I had second thoughts. How could I resist a peek?'

'Do I even want to know what you said to the bouncer to finagle your ass in here?'

'I'm heading out now,' she said, jingling a set of BMW keys. 'I know you've got to work. Are you the partner?'

'That'd be me. Ellie Hatcher.'

'Sydney Reese. He's been good to you so far?'

'The best.'

'A-hem,' Rogan said pointedly. 'I hate to interrupt the girl talk, but we sort of have a homicide investigation going here.'

Sydney waved good-bye and blew Rogan a kiss before leaving.

'What have you got so far?' Rogan asked.

Ellie led the way toward the rear of the club. With the help of two uniform officers from the Tenth Precinct and the cooperation of Scott Bell, the assistant club manager, she had gathered everyone from the Capital Research Technologies VIP lounge into the back office. She had also called Chelsea's friends, Stefanie Hyder and Jordan McLaughlin, and asked them to come down right away.

In the process, she'd lost her unofficial partner. Once the amateur sleuthing had been replaced by official police work, Jess had given up all interest in Pulse and left to meet an ex-girlfriend in SoHo.

'We need to interview these people fast,' Ellie said. 'Some of them are already talking about lawyers and their rights and when they can leave.'

'Rich folks are so difficult,' Rogan said.

At best, Ellie had only enough suspicion to justify a

135

brief detention of the customers in the VIP room. Anything beyond that would require probable cause.

'I've already talked to the guy who set off my radar in the first place.' She pointed to the blond guy with shaggy hair. 'His name's Nick Warden. It's his Am Ex holding the VIP room. I saw him connect one of the club's bouncers – that guy Rodriguez – and some model for a drug deal, then take a piece of the profits afterward. And, you're gonna love this. He's twenty-five years old. Has his own hedge fund company.'

The look on Rogan's face made it clear he knew the type but didn't have to like it.

'He's of course denying the drug deal, but he admits he was here last night. He tells me these two' – she pointed to two men whom she had separated on opposing sides of the small office – 'were here with him last night as well. The big one's Tony Russo, a financial analyst. The skinny guy, Jake Myers, works with Warden at his hedge fund. Warden insists the rest of these folks weren't around last night, at least not with him.'

'And Chelsea?'

'I showed him the picture we got out of Jordan's cell phone. Our Nick said right away he remembered her. At least he knows not to pull any obvious bullshit. "The party girl" is what he called her.'

'A girl from Bloomington struck *this* guy as a party girl?' Rogan asked. 'She had to be a bigger player than her friends let on.'

'Or more so than they realized.'

A quick and dirty test of Nick Warden's credibility was to ask everyone else in the room whether they'd been at Pulse the previous evening. Ellie had separated the VIPs quickly, so there'd been no time for them to sync their stories.

They started with the friends who, at least according to Nick, had not been partying with them the night before. To a person, they denied having been at the club. After getting their basic contact information and head shots for good measure, Ellie and Rogan had cut them loose. They had to. No choice.

With one exception. The model. Her name turned out to be Ashlee Swain. Ellie had requested consent to search her purse, but she refused. Swain's fortitude earned her a pair of handcuffs, her Miranda warnings, and a search incident to arrest.

'Word to the wise,' Ellie said, removing a small ziplock bag from Swain's purse. 'There's always an easy way and a hard way.'

'Whatever,' Swain said. 'I want a lawyer.'

Ellie held the bag up toward the office's overhead fluorescent lights. She recognized the crushed tan crystalline substance as a snortable form of crystal meth. Same euphoria, agitation, and sexually compulsive behavior. None of the mess and paraphernalia required for smoking. None of the hypodermics that came with slamming.

'What's the matter? Afraid of needles and fumes? You sure you don't want to corroborate my testimony that the bouncer over there sold to you?' Ellie took a look at Jaime Rodriguez, who was playing it cool. 'Remember: easy way and hard way.'

'Are you sure you're supposed to be talking to me?

Because what I remember is that I'm a two-L at Cardozo Law School who has read the Supreme Court's opinion in *Edwards* v. *Arizona*, and I know I just asked for a lawyer. And for a first-time buy, the hard way, as you call it, is a heartfelt apology, a stop at drug court, and a clean record once I'm done.'

The woman was six feet tall, drop-dead gorgeous, and knew her legal rights. At that moment, Ellie really hated her. But Ashlee Swain's recreational drug use was not her current priority. She turned the woman over to one of the uniformed officers to process the drug case.

'Two VIPs to go,' she said, looking at Tony Russo and Jake Myers. 'You want the financial analyst or the hedge fund dude?'

'I'll take the hedge fund prick,' Rogan said.

Tony Russo had a thick body and a square head that was losing its black hair. Combined with his large facial features, he might have been typecast as a Brooklyn butcher were it not for the wardrobe, a black sports coat over a sky blue dress shirt and dark gray pants. Ellie began by asking him when he was last at Pulse.

'What do you mean? I'm here right now.'

'Before now,' Ellie clarified. 'When was the last time you were here before tonight?'

'I don't know. I come here all the time. Wait. Last night. That's how much I'm here. I was here last night.'

'Who was with you?'

'A bunch of people. What is this about? What do you mean, who was with me?'

'I'm just asking you who generally you were with.'

'Well, the same people who were with me are the same people I was with. How's that for esoteric?'

'You're making my head hurt, Tony. Who was in your company last night?'

'It's always Nick's friends. Nick was here. Jake – that dude over there, Nick's partner – he was here.' Russo looked around and saw that the others were all gone from the office or leaving. 'That was it, I guess. Most of those other people, they were just girls Nick waved in from the dance floor, you know? Or maybe he knew a few of 'em, I don't know. You gotta ask him. He's always the ringleader, you know?'

'But you didn't just get waved in. You and Nick are friends?'

'Yeah, tight. Him and Jake, too. Are you gonna cut me loose here pretty soon, babe?'

'Hey, J. J., Tony here thinks I'm a babe.'

'Man's got good taste,' Rogan said, keeping his attention fixed on Jake Myers.

'Yeah, we're about done. I just need to know whether you remember seeing this girl last night.' Ellie showed him the photograph of Chelsea, monitoring him closely for his reaction.

Despite his seeming indifference, Russo took a good look at the picture. No nervousness. No evasiveness. Same breezy, cocky demeanor.

He tapped the photograph a few times with his index finger. 'Yeah, yeah, I remember her. Go Hoosiers. She was a real babe. Not as good as you, of course.'

'Did you talk to her at all?'

'Nah. I got a girl. She's out of town, but I'm not stupid, you know?'

'Not even on a night out with Nick?'

'Not even. Altar boy. Can't you tell?'

Actually, Ellie could.

'So, who was she with?'

Now, for the first time, she did sense a change in Russo's easygoing manner. His smile fell as his brow furrowed.

'Seriously, what's going on? I just want to get out of here.'

'This girl was murdered last night.'

'Ah, Jesus. Nick, did you hear this, man? One of those Indiana chicks last night –'

'Hey,' Ellie said, 'I can't have you guys talking to each other right now. Talk to me,' she said, pointing to herself. 'No one's accusing anyone. I just need to know who this girl was talking to last night.'

'Everyone, man. I don't know. She was toasted, you know? Partying. Getting her freak on.'

'Did she talk to Nick?'

'That's bullshit. It wasn't like that. She wasn't *talking* to anyone. She was just dancing and hanging out – with anyone and everyone.'

'So she was dancing and hanging out with Nick?'

Russo shook his head in frustration, apparently finding Ellie considerably less babe-ish now. 'Yeah, fine,' he said, lowering his voice, 'she was dancing with Nick. But she was also dancing with Jake. And our buddy Tom. And some other dude – um, Patrick, another friend of Nick's.'

'But she didn't dance with you.'

'No, but that's only because I don't dance. Seriously, it wasn't what you're thinking. She wasn't *with* anyone. That's how Nick nights are. Girls come in for the free booze and to be our eye candy for the night. No one's looking for a girlfriend.'

'Not even for one night?'

Russo didn't respond.

'When you left, did you leave alone?'

'I told you. Altar boy.'

'I didn't mean with another woman. I want to know if you saw your friends leave.'

'I don't like where this is going. My friends are decent guys.'

'Then you shouldn't mind telling me who left and when.'

'You just don't get it,' he said, shaking his head. 'Don't take this the wrong way. I'm not trying to be a prick, but I don't want to say anything that's gonna bite one of my boys in the ass. I want a lawyer, like that Cardozo chick said.'

Great. The model had not only invoked her own rights, but had done so loudly enough for Tony Russo to get an introductory lesson about his own.

Ellie turned to check on Rogan. With the pace of the last thirty minutes, this had been her first opportunity to take a look at Jake Myers, who was trendier than his preppy friends. He was about six feet tall. Thin. Dark brown hair. He had an interesting face – long and narrow with a prominent chin and sleepy eyelids. He reminded Ellie of someone. She was just about to put her finger on it when she heard a high-pitched female voice behind her.

'That's him. That's the guy who looks like Jake Gyllenhaal.'

Chapter Seventeen

'How many times do I have to tell you?' Jake Myers's voice was strained. Twenty minutes in, and he was sticking by his story. 'She told me she had an early flight and left the club before I did. I haven't heard from her since.'

'What time did she leave?' Rogan asked.

'I don't know. I remember that bitchy friend of hers coming by and trying to get her to leave right before.'

'Well, that bitchy friend just ID'd you as the last person to see Chelsea Hart alive. You might want to start coming up with specifics.'

Myers licked his lips nervously. 'My guess is she left about half an hour after that, but I'm not sure. It was a late night, and I wasn't checking my watch.'

'Did you walk her out?'

'No. She left by herself, as far as I could tell.'

'Were you outside of the club with her at all?' Rogan asked.

'No.'

'Not at any point?'

'I told you, we were just dancing and hanging out.'

'When did you leave?'

'Late. Ask Nick. He was with me.'

'Anyone else leave with you?'

'No, just me and Nick.'

'Here's the problem with that, Jake. Nick's not talking. Neither is your friend Tony Russo.'

Myers had a hard time hiding the slight smile. 'Well, I don't have any control of that, do I? We left at closing time, so I'm assuming it was four, but sometimes the clubs go a little later if they don't think they'll get caught. Like I said –'

Rogan completed the sentence for him: 'You weren't checking your watch. Did anything happen between you and Chelsea before she left?'

'What do you mean?'

'You know what I mean. Single guy. Hot girl. Flirting. Did anything come of that?'

'No, man. I was just dancing with her.'

'You didn't have any sexual contact at all?' Rogan was making sure to lock down all of Jake's various denials, no ambiguities to exploit down the road if they caught him in a lie.

'No. I kissed her – not even, just a peck – when she left. That was it.'

'And no drugs?'

'I told you. I could tell she was drunk, but I didn't take any drugs. I didn't give her any drugs. And I didn't see her with any drugs.'

Ellie interrupted. 'Her friend says you were pretty eager to have Chelsea stick around. You didn't want her to leave.'

'We were having a good time. Did I think maybe it was going somewhere? Sure, but when she said she had to go, she had to go. No means no, right?'

'Not always,' she said.

'It does with me. There's always another girl.'

'Was there one last night?' Ellie asked.

'No,' Jake said quietly, some of the attitude falling into line.

'All right. Let me talk to my partner for a second,' Rogan said. He waved Ellie to the front of the office, and she followed. 'What do you think?'

'I think he's lying.'

'Well, he's not coming up with any details.' Innocent people tended to have excellent memories when it came time to account for their whereabouts.

'And I'm not buying all that indignation. Fear? Nervousness? That's what I would understand from him right now. But he's so put out by half an hour of conversation?'

'That's 'cause lying is hard work.'

'And we *know* he's lying about the drugs. It's too much of a coincidence that Chelsea had meth in her system, and we just happen to catch these guys hooking up a girl with meth through Rodriguez.'

'But Rodriguez wasn't working last night.'

'Doesn't matter. If he's dealing out of the club, then he's probably working with someone else who supplies on his days off. These clubs have more drugs going in and out of them than a Duane Reade. A club can't be known as a place to score unless they've got every night covered. And if Myers is lying about the meth –'

'Then he's also lying about the girl leaving alone, him leaving without a girl, and everything being Doris Day innocent.'

'Otherwise his friends would back him up,' Ellie said. 'Instead, they invoke, and he's sitting pretty. He's rolling the dice that we don't have enough to hold them. The minute we cut them loose, they'll get together and line up their stories.'

'Not exactly a high-stakes bet,' Rogan said. 'No PC for the murder, and the ADA will shoot us down on material witness warrants.'

'So let's give Mr. Myers what he wants. Let's go ahead and spring him.'

'So he can get his buddy Nick to vouch that they left together?'

'Nope. Because we're about to introduce Nick Warden to the overnight comforts of the Tenth Precinct.'

'Jaime Rodriguez. Nick Warden. You're both under arrest for criminal sale of a controlled substance and conspiracy to commit criminal sale of a controlled substance.'

Ellie placed her cuffs on Nick Warden, while Rogan pulled Rodriguez's wrists behind his back. They might not have probable cause to hold anyone for Chelsea Hart's murder, but she'd personally witnessed Warden negotiate the drug deal between Rodriguez and that Amazon of a law student.

They walked the two men toward the back of the office, where officers from the Tenth Precinct would take them out a rear exit to complete the booking process.

Jake Myers took a step in their direction. 'Whoa, what are you doing?'

Ellie pointed him back toward his corner at the front of the office. 'Stay over there. Move again, and I'll arrest you for obstructing. Someone get Mr. Myers a glass of water to keep him busy, all right?'

The decision to book Warden entitled her to conduct a search incident to arrest. She pulled a money clip from his jacket pocket, and slipped the entire wad into a baggie. If some of the cash came back with Rodriguez's fingerprints, it would at least corroborate the deal she'd seen go down between them.

'Smile for the camera,' she said, snapping a quick head shot with her cell phone.

Rogan finished a check of Rodriguez's pockets and gave her a slight head shake. No drugs. Either Rodriguez had sold the last of the ice he was holding to the model, or he had managed to pass off his stash to someone else in the club before he was herded into the back office.

Without anything to corroborate Ellie's testimony, the defense would argue that she had misinterpreted a harmless conversation between Warden and Rodriguez. Not that it mattered.

As a uniformed officer led Warden through the back door, he shot a look at Myers, who was drinking his glass of water as directed. A night in jail would be a good test of Warden's loyalty.

Rogan passed Rodriguez off to another officer. 'Maybe Warden will wake up tomorrow telling us he didn't leave with Myers after all.'

'At the very least we've bought ourselves some time until tomorrow afternoon's arraignment. The labs might be back by then.'

'Maybe we'll get lucky and find a witness placing Myers with Chelsea after she left the club.'

'Oh, and by the way,' Ellie said, 'that glass of water Myers is drinking from as we speak? He might just leave behind tidy little fingerprints to match the latent on Chelsea Hart's button.'

'Detectives?' A uniformed officer looked at them apologetically. 'I'm sorry to interrupt, but there's an older couple here asking for you. They're refusing to leave.'

Paul and Miriam Hart looked out of place at the club's entrance in their wool sweaters and matching khaki pants.

'Those two men,' Miriam said. 'The men who were pulled out of here. Were they the ones?'

Ellie placed a hand gently on Miriam's forearm. 'Tonight we made real progress. But we arrested those two men – for now – only on drug charges. We believe one of them may have information about what happened to Chelsea last night.'

'What about the man Stefanie identified?' Paul asked. 'Stefanie called us from the cab. She said she left Chelsea alone with him, and that you'd found him here.'

Ellie swallowed. 'We are following up on that.'

'What do you mean, following up?'

She didn't want to tell them that Rogan was currently cutting Myers loose out the club's back exit. 'I would call him a person of interest for now.'

'You're arresting him, then?'

She did her best to explain the legal requirements for an arrest and all of the ways that making an arrest too early would jeopardize the chances of a conviction down the road.

'So he just goes home?' Paul said. 'We go back to our hotel room and turn off the lights and go to sleep with the knowledge that your "person of interest" is out there doing God knows what?'

Ellie had tossed and turned her way through countless numbers of those kinds of nights, and she wasn't going to lie to these people. 'Yes, that's exactly what you need to do. And you'll probably have to do the same tomorrow, and maybe the next day. But I promise you, I would not ask something so painful of you if it weren't absolutely necessary. We are making progress. I promise.'

'A drug arrest is progress?'

Miriam began to apologize for her husband, but Ellie stopped her. 'I know I have no right, but I'm asking you to trust us.'

As she helped the Harts into the back of a patrol car that would carry them to their complimentary suite at the Hilton, she told herself that Nick Warden's night in the Tenth Precinct would turn out to be more than just another drug bust. It had to.

Sleep. What Ellie needed next was sleep. She had been awake for twenty-two hours and desperately needed to catch a few hours of shut-eye. The thought of a soft pillow and clean-ish sheets was paradise.

What welcomed her instead was Peter Morse, sitting on the step that led to her building's doorway, staring at his cell phone. His brown hair was tousled, as usual, and he looked cold in a fashionably crumpled corduroy jacket thrown over a T-shirt and jeans.

'Hey, you.' He stood to greet her, as if waiting outside her door in the middle of the night was perfectly normal. 'I've been calling you.'

'I know. Didn't you get my text?' After Peter's name popped up twice on the screen of her cell, Ellie had sent him a text around midnight, telling him she was wrapping up some work on a case.

'Yeah, that's why I figured I had a chance of finding you awake this late. I didn't realize you'd be out all night and coming home wearing – wow, you look frickin' amazing.'

'Thanks. It's borrowed.' Ellie slipped her key into the building's security lock, and Peter followed her inside and into the elevator. 'Not to be rude, but what the heck are you doing here?'

'I was hoping to exploit a technicality in your two-nights-alone rule. I figured after midnight, we had achieved formal compliance.'

'It's nearly three in the morning,' she said.

'It was only two when I got here.'

'You waited in the cold for *an hour*?' As she opened the door, she called out Jess's name, but the apartment was empty. 'I suppose it's romantic, in a stalkerish sort of way. So are you coming in?'

He paused at the doorway.

'Peter, I don't have a lot of experience with men

150

showing up at my doorstep at three in the morning, but I sort of figured an invitation to spend the night would have been way up there on the best-case scenarios for you.'

He followed her inside and gave her a soft kiss on the lips.

'Seriously, where were you?'

She pulled her head back. 'Seriously? I was working on a case. Oh, my God, is that why you sat outside my building for an hour? You thought you were going to catch me with someone else?'

'I don't know what I was thinking,' he said. 'All I know is that when you didn't answer your door, I couldn't bring myself to leave. I just sat there like some lovelorn teenager waiting for my phone to ring.'

'Sad.'

Peter leaned in for another kiss, but she pulled away again.

'So when do you explain why you just asked me where I was, even though I told you three hours ago I was working?'

'Can we just forget about it? I'm exhausted, and that best-case scenario you mentioned is sounding pretty appealing right now.'

'Did you think I *lied* to you?'

'No, of course not. I just – I don't know. I mean, it's not like we ever said anything about being exclusive. So, yeah, the thought crossed my mind.'

'But I told you I was working.'

'Ellie, people offer all kinds of explanations when they're dating around. Things are still pretty new with us. You wanted the night off. You were out late. You texted instead of called. All I said was that the thought crossed my mind. Can we please drop the subject?'

'Have I acted like a person who's still on the market? I thought everything was fine.'

'Everything *is* fine. I shouldn't have asked where you were. It was a slip of the tongue. Chalk it up to being tired, or recovering from the emasculation of waiting outside your door.'

'But it wasn't a slip of the tongue,' Ellie said. 'You were very clear about wanting to know where I was, even after I told you. And if everything were really fine, I don't think a thought like that would cross your mind, as you called it. If something is bothering you about the way things are between us, I wish you'd talk to me about it.'

Peter gave her a patient smile. 'Nothing's bothering me. Let's go to bed, okay?'

'See? You say that like we're skipping over something. Like there's something you want to get off your chest but it's easier to let it slide.'

He let out an exasperated groan. 'How do you do that? How do you know exactly what a person is thinking?'

'If I knew what you were thinking, I wouldn't be pressing you to tell me.'

'Pressing? More like waterboarding. Trust me, Ellie. You don't really want to have this discussion with me.'

'Well, you can't just leave it at that. Is this about your book?' She thought she had done a good job of keeping her apprehensions to herself.

'No, that's just pie in the sky. I'm talking about Kansas. About your dad and that case. About you going to Wichita for a month. I shouldn't have had to learn the details on *Dateline* like the rest of the country, Ellie. You never even talked to me about it. You'd stay up late talking to Jess – I'd hear you out here in the living room – but never once spoke about any of it with me.'

'You're jealous? Jess is my brother. My father was his dad, too. And it's our mother.'

'You don't need to explain to me that you and your brother share the same parents. I'm not jealous. I wish you would have let me in, just a little. And, yeah, I guess it sort of made me wonder what exactly we were doing.'

Much of what Ellie had learned about the College Hill Strangler during her trip to Wichita was now part of the public record, easily attainable with a few Google searches. After believing for nearly two decades that the killer who'd haunted her father for his entire career had been responsible for his death, Ellie finally received concrete proof from the Wichita Police Department: on the night of Jerry Hatcher's death, William Summer had been the best man at his sister's wedding in Olathe, more than 175 miles from the country road where Ellie's father died in his Mercury Sable after a single bullet was discharged from his service weapon into the roof of his mouth.

The implication was clear. If Summer hadn't pulled the trigger, then her father had. He had chosen to end his life, leaving behind two children and a mother who was incapable of caring either for herself or them on her own. Ellie was still learning how to accept a version of history she had always rejected.

She poured herself a glass of water from the Brita pitcher in her refrigerator and carried it to the coffee table. And then Ellie did something she rarely did. She apologized. 'I'm so sorry. You should have heard it all from me, in my words – not in sound bites from a television show.'

Peter pushed her hair from her eyes and kissed her forehead, then her lips. 'Let's get some sleep.'

For the first night since she returned to New York from Kansas, Ellie Hatcher did not dream about William Summer.

Three hours later, a man closed the door of his Upper East Side apartment behind him and used two different keys to secure two separate locks. He walked the two flights of stairs down to 105th Street.

It was still dark, the streets relatively deserted, but the man could see when he turned the corner that the Chinese man who operated the newsstand at 103rd and Lex had just unlatched his makeshift storefront and was using a pocketknife to free stacks of newspapers from the constraints of cotton twine.

The man slowed his pace. He did not want to be in a position where he either had to wait for the news man or help him. Then he might be remembered as the impatient man who was waiting for the morning's papers, or the friendly man who had assisted with the twine. He preferred not to have any adjectives associated with him.

Once the papers were stacked and the Asian was back in his booth, the man allowed himself to approach. He selected three local papers – the *Daily Post*, the *Sun*, and the *Times*. Extended three dollars across the row of candy bars – exact change.

He folded all three newspapers together, tucked them under his arm, and made his way back to 105th Street. Turned the corner. Into the building. Up two flights of stairs. Past the locks.

Inside his apartment, he unfolded the papers and placed them side by side on the small dining table in the corner of his living room. Chelsea Hart's murder was splashed across the front page of both the *Sun* and the *Daily Post*. Front page of the *New York Times* Metro section. This would not have happened if she were not a college student from Indiana.

He recognized the photograph used by both the *Post* and the *Times*. It was the same picture Chelsea had used to make her fake ID card. The photograph in the *Sun* was different – candid, casual, less professional.

The man began to read the text of the *Sun* article but then looked again at the image of Chelsea Hart. Even with the cropping, he understood the photo's significance. The red shirt. Collar necklace. Beaded earrings that matched the one buried beneath his floorboards.

He knew precisely when and where that photograph had been taken. He even remembered the limoncello-shooting tomcat who'd snapped it.

Chapter Eighteen

The coverage of Chelsea Hart's murder had hit full throttle by Tuesday morning. It was the lead story on NY1's morning show, and Chelsea's photograph dominated the front page of both the *New York Sun* and the *Daily Post*. The case even warranted a story in the Metro section of the *New York Times*.

Ellie noticed that the *Sun* had run the photograph with which she was now long familiar – cropped around Chelsea's smiling, happy face while she waited for a table at Luna, the last restaurant she'd ever frequent. She wondered whether the *Sun* had paid Chelsea's friend Jordan for the picture or simply given her the standard line about how important it was for the public to see Chelsea as she had actually lived.

In contrast, both the *Daily Post* and the *New York Times* ran the same formal, posed headshot – Chelsea's senior high school portrait, provided directly by the Hart family. After their talk the previous day with a caseworker from the Polly Klaas Foundation, Paul and Miriam Hart had apparently taken a page from the parents of Elizabeth Smart and Natalee Holloway, marshaling all of their resources to launch an orchestrated public relations campaign to ensure that their daughter's case was at the top of every news cycle until they found something resembling justice. Press releases. Photographs. Tearful public statements from designated family representatives.

Ellie didn't blame them. Given the symbiotic relationship between the media and law enforcement, nothing put the screws to the criminal justice system like a watchful public. She had taken advantage of that reality in her own life to call attention to her father's death. She could not imagine the lengths she would go to as a parent who had lost a child.

The publicity surrounding the case had no doubt influenced Lieutenant Dan Eckels's decision to summon them once again into his office. He sat. They stood.

'We're more than twenty-four hours out,' Eckels said, steepling his fingers. 'Tell me what we've got.'

Rogan spoke up first, giving the lieutenant a rundown of the investigation, ending with the events of the previous night.

'Good call arresting the friend instead of Myers,' he said, clearly directing the comment to Rogan. 'If you'd hooked up Myers and he broke on what you had, the DA wouldn't have run with it.'

'Thanks, Lou, but it was Hatcher's idea.'

The idea earned Ellie a nod of acknowledgment. To the untrained eye, it was just a tilt of Eckels's chin, but to Ellie it was the Thirteenth Precinct equivalent of Armstrong's one small step from the *Apollo 11*.

'That explains the call from Kluger in the mayor's

office this morning. Apparently he got wind of some kind of arrest last night from the parents. What the hell kind of luck do we have that our vic's somehow related to the deputy chief of staff?'

'Actually,' Ellie said, 'I think he's a frat brother of the father's brother-in-law.'

Eckels gave her an annoyed look, and she decided it was best to move on.

'I just got a call from the city's taxi commission,' she reported. 'They circulated the picture I sent them yesterday of the victim. One of the drivers thinks he may have seen her that night outside Pulse. We'll follow up.'

'Good, because we've been popular this morning. I also heard from the DA's office. They want to get in early, so I'd start by having them set up a face-to-face with your Nick Warden before his arraignment. A night in jail might have given your hedge fund boy some different priorities.'

Eckels peeled off the top sheet of a Post-it pad next to his phone. He started to reach toward Rogan, but then handed the yellow square to Ellie. *ADA Max Donovan for Knight*, followed by a phone number. 'Some kid called Donovan was the one to reach out, but it'll be Knight's case.'

Ellie had no idea who Max Donovan was, but anyone who followed New York City criminal trials knew about Simon Knight, the chief prosecutor of the trial unit at the district attorney's office. His day-to-day job was to run the busiest trial unit in one of the nation's largest prosecutor's offices, break in the newbies, and ensure that the other assistants didn't wuss out. His personal and early attention to the Chelsea Hart case was yet another indication that this one was big.

'We'll call this Max Donovan straight away, sir.'

'Very good.'

Ellie and Rogan meted out tasks on the short walk back to their desks. She'd track down the cabdriver while he checked in with ADA Donovan, the medical examiner, and the crime scene unit.

She'd just plopped down into her chair when Eckels called out after them. 'And, in case this wasn't clear, don't screw up.'

Nothing like a pep talk to kick-start the day.

According to the taxi commission, the driver who last saw Chelsea Hart alive was one Tahir Kadhim. Ellie dialed his number, then flipped open the *Daily Post* and checked out the byline: reporting by George Kittrie and Peter Morse.

Last night Peter had mentioned staying late at the paper to write something up with his editor. Now she saw that Kittrie had taken first billing for himself. Given the history there, she could only imagine Peter's aggravation. A few years earlier, Kittrie had made the leap from career crime-beat reporter to author, and then editor, when he published a book about all of the opportunistic crimes that had been perpetrated in the chaos following September 11. From what Ellie understood, the book had put enough extra cash in Kittrie's pocket to pay for a cottage in East Hampton. In the back of Ellie's mind, she wondered whether George

Kittrie was in part responsible for Peter's excitement about writing a true-crime book. She also wondered if Kittrie's success as an author might explain why Peter harbored such resentment toward his boss.

'Balay!'

Ellie held the phone away from her ear. The man on the other end of the line was yelling over some kind of Persian music in the background.

'This is Detective Hatcher. NYPD. Is this Tahir Kadhim?'

The music immediately quieted. 'Yes, this is Tahir. This is about the picture, yes?'

Ellie was relieved she wouldn't need a translator. The city's taxi drivers sometimes appeared to have problems with the English language when you told them to turn on the air conditioning or turn down the radio, but their difficulties often faded away under less convenient circumstances.

'That's right. The taxi commission told me you recognized the girl in the photograph?'

'I was not certain last night when I first saw it because of how it was printed from the fax, but I sent in a message nonetheless because I did think it was the same girl. But now that girl is the one in the newspapers. It is most definitely the same girl I saw yesterday morning.'

'We're going to need to talk to you in person, Mr. Kadhim. Where should we meet you?'

'Where are you located?'

'Thirteenth Precinct. Twenty-first and Second Avenue.'

'I am ten blocks away. You will help me with parking?'

'I think that can be arranged.'

Rogan was still on the phone when Ellie hung up. He covered the mouthpiece with his palm. 'Asshole put me on hold and never came back.'

Ellie scanned the DD5 containing the information that had come in about the case on the department's tip line. The vast majority of calls were complaints about the city's 4:00 a.m. closing time for bars – thirteen separate calls, by her count. Every time some crime was even tangentially associated with the late-night bar scene, the same people who complained on a weekly basis about the noise at the clubs in their neighborhood used the case as an opportunity to lobby against their favorite pet peeve.

Then there were the usual crackpots: three – count them, three – psychics offering their abilities to communicate with the dead; a woman whose schnauzer got sick early the previous morning, certainly a sign that he shared a karmic connection with Chelsea Hart; and some crank call from a guy who wanted to know if the girl had any cute midwestern friends heading to the city for the funeral.

No false confessions yet, but there was still time.

One entry tucked in among the rest caught her attention. 'Bill Harrington. Daughter (Roberta, aka Robbie) murdered 8 years ago. Similar. Flann McIlroy thought there were others.' At the end of the notation was a ten-digit phone number. Ellie recognized the Long Island area code.

She found herself staring at two words: *Flann McIlroy.*

Detective Flann McIlroy had been famous – infamous, many would say – for his creative theories about investigations, creative enough to earn him the nickname 'McIlMulder' within the department, an allusion to the agent who chased space aliens on the television show *The X-Files*. Ellie's own experience with him had been far too brief, but she had come to trust him as both a man and a cop. If Flann had spoken to a murder victim's father about his suspicions of a broader pattern, then Bill Harrington at least deserved a return phone call.

She wrote down the name 'Roberta Harrington' and walked the slip of paper down to the records department. She was still trying to learn the names of the Thirteenth Precinct staff, something that had paid off in her previous assignments. A clerk who introduced herself as Shawnda promised she would order the old police reports from the Central Records Division immediately. Ellie thanked her for her time and made a point of repeating her first name.

Rogan was just hanging up his telephone when Ellie returned to her desk. 'Something better shake soon, because the lawyers want us at the courthouse in two hours.'

Tahir Kadhim was dark, slight, and reluctant to leave his taxicab in front of a fire hydrant on East Twenty-first Street.

'It's the only spot on the street, Mr. Kadhim,' Ellie said. 'I'll leave a permit on the dash.'

'Some meter maid will not believe that a taxicab is

with the police. If the city tows my car, that is my entire day, not to mention the record I get on my medallion number.'

'We really need to speak with you.'

'Must I go inside? Why can we not speak out here?'

Ellie didn't see the harm in getting the quick version of the driver's story now, to avoid what she could foresee was going to be a headache-inducing conversation about the lack of adequate parking, the ineptitude of municipal employees, and the financial burdens of cab-drivers. She hopped into the passenger seat, and Kadhim hit his emergency blinker. At least it wasn't the meter.

'You said you recognize this girl?'

She pulled an eight-by-ten printout of Chelsea Hart from a manila folder.

'Yes, that is right,' he said, tapping the photograph for emphasis. 'I stopped Sunday night for her. She hailed me down, I think it was at Fifteenth and Ninth Avenue.'

'Where did you take her?' If Chelsea had left Pulse and headed to another club by herself, she would have an even tougher time linking Jake Myers to the murder.

'I did not take her. She stopped my cab, but I did not drive her.'

Ellie waited for Kadhim to explain, but he did not. 'Did she change her mind?'

'No. See, there is a bit of a problem here. I want to help. That is why I called when I saw the picture. I did not have to call, you know.'

'What are you trying to say, Mr. Kadhim?'

'The Taxi and Limousine Commission. They are

163

crazy. They have these rules, and they think nothing of shutting us down.'

'Mr. Khadim, I assure you, I am not trying to jam you up about some taxicab regulation. I just need you to tell me everything you can remember about this girl. Her name was Chelsea Hart. She was from Indiana. Her parents flew here yesterday to identify her body. I'd like to have something to tell them, sir.'

'You do not report to the commission?'

Ellie shook her head and waited for him to speak.

'She got inside the cab and told me to take her to the Hilton at Rockefeller Center. Before driving away, I checked to be sure she could pay me in cash. She could not. She asked me if I could take her Visa card instead.'

'But aren't you all upgraded? The GPS, automation, credit cards.' The cabdrivers had gone on strike twice to try to prevent the change, but ultimately the commission had prevailed. Ellie peered over the partition into the backseat and saw the required equipment in Kadhim's taxi.

'The credit card processing is broken,' Kadhim explained. 'I told that to the young lady, but she said she had spent all of her cash. It happens a lot in that part of town at that time of night.'

'What time was it?' Ellie asked.

'It was not quite closing time, I remember. It was probably three thirty.'

An hour after Stefanie and Jordan left. Thirty minutes later than Jake Myers's faltering estimate of when Chelsea had supposedly walked out alone.

'So what happened when she said she couldn't pay cash?'

'I told her I would not drive her.'

Ellie now understood why Khadim had been nervous. She remembered from the taxi strike that the drivers were especially upset about a rule that required them to pull their cabs out of service if their credit card machines malfunctioned.

'Then what?'

'That is when the man offered to give her the money she needed.'

'Wait a second. There was a man with her?'

'She was alone. At first. But then when we were talking about how she was to pay her fare, a man came and knocked on the window. He . . . he propositioned her, if you understand.'

'Yes, okay, I think I know what you mean by that,' Ellie said, nodding even though she was having trouble picturing the scenario. 'A man came up out of nowhere and knocked on your taxi window and offered to pay her for sexual favors?'

'No. It was not like that. She was talking to me, but then when the tapping began at the window, she lowered the glass and spoke to the man. I do not recall all of it, but it was along the lines of persuading her to stay with him, wherever she had been prior to coming outside. She told him she needed to go to her hotel – that she had an early flight in the morning – but that now she didn't have any money, and I would not take her credit card. I remember that: she said, "And now this guy won't take my fucking credit card." Not angry, but as if she were trying to be humorous. They both seemed intoxicated.'

'And what did the man say?'

'That is when he propositioned her. He said something like, I can give you the money. But then when she reached out of the window, he said she would have to earn it. I did not want them in my cab any more after that. Not every driver allows Taxicab Confessions in the back of their car, you know. I was about to order her to get out, but then she left on her own with the man. They were laughing, like it was a game.'

'Do any of these men look familiar?'

Ellie handed Kadhim four photographs. Kadhim flipped through them quickly and apathetically, past Nick Warden, Tony Russo, and Jaime Rodriguez – until he landed on the final picture. Jake Myers. 'This man,' he said, handing the photograph to her. 'This is the man she left with.'

'You're sure?'

'I am positive. He was wearing a thin black tie, and his clothing was too tight. Pardon my French, but he looked like an asshole.'

That description alone left no doubt in her mind that the person Kadhim had seen with Chelsea Hart had been Jake Myers. But it was the two calls J. J. Rogan had placed while Ellie was wrapping up her conversation with Kadhim that persuaded her they had their man.

One call was to Mariah Florkoski at the crime scene unit. The fingerprint on the top button of Chelsea Hart's blouse was an eight-point match to a latent print pulled from the glass of water Ellie had so generously offered to Jake Myers last night. And she'd found seminal fluid in the stain on the same shirt.

The other call was to the medical examiner. The rape kit was back. The oral swab was also positive for seminal fluid.

Now all they needed was a DNA sample.

Chapter Nineteen

One Hundred Centre Street not only famously houses many of the city's criminal courts, but is also home to most of Manhattan's five hundred assistant district attorneys. Rogan and Ellie checked in with a receptionist on the fifteenth floor and were directed to the office of ADA Max Donovan in the Homicide Investigation Unit.

Ellie already knew that the professional lives of ADAs were not glamorous. She had met with enough of them to know that the spacious, mahogany-highlighted offices, complete with brass lamps, antique scales, and matching volumes of leather-bound books, were the stuff of fictional lawyers on television. Most prosecutors worked long hours out of cubbyhole-sized cubes of clutter, all for a paycheck that wasn't enough to cover both Manhattan rent and law school student loans.

Still, she would have thought that an attorney who'd been in the office long enough to earn a slot trying murder cases would warrant digs better than these. An ornately framed diploma from Columbia Law School stood out alongside Max Donovan's metal desk, ratty chairs, and dented file cabinet. Apparently any luxuries to be found in the office were enjoyed even further up the food chain.

Donovan was tall, with broad shoulders and dark curly hair. If he felt any self-consciousness about his humble surroundings, he didn't show it. He rose from his desk to welcome them with hearty handshakes, and then gestured for them to have a seat themselves. Ellie noticed the lawyer watching her as she crossed her legs in the charcoal-colored pencil skirt she'd chosen that morning. She also noticed a subtle smell that reminded her of white truffles.

'So I've already received a call this morning from Mr. Warden's lawyer, looking for a deal.'

'So a night in jail did work wonders,' Rogan said, smiling.

'I assume you two don't care about the drug charges on Warden. We're just looking for cooperation in the event he's covering for Jake Myers.'

'We're more certain of that now,' Ellie said. 'CSU matched Myers's prints to a latent they pulled from the victim's shirt. We also located a cabdriver who can place Jake Myers outside the club with the victim just before closing time. That contradicts his statement in two ways: he said Chelsea left earlier, and he said he was never outside the club with her.'

'Good,' Donovan said, straightening his blue-striped tie. 'We're getting somewhere. And we're going to have some leverage against Warden. I just got the crime lab reports from last night.'

'That was fast,' she said. In the bureaucratic world of NYPD, evidence related to Warden's drug bust had to be processed by a separate – and typically slower – unit than the physical evidence in the Chelsea Hart murder case.

'It's amazing what they can do when you tell them Simon Knight needs something yesterday. The drugs you took off the girl –'

'Ashlee Swain,' Ellie reminded him.

'Right. The drugs came back positive as crystal meth, with Jaime Rodriguez's fingerprints on the baggie. We've also got Warden's prints, plus Rodriguez's, on the money you seized from Warden's pocket. And the weight came in at precisely an eighth of an ounce.'

'Hot damn,' Rogan said. The prints corroborated Ellie's version of what went down between Rodriguez, Warden, and the model. And thanks to the Rockefeller drug laws, an eight ball of meth could get Warden up to nine years.

'Warden's lawyer is ready to deal,' Donovan said. 'Her client went through drug court once already as a college sophomore after he got popped for DUI on Christmas break and the police found a small amount of cocaine in his impounded car. That, combined with the drug weight and his current participation in distribution, will keep him out of drug court and on the felony docket.'

Ellie smiled. After news like this, the preppy rich kid with the surfer haircut would not be so protective of his friend.

'Shoot,' Donovan said, checking his watch. 'I better run if I'm going to talk to this lawyer before arraignment.'

'Who's the lawyer?' Rogan asked.

'Her name's Susan Parker. I expected one of the big gun criminal defense lawyers, but she's an associate at one of those fringy finance firms. They've got a reputation for pushing the envelope-moving business offshore, hiding conflicts of interest, just about anything to avoid oversight from the Securities and Exchange Commission. I assume they represent Warden's hedge fund. Parker's not much older than Warden himself. She was probably sent over here to work something out. If it gets complicated, they'll bring in a shark. But not to worry. We're not going to let it get complicated.'

'Real quick, before we go: we drafted an affidavit based on Jake Myers's statements last night and the cabdriver's ID,' Ellie said, holding up the four-page document she'd hammered out at the precinct. It was accompanied by an application for an arrest warrant and a search warrant for Jake Myers's apartment, car, and a DNA sample. 'We figured it was enough for PC. Do you want us to hold off until you get Warden's story, or go ahead and get it signed while we're here?'

'May I?' Donovan asked. She handed him the document and watched as Donovan scanned the pages, nodding occasionally. 'Nice work. You write better than half the trial lawyers in the office.'

'That's not exactly high praise for your coworkers.' As Donovan handed the affidavit back to her, Ellie noticed Rogan eyeing her with a smirk. 'So what were your thoughts on the timing?'

'Right. Go ahead and get the warrant signed. Better

to pick Myers up now. You never know where a guy like that might run off to.'

'That was quite the mutual admiration society up there,' Rogan said as they jogged down the courthouse steps on Centre Street. It had required all of fifteen minutes to get the warrants reviewed and signed.

'What are you talking about?'

'What are *you* talking about? I felt like I was standing in between Angelina and Billy Bob back in the old dirty days.'

'Please, because he said that stupid thing about my writing? He's just a typical lawyer trying to get on our good side so he can screw us over down the road.'

'Excuse me, but I've been shined on by half the ADAs in the county, and that's not what all that was about. I saw the way he was looking at you.'

'You are having far too much fun teasing me,' Ellie said.

'I'd say that from the looks of things, it was more like you were having fun teasing him. Crossing your legs. Getting his advice about the warrant. I think I even caught a hair twirl in there.'

'All right, that's enough.' It was *not* a hair twirl. Maybe a flip, at most. Ellie did have to admit that she'd noticed Donovan looking at her.

She'd noticed other things as well during their brief introduction: Donovan's height – he must have been about six-one – and solid build. Cool gray eyes and square jaw. A thin-lipped smile that was cute without being cocky. Sort of a John Kennedy Jr. look. No wedding band. That nice truffle smell.

That really *was* enough, she thought to herself. These loopy teenage daydreams were clearly the result of clinical levels of sleep deprivation. She felt a slight pang of guilt recalling one of the reasons for her sleeplessness – her late night with Peter Morse.

'Ready to pick up our boy Myers?' Rogan asked.

'I've been ready since the second he called Chelsea's friend a bitch.'

The sign that welcomed them was black marble with silver letters. Capital Research Technology.

It sounded serious. Large. Trustworthy. Established. In truth, it was a ten-month old, four-man shop occupying only half a floor of a midlevel office building on Fifth Avenue and Forty-third Street.

The receptionist informed them they would need an appointment to see Mr. Myers, but Ellie and Rogan ignored her and found their way down a narrow hallway leading to four offices. The first was empty. A nameplate on the desk read Nicolas J. Warden.

At door number two stood a man with a familiar face.

'Detectives. I didn't realize you'd be coming here.'

Jake Myers apparently left his New Wave wardrobe at home during business hours. In a conservative navy suit and red power tie, and without mass quantities of gel to mold his hair into a gravity-defying shape, he almost didn't look like an ass.

Rogan grabbed Myers's arm, pushed him against the

hallway wall, and began patting down his suit. 'We don't usually give people a shout-out before arresting them for murder.' He read Myers his Miranda rights while placing him in handcuffs.

'You're making a mistake,' Myers said. 'I didn't kill anyone.'

Ellie pulled Myers around to face her. 'You're the one who made a mistake. Last night, you were sure your boys would cover for you. Well, tomorrow Nick Warden will be selling short and trading swap futures in his office next door, looking for someone else to help him run the company while you spend the rest of your life in prison.'

'I thought cops were supposed to investigate. You won't listen to anything I tell you.'

'Let's take a look at what you've told us so far. You told us you didn't leave the club with Chelsea Hart, do drugs with her, or have sexual contact with her.' She ticked off his lies on her fingers. 'So, as far as we're concerned, everything you've ever said to us is a lie.'

Ellie was new to homicide cases, but she had arrested enough suspects to be familiar with the typical responses to confrontation. Regret. Panic. Anger. Defiance. She also recognized the physical acts that tended to accompany these emotions. Regret and panic tended to trigger tears, while anger often brought violence. Defiance was usually accompanied by either an adamant and detailed story of innocence or an invocation of counsel. And sometimes spit. Spit paired well with anger, too. She hated it when the angry and the defiant spit.

But Jake Myers caught her by surprise.

He smiled. He grinned like a man with a well-kept

secret. Whatever apprehension they had temporarily instilled in him was gone, and the arrogance she'd initially witnessed at Pulse was back in its full glory. 'Fine. Do what you have to do, beautiful.'

Ellie pictured herself delivering a knee strike to Myers's groin, followed by a left jab into his skinny head. *That's* what she had to do. At least a good smack. Something.

Instead, she said, 'I take it you're not answering any questions.'

'Not without a lawyer. You're welcome to my DNA, however.'

It was Rogan who delivered the slap to the back of Myers's head, and it wasn't just in Ellie's imagination. 'Not another word.'

And that was the last they heard out of Jake Myers for three days.

That evening, at precisely 5:30 p.m., the man watched the entrance of Mesa Grill from a counter at an Au Bon Pain across the street.

He had come across the bartender accidentally the previous night. He had been walking downtown, looking for his next project; given the changes in the city over the last several years, it was his impression that downtown was the best place to look for the kind of girls he liked – girls who had fun, too much fun.

He started in Washington Square Park. A lot of NYU girls there. Hippie chicks. Down-and-outs. But compared to Chelsea, none of the girls he saw had that kind of spark.

175

From the park, he'd made his way over to the West Village. Spent some time in three different sex shops. He figured any woman who worked in a place like that would eventually be easy to grab. But to his disappointment, the employees had all been men. Most of the customers, too. It was the neighborhood, he figured.

He'd gotten his hopes up at a store called Fantasy when he'd spotted one of the employees from behind. She'd been reaching for a foot-long purple dildo from a top shelf. She must have been six feet tall. Thin. Long, white-blond hair. Then she had turned around, and it was clear that she was a he. Not his type.

From the Village, he had headed to the Flatiron. The district had once been known as Ladies' Mile, famous for the department stores that drew the country's most elegant women, shopping for the finest luxuries. First ladies frequented Arnold Constable at Nineteenth Street and Broadway. Tiffany & Co. had sat at Fourteenth Street and University before the jeweler decided that Union Square had coarsened. A century ago, this neighborhood had catered to the choosiest of women. Now, a hundred years later, he hoped that he might find precisely what he was searching for, somewhere on Broadway before he reached Madison Park.

The sidewalks were crammed with hundreds of interchangeable girls in blue jeans and winter coats, carrying shopping bags and designer purses. Most were in groups. Those who weren't were attached to their cell phones – so uninteresting that they couldn't stand the idea of being alone with their own thoughts for the handful of minutes it took to move on to the next purchase.

The man wondered if perhaps he was too spoiled in New York. He suspected that in any average city, the majority of these girls he'd written off would shine like flawless D-grade diamonds. Maybe his problem was that he had it too good. So many, many girls, not paying attention.

So he had tried again once he reached Twenty-third Street, making the turn where Broadway met Fifth Avenue. If anything, Fifth Avenue was even more crowded than Broadway. More girls. More shopping. More vacuous phone calls: 'Nothing. What are you doing? Where are you? I'm going into Banana.'

He tried to remind himself that this was only his first attempt to find his next project, and less than twenty-four hours since Chelsea Hart. He had decided to call it an evening when he passed a busy restaurant. The brightly painted letters on the front window read 'MESA.' High ceilings. Big crowd at the bar. Probably expensive. He was looking in the window, wondering whether it was expensive-stupid or expensive-good, when he noticed the bartender with the blond ponytail. She was pouring from two bottles into a martini shaker and talking to a middle-aged couple at the bar.

He spent a lot of time in bars. Despite the stereotype about bartenders, they really weren't good listeners. If they were, he'd spend less time in bars. But this girl, she was really listening. She was nodding, laughing, looking the female half of the couple right in the eye, even as she frantically mixed away. Giving the mixer a vigorous shake, she scratched her cheek with her sleeve. Then she laughed about something. He could tell it was a real laugh, from the belly.

A margarita sounded good.

He'd waited until the seat next to the couple was empty before he ordered. *House margarita, rocks and salt.* Good, generic, forgettable order. As he sipped his drink, he'd learned more about the bartender, eavesdropping on her conversation with the couple. She was an aspiring writer. Two published short stories, a few magazine essays, and one unpublished novella. Now she was working on her first thriller, an attempt to go commercial at the suggestion of her agent. The setup featured a small-town female cop who realized her son was a serial killer.

He also overheard the bartender swap shifts with her bald male colleague for Tuesday and Thursday. She'd be covering his 11:00 to 5:30 shift; he'd take her usual 5:30 to midnight. 'Thanks a lot for doing that,' the bald guy had said. 'Not a problem,' she'd replied. 'It'll be nice to actually have a night to go out like a regular person.'

Only one pop-in, and he'd already nailed down a big piece of her schedule.

After he'd signaled for the check, he noticed that the top of the computerized slip of paper listed the name Rachel next to the date and time. He owed her twelve dollars. He opened his wallet and fingered a hundred-dollar bill inside, smiling as he remembered finding it in Chelsea's purse. He removed a ten and a five instead and left both bills on the bar. Not too cheap, not too generous.

Now it was Tuesday evening, and the bartender should have just wrapped up the first of her two day-shifts this week. He watched from the bakery window, coffee in hand, as the girl he presumed was called Rachel buttoned up her beige peacoat and dashed across three lanes of traffic on Fifth Avenue.

Taking the corner onto Fifteenth Street, she passed directly in front of him. He lowered his gaze and then made his way to the exit, also turning at Fifteenth.

He was thirty feet behind her. He caught a whiff of musky perfume. He figured she probably spritzed herself on the way out of the restaurant to mask the smell of southwestern food.

He noticed she wore flat black loafers. Hopefully she would turn to something less practical when she wasn't working. A healthy girl like her could run in loafers.

She reached her right hand to the nape of her neck, slipped off her ponytail elastic, and shook her blond waves loose. He stole a glimpse of her profile reflected in the window of a sushi restaurant as she passed. She looked good with her hair down.

Before she reached Union Square Park, she turned and disappeared into a storefront.

He crossed Fifteenth Street and kept his head down as he walked directly toward the park. He glanced in his periphery as he passed the spot where she had disappeared. 'Park Bar.'

When he reached Union Square West, he found a seat at an unoccupied picnic table near the curb. He would sit here, and he would wait. And watch.

Patience. Diligence. Dedication. Timing.

He had found his project. Now he had to nail down the routine, learn the habits. Chelsea had caught him off guard. This time, nothing should be unexpected.

As he sat at the picnic table, watching subway riders dash to their trains at Union Square, he found himself smiling and remembering a line from Jack Finney's classic novel *Time and Again:* 'Suddenly I had to close my eyes because actual tears were smarting at the very nearly uncontainable thrill of being here. The Ladies' Mile was great, the sidewalks and entrances of the block after block of big glittering ladies' stores . . .'

He too had a very nearly uncontainable thrill of being in the Ladies' Mile.

Chapter Twenty

'What can I get you, Hatcher?'

'Johnnie Walker Black. Rocks.'

'A week on the job together, and I still don't know your drink,' Rogan said. 'That ain't right.'

As much as Ellie wanted to go home, flip on the tube, and crash on the couch, this had been her first invitation for a group drink out of the Thirteenth Precinct, and she was not about to blow the opportunity. They were celebrating Jake Myers's arrest at Plug Uglies, a cop bar on Third Ave. between Twentieth and Twenty-first.

Even though this wood-paneled pub – originally named for one of the city's old Irish gangs, now accessorized with the shoulder patches of hundreds of police and firemen – was the official hangout of the Thirteenth Precinct, this was Ellie's first visit with other cops. Her only previous invitation had come from Jess after her first day in the homicide squad – not his sort of place, but it was close to work, and with a $2 happy hour, it was one of the few spots in Manhattan where her brother could afford to pick up a tab.

Tonight, drinks were on Rogan, and that meant that half the squad tagged along, even though they had nothing to do with the Chelsea Hart case. When it came time to celebrate, a case clearance for one was a win for all.

She spotted a familiar face at the end of the bar and indicated to Rogan she'd be right back.

'Hey, stranger.'

Peter Morse greeted her with a peck on the cheek. Ellie automatically looked around to confirm that the other cops were pre-occupied.

'How'd you know I'd be here?' she asked.

'I didn't. I'm meeting Kittrie.' Peter glanced at his watch. 'His idea to be here, and now he's fifteen minutes late. Typical.'

'He made you stay late last night, took top billing on this morning's story, and now you're having a drink with him? I thought you hated that guy.'

'Doesn't matter – he's the boss. Everyone's tiptoeing around him anyway these days, ever since Justine accidentally connected to his line and heard some doctor saying something about a tumor. I'm convinced she made up the whole thing to fuck with me, but I'm not going to risk being an a-hole to the guy. He wanted to work together on the Hart story, we worked together. He wants to have a drink, I'm having a drink.'

'And he just happened to pick Plug Uglies out of all the bars in Manhattan?'

'Of course not. He's convinced you pick up the best dirt at cop bars. Little does he know I have found a much more pleasurable method of cultivating inside sources.'

Peter placed his palm on the small of her back, and she pulled away. Enough PDA for one night.

'Ah, except I *don't* actually give you any inside information. I just use you for the sex.'

Peter snapped his fingers. 'I knew there was a problem with my plan. That probably explains why I'm in the doghouse with Kittrie. He's pissed we didn't get a better picture of your victim.'

'You had the same one as the *Times*.'

'Exactly. But the *Sun* didn't. Now he says I shouldn't have just taken whatever the family handed us. He says the graduation shot was too *controlled*.'

'What did he expect you to do? Go to her MySpace page and steal pictures off the Web?'

'That's actually not a bad idea.'

'Too late. We already told the family to pull down the profile. But it would still be less tacky than nagging Chelsea's friends. That's how the *Sun* got their picture.'

'You're tracking journalists' practices now?'

Ellie got the impression he didn't agree with her assessment about the tastelessness of chasing down a murder victim's loved ones to help a story. 'No, but it's the only way they could've gotten it. One of Chelsea's friends snapped it with her cell phone the night before the murder.' She was still annoyed that the photograph had run on the front page of tens of thousands of newspapers, with Chelsea's missing earrings on full display.

She felt a hand on her right shoulder and turned to find herself in the middle of an enthusiastic handshake. The man pumping her arm was about forty years old, medium height and build, with wire-rimmed glasses and not much remaining hair.

'Hi there. George Kittrie. I believe you're the famous Ellie Hatcher?'

'Hopefully less famous by the day.'

'Not if we have anything to say about it, isn't that right, Peter?' Kittrie nudged the visibly uncomfortable reporter. 'Ignore me. I'm being a jerk, even if I was only kidding.'

Kittrie looked familiar. She tried to place him – probably the author photo on his book. 'Have we met before?'

'Nah, but you may have seen me around. I'm a big believer that any crime-beat reporter worth his salt has got to hit the cop bars. It's all about contacts. I had a real good relationship with Flann McIlroy, by the way.'

Given the circumstances of McIlroy's death, Ellie supposed her name would always be linked with his in New York City law enforcement circles.

'What kind of drink can we get you?' Kittrie asked.

She turned to see J. J. Rogan encircled by Thirteenth Precinct cops, a lonely Johnnie Walker Black on the bar next to him, getting more watered down by the second, calling out to her: *Drink me.*

'I've got some friends waiting for me,' she said.

'Sounded like a celebration when I passed. I don't suppose there's a break in the Chelsea Hart case.'

'Just an after-work drink is all.' The *Daily Post* would get wind of Jake Myers's arrest soon enough from the Public Information Office. She said her good-byes and left poor Peter on his man date with Kittrie.

As Ellie made her way over to Rogan, she saw that

the first patrol officer who responded to Chelsea's crime scene was holding court. If she had to guess, he was probably leaving out the part where he tossed his cookies and was sent off to fetch her clothes.

She plucked her drink from the bar, and Rogan nodded his head in her direction.

'Capra here was just telling everyone about being first on the scene this morning.'

Ellie saw a hint of color creep into the cheeks of the young officer. 'First *uniform* on the scene, Detective. Your partner, of course, was first man there. Or woman, or –'

'Someone get this officer another drink,' she said with a laugh. John Shannon, the detective whose desk was behind hers, raised his glass in a toast. The rest of the crowd, however, greeted her with stony stares and uncomfortable glances. It was apparently going to take more than one arrest and a round of drinks to win some folks over.

Her cell phone vibrated at her waist. The screen read, 'Unavailable.'

'Hatcher.' Ellie plugged one ear shut with her index finger.

'Hi, it's Max Donovan from the DA's office.'

'You got our message?' She maneuvered her way to the front of the bar.

Their message had actually been left by Rogan. She stole a look at her partner.

'Yeah, this is my first chance to get back to you. The good news is, well, it couldn't be any better. I cut a deal with Nick Warden.'

'He's flipping on Jake?'

Ellie opened her backpack and pulled out a manila folder that the Central Records Division had delivered that morning. It contained the file on the murder of Roberta Harrington, aka Robbie. The original reports dated back to the summer of 2000. Given that Jake Myers was barely out of middle school at the time, any connection between the two cases now seemed impossible.

She skimmed while Donovan brought her up to speed.

'No question. It helped that I could go in there this morning with the fingerprint match and the cabdriver's ID. I told him, "Look, we've got our case against Jake. The only question is whether we're going to have one against you, too." Once he and his lawyer heard what we already had on Myers, and what Warden was looking at on his drug case, it was easy. The guy's got loyalty, though. He wanted a deal for Jaime Rodriguez, too.'

'You're kidding me? White-collar recreational drug user taking care of his dealer? Who's ever heard of such a thing?'

'I know, right? I guess Warden feels bad about getting the guy in trouble. He said Rodriguez hooking up the girl with some dope was kind of like helping him out, too. This isn't exactly politically correct, but I got the impression she was quite the box of chocolates?'

'If tall, thin, and ridiculously sexy is your kind of thing.'

'Absolutely not.'

'So you made the deal? I thought Rodriguez would

be looking at some serious time with his prior conviction.'

'His prior for Burg of a dwelling with a gun counts as a violent predicate. He was looking at six years minimum under the second felony law. But we made the deal. He and Warden both get dismissals. Rodriguez will lose his job with the club just for the arrest, and he'll have a hard time finding work anywhere else.'

'You don't need to sell me on it,' Ellie said, her eyes still scanning the Harrington file as she flipped to the next report. She hadn't known a prosecutor to ever care in the past whether she approved of a plea deal. Besides, she had learned a long time ago that drug cases – no matter what quantities, no matter how many priors, and despite all the rhetoric about the war on drugs – were all expendable when the prosecution of a violent crime was at stake.

'Our case against Myers is looking strong. Warden's not only going to testify that Jake left with Chelsea alone, well before closing, but he's got real corroboration. And it's good.'

Ellie stopped multitasking so she could focus on Donovan's news.

'His lawyer produced a photograph that Warden took with his cell phone that night inside the club. He was snapping the picture because some cow – Warden's words, not mine, I swear – was making an idiot of herself on the runway, but guess who pops up in the background? Jake Myers walking hand in hand with Chelsea Hart out of the front doors of Pulse. And the time stamp says 3:03, almost an hour before closing.'

Sex. Alcohol. Drugs. Now they'd caught Jake Myers in a lie on his alibi, proving not only opportunity, but consciousness of guilt. Unless the DNA on Chelsea Hart's shirt belonged to someone else, Myers was done.

'How long will it take for the crime lab to give us DNA results from the stain on Chelsea's shirt?'

'A couple of weeks, but Simon Knight swears he can find a shortcut. The mayor's office is breathing down our necks.'

'Too bad Myers invoked,' she said. 'With Warden flipping on him, we might've been able to get a confession.'

'We're going to get him anyway. If all cops were as good as you and your partner, my job would be a lot easier. I was just telling Knight what a dream witness you are. Smart. Articulate.'

'For a cop.'

'Sorry. That's not what I meant. It was actually my insanely awkward way of trying to transition into asking if you wanted to get something to eat. I don't know about you, but I've been running around all day, and I'm starving.'

In Ellie's mind, she could feel laser beams from Peter's eyes penetrating the back of her skull and piercing her neocortex where the words of their phone conversation were being processed.

'Sorry, I've got plans tonight.'

'So, does that mean maybe some other night, or should I take that as an extremely polite shutout?'

'It doesn't sound very polite when you put it that way,' she said with an embarrassed laugh.

'Okay, I think I can take a hint. I hope it's not weird I asked. Knight will kill me if I alienated our star witness.'

'Consider me wholly unalienated. People get hungry. They eat, sometimes together. Not a problem.'

If Peter had been eavesdropping on her neocortex, she was pretty sure she'd passed with flying colors. Still, Ellie couldn't help but notice that she was still smiling as she flipped her phone shut, took a sip of her drink, and returned to her reading.

Ten minutes later, she had finished reviewing the Robbie Harrington file. Her smile was gone. She drained the rest of her whisky, tucked the file into her backpack, and sent a quick text message to Peter, who was still with his boss, chatting up a couple of cops who looked familiar from the Thirteenth Precinct: 'I've got a little work left, but call me later.'

When she returned to the squad's huddle, John Shannon was in the middle of some story about a witness who'd made the moves on his partner that day. 'She was a ten all right,' he said, taking a swig from his mug of amber-colored beer. 'As in four teeth and a six-pack.'

Ellie cut through the laughter and thanked Rogan for the drink.

'You're heading out already?' he asked.

'Yeah. Another drink, and I might fall asleep right here in the bar. That call before was from Max Donovan at the DA's office.'

Rogan snuck a peek at the cell phone clipped to his waist.

'That's funny. He didn't call me. Hey,' he said to anyone within earshot, 'why do you think a young, single ADA might have called Hatcher here for the case update instead of her more senior, and equally fine-looking, partner?'

That got a laugh out of the crowd, but not as much as Ellie's follow-up: 'He was asking for your home number.'

'Nice,' Rogan said, giving her a high five.

She ran through a quick summary of Donovan's update, pulling on her coat as she talked.

'News like that, and you can't stay for another drink? Come on.'

'I can't keep up with you. I've got to go home and hit the sack.'

But as Ellie walked out of the bar, she knew she wasn't going home anytime soon. The case against Jake Myers was sealed up tight. But she had just read the police reports on the murder of Robbie Harrington, and now she was wondering if perhaps it had all been a little too easy.

Chapter Twenty-One

On the night of August 16, 2000, a homeless woman named Loretta Thompson thought she had found a safe place to sleep when she passed a pile of Mexican serape blankets tossed into the basement entrance of a Chinese massage parlor on the corner of Fourth Street and Avenue B.

It was a warm, dry night, and Loretta had decided not to check into one of the shelters, filled as they were with strung-out and angry women. She was not like the others. She just needed a break – a friend to take her in for a few weeks, an employer to take a chance on her – some way to get back on her feet after leaving the man whose beatings had caused her to miscarry the only child she'd ever managed to conceive.

When she reached the bottom of the unlit stairwell, she realized that the blankets were wrapped around something firm. Her hope was that it was a rug – something she could use as padding between her body and the filthy concrete. But when she pulled one of the blankets loose from the bundle, she felt something heavy shift beneath it. She tugged at the blanket with more force to get a better look.

Her screams awakened multiple Fourth Street residents. The 911 calls followed.

It took police three days to identify the body as Robbie Harrington, a twenty-four-year-old artist who paid her bills working at a tattoo parlor on the Lower East Side. She was last seen having a drink alone at a dive bar a few blocks from her job. She had been strangled with a brown leather belt that was left wrapped around her neck.

According to the log notes on the outside of the Harrington file, the active investigation had been put to rest about a year after Robbie's body had been found, and her murder joined the legions of cold case files that gather dust until a new lead lands unexpectedly in the department's lap. But three years ago, someone had brushed off the dust from the case. Three years ago, Detective Flann McIlroy had requested this file and read the same reports that Ellie had just finished reviewing for the second time at her desk.

She could see why the media reports of Chelsea Hart's murder would have caught Bill Harrington's attention. Like Chelsea, Robbie was a very young, white, blond female murdered after leaving a New York City bar, although her club of choice on the Lower East Side was significantly less glitzy than Pulse.

Ellie picked up the phone and dialed the number that Harrington had left that morning when he contacted the department's tip line. She took note of the Nassau County area code, a change from the Pittsburgh number listed for the Harringtons at the time of their daughter's death.

'Hello?' The man had a smoker's voice.

'This is Detective Ellie Hatcher with the New York Police Department. I'm calling for Bill Harrington.'

'This is him.'

'You called the tip line about a recent case of ours?'

'I did. I'm feeling foolish about it now. I don't know anything about that poor girl's murder other than what I heard on the news. The minute I called, I regretted it. Some old man's imagination could keep you from leads that might actually get you somewhere.'

Ellie realized that the man had probably experienced his share of false leads and crank calls eight years ago. 'Why don't you go ahead and tell me why you called.'

'This is going to sound crazy, but I had a dream the other night, and I think it was a message from Robbie. I wasn't calling the tip line for myself. I was calling for her.'

It took the man some effort to get the words out, but Ellie eventually put the picture together. Flann McIlroy had tracked Bill Harrington down out of the blue three years earlier, looking for additional information about Robbie's murder. By then, Bill had retired, and he and his wife, Penny, were living in Mineola on Long Island. It had been a year since they'd communicated with anyone from the NYPD about their daughter's case.

'At first, when the trail went cold, we'd call every month or so. Usually it was me, not Penny. Then every month became every season, and then just every August on the anniversary. Ultimately, it was our older daughter Jenna who convinced us that to move on with our lives, we needed to accept the probability that we would never know who took away our girl from us. I think that most of Penny's reason for wanting to move closer to New York was to show that she hadn't forgotten about Robbie. Being near to the city that Robbie had insisted on living in was my wife's way of being close to our daughter after it was too late.'

'I'm sorry if my call has dredged all of this up for you again, Mr. Harrington.' Ellie hoped she had made the right decision contacting this man.

'I told you, it was the dream that did the dredging. I called you, remember?'

'You said in your message that Flann McIlroy told you he thought there were others. What did you mean by that?'

'That's what he said when he called us three years ago. He had been working a few months before that on a different case and had pulled up a mess of cold cases looking for patterns, I guess. He told us it turned out the case he was working was some kind of a domestic thing. But in the process of looking at all those old cases, he thought he'd noticed some connections between Robbie's death and a couple of other unsolved murders.'

'Did he tell you anything about the other cases?'

'No names or anything. He said the others were girls around the same age, and they had been out on the town before – well, before someone got to them.'

'Did he have any leads? I'm trying to understand

why he would have called to tell you all this if he didn't have any developments to report.'

'I remember exactly why he called. He said the same thing, in fact – that he was sorry for calling us and wouldn't have done it if he didn't think it might be important. It was the strangest thing, though. I couldn't imagine how an offhand comment could possibly matter.'

An offhand comment. Ellie's fingers involuntarily clenched the handset of the telephone as she braced herself for what Harrington was about to tell her. She did not want the nagging feeling that had pulled her from the bar tonight to go any further. She wanted Flann to have had another reason for calling.

'He wanted to talk to Penny about something she said when we identified Robbie's body.'

Ellie knew immediately which single sentence in the voluminous police reports had triggered Flann's phone call. It was the same line that had caused her to leave the bar earlier than she'd intended. *Victim's mother confirmed ID but said victim's hair looked odd.*

'What exactly did Detective McIlroy want to know?' Ellie asked. 'Would it be better for me to speak directly with your wife?'

'Penny's not in a position to answer any questions. She has early-onset Alzheimer's. It's advanced.'

'I'm so sorry.'

'It is what it is. She recognizes me on good days but doesn't understand why I look so old. The only silver lining I've been able to find in my wife's condition is that she seems to have no memory of Robbie's murder.

She either forgets her daughters altogether, or remembers them as they were when they were young and we were still living as a family in Pittsburgh.'

'Were her memories gone by the time Detective McIlroy contacted you?'

'They were fading, certainly, but she was still home with me then. She did speak with him directly, and I tried a couple of times to work with her on the information the detective wanted. I never did quite understand what the issue was.'

'What about at the time she made the comment, after the two of you identified the body. Didn't she give some idea of what she meant back then?'

'Not to be specific. She just blurted out that Robbie's hair looked funny when she saw her lying like that on the table. She brought it up later when we were driving back home, but it was just this observation that made her realize how little we'd seen Robbie since she moved to the city. I guess a mother is like that – figures she should know when her own daughter changes her appearance.'

'But you don't know exactly what the change was?' The fact that Chelsea Hart's hair had been crudely chopped off had not been released to the public, and Ellie did not want to share the information with Harrington. But she had to think that such a brutal transformation would have been noticed by more than just one of Robbie's parents.

'It looked a little shorter to me, but Penny was just so bothered by it, saying it didn't seem like a style Robbie would go for. I don't know enough about those kinds of things to be any more specific than that, and by the time anyone asked Penny about it, it was too late. I tried and tried, but all she could say by then was that Robbie liked her hair long. No, wait, that wasn't it – because Robbie did sometimes keep her hair a little neater, cut up above her shoulders, I guess.'

'So, I'm sorry – what is it your wife meant?'

'I don't know what it's called, but Penny was saying Robbie liked her hair to be – you know, even. All the same around, how most of the girls wore it back then. She didn't like it being different lengths, the way you see it now, with all the long hair, but then short on the top.'

'Do you mean bangs, where it's cut above the eyebrows?'

'Yeah, that's it. Bangs. When Detective McIlroy called a few years ago, I finally got Penny to focus, and she told me that Robbie didn't like bangs. Apparently she was wearing her hair that way when she was killed.'

'And you passed that on to Detective McIlroy?'

'I did. But what does any of this have to do with that girl who was found in the park? I called because she'd also been out all night like my Robbie, and there was something about the picture that reminded me of her, and, well, I told you about my dream.'

If Robbie Harrington really had sent her father to the NYPD tip line, perhaps it was because she was in a position to know something that her father could not – that whoever strangled her on August 16, 2000, may have claimed another victim yesterday morning.

Part III

No Surprises

Chapter Twenty-Two

'I told you. Detective McIlroy would check out stacks of cold cases at a time. There was no rhyme or reason to any of it, and you can stand here all morning while I pull files, and none of that's going to change.'

Ellie looked at her watch. She didn't have all day. She had a precinct to go to. But her first stop on Wednesday morning had been to the Central Records Division at One Police Plaza.

She had come in the hope that it would be easy to identify which cases Flann McIlroy had been reviewing along with Robbie Harrington's. The task was anything but. Flann had a penchant for checking out old files and looking for patterns. It had been his imaginative theories – connecting seemingly unrelated cases – that had earned him both praise and ridicule from his peers in the department, along with the nickname McIlMulder.

'He had all of these cases checked out at the same time as the Roberta Harrington file?'

She had asked the clerk to pull up any case files McIlroy had checked out in the three months preceding his phone call to Bill Harrington. The resulting printout was pages long.

'Like I said, he didn't have all of these at the same time. He had up to fifteen cases checked out at a time. And, as far as I can tell, in that three-month window, he pulled a total of a hundred and seven.'

Once again, Ellie scanned the list of files. Once again, total disbelief.

'That's actually a little light,' the woman remarked. 'I used to joke he had a ten-file-a-week habit.'

Ellie had already asked the clerk to pull a random sample of the different files, and, on a brief skim, she had been unable to figure out which cases had been linked in McIlroy's mind to Robbie Harrington's murder, and which had been of interest for any number of other, unknowable reasons.

'You want me to pull some more reports or not?'

Ellie looked at the two-foot-high stack the clerk already needed to reshelve because of her morning research project.

'Don't feel bad. God knows McIlroy never did.'

It wasn't that Ellie didn't want the woman to work. She just didn't want the work to be futile.

One hundred and seven files? Ellie had only known Flann for a week before his death. During that time, she'd become a staunch supporter, but now she was beginning to wonder if he really had been certifiably insane. Even when she narrowed the list to female victims under thirty-five years old, seventy cases were left taunting her.

'What day did Flann return the Harrington file to CRD?'

The clerk entered a few keystrokes on her computer and recited a date about nine months after Flann had reached out to Robbie's father. He had let the theory grind around in his brain for nine months after that phone call, until he'd apparently given it up. She wondered what more she could possibly add.

'Can you figure out which of these other cases he turned in on the same day?' Ellie asked.

More keystrokes. 'He turned in three files all together. Your Harrington case, plus two others: Lucy Feeney and Alice Butler.'

'And how old were the victims?'

'Feeney was twenty-one. Alice Butler was twenty-two. Feeney was killed two years before Harrington. Butler, almost two years after.'

'I'll take those, please.'

One by one, the men filed into the Thirteenth Precinct's lineup room.

Watching from the other side of the viewing window, Ellie recognized number 1 as Jim Kemp, a desk clerk from downstairs. Number 2 was Toby Someone, who worked behind the counter at the bagel shop on Second Avenue. Number 3 was Jake Myers. She maintained a neutral expression, lest Myers's attorney accuse them later of a biased process. Number 4 was another desk clerk, Steve Broderick. Number 5 was a kid they'd found playing guitar outside Gramercy Park.

All young, thin, and brunet. Decent looking. Similar heights and builds. She was just giving herself a silent congratulations on a well-built lineup when number 6 entered, provoking a skeptical laugh from Willie Wells, the defense attorney Jake Myers had retained after his arrest the previous night.

'You're kidding me, right?'

Number 6 was the homicide squad's very own civilian aide, Jack Chen. Young, thin, brunet, decent looking – and noticeably Asian.

'The kid we pulled from the holding room backed out,' Rogan explained. 'A sudden worry he might be falsely accused.'

'So you found this guy?' Wells said, pointing at Chen. 'What? Fat Albert wasn't available? How about the Abominable Snowman? He'd probably fit in.'

'Is that your way of saying you'd rather proceed with five?' Rogan said.

'I'd rather have a good six.'

Max Donovan intervened. 'And you know that any court would say the first five will do.'

'It's not my job to help you sink my client. Do what you're gonna do, and if you screw it up, you'll hear about it at the *Wade* hearing.'

Donovan looked to Rogan, who pressed a speaker button next to the glass and excused number 6.

'We're ready?' Ellie asked, once the lineup was down to Myers and the four suitable decoys. She wished she hadn't noticed Donovan's sleepy gray eyes. If he was at all embarrassed about asking her out to dinner the previous night, he wasn't showing it.

He nodded, and Ellie opened the door to the hallway. Tahir Kadhim sat by himself on a metal folding chair outside the viewing room. Stefanie Hyder, Jordan

McLaughlin, and Miriam Hart stood huddled together a few feet away, Paul pacing next to them.

Ellie called in Kadhim first. The taxi driver had not even made it to the glass before pointing to Jake Myers. 'That's the man,' he said. 'He is the one I saw take the girl from my taxi.'

'You didn't actually see anyone *take* Ms. Hart anywhere, did you?' Wells asked.

Donovan held up a hand. 'We're here for a lineup, Willie. If you want to have an investigator chat with Mr. Kadhim on your own time, that's your call.'

'And by then you will have no doubt had your standard talk with him.'

'I am under no obligation to speak to you,' Kadhim said. 'You can ask your questions of me at trial.'

'Ah, I see I'm too late,' Wells said.

Donovan smiled, and Ellie walked the taxi driver to the door. Next up was Stefanie Hyder.

Unlike Tahir Kadhim, Chelsea's best friend took her time at the window, but it was not out of apprehension. Her eyes did not dart from person to person. Instead, they remained focused solidly on the middle of the lineup. As she stared at Jake Myers, her face became contorted with hatred.

Finally, after a full minute, she spoke. 'It's number three. No doubt.' She used the sleeve of her sweatshirt to wipe a tear from her cheek, and Ellie placed an arm around her shoulder and walked her out of the room.

Paul and Miriam Hart were waiting in the hallway with expectant eyes.

'No question,' Stefanie said. 'It was definitely him.'

Miriam and Jordan wrapped their arms around Stefanie, while Mr. Hart shook Ellie's hand with both of his, thanking her for catching the man who had killed their daughter.

'I just want to go home,' Stefanie said, crying into Mrs. Hart's shoulder.

'You can go back to Indiana whenever you're ready,' Ellie said. 'We needed you to identify Myers, and you've done a great job. The trial won't be for at least a couple of months, and the district attorney's office will stay in touch with you about any hearings that come up beforehand.'

Mrs. Hart wiped her eyes with a tissue. 'The girls have something they want to do this afternoon to remember Chelsea – a way for them to close the door on all this, at least in New York. But we're going to fly home tomorrow. It's time for us to take Chelsea home.'

As they told her once again how grateful they were for her help, all Ellie could think of were the three cold case files in her blue backpack and the damage a lawyer like Willie Wells could do with them in front of a jury.

Lying on her couch that evening, Ellie closed the files and tossed them on the coffee table. By this point, she had read them enough times to have memorized the critical details.

Lucy Feeney had been killed nearly a decade ago. She was three months past her twenty-first birthday, still in that phase where making full use of one's legal age was a top priority. She and three roommates shared a converted two-bedroom in Washington Heights, but

Lucy could be found downtown during most of her waking hours, where she'd spent the last two years waiting tables at six different restaurants.

The week of Lucy's murder, she and her roommates, in various combinations, had gone out partying on each of the previous four nights. The roommates' appetites for adventure had been sated. Lucy's had not. On the evening of September 23, 1998, she hit the bars on her own. According to her roommates, it wasn't an unusual move for any of them. They enjoyed semi-regular status at a sufficient number of places that they could be comfortable on their own.

The last time anyone saw Lucy Feeney alive, she was at B Bar on Bowery, enjoying a Cosmopolitan. The bartender remembered her. He also recalled sneaking her a couple extra shots of Stoli, one of the privileges of semi-regular bar status. He did not, however, spend enough time with her to recall anything about the man with whom he saw her leaving shortly before closing time.

Lucy's roommates did not report her missing for two days, another indication of the kind of lifestyle the girls considered to be normal. Lucy's naked body wasn't found until three days after that, wrapped in black plastic garbage bags and dumped in the Bronx near the Harlem River.

She'd been strangled. Stabbed four times in the chest and stomach. And her blond hair had been chopped off in blunt chunks near the roots, just like Chelsea Hart's.

The second of the three files was Robbie Harrington's.

She too was strangled after a night of barhopping, nearly two years after Lucy Feeney. And if Robbie's mother was correct in her observation about her daughter's changed hairstyle, Robbie's killer may also have tampered with her hair, albeit with more subtlety.

That left the third file, Alice Butler. Alice disappeared a year and a half after Robbie Harrington's murder. She was twenty-two years old at the time – slightly older than Lucy Feeney, a couple of years younger than Robbie Harrington. Alice had been an on-and-off student at the City University of New York for two and a half years, earning barely enough credit hours to be considered a college sophomore by the time she dropped out for good a year before her death.

She worked behind the counter of a New York Sports Club on the Upper East Side, but lived with her sister in Elizabeth, New Jersey. On the night of her murder, Alice borrowed her sister's Toyota Corolla for a night of partying in the city with a girlfriend. When she parked on the corner of Thirty-ninth Street and Ninth Avenue in Hell's Kitchen, she failed to notice the adjacent fire hydrant. By the time she and her friend returned to the spot at three in the morning, the Corolla had been towed.

According to Alice's friend, Alice grew increasingly angry while they waited to claim the car at the city tow lot. No doubt fueled by alcohol, she began muttering about abandoning her sister's car and walking back to Jersey if necessary. The friend left an impatient Alice by herself in line while she sought out a restroom. When she returned five minutes later, Alice was gone.

Ellie recognized a familiar name in the Alice Butler file: Dan Eckels. Six years earlier, shortly before he'd earned his white-shirt status, her lieutenant had been the lead detective on the Butler murder case. As far as she could tell, he'd worked the case as well as possible. The best leads in the days following Alice's disappearance were three separate phone calls from drivers reporting that they'd seen a blonde matching Alice's description walking alone on the West Side Highway. Alice's deteriorated body was found ten days later in Fort Tryon Park, dumped in a ravine between the Cloisters and the Henry Hudson Parkway. Bruises around her throat suggested she had been manually strangled, but the official cause of death had been the eighteen stab wounds to her neck, chest, and abdomen.

Including Chelsea Hart, Ellie was looking at four victims. All were young and blond, killed after late nights in Manhattan bars. But she knew that wasn't enough for a pattern. Thanks to the inherently dangerous mix of sex, drugs, and alcohol at four in the morning, the sad reality was that several women were killed in the city each year under similar circumstances. Based solely on their demographics, Lucy Feeney, Robbie Harrington, Alice Butler, and now Chelsea Hart were just four of many.

But she could not get past the hair.

Lucy Feeney and Chelsea Hart both had had their hair hacked off, leaving portions of their scalps exposed. Robbie Harrington, in contrast, had been wearing new and unexpected bangs.

Snipping off a few fringes of hair around the victim's

face was a far cry from the kind of angry chop job she'd witnessed on Chelsea.

Since her first skim through the files that morning, Ellie had known there was only one way to determine whether there was a pattern, but she'd forced herself to hold off. She told herself she should sit on it for the day before digging up the past for a murder victim's family. Flann had been known for his far-fetched theories. This could all be yet another McIlMulder wild goose chase.

She looked at her watch. It was seven twenty. Eleven hours since she'd left One Police Plaza with the cold case files. Eleven hours since she'd taken her first browse of them in the elevator. Eleven hours since she'd opened her cell phone and entered a New Jersey telephone number. Eleven hours since she'd flipped the phone shut without hitting the call button.

Eleven hours, and there was still only one option. She picked up the phone and dialed before she changed her mind.

Chapter Twenty-Three

The woman who picked up on the fourth ring seemed put out. Ellie could detect a television playing in the background, along with the sounds of children's voices. Someone was accusing someone else of hogging something or other.

'Hi. I'm looking for Michelle Butler?'

Ellie realized she should have run Alice's sister through the system. After six years, she could be anywhere, and this phone number could belong to anyone.

'It's Trent now. Has been for a while. I've really got my hands full –'

'My name's Ellie Hatcher. I'm a detective with the NYPD. I'm calling about Alice.'

Five full seconds of background noise, then the woman said, 'Kids, in the family room.' The kids protested, but apparently realized that Mom meant business when she followed up with, '*Now*. I mean it.'

'Have you found someone?'

Ellie swallowed, hearing the hope in the woman's voice, picturing the tears that were probably already welling in Michelle Trent's eyes as she braced herself for words that were long overdue.

'No. And I'm very sorry to call under those circumstances, Mrs. Trent. But your sister's case came to my attention in the course of another investigation.'

'Is this going to happen every time some other girl gets killed after drinking too much? Another detective called me – it must have been three years ago.'

'Flann McIlroy?'

'Something like that. Yeah.'

'Why did he call you?'

'Jesus Christ. Don't you people talk to each other?'

Ellie silently cursed McIlroy for not making any notes in the case files. 'I'm very sorry,' she said once again. 'I would speak to Detective McIlroy directly, but he's passed on.'

Michelle either hadn't seen the stories about Flann's murder in the papers, or hadn't made the connection to the detective who'd phoned her three years earlier.

'Well, I'm sorry to hear that. When he called me, he was asking questions about Alice's hair. He wanted to know whether whoever killed her might have cut her hair.'

'And what did you tell him?'

'I told him, How could I know? I took one quick look to identify her, and then they had my sister on ice for days. We couldn't get the body. We couldn't have the funeral. They had to cut her open for an autopsy so they could explore every little part of her insides, and for what? No evidence. No arrests. Nothing. With all that poking and prodding, if whoever killed her cut off her hair, shouldn't you people have noticed that?'

'I know this is very upsetting for you, Mrs. Trent.'

'Damn right it's upsetting. I'm married now. I've got kids. My sons sleep in the room that was Alice's when she was here. My own children don't even know their mom used to have a sister. They think Mommy was an only child. I've moved on. And now I'm going to keep getting these phone calls when you've got nothing?'

'If I thought it was nothing, I wouldn't have called you. I assumed you would want us to do whatever we could.'

'Okay, fine. So if you have something, it's going to be news that whoever killed my sister has been out there for the last six years, breathing, eating, sleeping, and now killing other women. I've been able to get on with my life by convincing myself karma caught up to this guy. He stepped into the wrong fight, or was burned to ashes in some terrible car accident. Maybe in prison for something else. And now I have to go to sleep tonight wondering if he's still out there and what he's thinking and whether he even remembers anything special about Alice.'

Ellie noticed that Michelle had calculated the number of years since her sister died without missing a beat. She'd heard other family members of murder victims say the same thing – that the worst part of it in the long run is realizing that the killer lives in real time with the rest of us. That for every happy moment you have, he might have two. That he might be watching the same television program, or admiring the same

213

sunset, or boasting to his friends about your loved one's murder while you are putting the kids down for the night.

'If he's out there, Michelle, I'm going to do everything I can to find him. And that's the only reason I would make this phone call. The chance – however small – that I might be able to call you six months down the road with some answers is the only possible reason I would ever ask you to revisit these kinds of questions.'

The line fell silent, and Ellie wondered whether she had missed the click of a hang-up. Then she heard a quiet sniffle.

'So what do you need to know about Alice's hair?'

Ellie felt the tension leave her fingers, wrapped so tightly on the handset. 'In the file, it says you were the one to identify your sister's body.'

'That's right. Our mom died a few years before Alice, and our dad – he wasn't around.'

'When you saw her, did you notice anything unusual about her hair?'

'I wasn't paying attention to her *hair*. It's really hard to see your kid sister like that. I made myself look at her face, saw it was her, and made a point not to turn away. But, like I told the other detective, I think I would have noticed if someone had chopped off all Alice's hair. I assume you have pictures of her like that. Can't you check?'

'I'm sorry. I don't have anything to compare the medical examiner's photos against.'

'I'm sorry I sound so angry. It's just that I don't understand how this can possibly matter. Back when it all happened, I told the detectives that Alice had thought something was wrong. She told me she was being followed. Why couldn't they find the guy?'

Ellie recalled a mention in one of Eckels's reports that, according to Alice's sister, Alice had complained a week before her murder that a man was following her on the street. Eckels was never able to identify who the man might have been, or even to confirm whether he in fact existed.

'It was my understanding from the crime reports that your sister didn't give you any specific information about the person she thought may have been watching her.'

'What was she going to say? Obviously she didn't know who it was.'

'But there was no physical description, no identifying information, nothing to give us a lead on the man. You told the police that this happened somewhere near the health club where she worked?'

'Right. It must have been a couple of weeks before she was – well, you know, it was a couple of weeks before. She came home from work and told me she might be going crazy, but that she thought someone was tailing her. She said she noticed some guy behind her on the street when she was a few blocks from the gym. Whenever she'd turn around to look at him, he'd check out a store window or a newspaper or whatever. She was pretty creeped out about it.'

'But she didn't file a report at the time?'

'You know, I still blame myself. Once she said she didn't see the guy again after she got to work, I told her it didn't sound like a big deal, and she seemed to calm down. Obviously it took on more importance after what happened.'

Ellie knew from the reports that police had canvassed a five-block radius around Alice's branch of New York Sports in an attempt to find a witness who might have noticed anyone suspicious watching either Alice or the club. It had been a long shot, and, as one could have predicted, it hadn't panned out.

Something was bothering Ellie, though, about Michelle's recollection of her sister's complaint. 'You said she was on her way *to* work when she saw the man?'

'Yeah. Near Eighty-sixth and Lex.'

'The file said she usually worked days, eleven to seven, but that she spotted the guy at night. I assumed she was on her way home.'

The canvassing had focused around evening hours on the assumption that people in the neighborhood likely followed the same weekday routines. If the police had searched at the wrong time of day six years earlier, they may have blown their best chance at locating a witness who might have spotted the man who had been stalking Alice two weeks before her murder.

'No, that's right. She did work days. But she got home late that night, and told me she saw the guy on her way to the gym.'

'So it was in the morning.' Ellie was getting seriously confused.

'No, I'm sure it wasn't. I even asked her because it just didn't seem like anything creepy was going to

216

happen in the middle of the morning. She told me it was around eight o'clock. Not late, but dark. She said, "It was dark, Shell. I didn't get a good look at him, but I really think he was following me." I'm absolutely positive. For so long I blamed myself for not making her call the police. I'd replay her voice over and over in my head. But you're right. She worked days. And she was home and telling me this story by, like, ten o'clock.'

'Don't beat yourself up over it. It's natural for us to fill in memory gaps over time.'

'But here's the thing. She *was* on her way to the club. She told me the route and the various places she spotted him watching her. I remember now. She got off work at seven, ran some errands, and then went back to the club for her bag. Oh, shit. Oh, this is weird. Her errands –'

Ellie took a deep breath.

'She went to her hairdresser's. She wanted a change.'

'How much of a change?'

'About five inches worth. She got her hair cut into a bob, and the guy was following her when she left. I completely forgot about that. It's coming back to me now, though. I remember telling the detective about it.'

'You told this to Detective McIlroy?'

'No, I mean the detective at the time.'

'Detective Eckels?'

'Yeah, that was the one. I told him the guy had followed my sister on her way back to work from the hairdresser's. I'm sure of it.'

There was no mention of the hair salon in any of Eckels's reports, but that was the kind of detail that some cops might not jot down. What troubled Ellie more was the certainty that, in the nine months he had carried around these three cold case files, McIlroy would surely have approached the lieutenant who had been the lead detective on one of the cases. And if McIlroy had run his theory by Eckels, why hadn't Eckels been the one to point out the resemblance between these cases and Chelsea Hart's?

Chapter Twenty-Four

Peter was waiting for Ellie at the bar when she walked into Dos Caminos at eight o'clock. The popular restaurant was a bit of a scene, especially for the relatively sedate Gramercy neighborhood, and was much fancier than her usual take-out Mexican fare, but she supposed that had been the point when Peter had selected it.

He handed her a margarita on the rocks, with salt. 'I took the liberty.'

'You dear, wonderful man.'

They followed the hostess to a small table in the back dining room.

'So hopefully today was slightly better than the rest of your week?' Peter asked once they were alone.

Ellie used a chip to scoop up an enormous blob of green salsa, and popped it into her mouth. She nodded happily while she swallowed. 'No new bodies. No new arrests. Just tying up the loose ends against Myers.'

'Well, as much as I've appreciated your willingness to allow the late-night pop-ins –'

'I believe the young people refer to them as booty calls.'

'Yes, right. Lovely. Despite my appreciation for the time together, it's nice to see you while the hour is still in the single digits. You holding up okay? I think you've put in more time in your first week in that unit than I have all month.'

'I'm good. The truth is, I put in a ton of time off the clock even when I was working garden-variety property cases.'

Finally, for the first time in forty-eight hours, Ellie had a chance to breathe. She was in a great restaurant with a terrific guy and a tasty margarita. She could finally think and talk about something other than Chelsea Hart, Jake Myers, and the little mistakes that had turned a night of spring break into a tragedy.

She should have been appreciative. She should have been bubbling over with non-work-related chatter. But she found herself thinking about those cold case files. She finally allowed herself to raise the subject over her pork tacos.

'I was following up on some old cases Flann McIlroy had been looking at,' she said.

'You get ten minutes of downtime, and you start poking around in someone else's cold cases?'

'I know. I'm a glutton for punishment. But, you know, he meant a lot to me, and so –'

'No explanation necessary.'

'Anyway, he had these three cases he thought might be connected. I was wondering if he ever reached out to you about them. It would've been about three years ago.'

'Why would he call me?'

'That was just his way. He'd plant stories in the press as a way to stir up public attention. Maybe turn up a witness who'd never come forward.' Of course, McIlroy's critics would have said it was a way of calling attention to his own career.

'No, I never spoke to the man until I met you. But I'm still pretty new to the crime beat. If he was going to call someone at the *Daily Post*, it would've been Kittrie. You should ask him.'

'Your editor? You haven't exactly described him as the most accessible man on the planet.'

Peter shrugged. 'He's not that bad. Just a little rigid. I might be, too, if I was a boss.'

'Oh, my God. You look like you're in physical pain trying to say something nice about the man.'

'Fine, he's a fuckstick.'

'I don't think you're allowed to say that about a guy with a tumor.'

'I told you, I think Justine's just screwing with my mind, trying to force me to be nice to him.'

'I wouldn't be so sure of that,' she said. 'You know what they say: People live longer, we've got crummy lifestyles, the environment's going to hell. Cancer rates are up, my friend. We're pretty much all dying as we speak.'

'Jesus, you're depressing. I'm telling you – Kittrie's fine, in that respect, at least. Just call him, okay? He's a tool, but he definitely would've had a line in to a guy like McIlroy.' Peter pulled out his own business card and scribbled George Kittrie's name and number on it. He extended it toward Ellie, then pulled it back. 'I don't need to be jealous now, do I?'

'Oh, definitely. Because, as you know from my own history, I have such a weakness for overbearing, micromanaging bosses.'

He handed her the number. 'If McIlroy had a story to plant, it would have been with him.'

'Okay, now I have a single remaining demand of you this evening.'

'Ooh, a demand? Daddy likey.'

'Okay, two demands. One, don't ever say that again. And two, don't let me talk about work anymore.'

'But, Detective, what in the world would you talk about if not work, when that's all you ever do?'

'Fine, I can talk about normal-people work stuff – my partner, my boss, the heroin addict who left behind his prescription methadone during a burglary –'

'You're kidding.'

She shook her head. 'But I don't want to talk about my cases.'

'I think we can work around that.'

And for the rest of the evening, Ellie forced herself to be normal. No talk of killers, either past or current. She and Peter were on a date like two regular people.

And when Peter offered to walk her home, she had anything but work on her mind.

Chapter Twenty-Five

There's always an easy way and a hard way.

Ellie had spoken those words to the drug-buying law student at Pulse as a warning that there were two ways she could search her purse. Now it was Thursday morning, and she repeated the phrase to herself as an entirely different kind of warning. She had three cold case files tucked discreetly in her top drawer, and she had a decision to make.

She could return the files to Central Records and pretend she had never received a call from Bill Harrington. Or she could try to retrace Flann McIlroy's steps, a task that was probably impossible and would only complicate the case against Jake Myers.

She sat at her desk nursing a spoonful of Nutella, looking at the handwritten phone number on the back of Peter's business card. An easy way or a hard way.

The dream witness in the solid case against Jake Myers. Easy. Cherry pie. Or the cop who breaks the news to Rogan, Dan Eckels, Simon Knight, Max Donovan, the mayor's office, and – worst of all – Miriam and Paul Hart that there's a problem. Not easy.

One more phone call.

'George Kittrie.'

'This is Ellie Hatcher. We met the other night at Plug Uglies, with Peter Morse?'

'You finally dumped that kid?'

'Nope. Not yet, at least. I'm actually calling about another mutual acquaintance – Flann McIlroy?'

'I'm just giving you a hard time. Morse told me you might reach out. I think he was afraid I might tear your head off if you called without notice. Something about three girls?'

'Yes, sir. I've got a murder victim's father calling the department for an update, saying McIlroy thought his daughter's death was related to a couple of others. I figured I'd try to piece together what McIlroy was up to.'

She was walking a fine line here. She wanted to know if McIlroy had contacted Kittrie, but she didn't want to tip him off to a story in the event that he hadn't. The vaguer the information, and the more innocuous the request, the less likely Kittrie would go digging.

'Yeah, that rings a bell. He called, what, it must have been a few years ago – definitely after my book came out, so 2004? 2005?'

'That sounds about right,' Ellie said. She wondered if Kittrie had a regular habit of dropping references to his book.

'He wanted me to write a piece speculating a connection between three murders, all a few years apart. All the girls had been out on the town.'

'Do you have any notes?'

'Nah. It sounded like garbage at the time. The city's a dangerous place at night, you know? And he wasn't giving me anything to tie it all together. I realized by then that Mac wasn't above using us. I figured he had an agenda of some kind.'

'So the club angle was the only thing tying the murders together?'

'Yeah. You know, same demographics, I guess – young women. But that was it. I've always been pretty cautious about what I'll print under my byline. There was nothing to verify, so I wasn't going to run with it.'

'Well, I can see why you'd pass. Thanks a lot for your time. I'll get back to the victim's dad and let him know there's nothing new.'

'Glad to help those who protect and serve. Maybe I can hit you up for a return favor?'

Ellie had known when she called a reporter that there'd be a quid pro quo. 'Yeah, shoot.'

'In the Chelsea Hart case, can you confirm that Jake Myers shaved the victim's head?'

It felt like Kittrie had punched her in the throat. His information was not a hundred percent accurate, but it was close enough. She couldn't remember the number of times the Wichita papers had printed something about the College Hill Strangler that may have started out as truth, but had morphed into something entirely different by the time it reached the press, like a fifth-hand message in a child's game of Operator.

She couldn't find words as her mind raced through Kittrie's possible sources. She finally mustered a 'No comment.' She was surprised by the force of the handset as she returned it to the carriage.

She was still processing Kittrie's bombshell when Rogan showed up, a cup of Starbucks in one hand, his cell in the other.

'You seen the Lou yet?' He used his jaw to flip the phone shut.

'Huh-uh. You got a sec? We need to talk.'

'It's gonna have to wait. Eckels just called me, pissed off about something. He wants us in his office, like, ten minutes ago.'

Rogan led the way, waving off her attempts to slow him down. He rapped his knuckles against the glass of Eckels's closed door, then helped himself to the doorknob. Ellie caught a brief glimpse of their lieutenant speaking animatedly into his phone. He held up a hand momentarily, then gave them the all-clear.

'Ah, Rogan. I see you didn't come alone.'

'You said it was about the Myers case. I figured you wanted me and Hatcher.'

'Sure. Why not? This is, after all, something that should definitely concern her. Have a seat.'

Rogan threw her a worried look.

'So, I got a phone call from the Public Information Office this morning,' Eckels announced. 'Seems they just heard from a reporter at the *Daily Post*. You two know anything about this?'

'I just gave a no-comment to George Kittrie about five seconds ago.' Another worried look from Rogan.

'He wanted confirmation that Myers shaved the vic's head.'

'Shit.' Rogan bit his lower lip.

'Yeah, no shit, shit. So is one of you going to tell me why we're losing control of this investigation?' Although the wording of the question was aimed at both of them, Ellie felt Eckels's eyes fall directly on her. 'And, by the way, the reporter who called the PIO wasn't Kittrie, it was one Peter Morse. I want to know who let this leak.'

The insinuation was obvious. Ellie's case. Ellie's boyfriend. Ellie's leak.

Before she could defend herself, Rogan was doing it for her. 'Hatcher wouldn't do that.'

One simple sentence. No hesitation in his voice. No question mark. Rogan wasn't simply backing her up out of mandatory partner loyalty. He had no doubt at all about her innocence.

'I wouldn't,' she confirmed. 'And I didn't.'

'Who the hell was it, then?' Eckels demanded. 'Even inside the house, we kept a lid on that. It was our ace in the hole: the killer took the hair and the earrings, and that was how we'd head off a bunch of whackadoos trying to give us fake confessions.'

'With all respect, Lou,' Rogan said, 'now that we've got Myers dead to rights, what does it really matter? The press was going to get hold of it eventually.'

'It matters because I expect my detectives to show a little discretion.'

'Maybe it was the girl's family,' Rogan said. 'They've been talking to the media.'

'They were using the media to put pressure on us.

Telling the world that their daughter was mutilated, after we've already caught the guy, wouldn't appear to fall into that game plan. Only a handful of us knew the condition of that girl's body when she was found. And it just so happens that one of them's boinking the very same reporter who seems to be a leg ahead of every other reporter in the city.'

Ellie wanted to tell Eckels he was out of line. That she didn't have to sit here and take his abuse. That he wouldn't make the same assumption if one of his male detectives was dating a female reporter.

But she knew she couldn't do any of it. He was drawing the same inferences she would in his position. Her case. Her boyfriend. Her leak.

Once again, it was Rogan who spoke up. 'Hatcher and I – we've kept it in the vault. But other people saw the girl. The joggers. The medical examiner. The EMTs. Could be anyone.'

Ellie's memory flashed to Officer Capra, the first uniform on the scene, holding court the night of Jake Myers's arrest at Plug Uglies. Peter and his boss, George Kittrie, had gone to the bar that night for the express purpose of finding loose-lipped cops. She would've cold-cocked Capra on the spot if he were in the room, but she still wasn't going to dime him out to Eckels.

'I knew Peter Morse when everything went down with Flann McIlroy, and you know I didn't give him any tip-offs on that. It's your choice whether to believe me, Lou, but I would hope you'd give me the benefit of the doubt.'

Rogan leaned back in his chair. 'You said the reporter

asked if Chelsea Hart's head was *shaved*? See, now that shit's not even right. No one who saw that girl would've said that. Myers hacked that shit up. Sounds like the paper's heard something third- or fourth-hand.'

Ellie had been wondering whether to point out the discrepancy to Eckels herself, but it sounded more persuasive coming from Rogan. She was finding it hard to focus on anything beyond the question that kept echoing in her mind: Why hadn't Peter mentioned any of this last night?

Whether Eckels was persuaded or simply acquiescing to the fact that he couldn't prove his suspicions, he moved on. 'For what it's worth, I told the Public Information Officer to shell out a no-comment to Morse. I expect you – *both* of you – to do the same. I just got off the phone with Simon Knight to give him a heads-up on the story, and I assured him that we will keep control over this case. The last thing we need is a media circus around Myers's trial.'

Eckels picked up a newspaper that was open on the corner of his desk and dropped it in front of the detectives. 'This, of course, didn't help.'

It was a copy of the morning's *New York Sun*. Most of the page was occupied by a photograph of Jake Myers's perp walk, snapped while Rogan and Ellie escorted him from the back of a squad car to be arraigned after his lineup at 100 Centre Street.

But it was a smaller headline on the sidebar that Eckels was tapping with a meaty index finger: 'For Victim's Friends, Another Encounter with NYC Crime.' Ellie skimmed the first paragraph. As Jordan

McLaughlin and Stefanie Hart had sat on the front steps of the Metropolitan Museum of Art the previous afternoon, an armed assailant had snatched their purses from the sidewalk and escaped through Central Park.

'Oh, Jesus,' Ellie said. Those girls had been put through enough.

'You mean to tell me you haven't seen this?' Eckels asked.

'I've been catching up on other work,' Ellie said. She'd scanned the coverage of the Hart case this morning, but hadn't noticed the ancillary sidebar.

Eckels looked at Rogan for his explanation.

'I just walked in,' Rogan said. 'I had some personal stuff I'd pushed off during the heat of the case.'

'Why didn't we hear about this yesterday?' Ellie asked. 'We spent a lot of time with those girls.'

'They reported it to museum security,' Eckels said. 'The museum turned it over to Central Park precinct, where some uniform took a complaint without thinking to reach out to us.'

She shook her head. 'I'll call the girls right away.'

Eckels held up his hand. 'Already done. Public Information's getting a victim's advocate in touch with them for damage control. Make sure they've got all their credit cards canceled, that kind of thing. We'll get them to the airport for their flight later this morning. They're more than ready to go home. Just promise me you'll do everything you can to make sure no more shit sandwiches.'

She and Rogan both nodded. Ellie was beginning to detect a pattern: Eckels liked to blow off steam but generally calmed down before breaking the huddle.

Unfortunately, she wasn't quite ready to break. Easy way and a hard way. All things being equal, she was one to opt for ease. But she saw no detour around this one. She didn't want to be that cop who twenty years down the road – after an innocent man had been exonerated – had lacked the courage to challenge the conventional wisdom.

'Sorry, sir. One more thing, while we're here. We got a phone call off the tip line from a victim's father on a cold case. His daughter was also killed after getting a little wild, on the Lower East Side in 2000.'

'So call him back and make nice.'

'I did, sir. But here's the thing. His daughter also had her hair chopped off. And if the news is going to come out about Chelsea, then he's going to see the resemblance between the two cases.'

'He's going to see the resemblance, or you are?' Eckels shot her an annoyed look, but then a glimmer of recognition crossed his face. 'Please tell me this isn't that same case McIlroy bothered me about a few years ago.'

'Probably,' she said. 'He apparently was looking into three different cases – all young blondes, all killed late at night, all possibly having to do with their hair.'

'Emphasis on *possibly*. As in *im*possibly. You really are McIlroy's long-lost love child. The case I had didn't fit the pattern at all, as I recall.'

'It depends what you mean by the pattern. The victim thought someone was stalking her when she left Artistik, a salon on the Upper East Side. Her hairdresser took off five inches. We could be talking about one killer –

someone with a hair fetish. He cuts his victims' hair. In your case – Alice Butler – he could have been set off by the haircut. Or he could have taken more of it when he killed her, and no one noticed because she'd just had the big change.'

Eckels shook his head in frustration. 'Our job, despite what you may have learned from McIlroy, is not to work cold cases. If you think you've got something, send it to the Cold Case Squad and listen to them laugh at you. Until then, Rogan, please get your partner out of my office. I believe you have grand jury today on Jake Myers?'

Rogan looked at his Cartier watch. 'In an hour.'

'Fingers crossed, guys. And, Hatcher, no surprises.'

Chapter Twenty-Six

Rachel Peck had been forced to alter her usual writing routine. Today was the second of two days this week she'd agreed to switch shifts with Dan Field, the afternoon bartender. Dan's request had been accompanied by an explanation that his agent had lined up afternoon auditions for him, but Rachel suspected it was just another ploy to get access to her more lucrative peak-hour tips and to stick her with the lunch crowd. Still, Dan was generally a nice guy, and she didn't want to be seen as an inflexible bitch, so she'd made the swap.

Her usual routine was to sleep late, do some yoga, and then write until it was time to show up to the proverbial day job, which, in her case, was a night job. Her goal each day was eight hundred words, even if it sometimes meant gluing herself to her keyboard at 2:00 a.m. when she returned from the restaurant.

This morning, however, she'd set her alarm for eight and had skipped the morning yoga so she could work in a couple of hours of writing before covering Dan's lunch shift.

Rachel was twenty-six years old and had already

thought of herself as a writer for a decade. Her literary dabblings began even earlier, when, as a kid in Lewiston, Idaho, her only escape from a household dominated by her angry and possessive father was a spiral-bound journal.

The Reverend Elijah Peck had found himself a single father one night when Rachel was only seven years old. Rachel's mother had run to the corner market for a quart of milk and never returned. Her one-way Greyhound ticket to Las Vegas turned up on the family MasterCard, but the Reverend didn't bother trying to chase her down.

Her father's willingness to let go of the wife who had abandoned him did not, however, extend to the daughter. Rachel had begun running away when she was only thirteen. She hitched rides to Spokane, Missoula, Kennewick, Twin Falls, Seattle.

Elijah would track her down every time. The last time she'd been brought home by her father, he'd found her working at the door of a Portland strip joint, scantily clad and impersonating a hostess of legal age. He hauled her back to Lewiston and told her that if she didn't stay put and complete her senior year, she'd be dead to him.

When she asked her father what he meant, he looked her straight in the eye and said, 'I'll deliver you home to the Lord myself before you set another harlot's foot in a sinner shack like that.'

Rachel had never understood her father, but she knew him well enough to believe he just might follow through on his promise. For a full year, she stuck to his drill. No more missed classes, no hitchhiking. She even kept curfew. Then the Saturday before her high school graduation ceremony, she packed a bag, found the principal, and did what she needed to do to convince him to let her take her diploma away with her. She hadn't heard from her father or Lewiston since.

For the first time in years, Rachel was thinking about the Reverend Elijah Peck. The yellowed pages of her old journals lay before her on the dining table she used for a desk. Her eyes were still wet from the intermittent tears that had formed as she'd read her own teenage words and relived all those same emotions.

She was always surprised at how the quotidian details of everyday life crept into her writing. The way a woman at the next table checked the coverage of her lipstick in the reflection of a coffee cup. The pug in her building who wore an argyle turtleneck. The taste of cigarettes and dark chocolate.

But this was the first time she had made a conscious decision to draw on her own biography. The characters were fictionalized, of course. The defiant teenager would be a boy who developed into a killer. The oppressive parent would be a mother whose law enforcement career – always so resented by her always-resentful son – would now become the one means of helping her child, if she chose to do so.

Rachel was in the middle of a pivotal scene between mother and son – the one where the detective finds critical evidence beneath her own roof, implicating her own son – when she caught a glimpse of the time on the lower right hand of her computer screen.

Ten-fifteen. Time to earn a paycheck.

Her fingers tapped away at the keyboard as quickly as she could force them, pulling all of the thoughts stacked in her short-term memory and throwing them onto the screen. Spelling and syntax be damned. As long as she could piece it all together when she returned tonight, she'd be fine.

Chapter Twenty-Seven

Rogan had driven past Cooper Square and was on the Bowery by the time he permitted Ellie to speak.

'What I've been trying to say is that I'm sorry I didn't give you advance warning. I tried, but you were in such a hurry –'

'So this shit is my fault?'

'No, of course not.'

Rogan shook his head and kept his eyes on the road as he changed lanes to pass a minivan with Virginia plates. 'What are the chances you're actually going to listen to Eckels and leave this shit alone?'

'Mmmm, thirty-five, forty percent?'

'Higher than I would've thought. All right. Lay it on me.'

Ellie mapped out all three cases for him. Robbie Harrington and her unlikely bangs. Alice Butler and her new haircut. And Lucy Feeney, whose hair had been hacked off just like Chelsea Hart's. She pulled Feeney's autopsy photograph from her bag, but Rogan didn't bother to look at it.

'Like the Lou said, it's all for the Cold Case Squad.'

This time, she held the ME's photograph above the dash, forcing Rogan to see the resemblance. 'J. J., it could be the same guy.'

'And what year did all this go down?' he asked, eyes back on the road.

'Three women, all killed between '98 and '02.'

'And how old was Jake Myers at the time?'

Myers was currently only twenty-five years old. 'I know. I've done the math.'

'So then you know those cases can't be connected to ours.'

'The problem is, I don't know that. What I know is that if there *is* a connection, we might have jumped too soon with Jake Myers.'

'When a pretty white girl from Indiana gets sliced up like a roast beef, there's no such thing as jumping too soon. We've got a good case, a thousand sets of eyes on us, and once that DNA match comes in, we'll have it locked and loaded.'

'Unless we missed something, in which case it's a hell of a lot better to figure that out now instead of in the middle of a trial. It really disturbs me that Eckels didn't say anything earlier. He told us himself that McIlroy went to him about these cases three years ago, so he knew the theory was out there. Then we catch the Chelsea Hart case, and he doesn't bother mentioning any of this?'

'Because Jake Myers is our guy, and he couldn't have done any of those other girls.'

'But what about when we first caught the case? When we didn't have a suspect yet? You'd think Eckels would have taken the time to say, Oh, yeah, by the way, there's some old cases you might want to look at.'

'Except the cases don't make a pattern, Hatcher. Killers don't murder three girls within four years, then lay low for the next six.'

She gave him a you've-got-to-be-kidding-me look.

'Fine, with the exception of William Summer, killers don't stay dormant for years on end. And you're blowing this whole thing with the hair out of proportion. Cutting bangs on a victim, or snipping off a few pieces from a new hairdo? That sounds like a serious fetish. Hacking it all off with a knife is anger, or maybe destruction of physical evidence. It's not the same. And Chelsea's not like your victims. They were all pretty rough city chicks. Hard-knock-life, round-the-way girls, not wide-eyed college students from Indiana.'

Ellie wasn't persuaded, however, and Rogan knew it. They were nearing their turn onto Worth Street, but he had slowed the car in the right lane. 'You never heard the term "exculpatory evidence" on patrol, Hatcher?'

'Of course I did. It's evidence suggesting that we may have gotten the wrong guy.'

'Nope. All exculpatory evidence means is some bullshit that a defense attorney could use to confuse a jury into thinking we got the wrong guy. And if the prosecutor finds out about so-called exculpatory evidence, they've got a duty to turn it over to said defense attorney. But we don't. And that's why we don't give so-called exculpatory evidence to prosecutors.'

She returned the photograph of Lucy Feeney to her bag and zipped it shut.

'So we're keeping that to ourselves?' he asked.

'Was that a question or a conclusion?'

Rogan pulled the car into a spot across the street from the courthouse. 'Let's get something straight here. I'm not your boss, Hatcher. I'm your partner, so I'll back you, even when you do something stupid.'

'Don't you mean *if* I do something stupid?'

'No. I mean when, whether it's this or some other thing a year from now.'

'Well, I appreciate that.'

'Wait, I'm not done. I'm saying this because that's the kind of partner I am, no matter who I'm paired up with. And, I'll be honest with you, before Casey, I had some problems in the partnership department.'

Ellie waited for an explanation.

'My extra pocket change was an issue for some people.'

'Jealousy?' Then another possibility dawned on her. 'You didn't have another cop go to IA on you? Talk about assuming the worst.'

Rogan shook his head. 'I guess you could say they assumed the worst, but they didn't go to the rat squad. They wanted a piece of the action. And it happened more than once. I became a magnet for trouble. Then, two partners ago, I wound up on IA's radar for something I had nothing to do with.'

'What happened?'

'I showed them bank records, my grandmother's will, everything I had to prove I was clean. But it wasn't enough. It didn't explain why my partner was living just as well as I was, and they knew I had to have suspected what was going down.'

'So you cooperated.'

'The man deserved it.'

To a lot of cops, that wouldn't matter: anyone on the job who went along with Internal Affairs was a turncoat.

'Then I got paired up with Casey, and it was all good. And now I've got my whole you-think-a-brother-can't-have-money riff, and that puts the issue to rest.'

'I'm sorry, J. J.' She had a better idea now why Rogan might have been willing to roll the dice as her partner.

He waved off her apology. 'All I'm saying is that I want things to work out with you, Hatcher. But, that said, it's a hell of a lot easier to be a good partner when it's a two-way street. Just know that any decision you make, it's for both of us. And I'm telling you, Myers is our guy.'

He stood on the corner of Grand and Ludlow on the Lower East Side, watching Rachel Peck emerge from a four-story brick walk-up. Based on the blankets and stained sheets that served as makeshift curtains for most of the building's windows, he gathered that it wasn't the homiest place to live. A bartender probably couldn't afford much better in Manhattan these days, however.

He had followed Rachel home last night and had come back this morning to check on her. Ten thirty-five. It would take her twenty minutes, max, to get to Mesa Grill on the F train.

She kept her word about covering her coworker's shift. He liked loyalty. And she was prompt. He liked that, too. Good old reliable Rachel. He was beginning to feel like he knew her. He was looking forward to her night off.

In the meantime, he had places to go. In ten minutes, he would meet a man called Darrell Washington in Tompkins Square Park. It was an important meeting. It would determine whether Darrell lived or died.

Chapter Twenty-Eight

Simon Knight had wanted to meet the two cops he was calling his 'dream team' on the Jake Myers case before presenting their testimony to the grand jury. Just as Knight had already apparently decided that he loved his investigative team, Rogan had already decided that he hated the team leader.

He made his feelings known in the elevator ride to the seventh floor. 'Are you kidding me? The dream team? He sees a black detective, and so his mind jumps to O. J. Simpson?'

'Oy. I wish I'd never mentioned it to you. I think it evolved because Max Donovan was calling us dream witnesses.'

'Correction. I believe your new boyfriend called *you* his dream witness. And if his boss is now calling us the dream team before he's even talked to us? It's because he's having a wet dream over the idea of a pretty blond girl detective and what I'm sure he'll deem to be a – quote – *articulate* black man to testify against a rich, preppy white boy in front of a New York City jury. It's got nothing to do with who we actually are.'

243

'J. J. Rogan, I had no idea you were so profound.'

'No, just a pissed-off token,' he said with a smile that indicated he wasn't really so angry after all.

Simon Knight's office reflected his seniority over Max Donovan. Not only was it twice the size, it was furnished with leather chairs, a Persian rug, and what at least appeared to be an antique mahogany desk.

The man came across as equally dignified. Ellie took in the dark, graying hair, the fine lines etched into his thin patrician face, and the conservative navy blue suit. If someone had told her he was a four-star army general, she would have believed it, but chief prosecutor of the trial unit of the New York District Attorney's Office suited him just as well.

Max Donovan handled the introductions, and Ellie and Rogan took a seat across from the two lawyers, who settled into a brown leather sofa. She and Donovan exchanged a glance, and she found herself wondering who had looked first at whom.

'Well, detectives' – Knight clasped his hands together in front of his chest – 'there's nothing better than being able to introduce myself to the both of you with a piece of excellent news. I told the crime lab I wanted preliminary DNA results before grand jury. They said it was impossible, but I got the call half an hour ago – the semen on the victim's blouse and in the oral swab is a match to Jake Myers's. One in 300 billion.'

'I guess you'll have to add the criminologist to the dream team.'

Ellie shot a disapproving look at her partner, but

somehow Rogan was actually pulling it off with a broad smile and seemingly earnest enthusiasm. Had it not been for their conversation in the elevator, she would have thought that he was proudly owning his spot on the team.

Knight was eating it up. 'Yes, I will, Detective,' he said, with an extended index finger. 'Yes, I will.'

She could already picture Rogan impersonating Knight to the rest of the house over drinks at Plug Uglies.

'So,' Knight said, continuing his rundown of the case, 'we can place the defendant with the victim shortly before her death. We have ironclad proof of sexual contact, also shortly before time of death. We have the defendant's attempt to create a phony alibi, now contradicted by his friend Nick Warden. We have the photograph of the defendant leaving the club alone with the victim. We've locked down all the other folks who were with him that night, and no one saw him again after three – oh – three a.m., the time stamp on the photograph. And of course now we have the other girl.'

'What other girl?' Ellie asked.

'They haven't heard?' Knight asked.

Donovan shook his head. 'I knew we were meeting this morning.'

'Donovan here worked his ass off yesterday making some calls to Cornell.'

'Myers's alma mater,' Max explained. Ellie didn't need the reminder. Even seemingly irrelevant details about suspects were cataloged in her memory. She still remembered the date of birth of the first person she ever arrested.

'Five years ago, when Myers was a junior in college, it seems he had a little too much to drink at a party and tried to rape a girl after offering to walk her home,' Knight said. 'The girl didn't file a complaint, but we've got two of her friends who say she reported it to them the next morning.'

'You can use that at trial?' Ellie asked. A decade had passed since her on-and-off pre-law classes at Wichita State University, but she recalled serious evidentiary restrictions on using a defendant's prior acts against him.

Knight nodded. 'We'll argue it forms a pattern. Alcohol. A little flirting. It helps that the previous girl was the same age, also a blonde. She says he was very rough with her and grabbed her neck. He ran out of her dorm room when she grabbed a bottle of hair spray and shot him in the eye with it. We'll argue that this time he didn't give up so easily.'

Knight's argument sounded like a stretch to Ellie, but she kept her thoughts to herself.

'As the two of you know, grand jury will be a breeze. Just us and twenty-three regular New Yorkers. And, no, that's not an oxymoron.' The joke was obviously one of Knight's old chestnuts, but Ellie smiled politely anyway. 'Any questions?'

Ellie and Rogan shook their heads.

'Very well, then. It's time for the dream team to show 'em what we've got. No surprises, right?'

That was twice this morning that Ellie had heard the

phrase. Both times, she had felt a sinking in the pit of her stomach as she thought about Lucy Feeney, Robbie Harrington, and Alice Butler. Even as Ellie took her seat in the front of the twenty-three sets of watchful eyes in the grand jury room, she had not yet decided for herself what to do about the doubts she was carrying about Jake Myers's guilt.

The grand jury room, as Simon Knight had pointed out, contained only the prosecutors, their witnesses, and twenty-three regular New Yorkers. The grand jury foreman, a barrel-chested man in a plaid shirt and glasses with thick lenses, asked Ellie if she swore to tell the truth, the whole truth, and nothing but the truth.

No defendant. No judge. No defense attorney. No cross-examination. No difficult questions. *There's always an easy way and a hard way.* What in fact was the whole truth?

Ellie took her oath and, like a dream witness, spelled out the state's case against Jake Myers – every bit of it truthful. As it turned out, the surprises that day would not be of her making.

The first curveball was the attractive redhead waiting outside the grand jury room when Ellie had finished with her testimony. She wore a fitted black suit with patent leather high heels and carried an alligator attaché that must have cost more than Ellie took home in a month. She couldn't have been any older than Ellie, but, from all appearances, carried no insecurities about either her age or her corresponding lack of experience.

'Hey, Max. I was starting to wonder whether you were leaving us out of the party.' She gave Donovan the kind of smile women tend to give men who looked like Donovan.

Donovan cleared his throat. 'Everyone, this is Susan Parker. She's Nick Warden's lawyer.'

Simon Knight popped his head out of the grand jury room. 'What's going on? They're ready to hear from Warden.'

'Mr. Knight, you obviously need no introduction,' Parker said, extending her hand for a shake before introducing herself to Rogan and Ellie.

Ellie recalled Donovan mentioning that Warden's lawyer was a young attorney at an aggressive securities firm. The fact that criminal courts weren't her usual gig no doubt explained why she was considerably better dressed than the defense lawyers Ellie was used to.

'Where's your client?' Knight asked.

'He went to find the little boy's room. The problem is, he brought a friend with him.'

'The only friend of his we care about is at Rikers Island on a no-bail hold,' Knight said.

Then Parker dropped the second surprise. 'I'm talking about Jaime Rodriguez.'

'That's the bouncer?' Knight asked, looking to Donovan for clarification. Donovan nodded. 'I would have thought your client would be scared enough to just say no these days. I don't need him taking another pop before Myers's trial.'

'We have a problem,' Parker said, any playfulness in her tone gone now. 'Much to my considerable consternation, there is apparently still contact between Rodriguez and my client. And that's how I've come to learn that Rodriguez has a story to tell that you might find interesting.'

'Enough with the teasing,' Knight said. 'Get to the part where we have a problem.'

'According to Rodriguez, another employee at Pulse knows a little too much about the murder of Chelsea Hart.'

'What's there not to know?' Knight asked. 'The press has been all over this from the second that girl's body was found.'

'So you're saying everything's out there? There's nothing left that only the real killer would know?'

'Jake Myers is the real killer,' Donovan said.

Parker held up her hands. 'Not my job to figure this out. Apparently someone at Pulse says the killer took something that belonged to the victim. I for one had not read that in the paper, so I thought I was doing a good deed by persuading Rodriguez to come here and talk to you. If you don't care about that, send the guy home.'

'Rodriguez doesn't even work at Pulse anymore,' Rogan said.

'No, but he still has friends who do. And one of those friends talked to this janitor who seems to think he knows something.'

'It's a janitor who said this?' Ellie asked. Besides Rodriguez, the only other employee at Pulse who had a conviction was the janitor, Leon Symanski.

'That's right. Why? That means something to you?'

Ellie didn't have a chance to respond, because apparently Simon Knight had heard enough. 'I think we need to have a little chat with Mr. Rodriguez before we ask for our indictment.'

Chapter Twenty-Nine

An hour later, without a word to the other three people in the room, Simon Knight picked up the telephone in a conference room in the District Attorney's Office and dialed an extension.

'Call the clerk to give the grand jurors their lunch break. We won't be presenting any further evidence this afternoon in the Myers case.'

Knight had just closed the door behind Jaime Rodriguez, Nick Warden, and Susan Parker, and apparently had heard enough.

Rogan was the first to speak up. 'We came down here because the case was ready for grand jury.'

'And that was before Rodriguez told us that a janitor with a past sex offense somehow knows more about Chelsea Hart than what's been reported by the media. So far, of course. I'm told the *Daily Post* is onto the fact that the victim's hair was cut. And that's why the two of you need to go see this Symanski while we still have some control over that information.'

'As far as the NYPD is concerned, the case has been cleared.'

'You're telling me you want me to call your lieutenant and notify him that you're refusing to investigate your own case?' Knight asked.

'I was giving you my opinion that the case has been fully investigated. We're a team, right?'

Ellie could see where Rogan was going. There had been cases in which the department had pressured the DA's office to pursue charges by threatening – implicitly or explicitly – to portray prosecutors as obstructionist if they delayed. But Rogan wasn't necessarily packing the heat he'd need to win this fight.

Knight turned to Ellie. 'What do you think, Detective Hatcher?'

Ellie looked at Rogan. Rogan looked at Ellie. Ellie looked at her bag, still holding three files about murders that had occurred when the janitor named Leon Symanski was in his thirties – still well within the window for serial violence.

'The man asked for your opinion,' Rogan said.

'I think we should check out Symanski, but only so Myers's lawyer can't spring anything during trial. We've got the right guy,' she said, doing her best to sound convinced.

Donovan backed her up. 'The whole thing's going to turn out to be bullshit. Rodriguez probably heard about this guy's prior and is making all this up to help out Myers. It's payback, since Myers's pal got him his deal on the drug case. "The killer took something from the victim?" What does that mean? It could be a robbery, a souvenir, her virginity. Say it in any case, and it's bound to be true. It's like those so-called psychics who say, "I'm getting a message from someone, and I see the letter B." It's vague, meaningless P. T. Barnum stuff. It lets us see whatever we want.'

'So we'll have a chat with Symanski,' Ellie said. 'We'll find a way to prove Rodriguez is lying.' Or they could find something to tie Symanski not only to Chelsea Hart's murders, but to the other cases as well.

'Very well, then. Are you all right with that, Detective Rogan?'

'Right as rain.'

'Call me when you've got something. And by the way, Hatcher, I saw you last month on *Dateline*. You were terrific.'

As they left the district attorney's office, her cell phone rang. She flipped it open. It was Peter.

'I need to take this,' she said, holding her palm across the mouthpiece. 'I'll meet you outside?'

This was a conversation that would require some privacy.

She found relative solitude and decent cell phone reception next to a window in the courthouse hallway.

'Hello?'

'Hey, it's Peter. I need to talk to you –'

'Too late,' she said. 'You might've given me a heads-up before you called the Public Information Office three hours ago. Or how about last night over dinner, or on the way home? Or, oh yeah, while you were reenacting the *Kama Sutra* in my bedroom?'

'That's not fair, Ellie. I didn't even know about it until this morning. And I couldn't call you.'

'Your phone suddenly stopped working?'

'Did you call me when you found a body by the East River? Did you bother mentioning that you'd made an arrest when I saw you Tuesday night?'

'That's not the same.'

'It's *exactly* the same. And don't think I didn't start to call you. I did. But even if I had, it would have been like I was feeling you out for information. And the last thing I've ever wanted to do since we met is to take advantage of you as a source. But you can't expect me to notify you any time we unearth something the department wants to remain secret.'

'Well, as it stands, my lieutenant assumes I *was* your source. He knows about us, and now you know something you're not supposed to know.'

'But that's ridiculous. I'm on the crime beat. Is he going to think you're helping me on every case I cover?'

'Yeah, probably. If it's a case of mine.'

'So I'll talk to him. I'll tell him –'

'You'll tell him what, Peter? The only thing that's going to convince him I'm not the leak is if you give him another name.'

'You know I can't do that.'

'You don't need to. I already figured it out. It's that kid Jeff Capra. I checked him out. He's not even in the Thirteenth, but he shows up at Plug Uglies to tell everyone he was first uniform on the scene. He's one of about ten people who knows what was done to Chelsea.'

'So it *is* true. Her head was shaved.'

She resisted the temptation to tell him that he wasn't quite accurate. 'I can't believe you. You just did exactly what you said you didn't want to do, your supposed reason for not calling me this morning before I got bombarded by Eckels.'

'I'm sorry. That's not what I meant. Can you please just stop and look at this from my perspective? I'm a reporter. Just like you can't tell me inside information about your case, I can't tell you a source, or even whether I know the source.'

'Oh, so now you don't even know your own source.'

'Look, this one wasn't even my call. Kittrie's been all over it. He's got a really quick trigger finger. He'll go to press with anything to get a head start on the other papers.'

Ellie felt like screaming into the telephone. She had spoken to Kittrie herself that morning. She had listened while he'd explained how cautious he was in his reporting. It was the reason why he hadn't run with McIlroy's story about the three cold cases.

'Don't try to blame this on your boss, Peter.'

'Look, I've already said more than I should. Please don't jump to conclusions. And stop treating me like a suspect. Haven't I earned even a little bit of your trust by now?'

She remembered her own anger that morning in Eckels's office, her outrage that her lieutenant had not given her the benefit of the doubt. She and Peter had a lot more between them than she and Eckels did.

'So when are you going to print?' Ellie asked, her voice calmer now.

'Afternoon edition. It'll be on newsstands in a couple of hours.'

'Okay, thanks for the heads – up.'

'We can talk about this more later?'

'Yeah, okay. I'll call you when I free up. It might be late.'

'You know me. I like late. Need a guy on the porch at three a.m.? I'm your man.'

Rogan began deconstructing the morning's developments the second Ellie hit the passenger seat. His assessment was blunt: 'Simon Knight's a fucking prick.'

'He wasn't *that* bad.'

'Are you kidding me? I hate guys like that. Pretend they're down with the cops. Equals. Part of the *team*. The minute there's a disagreement, he threatens to pull rank.'

'But, J. J., I thought you were "right as rain" with all of this.'

'You don't think sarcasm suits me, huh? And what was that shit when we left about *Dateline*? Like you're some monkey performing a trick. You're Heather Fucking Mills crying on the *Today Show*. Does he think that's easy, for you to go on national television and talk about that shit with your father, and then all he can say is you were great, like it's appropriate for some passing conversation?'

Ellie had never heard anyone but Jess acknowledge that her occasional forays into the media had not been for her own enjoyment. Rogan, however, apparently got it.

'So, at the risk of getting all relationship-y on you again, are we okay?'

'Yeah, we're cool. Honestly, you saved my ass back there. I almost stepped in it, huh?'

She laughed. 'What? You don't think Eckels would've backed us up if we'd gone on strike from the investigation?'

'Right, because whenever I think of Eckels, that's what I picture – backup. There was a minute there, though, when I thought you were going somewhere else. I'm starting to get a read on you. You had to be doing the math. Jake Myers is too young to have killed those other women, but Symanski's not. He's in his forties now, right?'

'Forty-six.'

'But you didn't say anything.'

'Better for us to take a look at it first, right? Just the two of us.'

'You're actually having doubts about Jake Myers?'

More than doubts. 'I don't want to, but, yeah, honestly, I am. I'll feel a whole lot less guilty about it if it turns out Symanski's good for all four of the murders.'

Ellie used her cell to call the records department for Leon Symanski's contact information, then dialed the phone number. A man who sounded of the right age picked up.

'Is this the pharmacy?' she asked.

'You've got the wrong number,' the man replied.

She apologized and flipped her phone shut. 'He's home,' she said. 'You ready to roll?'

'Twenty bucks says this is nothing. Symanski's either some loudmouth talking out of school, or Rodriguez made the whole thing up. You want a piece of that action?'

She took the bet, unsure whether it was one she wanted to win.

Chapter Thirty

Darrell Washington flicked his favorite lighter, the one shaped like a bullet. He ran the flame up and down the length of the Optimo, spinning the blunt slowly to give it a good bake. They cost a little more than Swisher Sweets, but Optimos burned forever and were so mild that, with strong weed, you could barely taste the cigar.

Darrell lay back on a bare mattress on the floor of his mother's living room on the eleventh floor of LaGuardia House 6 and gave his lighter another flick. He took a long toke off the fat blunt and held his breath, deep inside his lungs, before letting it go.

His mom would go ape-shit if she caught him smoking inside again. Some noise about how she could lose her public housing, all because of his weed. That didn't sound right to him.

Besides, even if she smelled it when she got home, he'd deny it. Darrell wasn't good at much, but he was good at lying. His whole life, no one had ever been able to get a read on him.

It wasn't likely to come up anyways. His mom was working uptown today, taking care of some rich old white lady in a wheelchair. Then she usually walked his nieces home from P.S. 2 at the end of the day, even though it was only three blocks away. As far as Darrell could tell, there wasn't nothing his mom wouldn't do to make sure those two little girls didn't wind up like his sister.

Compared to Sharnell, Darrell was the one who'd turned out right. He was twenty years old. No prison. No guns. No gangs. Compared to everyone else he knew, he was doing all right.

He just didn't have the dollar bills they had. Coming up, his friends would all say to forget those by-the-hour jobs he was always working and losing. They'd make more slangin' in a day than he'd bring home in an entire two-week paycheck. But Darrell still lived a life that made him a chump as far as most of the people around LaGuardia saw it. His most recent job was at the new Home Depot on Twenty-third Street, but he lost that when he spilled a can of paint on aisle 8 and forgot to clean it up before his break. He stayed with his mom. He helped out with his nieces. He did day work here and there as a mover for a couple of companies who took work off of Craigslist.

Today's Optimo and its skunky contents came out of cash he got for doing a job for this guy he knew. He called the guy Jack but had no idea if that was the dude's real name.

About a year ago, Jack had shown up with a tape recorder, asking questions about gangs in the projects. Most folks either laughed at him or gave him the stink eye, but Darrell saw an opportunity. He told Jack he'd talk to him as long as no one knew about it. They'd meet every once in a while at Tompkins Square. Darrell would talk and leave with some easy cash in his pocket.

Darrell figured the dude for a cop, but Jack never pressured him to name any names. Instead he'd just sit and listen while Darrell explained the difference between the genuine article, hard-core gang members, and poo-butt juvenile wannabes. And the various factions – Bloods, Crips, MS-13, Saint James Boys – weren't about turf, like something out of *West Side Story*. With new condos and clubs popping up every week, there wasn't no turf left to fight over. Instead, it was all about the rock. The chronic. The X. The horse. You name the drug, you could find it in the projects. And with each new condo or club, the market expanded, and there was more to fight over.

Sometimes Darrell would talk about stuff that had nothing to do with gangs or drugs. Life in the projects. Life on the streets. Just life. Jack would still pay him, and for a while Darrell wondered if maybe Jack was a faggot.

About eight months back, Jack stopped coming around. Then he showed up again yesterday morning with another job. This time Darrell had to do more than talk, but he also got paid a lot more.

The job wasn't exactly legal, but Jack had learned enough about Darrell in their earlier talks to know he wasn't squeaky clean. He just didn't do any major thugging. As far as Darrell could tell, the police had their hands full. As long as he stayed away from drugs, gangs, and guns, he'd stay alive and out of prison.

261

After frisking Jack for a wire, Darrell did the job for the man, just like he asked, and gave him what he was wanting today in Tompkins Square. But something was off. It was like he didn't believe Darrell the ten times he'd told the man he'd turned over all of it. Even after he gave him the gun he had bought for the job, just like the man asked. It was like Jack knew more than he could, like he knew Darrell had skimmed a little something for himself.

Fuck it, he thought, drawing another toke. It was only one little credit card. Dude's probably some chicken hawk anyway. No way he could get a read on Darrell. No one ever could.

Chapter Thirty-One

Leon Symanski lived on the first floor of a split-level duplex in Queens. Ellie and Rogan had been watching the house for twenty minutes.

'I swear,' Ellie said, 'every time I'm in Astoria, I think of Archie Bunker. My father freaking *loved* that show. He'd watch the repeats at night, even though he'd seen them all five times. I'm sure it never dawned on him his daughter would be pulling a stakeout in the neighborhood where it was shot.'

'See, in our house, we loved the Jeffersons. That's what I think about when you say Archie Bunker – that Mr. Jefferson had to be damn happy to get the hell out of Archie Bunker cracker town and be moving on up to the East Side.'

'I never knew the words to either of those songs. I thought the first line of that song Archie and Edith sang was, *"Boil the weakling millipede"*.' Ellie wouldn't normally burden another human being with her horrible singing voice, but she figured there had to be an exception for botched television theme song lyrics. 'And I thought the Jeffersons went *"to a beat up apartment in the sky-y-y"*.'

'Now that's just racist.'

'Oh, and in the bridge –'

'The *Jeffersons* theme song had a bridge?'

'My brother's a musician. I thought it was, *"Key lime pie in the kitchen, Bees don't buzz on the grill"*.'

'That is so damn sad.'

'What do you want? I was five years old. Oh, check it out,' Ellie said, tapping on the dash. 'We've got something.'

Behind a screen entrance, a walnut door with a small stained glass window opened toward the interior. They couldn't see inside the house. Seconds later, the screen door opened, and a woman with long, light brown hair emerged in a bright orange peacoat. She held the screen, continuing her conversation with whoever was inside, and then finally let it shut behind her when she turned to walk away.

They had the same reaction.

'She's pretty young, right?' Rogan asked.

'Yeah, even with your self-proclaimed inability for cross-racial age identifications, yes, she's young. Really young. My guess is early twenties, maybe even younger.'

'And really pregnant?'

'It's hard to tell for sure under the coat, but, yeah, I thought the same thing.'

'Should we stop her?'

'No legal basis for it,' Ellie said. 'She's not in distress. And we run the risk that she makes a scene and tips off Symanski.'

They watched as the woman made her way down

the street, turned the corner at Thirty-first Street, and took the stairs up to the elevated N train.

'Should we go have a talk with the man inside?' Ellie asked.

'Ready when you are.'

A man in a plaid flannel house robe answered the door. It took him thirteen seconds after Ellie knocked. Long enough that she and Rogan exchanged a look and placed hands on their service weapons. Not so long that they unholstered.

She recognized Leon Symanski from his booking photo, even though the picture had been as old as the woman who'd left his house moments earlier. The man in front of her was less heavy and had thinning gray hair and whiskers on his chin. He had wrinkles, and his face was beginning to sag. But he also had the same broad nose and hooded eyes as the man who was arrested for sexual misconduct twenty years earlier.

'Leon Symanski?' she asked.

'That's right.'

'We're detectives from the NYPD. Mind if we have a word with you?'

'What is this about?'

'It's cold out here, sir. You think we could come on in?'

Symanski opened the screen door and stepped aside. The living room was small with a red brick fireplace and worn furniture. Ellie noticed two small framed photographs on the mantel, but could not make out the images from this distance.

'You work at a club called Pulse?'

Symanski nodded. 'Did something else happen there?'

'No, sir. It's about the murder we've been investigating. A customer named Chelsea Hart.'

He nodded again.

'You've apparently been talking about it,' Rogan said.

'Of course. One of the regulars in our club kills another customer? Everyone has been talking about it.'

'But only you seem to know more about the case than some late-night club janitor should know.'

'I don't know anything. Just what others have been saying.'

'The problem,' Ellie said, 'is that one of the others tells us that you've had some things to say about the case that aren't in the public domain. Obviously we've got to look into an allegation like that.'

'An allegation? Against me? I don't know anything.' Symanski seemed very interested in the threadbare carpet beneath his feet.

'Is it true that you told a coworker that Chelsea Hart's killer took a souvenir?'

'Like a New York City tchotchke?'

'No, I think you know what I mean, Mr. Symanski. A souvenir. Did you tell one of your coworkers that whoever killed Chelsea Hart took something from her? Because that's our understanding of the words you used: that the killer "took something" from her. What did he take?'

Symanski laughed nervously and scratched his

266

balding head. 'Is this a riddle or something? I don't understand what you're talking about.'

'It's not hard. Let's start with this: Did you say anything like that to anyone?'

Rogan was already giving Ellie an I-told-you-so look. He was apparently writing off Rodriguez as a liar and preparing to collect on his bet.

'No. I didn't – I don't even talk about the case, really. Everyone else does. I listen.'

'So if someone came to us and told us that they heard you say those words, you'd tell me they were lying?'

'Yes.' His eyes fell again to the floor. 'Or, I don't know, maybe they didn't hear me right.'

'And if I tell you I have a recording of you saying that?' Ellie asked. She pulled the digital recorder she kept on hand for witness interviews from her purse. 'You know how many of those new high-tech gadgets have things like microphones in them.'

'Maybe. Maybe I said it. I don't know. I may have repeated something I heard from someone else.'

'Tell us who you heard it from, Leon, and we're out of here. We'll go talk to them instead. We'll confirm that they were the ones who told you, and then we'll be on our way.'

'I don't remember. I don't even know the names of most of the people who work there. They all look the same.'

'What did he take from her?' Ellie asked again. 'Tell us what he took.'

She watched Symanski closely. She knew Rogan was

doing the same, because they were the same kind of cop. They trusted their instincts. They believed that a suspect's reaction under pressure could tell a good cop – in the gut, where it mattered – more than even the most damning piece of physical evidence.

And because they were the same kind of cop, she knew Rogan was seeing the same thing in Symanski that she saw. The slow swallow. The darting eyes. It was more than nervousness. It was an awakening, a realization. They were watching the man come to an understanding about his new reality.

He had a problem. And he knew that they knew.

'Let me propose a suggestion,' Ellie said. 'Why don't you let us take a quick look around the house, make sure we don't see anything that might have belonged to Chelsea Hart. That'll put our minds at ease, I think, and we can go back to the DA and assure him we did what we were asked. Is that all right with you?'

'If you go through my house?'

'Just to take a look around.' *Taking a look around* sounded so much less intrusive than *searching*. 'You don't have a problem with that, do you?'

'No. No, I don't have any problems with the police.'

'All right. Can we ask you to stay put right here while we do that? We can trust you not to run off, right?' She smiled at the ridiculousness of the thought.

'No, I'm not running anywhere.'

'And you're here alone?'

'Yes. I live alone. My wife died many years ago.'

'What about the woman who just left here? She doesn't live here?'

For the first time since they'd walked into the house, Ellie saw something dark cross Symanski's face. 'No. I live alone.'

'So who was she?' Rogan asked. 'The girl who left?'

'No one. You said you were going to look around and then leave me alone.'

'And we're going to do just that,' Ellie said. It was better to let the subject drop for now before Symanski revoked his consent to search. 'You just sit tight here for a second.'

The house was small, just the living room, two bedrooms, two bathrooms, and the kitchen. It was clean and uncluttered.

They started in the smaller of the two bedrooms. It was even cleaner and less cluttered than the rest of the house, apparently unused. The room's only contents were a nightstand, dresser, and double bed with baby pink sheets and a darker pink quilt.

Ellie opened a small drawer in the nightstand. 'Empty, unless you count a couple of rubber bands and an old Chapstick.'

'Same with the dresser,' Rogan said.

She walked to the closet and opened it. It contained nothing but empty hangers and a few items of women's clothing.

'His wife's?' Rogan asked.

'Depends what he meant when he said she died a long time ago. These look pretty new to me.'

'Right, because you've got your finger on the pulse of fashion.'

'Mean,' Ellie said.

They made their way to the master bedroom, with its own separate bath. Ellie opened the medicine cabinet. Heavy-duty psychotropic drugs might have been a tipoff, but instead, she found a razor, shaving cream, deodorant, aspirin, cough syrup, and all the other usual stuff. The only pills she found were some vitamin B supplements and two prescriptions she had never heard of. She was jotting down the names in her notebook when Rogan called to her from the bedroom.

'You better get out here.'

It took her a moment to recognize the object dangling from the pencil Rogan was holding out toward her in the master bedroom. It was a red beaded chandelier earring.

Beyond the bedroom, she heard a door slam.

'God damn it. He's running.'

And for the first time since she'd found Chelsea Hart, so was Ellie.

270

Chapter Thirty-Two

Ellie could hear Rogan yelling behind her, using all the major cuss words, but she wasn't thinking about her partner. She was focused on the back of Leon Symanski's head, bouncing on top of his plaid flannel robe, hauling ass a full block ahead of her. He apparently had found the time to pull on a pair of running shoes before slipping out the front door.

She didn't have to process the words coming out of Rogan's mouth to know why he was screaming at her. They had stopped by for a knock-and-talk. They weren't wearing vests. They didn't have backup. And they hadn't searched either Symanski or his living room for a weapon.

Rogan was telling her it wasn't worth it. They would set up a periphery. They'd bring out the dogs. They would find him within blocks.

But, at that moment – as she felt the rubber soles of her Paul Green boots slamming against the concrete of the street, the force of the impact shooting up through her knees and quads – all she could think about were the faces of four young women who had nothing in

271

common in life but were perhaps all tied together in death by the man in front of her. She had let his frail appearance and meek mannerisms fool her. They had left a killer sitting alone in his living room.

She pumped her arms harder at her sides as she picked up her pace. No way was a gaunt, gray-haired janitor in a bathrobe going to outrun her.

Symanski took a right on Thirty-first Street, then a quick left into the Astoria Boulevard subway station, taking the steps two at a time. He pushed his way through a crowd of commuters heading down the stairs, throwing two of them to the ground.

Ellie held out her shield, yelling, 'Get down! Get down!' She had to assume Symanski had a gun. He could open fire on the platform.

Terrified bystanders fell to all fours. Others slammed their bodies flat against walls and railings. Ellie dodged and weaved around them, surprised at Symanski's speed.

Inside the station, she came to a stop. She could feel her heart pounding like fists against her breastbone. No Symanski.

Separate sets of turnstiles stood on each side of her for the east and west sides of the tracks. He could have taken either one. This was the end of the N/R line. There were no northbound tracks. Nowhere to go on the east side of the platform.

She placed her right hand on the butt of her Glock. Twist, then up, she pulled the gun from her holster. She was about to hop the southbound turnstiles when she heard screams from a stairway behind her, on the opposite side of the station.

She followed the sounds of panic, sprinting down the stairs so quickly that she nearly tumbled from the momentum of her own weight. She hit street level and was wondering if she'd lost him when she saw a flash of Symanski's robe move into an alley past a four-story brick apartment building on the other side of Thirty-first Street.

She ran after him, drawing horn blasts from oncoming traffic. When she reached the alley's entrance, she pressed her back against the wall of the apartment complex, feeling her fingers wrapped firmly around the Glock, thumbs pressed together near the safety.

She needed to know if the alley cut through or was a dead end. Were there fire escapes that Symanski could reach from the ground? Businesses with unlocked back doors? She had no idea if she could even spare the seconds she was using to think through all of the unknowns. And where in the hell was Rogan and the backup?

She peeked her head around the corner – once quickly, then a more cautious look, two full seconds.

In two seconds, this is what she learned: no gunshots. That was good for the obvious reason, but it might also mean Symanski was gone. Two Dumpsters on opposite sides of the alley. A black Ford Explorer on the left. No accessible fire escapes. No signs of loading or unloading, so any back doors to businesses were probably locked. No visible exits, but the chain link fence at the end of the alley was easily scalable.

And no sign of Symanski.

Where was Rogan?

Ellie took a deep breath and swung her body around the corner.

'You're trapped, Symanski.' A false statement if he'd already jumped the fence, but true if he could hear her. She heard nothing but the hum of traffic on the BQE and a Poland Spring water bottle rolling on the concrete with the wind.

She crouched low and jogged to the Dumpster on the right, squatting against the end of it for cover. In her mind, she created a blueprint of the alley and pictured Symanski's available hiding places. Not behind the high-riding SUV. His legs would be visible. Inside, perhaps, but everyone in New York locked their cars. That left four spots: on the north side of each of the two Dumpsters, or inside the two recessed doorways on the ground floor of the apartment building to the east.

She mapped out her route.

Still squatting, she made her way like a crab around the side of the Dumpster, then sprang into an Isosceles shooting stance. Nothing but two black garbage bags.

She stepped sideways to her right, to the first doorway. It was clear. She checked the door. Locked.

From the safety of the doorway, she surveyed the alley again. Two spots remaining: the Dumpster or the last doorway. They were almost directly across from each other on opposite sides of the alley. There was no way to check them sequentially and still be covered.

Fifty-fifty odds.

She stretched farther, struggling to see inside the next doorway. Nothing but darkness.

If it were her, she would choose the Dumpster. It was deeper, invulnerable to angles. Behind a barrier of that size, her adversary would not have to expose himself to get to her. And a Dumpster wouldn't block her in. She could still bolt around her adversary. In the doorway, it was close combat. No escape.

She would definitely pick the Dumpster. Better than fifty-fifty. Where the hell was Rogan?

Crouching low again, she ran to the second Dumpster. She turned the corner, keeping a tight stance. It was clear.

She immediately rotated clockwise to get a look inside the final doorway. Also clear.

Damn it. She felt her shoulders drop as the stress fell from her deltoids. Her mistake had been pausing at the alley's entrance. Symanski had used the opportunity to jump the fence. She shifted her Glock to her left hand and unclipped her cell phone from her waist to call Rogan.

She had flipped the phone open and was scrolling for Rogan's number when she saw a blur moving next to her. She turned toward it.

Symanski had pushed open the metal lid of the Dumpster with his left hand and was reaching toward her with his right. She caught only a quick glimpse of the blade of his knife before her Glock and phone tumbled to the ground together and she felt a searing pain on the back of her right hand.

She saw blood.

Two steps, and she scooped up her Glock. She spun toward Symanski, who was pulling himself out of the Dumpster. Even with her cut hand, she had a shot. Symanski stumbled and fell to the ground. He knelt before her, knife in hand.

'Drop it, Symanski.'

'Just kill me. Shoot me.'

Ellie felt her finger against the trigger. Only five pounds of pressure. That's all it would take to put this guy down. *Not like this, not with him on his knees like this. Only if he takes another swipe at me.*

'Drop the knife.'

'I did it. I strangled her, and I cut her up, and I took her earring. I don't want to die in prison. Kill me.'

She heard sirens approaching and saw the knife in Symanski's hand begin to shake. She took a quick step toward him with her left foot, preparing to land a right heel against his knife hand in a push kick.

But as she lifted her leg, Symanski lunged at her and grabbed her ankle with his left hand while he raised his knife with his right. The weight of his body carried both of them to the ground. She saw Rogan in her periphery, running down the alley toward them, but there wasn't time.

There wasn't time to wait. There wasn't time to think. In a millisecond, her instincts processed the only information that mattered. Symanski was on top of her. He had a knife. She'd lost control over her service weapon once already. If it happened again, she was dead. There wouldn't be time to reach for the backup gun inside her boot.

Ellie was bracing herself for the kickback of the Glock when she felt Symanski's body weight leaving hers. She heard a crash as Rogan threw Symanski against the Dumpster, once, then twice, then a third time – all in seconds – before Symanski's body went limp and he dropped the knife.

'What about the others?' Ellie screamed. 'How many other girls did you kill?'

But Symanski wasn't answering. Rogan checked to make sure he was breathing. 'He's out.'

'He did it, Rogan. He gave it up. He killed Chelsea Hart.'

Rogan looked at her with a furrowed brow, then dropped his gaze to the concrete beneath his feet and shook his head.

And then Ellie understood. What Rogan had seen was a man on his knees in an empty alley at gunpoint. What the hell kind of confession was that?

Chapter Thirty-Three

'Does it hurt?'

From Ellie's vantage point on the ambulance floor, Rogan looked as sheepish as she'd ever seen him. She caught the eye of the EMT who was placing another stitch in the back of her hand.

'Will you be insulted if I don't say that you've managed to magically convert all of my pain into an unprecedented feeling of euphoria?'

The man shook his head.

'This very nice man is sewing, with a needle, into the back of my hand. As Samuel Jackson might say, yes, it mother-fucking hurts.'

'I'd feel less guilty if you said you had a thing for pain.'

'I don't, but you shouldn't feel guilty. You told me not to run. And you were right. We would have tracked him down anyway.'

After all that running – up into the subway station, back down on the west side – Ellie had made the arrest only two blocks from Symanski's house.

'When I saw you going after him, I went for the car.

I thought I'd have a better chance of catching up to you, but I lost you at the train station.'

'It's okay, J. J. It's not your fault. Besides, you saved me.'

'Yeah, right. Turns out I saved the bad guy. You would've blasted him pretty good if I hadn't come along.'

'Like I said, you saved me.'

Rogan took a closer look at her wounded hand. 'How many does she need?'

'Twelve.'

That meant four more to go. They both winced at the thought. 'She's gonna have one bitch of a scar.'

'Hello? The *she* is sitting right here and can handle a little mark on the back of her hand. It'll be a conversation piece. I can make up various tales of adventure to explain my mysterious defect.'

Rogan continued to mutter apologies until the twelfth stitch was completed, then asked the EMT to give them some privacy.

'What happened in that alley?'

She gave him a play-by-play, including Symanski's confession. 'I didn't get a chance to ask him about the other girls. We need to talk to him about Lucy Feeney. Robbie Harrington. Alice Butler. There could be others.'

'We can't talk to him about anything just now. He was still out cold when the wagon carried him away, and when he eventually comes to, the first thing he'll do is ask for a lawyer, and then we'll have a better shot at questioning Elvis. You really got him to cop to killing Chelsea Hart?'

'What do you mean, I *got* him to?'

'Hey, it's just us. I saw what I saw.'

A man on his knees in an empty alley at gunpoint.

'It wasn't like that. *He* attacked *me*. He cut me,' she said, holding up her patched-up hand for emphasis.

'And then you took control of the situation, pointed a gun at the man, and asked him for a confession?'

'No. He still had the knife. He was begging me to shoot. I wasn't even questioning him. He blurted it out. He couldn't have been more eager to confess. "I strangled her, and I cut her up, and I took her earring." That's what he said.'

Before she had allowed the EMT to stitch her hand, she had made him write down the exact words in her notebook, not because she thought she'd ever forget them, but so she could back up her testimony with a contemporaneous written record.

Rogan had her run through everything two more times to make sure he understood it all.

'The DA's still going to have a problem with that. Whether you were threatening to kill him, or he was begging you to do it, he was still under distress. They're going to argue that he just said that because he knew he was about to go down for life in prison, and he'd rather die. Maybe you pressured him because you had all those doubts about Myers.'

'The DA's going to say that, or you're saying that?'

'All Symanski said was that he cut her up. That doesn't bother you? What about the hair?'

The news about the killer chopping off Chelsea's hair had still not gone public.

280

'That's what he meant by "cut her up". He cut her body. He cut her hair. And what about the earring, J. J.? You've seen the picture. It's the exact same earring.'

'I talked to Eckels about that –'

'You called Eckels already?'

'He called me for an update. I couldn't exactly hide the fact that one of his detectives had been stabbed.'

'I prefer the word *cut*.' It didn't sound nearly so dire that way.

'Eckels pointed out that Symanski could have found the earring at the club.'

'And you believe that?'

'It's possible. Let's say Myers takes Chelsea into the alley for a little action after he finds her outside by the cab. He gets rough – we know he has it in him because of his past incident at Cornell. When he realizes she's dead, he tries to make it look like some crazy killer got to her. He throws her into his car, chops off her hair, slices her all over, and dumps the body under the Williamsburg Bridge.'

'And, again, the earring?'

'He notices when he chops off all that long hair that one of her earrings is missing. If someone finds that earring at Pulse, it's a link between the vic and the club, which would lead us to him. So he dumps the second earring.'

'And when Symanski finds the original at the club, he somehow realizes it belonged to Chelsea Hart and starts telling people the killer took something from her body? I don't buy it.'

'Look, I'm just talking out loud. No conclusions.

That's what investigations are for. We're going to tear up that house looking for more evidence, that's for sure. And once Symanski's got his lawyer, maybe we can get a sit-down with him.'

'Yeah, right.'

Ellie's cell phone rang at her hip. It was Jess. She let it go to voice mail, but it rang a second time and then a third. She struggled to get the phone open with her left hand.

'What's up, Jess? I've kind of got my hands full here.'

She waved her bandaged hand at Rogan and smiled.

'I need to talk to you, El. Can you come home?'

'No. I'm working. I can't just leave. Bad guys? Evildoers? You know, the whole I'm-a-police-officer thing?'

'Seriously, I really need to talk to you.'

'Where are you?'

'At home. The apartment.'

'I'll call you later.'

'Ellie –'

She hung up, knowing her brother would forgive her within seconds. They'd done far ruder things to each other but had never found a sin that couldn't be cured with a joke or a drink.

'If your brother needs you, you should go.'

'It can wait.'

Rogan placed his hands on his hips and sighed. 'I hate this as much as you do, but you need to take a break. Eckels –'

'You're fucking kidding me? He's sending me home?'

282

'He doesn't want you questioning Symanski or being part of the search, at least for now.'

'Because of what happened in the alley? He thinks I did something wrong?'

Rogan shook his head. 'You may prefer the word "cut," but you've still got twelve stitches because of this asshole. It makes sense for you not to be in the middle of the investigation minutes after something like that. Plus he got a call about that mugging of Chelsea Hart's friends yesterday. He wants you to follow up.'

He ripped a page from his notebook and handed her an address.

It sounded rational enough, but she could tell from Rogan's expression that there was more to the explanation. She had been hoping for even a modicum of progress with her lieutenant, but his opinion of her seemed to be falling by the hour. And he apparently thought she was the kind of cop who would coerce a confession out of someone just to prove she was right.

'Just let me finish going through the house. You can stay with me and watch my every move.'

Rogan looked down at the street. 'Please don't put me in this situation.'

Ellie realized she didn't have any good choices. 'Can I take the car?'

'Of course.'

'Promise me you won't let Eckels brush this off. Look for anything and everything, okay? And don't forget about the other girls. Symanski could be our guy. The timing is right.'

Rogan pressed his lips together.

'It's like you said, J. J. We're partners. Any decision you make, it's for both of us.'

He placed one hand on her shoulder. 'I'll look for anything and everything. I promise.'

Chapter Thirty-Four

Two hundred and fifty Madison – Street, not Avenue – was also known as the LaGuardia Houses, a nine-building brick cluster of high-rise housing projects erected in the 1950s when the Lower East Side was still dominated by squatters and hardworking immigrants. Now, if developers had their way, they'd evict the 2,600 residents, knock down the projects, and fill the space with more luxury condos.

Ellie ignored the suspicious eyes that followed her as she made her way from the Crown Vic, through the rundown courtyard, into House 6. She took the elevator to the eleventh floor. The moment the doors pinged open, she was welcomed by a giant X of crime tape across a door at the end of the hall.

She ducked beneath the tape and flashed her shield to the uniform officer at the door. He nodded toward the back of the living room.

One man in a suit stood out among the crowd of uniforms and technicians in the apartment. He was telling a woman with a camera to make sure she got plenty of photographs of dark burgundy splatter across the television screen and the wall behind it.

'Ellie Hatcher,' she said by way of introduction, struggling to hold up her badge with her left hand. 'I was told you had news for me about a robbery?'

'Ken Garcia,' he said, offering his hand, then quickly rethinking the gesture upon seeing Ellie's bandages. 'Your lou said someone might be coming by. Didn't seem necessary to me.'

'Why do I get the feeling you're not just here about a mugging.'

'Nope. Our RP's an eight-year-old girl upstairs. Called nine-one-one by herself over shots fired.' When schools taught children how to dial 911, they probably weren't envisioning them becoming the reporting party to a homicide. 'You just missed the body. Twenty-two-year-old black male named Darrell Washington. While the first responders were waiting for the homicide team, they found two brand-new handheld GPS devices purchased yesterday from the Union Square Circuit City.'

'That kind of loot out in the open and the shooter leaves it behind?'

'Hell, no. Stupid uniforms were snooping around where they didn't belong. The bag was in the refrigerator. Guess Washington was hiding them. Who knows. Anyway, the sales receipt was still in the bag. The charges came back to Jordan McLaughlin's credit card. Your lieutenant had a flag in the system for the Thirteenth to be notified on any developments, and I guess this counts as a development.'

'Any indication Washington's murder was related to the mugging?'

286

Garcia shook his head. 'Word so far – from the residents willing to speak to us – is that Washington was an outsider. A little too on his own. A little too quick to talk to cops. It could be a retaliation thing. Or we might be looking at a home invasion where the bad guy got his apartments mixed up. Narcotics has been monitoring some dealing going on next door. One thing's for certain: whoever did it was a lousy shot – two bullets in Washington, but three in the living room wall. No dummy, though. Left the murder weapon on the floor. No serial number. No prints.'

'Did you find the credit card?'

'Nah. Washington probably used it once and ditched it. I told all this to your lou about an hour ago so he wouldn't need to send a body over. No offense, but you must be in some kind of doghouse.'

Ellie took a quick walk through the apartment, just to make it look like there was a purpose to her being there. But she knew that Eckels had sent her here just to pull her away from Symanski's house.

There was nothing left for her to do but go home.

Jess was waiting at the apartment door for her with an open bottle of Rolling Rock. He helped her shrug her coat off around her bandaged hand.

'How bad is it?'

'I could show you,' Ellie said, 'but you've already puked once this week.'

She plopped herself onto the sofa and took a long draw from the beer.

'So are you going to stand there looking all sorry for

me, or are you going to tell me what was so important that you needed me to come home?'

He shrugged. 'This whole feeling-sorry-for-you-thing, my brain's having trouble processing it. It's usually the other way around. And I called you before I knew some crazy dude stabbed you.'

She was really getting tired of that word. 'Out with it.'

Jess took a seat next to her on the couch, and she knew it was serious. He had a determined, almost somber look on his face. She hadn't known her brother's facial muscles were physically capable of such an expression.

'You got a phone call about an hour ago. God knows how the wench got your number, but it was from an editor at Simon & Schuster. She was trying to verify facts in a book proposal she received from Peter Morse.'

Ellie didn't know what to say. It had been only three days since Peter had called the book pie in the sky. He certainly hadn't mentioned sending a proposal to any editor.

'What kinds of facts?' she asked.

'Well, it's not like she dictated a list of questions, but she was saying all kinds of stuff about Dad and the College Hill Strangler case. The book's not just about First Date, Ellie. It's about you. I don't get it, El. You've been a vault when it comes to that stuff and now it's in the hands of some reporter?'

Ellie wanted to defend Peter, to say he wasn't just some reporter. He was the first man she'd met in a long time whom she could actually picture herself with. He cared about her. He could be trusted. But instead she sat in silence on her sofa, wishing she had never spoken to Peter about William Summer.

'Ellie, are you listening to me? You need to call that editor and tell her Peter's full of shit and that you never said any of this to him.'

'I can't lie, Jess.'

'Oh, Jesus. Not this Girl Scout shit. He's the one who's the fucking liar.' He flipped open her laptop on the coffee table. 'There's something you need to see, Ellie. He's still online. I'm really sorry.'

And, sure enough, there he was. 'Unpublished,' the journalist and struggling author she'd first noticed online two months ago, was still listed on the very Internet dating service where they had first met.

Same profile. Same photograph. Same just-out-of-bed brown hair and piercing green eyes. All the same, as if he hadn't met anyone yet. As if they hadn't spent those nights together before she left for Kansas. As if they hadn't spoken every day while she was gone.

'I'm sorry, El. He's not the guy he pretended to be.' He placed a hand on her outstretched leg.

Ellie wiped her face, suppressing a sniffle. 'I'll call him first.'

'No. Don't call him. Don't talk to him. Ever.'

'I at least owe it to him to let him explain.'

'No, you don't. You met him, what? Two months ago? And you were out of town for almost all of it? Jesus, I'm sorry if this is harsh, but you're such a 1950s monogamist. Just because you go on a few dates with a guy doesn't make him your husband. You know how many women I've dated who just stopped taking my calls one day? I've been dumped by text message. My e-mail address is blocked from, like, half the women in Manhattan.'

She gave him a sad smile.

'Trust me, he'll get over it. I mean, it'll take a while. This is, after all, the one and only Ellie Hatcher we're talking about.' His tone became serious again. 'I mean it, El. You're one of the last single girls to make it to thirty without some asshole doing a number on your head. You know how many good guys are out there who'd kill for a chick like you? Don't let this guy turn you into a basket case for the next good one who comes around the corner. Save the drama for your mama. You need to cut him loose.'

Her cell phone rang. She recognized the prefix as a courthouse number.

'Hatcher.'

'It's Max Donovan. I heard what happened at Symanski's. Knight wants to talk to you.'

'I'm not sure that's going to work. My lieutenant seems to have sidelined me.'

'That's why Knight wants you to come in. It would just be the three of us.'

'I don't hide anything from my partner.'

'Fair enough. We're not trying to get in the middle of things. Knight just wants to make sure everything's getting a proper look. He can help you out with Eckels; he just wants to meet with you first.'

'What time?'

'He's tied up until six.'

That gave Ellie an hour before she would need to leave her apartment.

'Yeah, okay.'

'And, not to press my luck, but I'm pretty much sitting here waiting around with nothing to do until then.'

'Why do I sort of doubt that?'

'Okay, fine. But I do have time for coffee. If, you know, if coffee sounded good to you.'

Ellie looked at her brother's worried face. She pictured Peter boasting to some editor about his relationship with her to sell a book. She remembered his attempt that morning to blame his boss for the story about Chelsea Hart's shorn hair. She looked at his smiling photograph on her open laptop screen.

'Coffee would be good.'

An hour later, the man sat at his desk and watched another minute tick by on his computer's digital clock. He had a little time to spare.

He opened Mozilla Firefox and typed 'youtube' in the address box. Once he was on the site, he entered the search he had memorized as the quickest method for pulling up the clip he wanted: 'Dateline College Hill Strangler.'

A list of videos filled the screen. He clicked on the top one and waited while the data loaded. There she was, face to face with the anchor, Ann Curry, against a severe black set, in her white turtleneck sweater and black skirt. He'd seen the entire segment many times – her walking in front of the site of William Summer's first kill, kneeling at her father's grave, the childhood photograph with those little blond pigtails – but this was the part he liked best.

It wasn't about her childhood. It was about the present. It showed the woman she had become – smart, cocky, joyously uppity with that I've-got-your-number half-smile.

'How do you explain the fact that it took the Wichita police thirty years to capture this man? Was he that much of a master criminal?'

There was the half-smile. 'Oh, no. My father had a profile that was spot-on: he'd be a man who craved authority, maybe a badge bunny. Like a wannabe cop,' she said, quickly clarifying her use of the police slang. 'The people who worked with him would describe him as petty and autocratic. He might be in a relationship but would frequent prostitutes. All of it turned out to be right. The problem is, the WPD shut down the investigation. My father was one man working out of his basement around his other cases, and without any support. This person was no master criminal.'

'So if the department dropped the ball, how did they finally catch the killer?'

'He did himself in. It was his own desire for recognition and notoriety that led police to him. His desire to taunt and to show off – the letters, the drawings, the poems – were the equivalent of a billboard pointing directly to him. Killers like William Summer get caught because of their insatiable egos.'

The man hit the pause button at that moment. Such confidence.

Killers like William Summer get caught because of their insatiable egos.

On that point, he had to take issue. Summer got caught because he was stupid. He, however, was not.

Still, he hoped he had not made a mistake getting rid of the gun he'd fired only three hours earlier. In a straight contest of strength, he would always have the upper hand against a girl, so he had avoided guns until this afternoon. Too noisy. Too unpredictable.

But as he looked at the face of Ellie Hatcher, he wondered if he couldn't use the extra help.

He went to the Tools menu and clicked on the Clear Private Data command, erasing his search information on YouTube before closing the browser window. Rachel Peck would be leaving work soon and enjoying her night out on the town.

Chapter Thirty-Five

Ellie had sucked down half of her grande peppermint mocha by the time she finished giving Donovan the play-by-play of the events at Leon Symanski's house.

'Unbelievable. When Susan Parker showed up at the courthouse this morning with Jaime Rodriguez, I really assumed it would all turn out to be b.s. Either Rodriguez was lying, or his friend was lying, or maybe Symanski was some insane criminal wannabe.'

'Instead, he's some insane criminal actually-be who says he killed Chelsea Hart. Although,' she quickly added, 'Rogan did float the possibility that Myers is still our man.' As things stood, she had mixed feelings about meeting alone with Donovan. Until Rogan was around, the least she could do was to sound neutral.

'Well, with Symanski's confession, we've got enough to prosecute him, but whether we'd win at trial is another question.' Donovan broke off a chunk of the banana bread they were sharing. 'They'll argue the confession's coerced. And then even if we can use the confession, we need other evidence to corroborate it. At least we've got the earring. That would get the case to a jury, but convincing twelve people beyond a reasonable doubt wouldn't be easy.'

'Rogan thinks a good lawyer can argue the earring fell off while Chelsea was at the club and Symanski found it.'

'It also doesn't help that the guy who pointed us in Symanski's direction was a drug dealer who runs with one of Jake Myers's buddies. They'll argue Rodriguez was sending us in the wrong direction as a favor to his pal.'

'So it all comes down to Symanski's confession in the alley. Either it's real, or I forced it out of him at gunpoint. Terrific. Now I can see why Eckels sent me home.'

'That's why Knight wants to see you. Eckels thinks it looks bad if you're working the case after what happened between you and Symanski in the alley, but Knight thinks it looks a lot worse if you get pulled. If the department treats you like a bad apple, a jury might be inclined to see it the same way. The key is to keep you on this. You and Rogan work well together, right?'

'Yeah. No question.'

'All right. So you work it side by side. Two good detectives, backing each other up. That way there's not too much pressure on the word of either one of you. By benching you, Eckels is causing major problems for us at trial.'

'Between me and you, Eckels doesn't care if he causes problems for other people.'

'Hey, stop worrying about it. Knight will work something out. You saw that the *Daily Post* broke the story about the victim's hair being chopped off?'

'Although I believe they said "shaved". Salacious just the same, though.' She'd seen the update on the paper's Web site at her apartment. Byline: George Kittrie and Peter Morse. Ellie wondered if breaking the story had been worth it all to Peter.

'So, come on, you haven't given me your take yet. Is Symanski our guy or not?'

'I don't know.' Neutral. Report the facts. Present both sides. Let Donovan make up his own mind.

'Oh, come on. The guy told you he did it. What's in your gut?'

I strangled her, and I cut her up, and I took her earring. There were only two possible explanations for what happened in that alley. Either Ellie forced Symanski to speak those words, or he had murdered Chelsea Hart. And whether anyone accepted it or not, Ellie knew that Symanski hadn't simply recited that sentence. He'd looked her in the eye. He'd spoken with a pleading desperation that was unambiguous: he had truly wanted her to believe him.

'I know I didn't coerce that confession, so, yeah, I think he did it.' Ellie felt guilty that she might be biasing Donovan, but at least she was still keeping the cold cases to herself. She wanted to raise the subject once more with Rogan before she brought anyone else in on her theory.

'And Jake Myers is totally innocent?'

'It would follow. But are you really sure enough to drop the charges?'

Donovan shook his head. 'What a mess. I've got law school friends who make four times my salary, and all they have to think about is which enormous company should get how large a pile of cash. Why do we do this to ourselves?'

'Hey, speak for yourself, Mr. ADA. I get paid even less than you, but all I have to do is catch the perps and hand them over. You get to make all the decisions about charges and plea bargains and sentences and all that business.'

'Yeah, but I don't have to worry about getting stabbed in an alley.'

'Well, at least not at work.'

'Oh, and you're funny too. That's just great.'

'You've got something against funny?' she asked.

'No, in fact I'm a very big fan of the sense of humor.'

'So what's the problem?'

'It's yet another reason to wish this coffee wasn't just a coffee. But, that's all right. I'm good at keeping it strictly professional.'

'Is that what this is? A strictly professional coffee that's just a coffee?'

'I assumed so, what with the nondescript "plans" you had the other night and everything.'

'Actually, I don't think I'll have any plans along those lines in the future.'

'So, the extremely polite shutout from the other night —'

'Consider it retracted. If I'm permitted to retract, that is.'

'I think it can be managed.' He looked at Ellie with a cool smile that made her suddenly aware of the un-flattering overhead lights in Starbucks. 'Unfortunately, with that, our coffee that wasn't just coffee may have to end. Knight will kill me if we're late.'

Thanks to caller ID, Rogan didn't bother with a greeting.

'Let me guess. You're on your third drink and have pasted Eckels's picture to a dartboard.'

'One beer, one peppermint mocha. No dartboard, but an excellent suggestion nevertheless.'

'Beer and peppermint mocha? Disgusting.'

'Where are you?'

'St. Vincent's. Symanski's finally awake.'

'I'll be right there.' Ellie hung up before he could argue.

She found Rogan sitting in a wheelchair in the third floor hallway of St. Vincent's Hospital. A uniform officer stood guard at the door across the hall.

'You shouldn't sit on that when your legs work,' she said, kicking one of the wheels. 'Bad karma.'

'I'd lie in an empty casket right now. My ass is whooped tired.'

'Is Symanski talking?'

'Yeah, if "Get me a lawyer" counts as talking.' He used his hand as a puppet to act out Symanski's single sentence.

'Fabulous.' She used the wall next to Rogan as support and slid down into a crouch.

'Speaking of karma,' Rogan said, 'Symanski's in bad shape.'

'He's probably faking it. You didn't hit him *that* hard.'

'No, not from me. He's got some kind of melanoma.'

'Skin cancer?'

'No, like lung cancer or something. The doctor said it was from asbestos?'

'You mean mesothelioma?'

'Yeah, that's it. You've been attending med school on the side?'

'No, like almost everything I know, I learned it from the television.' She parodied a familiar ad for one of the city's omnipresent personal injury law firms. '"*If you've been diagnosed with mesothelioma, you know there are hundreds of questions about what steps to take. Let Datz and Grossman help you with your legal rights while you deal with this difficult diagnosis.*"'

'Damn, girl, you *do* watch too much TV. Now you better go and get your butt out of here. Eckels will go nuts if he finds out.'

'That's what we need to talk about. Simon Knight called me in and said he wants us both working on this – together. He's worried that if a jury hears Eckels pulled me from the case, it will taint me as a witness.'

'A witness against who?'

'Pick one. It's eventually going to be either Myers or Symanski. The whole point is, we've got to figure out which one of them killed Chelsea, and whoever it turns out to be, I'm already part of the picture of the case. They don't want me to be a problem at trial.'

'No, we couldn't let that happen to the dream team, could we now?'

'I know you're not a big fan of Simon Knight.'

'And you are? That guy doesn't give a shit about anyone. He just wants to win his cases. And he'd sell either one of us out in a heartbeat if necessary. Casey had a trial about eight years ago where the defendant said Casey planted evidence. Instead of proving the fat fuck was a liar, Knight went in front of the jury and said, "So what?" Detective Casey might be a bad cop, but all the other evidence showed the guy was good for it.'

'The rogue detective framed a guilty man,' Ellie said.

'Except Casey was a good, honest cop. And Knight didn't care what he said about the man as long as he got his conviction.'

'That's a DA's job.'

'That's bullshit.'

'Well, Knight's getting my back on this one. Bigtime.'

'As long as you realize that could all change, like that,' he said, snapping his fingers.

'I'm a big girl, Rogan.'

'Did you tell him about those cold cases?'

'No, not yet. I want to, though. It was different before we knew about Symanski. Now that he's part of the picture –'

'Okay.'

'Okay, as in, you're okay with it? Or okay, as in, you're pissed at me and want me to stop justifying my position?'

'Believe it or not, okay as in okay. I see the point. If we're taking another look at the case against Myers anyway, we should at least make sure we do it right.'

Ellie wanted to jump on Rogan's wheelchair and give him a big bear hug. Instead, she nodded. Nodding was always an acceptable way for cops to communicate with each other.

She was scooching her way out of her crouch when she spotted the woman in an orange coat step from the elevator. In the time it took Ellie to realize she looked familiar, the woman caught sight of the officer posted outside Symanski's door and stepped back into the elevator.

'Did you see that?' Ellie asked.

'What?'

'The woman at Symanski's house. The pregnant girl.' Ellie was already running down the hall. 'She got spooked and jumped into the elevator.'

Ellie pushed the call button, but the elevator was heading down. Slamming open the door to the stairwell, she took the stairs two at a time. She could hear Rogan's footsteps behind her.

'Try the second floor,' she yelled. 'I'm going to the lobby.'

On the first floor, she looked both ways, but there was no sign of the bright orange coat. She bolted out the hospital doors to Seventh Avenue in time to see the woman shut the passenger-side door of a gold Acura Legend.

And, once again, the day dealt Ellie a surprise. As the car drove off, she recognized Jaime Rodriguez behind the wheel.

Rogan was waiting for her when she emerged from the stairwell on the hospital's third floor.

'I asked the nurse whether a pregnant woman had been here earlier to see Symanski.'

301

'And?'

'No luck. But a guy delivering flowers from the gift shop overheard me. He says a pregnant lady in a bright orange coat was downstairs half an hour ago throwing a fit because her father had been taken here by the police.'

'Her *father*?'

'Yep. And for some reason Symanski didn't want us knowing who she was when we asked about her at the house.'

Ellie thought about the bare dresser drawers in Symanski's guest room. The empty hangers in the closet.

She removed her notebook from her bag. The most recent entry was Symanski's confession, scrawled at her command by the EMT: 'I strangled her, and I cut her up, and I took her earring.' Just above the confession were two words in her own handwriting: 'Pemetrexed' and 'Cisplatin,' the two prescriptions she had discovered in Symanski's medicine cabinet. She had no doubt they would turn out to be treatments for his mesothelioma. She recalled joking morbidly with Peter last night about the apparent ubiquity of cancer.

Symanski knew he was dying, but he hadn't called the law firm of Datz & Grossman to solve his problems. He had tried to handle them on his own.

'We need to look at Jake Myers's banking records.'

Chapter Thirty-Six

'Oh, come on, man. You have *got* to be kidding me. *Them*?'

The girl with the platinum blond hair and four-inch heels obviously wasn't happy that the bouncer had waved two other women past the velvet rope at Tenjune without a wait. Implicit in the girl's outrage was her belief that she was taller, thinner, and hotter than Rachel Peck and her friend Gina, a belief that was undoubtedly true, but which failed to take into account the network of friendships among the little people who kept the city's biggest hot spots up and running.

Rachel high-fived the bouncer at the door. 'Thanks, Rico. You're the best.'

Two years earlier, before a very active gym membership and his discovery of tight black T-shirts, Rico the bouncer was Ricardo the Mesa Grill busboy. News to the blonde in the stripper shoes: to get into a club like Tenjune, you either have to *be* somebody or *know* somebody.

They made their way down the stairs, past a lounge area of velvet seating, to the crocodile-skin bar. An old

Beastie Boys song blasted through the speakers, mixed and scratched together with a Madonna tune.

'Two Bombay Sapphire martinis,' Rachel asked once she finally got the bartender's attention. 'No vermouth. Up. Twists.'

The bartender looked annoyed when she handed him a credit card. Too bad for him. At thirty-five dollars a round, a splurge like tonight belonged on the Visa.

She tucked her card in the front pocket of her jeans and handed Gina her glass, then took a big sip from her own to bring the meniscus to a safer level. One good bump in the crowd could cost her half a cocktail. The gin was cold and smooth as it ran down her throat.

She followed Gina into the next room, where they found comfortable standing space not too far from the club's horseshoe-shaped dance floor.

'To girls' night,' Gina said, leaning forward to be heard.

Rachel clinked her glass against her friend's and took another swallow. The toast was a subtle reference to Rachel's recent breakup with a stockbroker she'd met three months earlier while she was bartending at the restaurant. She usually brushed off the advances of the drunken, overgrown frat boys knocking back tequila shots at the bar, but Hayden had seemed different. He'd flirted with her that night, no question, but he'd come back the next day at lunch, alone, to ask for her number. It seemed like a classy move on his part.

For a while, Rachel allowed herself to believe that she might have lucked in to one of those relationships girls somehow seemed to find in the city. Hayden was a decent guy with a good income. He was smart and fun and actually read her short stories and appeared to appreciate them. She even entertained the thought that if things worked out, she could quit bartending and focus on her writing full-time.

But like anything that seemed too good to be true, Hayden had an imperfection. A big one, too, unless you could look past an insatiable fondness for cocaine and the other women who started to look pretty attractive after a few lines. The first time Rachel found evidence of another woman at Hayden's apartment – maraschino cherries and sour mix in the refrigerator for some girlie drink Hayden would never imbibe – she forgave him. It was the coke, he said. He'd stop using, he said. It wasn't an addiction.

And then when she found his stash in the nightstand, she forgave him again. He had a bigger problem than he realized, he said. He'd get help.

But by then, Hayden had a read on her. She was a sucker and a doormat. She was the kind of woman who could be confronted with evidence that she'd been lied to and cheated on, and then simply forgive. She shouldn't have been surprised when she smelled Fendi perfume in his sheets four days ago.

But at least she hadn't bought Hayden's most recent round of apologies. He even cried. *I don't know what's wrong with me. I don't know why I can't just appreciate what I have with you.* As if she were supposed to feel sorry for him.

She'd seen another side of him when she walked out. His tears had turned to anger. It wasn't what Rachel would call violence, but he did try to stop her. Physically. She had some fingerprint-sized bruises on her left bicep, but nothing major.

So now here she was with Gina, back out on the scene from which she had hoped Hayden might save her. The men in these clubs were rich. The women were pretty. For most, there was an implicit trade-off in light of the gender preferences that drove Manhattan dating life. Men got the advantage on age and looks; women on finances.

'Shit,' Gina said. 'One martini and I have to pee already.'

They both knew that a pit stop to the ladies room could be a fifteen-minute wait, depending on the length of the line and the number of girls using the stalls to get high. Rachel held her index and middle fingers to her lips and puffed, indicating she'd use the time to smoke one of the cigarettes that Gina was always trying to get her to toss.

Outside, Rachel's ears felt cloudy from the sudden drop in volume. The blonde with the high heels was not happy to see her.

'Seriously? You waltz in, and now you're back out here *already*?'

'Rico, cut the girl some slack.' Rachel protected her lighter from the wind and sparked up a Newport. 'Poor thing's half naked and perched on top of some hardcore spikes.'

The bouncer formerly known as Ricardo gave the girl the cursory and disapproving look that kept a certain kind of clientele coming back for more. 'I didn't tell her how to dress.'

Rachel took a second, longer puff. 'I'm going to tell Carlita on you.'

Carlita was Rico's mother. Even when Ricardo had just begun his transformation into Rico, Rachel had overheard Carlita complaining at the restaurant about how 'fancy' her son had become.

Rico rolled his eyes and unhooked the velvet rope for the now jubilant blonde and her friends. 'Guilt trip much?' he said in Rachel's direction.

'Just keeping it real,' Rachel said with a smile. The optimistic eyes of the other expectant people in line now firmly on her, she walked east on Little Twelfth Street, then watched the bustle of Ninth Avenue while she enjoyed her smoke on the corner.

A blue Ford Taurus approached from Greenwich Street and pulled to the curb in front of her. The driver rolled down his window. 'You know where a club called P.M. is?'

'Yeah, you just passed your turn.' Rachel pointed to Gansevoort Street.

'I get so turned around down here,' the man said.

Rachel could see why. Greenwich, Gansevoort, Little Twelfth (not the same as Twelfth), and Ninth Avenue all merged together at this humble intersection.

'No offense,' Rachel said, 'but you don't exactly look like a P.M. kind of guy.'

'I'm not. It's a long story.'

'Sounds interesting.' Rachel liked hearing stories. It was one of the reasons she'd learned how to tend bar. Overheard conversations morphed into ideas that transformed into written words.

'Not really. Hey, don't I know you from somewhere? You look familiar.'

'Wow,' she said. 'You're really going to need better material if you're going for P.M.'

'Look at me. I'm in a Ford Taurus, for God's sake. I'm in no position to try a line. You really do look familiar.' He snapped his finger at the recognition. 'You make an excellent margarita. Mesa Grill.'

'Mesa Grill,' she confirmed, rubbing her arms for warmth.

'That smoking ban's harsh in winter. Here, hop in.' The man nodded toward the passenger seat.

'Do I look like the kind of girl who jumps into cars with strangers?'

The man shifted his weight to the left, pulled out a wallet with his right hand, and flipped it open. She took a close look at it.

'See? I'm legit. That long story behind my going to P.M.? I'm out here checking out the clubs on official duty. I'm dreading it. You're freezing. The least I can do for a woman who made me such a memorable margarita is to let you finish your smoke in my warm car. Then we'll both get on with our lives.'

She had a good half of a cigarette to go, and she *was* freezing.

When she got into the car, she nearly hit her head on the flipped-down sun visor.

'Here, let me get that for you.' When the man reached across the car with his left arm, she saw the blur of a piece of fabric in his hand, then immediately felt a wet towel pressed hard against her face. She felt her seat

308

recline abruptly. As she lost consciousness, she wondered who would call her father. She wondered if she would ever get a chance to finish that scene she was working on – the one in which she had hoped he would find the secret meaning.

The man flicked Rachel's cigarette out the window and pulled into traffic on Ninth Avenue.

Part IV
The Final Victim

Chapter Thirty-Seven

'Morning, Manny. Can I get a large coffee? No room. And a lemon Danish.'

'No room. You really think I need a reminder on that? Every morning of every day, you get a large coffee, no room. I got it now. We're good for life, sweetheart.'

'You're my kind of person to be good with, Manny.' Ellie didn't mind that the older man behind the deli counter called her sweetheart instead of the official titles he used with the other cops. She'd realized a long time ago that the occasional harmless byproducts of tradition actually made it easier for men of a certain generation to accept her.

Her cell vibrated at her waist. According to the screen, it was another call from Peter, the second already this morning, and it was only eight o'clock.

She'd called him last night when she'd gotten home from St. Vincent's. Just as Jess had predicted, Peter had an explanation for everything. He had only kept his profile on the First Date site because he thought it might come in handy while researching the book. He had only mentioned her to the Simon & Schuster editor as he was explaining why he was having second thoughts about the project.

An hour into the call, Ellie felt like she was on duty, interrogating a suspect who believed he could talk his way out of anything. She'd ended the conversation by telling him she needed a break. Peter had acquiesced, but he clearly had a different definition of the word. Just as she had earlier, she let the call go to voice mail. Once again, there was no beep alerting her to a new message.

Manny passed her a tall cup of coffee across the counter. 'What'd you do to yourself there? Those boys at the precinct aren't beating up on you, are they?'

She held up her hand, still wrapped in white gauze. 'Shark bite. Can you believe it? Jumped right out of the Hudson River.'

'Ah, we got a smart aleck over here now. Get a load of you, a shark bite.'

'It was just a misunderstanding yesterday. I'm fine.'

'The bad guy got it worse?'

Manny had enough cops go through here to know the lingo.

'That goes without saying.'

'Well, if you're gonna walk around with that humongous bandage on your hand, you need to work on your stories. The best tall tales are the ones you might actually believe are the truth.'

Ellie found herself thinking about Manny's words during the two-block walk to the precinct. She thought about Chelsea Hart, Lucy Feeney, Robbie Harrington, and Alice Butler. She replayed Rogan's argument that

Chelsea was different: *They were all pretty rough city chicks. Hard-knock-life, round-the-way girls, not wide-eyed college students from Indiana.* She thought about the murder of Darrell Washington just one day after he'd used Jordan McLaughlin's stolen credit card at the Union Square Circuit City.

By the time she was at her desk, retrieving her Danish from its greasy paper bag, she had decided that her jumbled thoughts at least warranted a phone call. She used the heel of her bandaged palm to flip through the pages of her notepad.

An electronic voice informed her that Jordan McLaughlin's cell phone had been disconnected. She tried Stefanie Hyder's number instead and got an answer.

'Hello?' It was barely seven o'clock in Indiana, but Stefanie sounded alert.

'It's Detective Ellie Hatcher from the NYPD. How are you holding up?'

'It's been pretty rough. You know what happened to us on Wednesday?'

'I heard. That must have been awful.'

'It's not like it was anything compared to Chelsea, but the whole reason we'd gone to the museum was to read this poem she liked in front of the place she had thought was so magical when we went before – well, you know. And then to have it ruined like that . . . We didn't get a good look at the guy. It's like all either of us could see in that moment was the gun.'

'Did someone from the department notify you that they found Jordan's stolen credit card at another crime scene?'

'Yeah, we got a call last night right after we landed. We were pretty freaked out by the whole thing.'

'It's probably good that you were finally able to go home. I was actually calling to follow up on something you mentioned the other day. You said Chelsea had a way of making up stories about herself?'

Ellie could hear the smile in Stefanie's voice. 'That was a classic Chelsea move. She didn't do it to be mean, but if someone really cheesy was hitting on her or something, she'd weave some crazy identity out of thin air.'

'Like what?'

'Whatever happened to strike her as funny. She told some guy at a diner our first morning in the city that we were there to audition for the Martha Graham Dance Company. By the time she was done talking, she had described some elaborate improv thing we were supposedly doing with bar stools. Other times, she'd say she was a stripper. When we were in high school, she'd tell people we were lesbian runaways.'

'Do you think she may have made up one of these stories the night she was killed?'

Stefanie paused. 'Not at Pulse. I heard her talking to a couple of guys about Indiana.'

Ellie remembered Tony Russo, Nick Warden's monogamous financial analyst friend, mentioning the Hoosiers when she had shown him Chelsea's picture.

'What about earlier in the night? At the restaurant?'

'Yeah. Maybe. The bar was crowded, and I know she wandered off to the bathroom at one point.'

'But you don't know who she might have talked to?'

'No. What's this all about? She met that Jake Myers at Pulse, not the restaurant.'

'I know. We're just making sure we didn't miss anything. Does Jordan still have that picture of the three of you from that night?'

'No. Her phone was in her purse when it got stolen, and most of our pictures from the trip were in there.'

'Do you know if she backed it up beforehand, or sent it to someone else?'

While Stefanie talked to Jordan in the background, Ellie opened Photoshop on her computer. Damn. Just as she thought.

'She doesn't have it anymore,' Stefanie said, 'and the only people she sent it to were you and that guy at the newspaper.'

Ellie flipped through the mess sprawled across her desk and plucked out a copy of the *Sun*'s first article about Chelsea's death. She looked at the byline.

'Was that David Marsters?'

More talking between the two girls.

'She says that's the guy.'

Ellie thanked Stefanie for her time, then made a quick call to the *New York Sun*. She got lucky: Marsters was at his desk. After a quick introduction, she gave him her cover story.

'Sorry to bug you, but the DA's office liked that picture you ran of Chelsea Hart and wants to get a copy of it for trial. Do you still have it?'

'Just a sec. Yep, it's right here on my computer. Want me to e-mail it to you?'

'That would be great.' She gave him her address. 'Do

you happen to have the original that Jordan McLaughlin gave you?'

'Hold on. Nope, I plugged her phone right into my laptop. I've only got the version I saved after I cropped it.'

'No problem. I'm sure the DA planned to crop it around the victim's face anyway.'

Ellie had followed the same process as Marsters. Instead of creating a separate file to crop Jordan's original photograph, she had cropped the only copy she had on her computer, then saved the changes to the same file. She vaguely recalled the faces of bystanders in the background of the original picture, but with the theft of Jordan's iPhone, there was no way to recover the complete image.

She made another call, this time to Detective Ken Garcia.

'This is Ellie Hatcher. My lieutenant sent me over yesterday to the LaGuardia Houses.'

'Bandage hand.'

'That's me. I was checking in to see if you have any suspects yet in the Darrell Washington shooting.'

'Nah. Between you and me, my hunch is it'll go down as an unsolved.'

'Did you find any other guns in the apartment?'

'We found the murder weapon. That's usually the one that counts.'

'I know, but my robbery victims said Washington was armed. I'm wondering whether you found the gun he may have used.'

'Good catch. I guess we'll need to look into the possibility he was killed with his own gun.'

As Ellie thanked the detective for his time, she wondered what other possibilities she had overlooked this week.

'How's the hand?' Rogan plopped himself down at his desk.

'Not bad,' she said. 'Okay, brace yourself for another argument with me: I think whoever killed Darrell Washington killed Chelsea Hart.'

'That's the dude from the projects?'

'Think about it. Street crime's down all over the city, especially in Manhattan. Two girls whose friend was murdered just *happen* to get robbed in broad daylight on the Upper East Side? And then the man who did it just *happens* to get shot? That's too many coincidences for me. Someone saw that picture of Chelsea in the *Sun* and realized he could have been in it. He hired Darrell Washington to steal Jordan's cell phone, but knew Washington couldn't be trusted to turn over all the loot. The minute we got a hit on Jordan's credit card, we would've been at Washington's door, asking questions. Our guy killed Washington to make sure there was no link back to him.'

Rogan nodded throughout her monologue, digesting every argument. 'You're making a whole lot of sense, Hatcher.'

'It's about time you came around.'

'All except one thing. Given Jake Myers's current custodial status, he can't be the someone you're talking about, correct?'

'No, but it could easily be Symanski. He could have

gotten to Washington before we showed up at his front door.'

'One problem with that: I just got off the phone with American Express. Capital Research Technologies took a cash advance of a hundred thousand dollars about four and half hours before we arrested Jake Myers for murder. And Myers signed for it, at the Mohegan Sun.'

The casino was at best a two-hour drive from the city. 'So either Myers plowed through a hundred grand in record time –'

'Or he used the company credit card and some casino chips to hide one big-ass payment to someone.'

'Then, lo and behold, two days later, Leon Symanski conveniently steps up and confesses to Chelsea Hart's murder.'

'The baby daddy's the missing link,' Rogan said.

She was picturing the same chain, one leading from Myers to Symanski. The connection between Myers and Nick Warden was clear: between their friendship and the hedge fund, the two men were practically inseparable. Warden was tight with his drug supplier, Jaime Rodriguez. And after last night's sighting of Symanski's pregnant daughter at the hospital, the safe bet was that Rodriguez was the father of Symanski's unborn grandchild. Combined with Myers's quick, covert, and well-timed disposal of a hundred thousand dollars, it all led to one conclusion: Myers had paid Symanski to take the fall for him.

Rogan tapped a ballpoint pen against his palm. 'I guess now we know why Warden wanted a deal for

Rodriguez as part of his cooperation agreement to flip on Myers: that was also part of the quid pro quo.'

'It also explains why Symanski was so evasive when we asked about the girl we saw at his house. If we'd gone to her, we might've found Rodriguez and started drawing the same connections.' Ellie shook her head. 'Jesus. First Rodriguez knocks up Symanski's daughter, then he asks him to go down for a murder he didn't commit?'

'Maybe he didn't ask him. Rodriguez spent a night in jail when we popped him on the drug charge. Symanski's daughter couldn't have been happy about that. She shows up back at Daddy's house, crying about the father of her child heading upstate for six to nine as a repeat drug offender. Daddy sees the chance to be a hero before he powers down in a few months anyway from the melathemiona.'

'Mesothelioma.'

Rogan rolled his eyes. 'Plus, you're going to love this. I was picturing how it must have all gone down, and I kept coming back to Nick Warden's smoking-hot lawyer.'

'Susan Parker.'

'Exactly. The junior associate at a law firm that doesn't even handle criminal defense. But she's the one who told us Warden wanted a deal not just for himself, but also Rodriguez. And she was the one who brought Rodriguez to us at the courthouse, pointing the finger at Symanski.'

'You think she was in on it, too?'

'I went to her law firm's Web site. Turns out she graduated from Cornell.'

'Jake Myers's alma mater.'

'Right again. She graduated one year ahead of him. They were both members of some club called the Entrepreneur Society. I still haven't figured out whose idea this was, but she should have known about it. They all did, every link in the chain.'

'Damn it,' Ellie said. 'Symanski was looking good for it all.'

'But now we're back to Myers – who couldn't have started killing nearly ten years ago.'

'You certainly had a busy morning while I was wasting my time trying to pull up the lost background of a photograph from the computer vortex. You didn't happen to cure cancer while you were at it, did you?'

'No. I'm saving that for the afternoon, but I do have a health tip for you.' He eyed the half-eaten pastry on her desk. 'Did it ever dawn on you to watch what you eat? You aren't *that* young.'

'I watch what I eat every day, right before I pop it into my pie hole.'

'Hatcher.'

Ellie looked up to see Lieutenant Eckels standing at his office door on the perimeter of the squad room.

'Morning, boss.'

'How's that hand?'

'A lot better. Thanks.'

'A word with you both?'

He closed his office door without waiting for confirmation.

'You hear that? He asked about my injury. My lieutenant cares about my well-being.' She used her good hand to fan away fake tears of emotion. 'I'm *verklempt.*'

'You really think Simon Knight saved your ass, don't you?'

'He said he would last night.'

'You know Eckels could be calling us in there to pull you off this case for good, right? He seems damn chipper about something.'

'Only one way to find out.'

'Where are we on this Symanski clusterfuck?'

Rogan gave Eckels a rundown on the previous night's events, carefully avoiding any mention of Ellie's presence at the hospital. He also walked him through Myers's hundred-thousand-dollar cash advance and their theory about the agreement between Myers and Symanski, all facilitated by Susan Parker.

'Now this, I like. Both guilty. Myers of the murder. Symanski of obstruction. We can get everyone in between as accomplices to the obstruction. Prove it, and we might actually come out of this OK.'

No department ever wanted to admit that they'd arrested an innocent man, but having to make such an admission about a rich kid like Myers would be even more costly – both in reputation and money.

'You're on board with all this, Hatcher?'

'I'm not working the case for now, but, yeah, Rogan's obviously on to something.'

'What do you mean, you're not working the case?'

'I was told last night that you wanted me off –'

'I sent you home because any cop needs a night off

after being torpedoed in an alley by a cutter. Are you saying you want off the case?'

'No. Not at all.'

'Good, because it's yours. Yours and Rogan's. Always has been. I'm sorry if you misunderstood that. Now, does this mean you're off that nonsense about McIlroy's cold cases?'

'We're working the Chelsea Hart case. I get that.'

Of course, if other files turned out to be relevant to the Hart investigation, she'd chase the evidence wherever it led. But she was beginning to wonder herself if the similarities she'd seen among the four murders had in fact been, in Eckels's words, nonsense.

'One more thing, guys. I spoke to Simon Knight earlier this morning.'

Ellie resisted the temptation to throw a smile in Rogan's direction.

'Since both Myers and Symanski are in custody, we've got to work this thing closely with the DA's office as they make their charging decisions. From now on, you'll be working directly with Knight and his assistant through the DA's Homicide Investigation Unit.'

'What does that mean exactly?' Rogan asked.

'I want you to treat them like your chain of command. Is that a problem?'

They both shook their heads, but Rogan didn't look happy about it.

'Very well, then. Don't be surprised when I'm still on your ass. I want updates.'

'Not a problem, sir,' Ellie said, before they both left the office.

'Holy shit,' Rogan said once they were at a safe distance. 'Everything last night was a so-called *misunderstanding*? You weren't kidding about Knight being smooth.'

'Downright silky.'

'Don't get too excited. What's that saying about out of the frying pan and into the fire?'

'All I know is that we need to call the rest of the dream team and tell them we want to have a word with Susan Parker.'

Ellie's phone buzzed. She checked the screen, worried it would be Peter again, but it was Jess.

'What's up?'

'I just got a call from Candy at Vibrations.'

'Oh, and I'm sure that's her real name.'

'They found a body in the parking lot last night.'

Her smile faded. 'One of the girls?'

'No, it's not that. It's – it's those files you were reading on the couch the other night. I thought you ought to know.'

'What is it, Jess?'

'When Candy called, she said the girl was all cut up and that her hair looked like part of a costume.'

Chapter Thirty-Eight

'Hank Dodge.' The detective waiting for Ellie in the medical examiner's office was probably in his late fifties. Tall. Bulky. Scruffy gray hair and a five-day beard. When she had called him to track down the details of the body discovered the previous night at Vibrations, he had insisted on being present if she were going to view the victim. 'Dr. Karr was just telling me he'd already met you.'

Ellie recognized the bearded pathologist who had conducted the autopsy on Chelsea Hart. She shook hands with both men.

'You were cutting it close on timing, Detective Hatcher. I was just about to start the autopsy when you phoned Detective Dodge.'

'I think that's the doc's polite way of saying he hopes you had a good reason for asking us to wait.'

'My brother works at the club where your victim was found. It sounded like there were similarities between this case and the Hart murder.'

'Your brother works at a titty bar?' Dodge asked.

'Long story.' It wasn't, really. The job at Vibrations

was the first Ellie could remember Jess holding down for two months straight. 'My impression is that any similarities had to do with the appearance of their bodies. That's why I was hoping to see the vic before the postmortem.'

'You want the basics first, or should we just head to the body?'

'The basics would be great.'

'Victim's name was Rachel Peck. Twenty-six-year-old white female. Works as a bartender. On-and-off party girl. Her girlfriend called police last night at one a.m. after Peck went out for a smoke and never came back.'

'Went out from where?'

'Some club.'

'It wasn't a place called Pulse, was it?' she asked.

The fact that Chelsea Hart had met Jake Myers at Pulse had been widely reported in the press, and Dodge could see where Ellie was headed.

'No,' he said firmly. 'Some joint called Tenjune.'

Ellie was familiar with it. 'In the Meatpacking District. Three blocks from Pulse.'

'You know how many kids are partying within a three-block radius in that neighborhood? This particular kid told her friend she was going for a smoke and never came back. As you can imagine, the friend's call – along with a hundred others just like it – got the blow-off at dispatch. Peck's body got called in at four a.m. from your brother's fine establishment.'

'Any witnesses?'

'Nope. She was behind a Dumpster at the back of the lot. The way the lot's situated, a car could pull in behind the Dumpster, ditch a body, and spin right back onto the West Side Highway. As long as they were fast enough, it would look like a car pulling in just to turn around. We do, however, have a suspect.'

Ellie's surprise must have registered on her face.

'I tried telling you on the phone,' Dodge said. 'But you were in such a hurry to get down here, I figured, what the hell. As we speak, my partner's holding one Hayden Holden Hammond, the victim's ex-boyfriend.'

'Hayden . . . Holden . . . Hammond?'

'Yeah, we'll see how cute the parents find the alliteration when their kid becomes known as the new Preppy Murderer. Not to mention the instant hit he'll be in prison.'

'You're sure it's him?'

Dodge nodded. 'The girlfriend who reported Peck missing says the two had a messy breakup earlier this week. She finally clued in that he was a cheater and a cokehead, and he got a little rough with her when she broke it off. When we found him this morning, he was coked through the ceiling and his apartment looked like he'd been on a three-day bender. I wouldn't be surprised if we had a confession within the hour.'

'Are you ready to meet Miss Peck?' Karr asked. Ellie nodded, and Karr led the way through the large, sterile room. As they passed two other covered bodies on stainless steel tables, she tried to rein in her curiosity. She had enough corpses to think about as things stood.

When they arrived at the third table, Karr stopped and folded down the white sheet.

'Dr. Karr was telling me a little bit about your case

before you got here. Based on what he told me, I think your brother might've missed the mark when he called you. About the only commonality is that they were both strangled. And, as you can see, my vic's still got all her hair. Our biggest problem with her body's going to be getting rid of it. When we called her father out in Idaho, he made it clear he wouldn't be coming to claim her.'

Ellie was listening to Dodge's words, but she could not take her eyes from Rachel Peck. She didn't need the medical examiner to explain the obvious signs of manual strangulation – the bruises around the woman's neck, the bloating in her face and eyes. But she did not agree that the similarities between Rachel Peck and Chelsea Hart ended there.

Rachel had been spared the repetitive cuts that had been etched into Chelsea Hart's entire body, but her face had been the target of the same kind of short, deep stab wounds – one hatched across each of her cheek-bones, along with a series of vertical and horizontal marks on her forehead.

But it was the hair that disturbed her most. Rachel's long, dark blond hair had been pulled into two girlish pigtails on either side of her face. Her bangs were thick and choppy – nothing like the soft, fashionable fringe that so many women were wearing these days.

Something about the look tugged at the back of Ellie's brain, but she couldn't quite pull from her memory whatever past image was troubling her. She did, however, know that something was very wrong.

'She may have all her hair, but look at it.'

'What about it?' Dodge asked.

'The stripper who called my brother said it looked like part of a costume. You can't see that?'

'I don't understand half the silly things women do in the name of fashion. Aren't bell bottoms back in?'

Ellie looked at Dr. Karr for support, but got nothing in return but a blank stare.

'No sane woman in Manhattan went to Tenjune looking like that. And if she did, she certainly didn't get in. Did you ask Rachel's friend whether she wore her hair this way when they went out?'

'She hasn't come in for the official ID yet. We found Peck's credit card in her front pocket. Got her DMV photo from there.'

'You need to get the friend down here.'

'Look, I let you come here because I figured if you wanted to waste your time, it was up to you. But don't barge in here accusing me of missing the boat because I didn't chat up the victim's friends about whether she was having a bad hair day. This is the real world, sweetheart, not a scene out of *Legally Blonde*.'

Sweetheart. The same term of endearment that she'd actually appreciated this morning from Manny the coffee guy lost all appeal in this context. Ellie forced herself to maintain a level tone. 'I apologize that it came across that way. There are other aspects to the Hart case that you would have no reason to know about. One of the angles we're looking into is the possibility our killer's a hair fetishist.'

'Isn't your killer already in custody?'

'Yes, we have a suspect. But we're also looking at some older cases. It's just an angle. But, I'm telling you,

330

as a woman, you're going to find out that your victim's hair did *not* look like that when she left the house with her friend.'

'Fine,' Dodge said, apparently mollified for the time being. 'We'll look into it. My guess is maybe she put it that way for some kinky schoolgirl fantasy that she and Hammond were acting out before the reunion went bad. Or maybe Hammond did it to her while he was coked up. What I do know is that we've got the right guy, and that he was high enough to have done just about anything. Take a look at these marks.'

He waved her over so they were standing by the victim's head, looking at her body upside down. 'See those cuts on her forehead? H-three. Hayden Holden Hammond. That cocksucker left us a calling card.'

Ellie could see the pattern now among what had originally looked like random lines. Three vertical marks. Four horizontal ones.

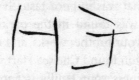

'One thing I will say,' Dr. Karr said, 'is that these cuts to Rachel Peck could have been made – and I emphasize the words *could have been* – by the same knife used on Chelsea Hart. They're of the same approximate width. My guess is a blade of about one and a half to two inches in both instances. Sharp, of course. We don't know how long, since the cuts were inflicted by slicing into the skin rather than deep plunges.'

'Sounds like eighty percent of the knives you'd find in any kitchen,' Dodge said.

'Fair enough,' Karr said with a nod. 'But I thought it was something I should share with you both. The other similarity, of course, is the manual strangulation, but you already knew that. As for anything else, that remains for the autopsy I am still waiting to begin.'

Ellie took the hint for what it was. 'Thank you for holding off on my account. You've got photographs of her in the event I need them later?'

'Of course.'

She had begun to make her way to the exit when she heard Dr. Karr behind her.

'You and your brother might want to be careful in the coming days,' he said.

'How so?' she said, turning around.

'No black cats or walking under ladders.'

Ellie still didn't understand.

'I'm sorry. That was in poor taste. It's just that this young woman was found in the parking lot of the business where your brother works, and I seem to recall that the two of you found Chelsea Hart while you were out jogging. I guess your family is another thing the victims have in common.'

And, with that, Ellie looked down at Rachel Peck's body and saw the marks on her forehead from a different angle and in a whole new light.

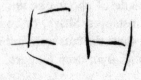

332

Dodge had seen H 3. Hayden Holden Hammond. But, right side up, the marks made an even clearer pattern: EH. Ellie Hatcher.

This woman had been dumped behind Vibrations, where Jess worked. Jess lived with her. He was sure to tell her about it. Chelsea Hart's body was left at the turnaround point on her regular running route – the route she and Jess took every day, at least five days a week, and never missed two days in a row. She'd been killed the morning after they had skipped a day. Chelsea's cell phone alarm had been set for 5:32 in the morning. It had been set to ensure they'd find the body.

As her own initials stared at her from the forehead of poor Rachel Peck, Ellie realized where she had seen the woman's awkward hairstyle before: that stupid fifth-grade class photograph that Jess had plastered throughout her apartment last year. The one for which she'd attempted to cut her own hair. The one that had been published in so many of the reports about her childhood.

Chapter Thirty-Nine

Ellie bypassed the crowd at the courthouse elevators and took the stairs to the trial unit on the seventh floor. She was still trying to catch her breath when the receptionist informed her that Mr. Knight was on the fifteenth floor in the Homicide Investigation Unit with ADA Donovan. This time, she opted for the elevator.

Her cell buzzed during the wait. According to the screen, it was Peter. Again. Add that to the call she'd received in the car, and this was now four calls before ten-thirty in the morning. If he didn't at least leave a message soon, he was about two attempts short of a serious conversation about restraining orders.

Ellie checked in with a receptionist at the Homicide Investigation Unit and was led to a conference room, where she found Simon Knight and Max Donovan seated across from each other at a cherry-veneer table, Rogan leaning against the matching credenza next to them.

'Excellent timing,' Knight said. 'I've just gotten off the phone with Celina Symanski. She has agreed to meet you and Rogan at her father's house in an hour.

We figured she'd be more likely to break than Rodriguez or Susan Parker. We'll work our way through the chain from there.'

'Very good,' Ellie said.

'Your partner told us you had a family emergency. I hope everything is under control.'

Rogan let out a small cough, and Ellie immediately filled in the blanks. Rogan was supposed to have informed Knight and Donovan about the body found at Vibrations, but he had held back in the event that the new case had nothing to do with their investigation. As he'd said, 'We don't give so-called exculpatory evidence to prosecutors.'

She was done with that tactic. She'd withheld her suspicions long enough. McIlroy had been onto something three years ago when he pulled those cold case files. When Chelsea Hart had been murdered, even Bill Harrington from his Long Island living room had sensed there was a connection. And now Rachel Peck's body had convinced her.

But she was not like McIlroy. She was not going to keep this to herself. She might actually get somewhere if she trusted others to help. Maybe if McIlroy had worked his theory with a partner, Chelsea Hart and Rachel Peck would still be alive.

'My family emergency was a call from my brother. They found a body last night where he works, at a bar off the West Side Highway. The woman's name was Rachel Peck. She was last seen at a club in the Meatpacking District, just three blocks away from Pulse. Like Chelsea Hart, she was manually strangled. She also had the same kinds of cuts across her face, and the ME says the same knife could have been used on both girls.'

'What the hell are you getting at?' Knight said. 'We just spent the last hour with your partner coming back to terms with our case against Jake Myers. You're telling me we've got another body to look at?'

'Another four, actually. A detective I worked with on a special assignment, Flann McIlroy –'

'I knew McIlroy,' Knight said.

'A few years ago, Flann was looking at three cold cases. All young women. All killed after late nights out.' She went on to explain Flann's theory that they were all connected by a single killer who collected the victims' hair, as well as how Chelsea Hart and Rachel Peck fit into the same pattern.

'Why are we just hearing about this?'

Knight must have noticed the look exchanged between Ellie and Rogan. He also understood its significance. 'Ah, I see. Another one of those situations where the police think it's better not to let the DAs know too much.'

'It sounded far-fetched until this morning,' Ellie said. 'Rachel Peck changes that. We've now got the three cold cases, plus two girls in the last week. Same pattern. Five girls, all within ten years.'

'And I still don't see the pattern,' Rogan said. 'The victims don't fit the same socioeconomic profile. We've got three murders all within a few years of each other, then we have nothing for six straight years. Now we've got two bodies in one week? Why the break? And the pattern with the hair isn't really a pattern. He chops off all of Chelsea Hart's hair, but leaves Rachel Peck's.'

'I agree with you that Chelsea wasn't living on the fringe the way the other girls were. But, remember, she had a habit of making up stories about herself. If she met someone at Luna, she could have made herself sound more like the other victims. And if whoever she met that night realized that Jordan McLaughlin might have caught him in the background of the picture taken at the bar, that would explain the very uncomfortable coincidence of her phone being stolen by a man who just happened to get killed himself the very next day.'

She had to back up to fill Knight and Donovan in on Darrell Washington's murder and the discovery of merchandise in his apartment that was purchased with Jordan's stolen credit card. She could tell they were having a hard time processing all of the new information.

'As for the hair, if he's a fetishist, it's not the process of cutting the hair that might be important to him. It's having the hair itself after the girls are dead. It's about having a souvenir. And look at the patterns within the patterns. The first of all the killings was Lucy Feeney. Her hair was hacked off, just like Chelsea Hart. The next was Robbie Harrington, where he cut only the bangs, just like Rachel Peck. The next was Alice Butler, where he may have somehow collected her hair after she had it cut at the hairdresser's, or maybe he only snipped a few pieces. But, each time, he was more subtle as he gained more control, trying to obscure the similarities. Now, he reemerges, and follows the same pattern.'

'So why does he reemerge, as you put it?' Donovan asked. There was no skepticism in his tone, but Ellie

337

wondered whether his formal demeanor was a sign of disappointment in her.

'Maybe he was out of state. Maybe in prison for something else. But there's another possibility, and this really is where I'm afraid I may sound insane. This is my first week in the homicide unit. I got that assignment after working an extremely high-profile investigation with Flann McIlroy two months ago – his last case, as we all know.'

Their eyes were all on her. They were following her but had no idea where she was taking them.

'I'm the one who found Chelsea Hart. She was on my regular running path. The alarm on her cell phone was set to go off right around the time I usually pass that spot. Rachel Peck was left where my brother works. Take a look at the incisions on Rachel Peck's forehead.' She dropped a printout of the photograph she'd snapped at the ME's office on the conference room table. 'Am I crazy?'

'Are those your initials?' Donovan asked.

'That's what I'm wondering.'

Rogan exhaled loudly.

'And look at Rachel's hair. There's a picture of me from when I was ten years old where my hair looks just like that. It was on *Dateline*. It was in *People* magazine. I'm more than a little embarrassed by the number of people who've seen me with precisely this hairstyle.'

Rogan cut in. 'We've got about half an hour before we're supposed to meet Celina Symanski in Queens. Did you forget that we have evidence *proving* that Jake Myers bribed a man to give us a false confession? We have Jake Myers's DNA on the victim. We *know* for a fact who killed Chelsea Hart.'

'Or else Jake Myers is innocent but wasn't so confident he'd get acquitted,' Ellie said.

'You two are making my head hurt,' Knight said. 'I'm trying to process the implications of what you're saying, Hatcher. If we've got a serial on our hands, it's someone with a beef against you?'

'As unsettling as that is, yes, that's what I'm beginning to think.'

'Any ideas as to who that person could be?'

She shook her head.

'No, of course not. Plus, it's someone who would have to know how to find the girl with the camera phone.'

'Jordan McLaughlin. Yes, I suppose that's right.' She was realizing that she sounded even crazier than she'd been prepared for. 'He'd have to know where Jordan was staying in the city, and then Darrell Washington could have followed them to the museum from there.'

Rogan shook his head.

'The two of you better go if you're going to make it to Astoria,' Knight said.

'So that's it? You're just ignoring everything I said?'

'No, Detective, because that's not how we work here. We're going to look at it all. That's what we have to do once something's been brought to our attention, which is why it wasn't raised with us earlier, I suspect. But first we need to nail down what Jake Myers did with his hundred thousand dollars. We can force the Mohegan Sun to pull video of Myers leaving with the chips if we

339

have to, but my guess is, you can break the daughter without it. We'll use her for leverage against Susan Parker. We then flip Parker to get another crack at Myers, and then maybe we'll be in a better position to know whether he's our man or not. Unless, of course, you think we have more attractive alternatives.'

'No, sir.'

'Very well. I'm sending Donovan with you. This woman needs to know that her boyfriend's immunity deal on his drug case is in jeopardy because of this bullshit. If a six-year mandatory minimum scared them into a stunt like this, a heart-to-heart about the potential maximums might actually get us the truth. In the meantime, I have obstruction charges to file against Symanski. Until we know what the hell's going on, I don't want either of these men out of our sight.'

Donovan must have sensed from the silence in the elevator that Ellie and Rogan needed a word in private. As they were leaving the courthouse, he found his excuse.

'I need to hit the men's room. Pull the car around, and I'll meet you out front?'

Ellie spoke up as they made their way to the Crown Vic.

'You think I torpedoed you.'

'Nope. If anything, I sandbagged you. We agreed I'd tell them where you went and what you were working on, and I didn't.'

'So what's the problem?'

'Honestly? I think you've got a wild imagination.

Even if those cold cases had something to do with each other, I don't think they've got anything to do with Chelsea Hart, or that girl you saw this morning. And I know for damn sure they don't have anything to do with some personal beef against you.'

Rogan's cell phone jingled. 'Damn it,' he said, eyeing the screen. 'It's Eckels.'

'Yeah, Lou . . . Hold on, I'm pulling into traffic.' He held the phone against his palm. 'I knew he'd bird-dog us,' he whispered to Ellie. 'He already wants an update.'

And then Ellie listened with as much gratitude as she could muster as her partner, despite his personal feelings, tried his best not to make her sound crazy.

They were waiting for Max Donovan at the curb in front of the courthouse when Ellie recognized the man crossing Centre Street. She watched as he pulled his cell phone from his pocket and flipped it open. A second later, her own phone vibrated.

'Un-fucking-believable.' She was out of the car before Rogan could ask for an explanation. She flipped open her phone. 'I'm twenty feet behind you,' she said.

Peter Morse was smiling when he turned to greet her, but his expression changed once he saw her face.

'How many times do you plan on calling me? I told you last night I needed some space, and this is how you respond?'

'Wow. I had no idea you were this angry at me.'

'So now I'm the problem. You get to write a book about me. You get to mislead me about your plans. You apparently even get to surf the Net for other women.

341

But when I say I need a break – and that's all I asked for, was just some time and space – then I'm angry, bitchy Ellie. That's really fair, Peter.'

'I just want to talk to you. This book is my chance to get somewhere as a writer. If you would just try to look at this from my perspective –'

'I can't do that right now, okay? And I explained that to you last night.'

'I hate the way we left things. Can we please just sit down and have a conversation about this?'

'No, we can't. We can talk when we're both ready. And your calling me over and over again does not help get me to a place where I want to talk things through with you.'

He raked his fingers through his hair, clearly frustrated.

'Damn it. I can't believe I have to ask you what I'm about to ask you.'

'What are you talking about?'

'My boss is a fucking asshole. Kittrie wanted me to call you this morning. I was trying to get around it, and he figured out we're having some problems. So now he's taking some perverse pleasure in my discomfort.'

'Jesus. You're about to ask me about the case, aren't you?'

He pressed his lips together.

'Go ahead and spit it out.'

'There was a body found last night at some strip club on the West Side Highway.' It dawned on Ellie that Peter hadn't spent enough time with her brother even to know where he worked. 'The girl's friend said she wandered off from Tenjune. I'm covering it, but Kittrie wants to write a separate piece. It's those cold cases you mentioned the other night. The ones Flann McIlroy was digging around in.'

Ellie felt a vein in her head starting to throb. She knew she shouldn't have mentioned those cases to Peter. She shouldn't have called George Kittrie. He wouldn't have connected the dots on his own.

'He's going to speculate about a connection?'

Peter nodded. 'He's working on it now. The three old cases. Chelsea Hart. Rachel Peck from this morning. I really hate this, Ellie, but he's my boss, and you *know* what an ass he is.'

'Tell him you were a good boy who did precisely what he asked of you, and I said "No goddamn comment".'

Chapter Forty

Celina Symanski opened the front door of her father's house before they had a chance to knock. She stepped aside, and they treated the movement as an invitation to come in.

She took a seat in the middle of a small worn sofa in the center of the living room, leaving only a single recliner for her three guests. Ellie helped herself to the spot. She was the obvious candidate to play the good cop in this scenario.

This was Ellie's first opportunity to view the woman without her coat. She wore a hip-length cable-knit sweater and leggings. Both were stretched tight across her belly. She was an otherwise small woman. Young, probably early twenties. Light hair. Fair skin. Ellie's best guess was that the baby would be coming in a couple of months.

'I'm Detective Hatcher. This is my partner, Detective Rogan. Max Donovan is from the district attorney's office. I think you know why we're here, Celina.'

She shrugged.

'Your father's not a murderer.'

'I never said he was.'

'No, but *he* did. And he did it to protect you. Now it's time for you to step up and protect him.'

'I don't know what you're talking about,' Celina said. So much for guilt.

'What your father's done is going to be all for nothing. We know about the payoff. You won't be able to spend a nickel of that money. In the meantime, Mr. Donovan can tell you about the potential criminal charges.'

Donovan uncrossed his arms and took a step toward Celina, as if preparing to cross-examine a witness. 'We're filing charges against your father this afternoon, not for murder, as he intended, but for obstruction of justice. We also intend to reinstate drug charges against Nick Warden and Jaime Rodriguez.'

That got her attention.

'See,' Ellie said, 'we also know about the father of your child.'

'He made a deal,' Celina said. 'The case got dismissed.'

'It was dismissed,' Donovan explained, 'without prejudice as a condition of Nick Warden's cooperation agreement to testify against Jake Myers. But with evidence that Warden was a part of a conspiracy to pay your father to undermine our case against Myers, I can get a judge to set aside the agreement. That means I can go after Rodriguez.'

He turned to Ellie, and she took it as her cue to jump in. 'And once your father, Jaime, and Nick Warden are codefendants for conspiracy to obstruct justice, who do you think's going to get the plea deal then, Celina? The convicted sex offender and janitor who stabbed a cop, the brown guy with a rap sheet and two prior drug pops, or the rich white hedge fund manager?'

Celina sniffled and wiped away a tear, and Ellie knew that one more push should do it.

'That leaves you and your baby alone,' she continued. 'No father for either of you.'

Celina stared at her with wide eyes. Ellie saw her upper lip quiver. One more push.

'And that's assuming the DA's office doesn't come after you, too. If you were an active participant in this, your kid might be born into the foster care system.'

Celina placed her face in her hands and began crying. The words were hard to decipher between the sobs, but Ellie got the gist of it. Her father. Her baby's father. Her fiancé. Poor them. Poor Celina.

Donovan cut in, and Ellie realized that Knight had made the right call in sending him. Pressure from a cop was one thing, but when it came time for cooperation, nothing worked better than a chat about the power of a prosecutor to determine who went to prison and for how long.

'I'll be in a better position to help everyone involved if we know exactly what happened. At the end of the day, what we really care about is catching Chelsea Hart's killer. All the rest of this is a distraction. The longer the distraction, the heavier the sentence my office is going to be looking for.'

This time when Celina spoke, her words were clear. 'What do you need to know?'

* * *

Susan Parker looked broken. As if a bulb had burned out. The batteries had gone dead. A processor had failed.

Ellie and Rogan were used to hitting defendants with the news that, despite their cagiest plans, they'd been busted. Sitting in Parker's office, however, Max Donovan was the one doing the talking.

Ellie was almost positive that what Donovan was asking of Susan Parker was wildly unethical. She represented Nick Warden, not Jake Myers. Pressuring her to convince her client to approach Jake Myers on their behalf was definitely not kosher. But Donovan had worded his request in a cagey way, so Ellie assumed he knew what he was doing. More importantly, if the DA's office didn't have a problem with it, she certainly wasn't going to object.

'We don't have all day here. Are you going to talk to your client or not?'

Parker's blank stare unfroze with a blink. The parts were turning back on. 'You know you've created a conflict of interest for me now. I should withdraw from my representation of Nick Warden so he can retain separate counsel.'

'You weren't so worried about conflicts of interest when you helped broker a deal for Myers to pay off Leon Symanski to give us a false confession.'

Celina had walked them through each step in the sequence of events. After the drug bust at Pulse, Rodriguez had phoned his girlfriend from the jail with the bad news. Distribution of an eight-ball of meth. With his record, he wouldn't be out until their kid was in first grade. She spent the night crying on her father's sofa.

By dawn, Leon had conjured up a way to solve his daughter's problems. He called Nick Warden's lawyer and proposed a deal. Nick could give the government what they wanted. He could flip on his friend with no remorse, because the so-called real killer would be caught within days. In return, Symanski needed a hundred grand and a walk for the father of his grandchild.

Ellie still didn't understand how a daughter could allow her father to make that kind of a sacrifice, but she'd long ago ceased trying to understand the inner workings of other families.

'I didn't *broker* anything,' Parker said. 'I have an obligation to my client to convey communications made to me in the scope of my representation of him.'

'Not when those communications make you a coconspirator,' Donovan said.

'I had no knowledge of the agreement between my client and Rodriguez. You offered my client a cooperation deal, and he was willing to take it. It is not a lawyer's responsibility to probe a client's motivations.'

'Give me a break,' Donovan said. 'The handover went down in this very office.'

According to Celina, the plan had been her father's idea, but Parker had overseen the details of its execution. Once the charges against Rodriguez were dismissed and he was freed from custody, he had gone directly from the jail to Parker's office. Jake Myers had been waiting for him with a hundred thousand dollars in casino chips and a red chandelier earring for Symanski to plant in his house.

'I am not aware of that,' she said, shaking her head. 'As you already said, I went to college with Jake. He came here to tell me he wasn't involved in that girl's death. Jaime Rodriguez showed up – uninvited, without an appointment – to thank me for getting the deal that he benefited from. If they passed something between them when I stepped out of the office –'

Donovan didn't bother masking his ridicule. 'Are you really ready to sell that story to the partners around here?' He glanced around Parker's office. 'Because I'm picturing you on the street within an hour, juggling all of your personal belongings in a cardboard box, with an ethics complaint brought by this firm against you with the bar. Pushing the boundaries for your white-collar clients is one thing in a place like this, but it won't seem so hunky-dory when it's a murder case at stake. The only way to distance yourself from the dirty laundry is to throw it out yourself. They'll make sure you're disbarred.'

Parker held Donovan's stare. She broke first.

'What do you want?'

'I want Jake Myers to take a polygraph.'

'And how am I supposed to get in touch with Jake?'

Once Parker had agreed to represent Warden, no court in America would have allowed her to simultaneously represent Jake Myers. Any attempt by Parker to contact Myers directly would show up in the jail's records, and she'd then have to explain to Willie Wells why she was contacting his client without his consent.

'You talk to Nick Warden,' Donovan explained. 'He visits Jake in custody. Tells him there's a problem. Convinces him to take the polygraph.'

'As long as you understand he can't make Jake do anything. And I can't make Nick do anything.'

'I understand.'

'Fine,' she said. 'I'll call him now. This all stays in this room? The firm doesn't hear about any of it?'

'You have my word,' Donovan said.

Ellie and Rogan nodded in silent agreement.

For the second time in a week in this same office, a conspiracy had been struck. The first had been to concoct a lie. Now they were conspiring to get the truth.

Chapter Forty-One

Five minutes after Nick Warden visited Jake Myers in custody, Myers called Willie Wells and fired him as his attorney. His next call was to Susan Parker, seeking her representation for the purpose of contacting Simon Knight and offering to take a polygraph examination to clear his name. By the time that call came in, Knight had already lined up the polygrapher.

They all knew, of course, that the so-called lie detecting machine was far less reliable than its name might suggest. The machines were only as good as their operators and, even at their best, were not entirely accurate. But the intangible value of a polygraph transcended the questionable science.

A defendant's willingness to sit for one said something in itself, especially if he managed to make it through an entire examination without breaking into a spontaneous confession. And a good polygrapher's opinion, while no guarantee, would do a lot to confirm the feeling in Ellie's gut that Jake Myers – although guilty of other wrongs – was no murderer.

The process was painstaking, with the most

important components transpiring before Myers was even hooked up to the machine. It started with an open-ended debriefing in which Myers was free to state his version of the facts – at his pace, in his own words. Then he was subjected to detailed questioning from Ellie, Rogan, and Donovan, until all three were satisfied they had asked every possible question that might trip Myers up.

Only after the conversation had been exhausted did the polygrapher hook Myers up to the instruments that would measure his physiological responses during innocuous inquiries such as 'Is your name Jake Myers?' and money questions like 'Did you cause the death of Chelsea Hart?' By the time the polygrapher announced that he had detected no signs of deception, Ellie could already replay the scene between Chelsea Hart and Jake Myers in her head.

'Holy shit. What the fuck did you give me?'

When Chelsea had snorted the line of whatever Jake had passed her in the VIP lounge, she had assumed it was cocaine. She'd tried it twice before and thought she could handle it, but tonight something was different. Whatever the powder had been, Jake and his friend had done a lot more of it than she had.

'Just a little speed. It's great for a second wind.' It was meth, actually, but he knew a lot of girls freaked out about the name.

Jake placed his arms around Chelsea's waist and pulled her closer on the dance floor. She treated him to a little grind and didn't object when he slipped his hands beneath the back of her shirt. His palms felt good against her bare skin, but she knew it was time for her to wrap things up before they went too far. She had promised Stefanie she'd be just behind them, and she knew what a worrywart her friend could be.

Chelsea pulled playfully on Jake's skinny black tie and leaned in so he could hear her over the music. 'I hate to be a tease, but it's time for me to go.'

He tried to persuade her to stay, just as they both knew that he would. She looked at her watch. Just past three a.m. 'Look at it this way,' she said. 'You let me leave now, and you've got an entire hour to line up one of these little sluts to go home with you. Waste all your time on me and, well, you and your friend there are on your own –'

She pushed up against him again.

'Damn, you're hot,' he said, kissing her neck and fingering the top button of her blouse.

'Occasionally. Want me to pick out a girl for you, or are you going to be fine on your own?'

Jake smirked and shook his head. 'Let me at least walk you out.' He took her hand and led her from the club. 'Do you have a car?'

Town cars and limos were parked and double-parked outside. 'Yeah, right. I used my entire student loan check to pay for a car service while we were in New York this week.'

'My car's in a lot in SoHo,' Jake said. 'Nick's driver's waiting out here somewhere. Let me just run in and check –'

They both knew a ride in his friend's car would start something they'd finish en route to her hotel. She was

353

tempted but decided against it. She'd been faithful to Mark the entire trip and didn't want to mess that up now.

'Really, I'm fine with a cab.'

Jake walked to the curb and tried to hail a taxi, but four yellow cabs passed them by, already taken, their rooftop medallion numbers unlit.

'I'll be fine,' Chelsea finally said.

He ignored her and remained in the street, one arm raised above his head.

'Tick tock, Jake Gyllenhaal. You're wasting that final hour. The other players are locking down all the pretty girls at Pulse as we speak.'

He touched her hair and leaned in for a kiss before thanking her for the fun and turning away. As Chelsea watched him return to the club, she still felt his lips against hers and wondered if it was a feeling of regret about turning down the invitation to go further.

Five more taxis passed her by before one finally stopped. She crawled into the back seat and shut the door. 'The Hilton at Rockefeller Center, please. Fifty-third Street at Sixth Avenue.'

The cab rolled a few feet and then stopped. 'You have cash?'

'Excuse me?'

'You have cash, right?'

'No. I'll pay by Visa.' Chelsea had spent her final bills on that last Angel's Tip at the bar. She was so messed up she'd forgotten about the free liquor in the VIP lounge.

'No credit cards.'

Chelsea knocked on the machine installed on the

354

partition in front of her. 'What's this thing for if you can't take a credit card?'

'It's broken. Only cash tonight.'

'I'll pay you when I get there – my friends have money, I promise.'

'I do not run a loan company, miss. I will not drive you if you do not have the money.'

'Well, I'm not getting out of the cab. What do you think about that?'

'The meter is still running, miss, and you don't have any money. You need to find another taxi.'

Chelsea was startled by a knock against the window. It was Jake.

'My savior,' she said, rolling down the window. 'I don't have any cash, and this asshole won't take my fucking credit card.'

'He wouldn't do that to you, now, would you, kind sir?'

'Tell him, kind sir,' Chelsea said. 'Tell him how you want to strand a girl here on the streets of New York City all by herself.'

'You need to get your drunk friend out of my car,' the driver said.

Jake touched the tip of his chin, as if pondering the situation. 'This is quite a predicament, isn't it?'

Chelsea knew Stefanie hadn't seen the appeal, but this guy really was incredible. The hair and clothes were too much, but the smile – those lazy eyes and the softness around his mouth – were irresistible.

'Can I borrow twenty bucks?' she asked. 'I mean, I know you're hurting for money and all, so I'll be sure to mail it to you from Indiana.'

'I tell you what. Get out of that cab and stay with me a little longer. I'll make sure you get home.'

'I told you I have to go. My flight's in, like, three hours.'

'Fine, here's your money.' He removed a hundred-dollar bill from the money clip in his pocket. Chelsea reached through the window to take it, but Jake snatched his hand back. 'As my father always says, there's no such thing as a handout. You've got to earn this money, young lady.'

Chelsea tilted her head to one side. 'And what would your father propose I do to earn it?'

'That is it,' the driver said. 'Get out of my cab.' He opened his door, and Chelsea knew it was only a matter of seconds before he was going to pull her physically from the car.

She and Jake were still laughing by the time they made their way to the entry stairwell of a basement apartment around the corner.

Chelsea felt the cold concrete against her exposed toes as she dropped to her knees and tried not to think about Mark. This was just a onetime thing. Spring break. New York. Jake Gyllenhaal. It was all a fantasy, and tomorrow, it would be as if nothing happened.

Jake was touching her hair softly at first, but by the time he got close, he was gripping her head firmly with his fingers, guiding her movements. He felt the wire hook in her right earlobe come loose. He did not want it to fall to the ground. Not now. Not at this moment. She might stop what she was doing. He slipped the earring into his pocket and replaced his hand on the back of her head.

When she had finished, he helped her to her feet and gave her a quick peck on the mouth. He loved girls who swallowed, but that didn't mean he needed to put his tongue in there afterward. She laughed when he brushed the dust from the knees of her pants.

'Where's my hundred bucks?' she said.

'Don't be ridiculous. We'll take Nick's car.'

'Don't you be ridiculous. Give me my money, or my pimp's coming after you.'

He slipped a hundred-dollar bill into her purse. 'Let's get you a cab before your pimp says I'm monopolizing you.'

'If I can turn tricks in doorways, I'm perfectly capable of hailing my own cab. And now I even have money to pay. You better get back.'

'You sure?'

'Go on. I mean it.'

He kissed her one more time before walking away. He was nearly back to Pulse when he placed his hands in his coat pockets to warm them. He felt the tiny glass beads of her earring. He thought of turning back to find her, but didn't want to spoil the perfect ending.

Chapter Forty-Two

Rogan looked like he'd just seen William Shatner walk through 100 Centre Street in a hula skirt.

'You figured you were innocent, so it was your God-given right to offer up another innocent man to take your place in prison?' Rogan was still coming to terms with Myers's newfound experimentation with honesty – and he wasn't happy about it.

Jake Myers stared at his hands. He was seated in the same District Attorney's conference room, at the same table, where, just yesterday, Jaime Rodriguez had told them about a club janitor who might be of interest.

Susan Parker was a sleazebag of a lawyer, but she was at least trying to protect her new client from Rogan's outrage. 'Give the guy a break. You had him on a murder he knew he didn't commit, and he freaked out.'

Donovan rose from the table and paced their side of the room. 'You could have told him to come clean, Susan. Instead, you orchestrated this.'

Jake looked up from his hands. 'You were going to send me to fucking prison for the rest of my life. What was I supposed to do?'

'You could have told us the truth that first night we talked to you at Pulse,' Ellie said.

'Fine. So kill me. I made a mistake. A bunch of cops barged into the club and started asking questions about some girl I got a little crazy with. I'd had a couple drinks – and more, as you now know – and I flipped, okay? I didn't see how anything I had to say could even matter. But then all I kept hearing about was the evidence you had against me. The cabdriver. My DNA. The time of death. I had *nothing*. For once, I did a decent thing – I went straight home that night so I wouldn't have to put up with Nick begging me for the details. I had no one to vouch for me.'

'Then along came Symanski,' Ellie said, 'ready to sell his last remaining months to take care of his daughter and unborn grandchild.'

Jake chewed on his lower lip. Without all the hair gel and ridiculous clothing, she could see how Chelsea Hart had found him attractive.

'When Susan first called me, it sounded crazy. But the guy was dying anyway, and he came to me. This wasn't *my* idea. He wanted the money. And when Susan told me he had a prior rape conviction, I figured, better him than me. Once I remembered about the earring, I knew we could use that so you'd believe him.'

'It didn't dawn on you that the person you were helping the most was Chelsea Hart's actual killer?' Ellie said.

He stared at his hands again. 'I wasn't thinking about that.'

'You were only thinking about yourself.'

'Maybe,' he said quietly, before glancing up at her. 'But it's not like you were looking for anyone other than me, were you?'

Rogan leaned across the table and pointed a finger at Myers. 'Don't put this on us.'

Myers slumped into his chair. Any remaining bravado was gone as he looked to Max Donovan with desperate eyes. 'You believe me, right?'

As Ellie scanned the faces in the room, she had no doubt that, at that moment, they all, in fact, believed him.

'Damn it.' Simon Knight slammed his fist against his desk. 'So now I have to explain to the mayor's office why Jake Myers is a free man?'

Donovan started to explain that they'd returned a protesting Myers to custody to face obstruction charges, but Knight waved him off.

'Are we absolutely positive about this? Why did Symanski run if the entire point was to take the blame? The guy stabbed a cop, for Christ's sake.'

Cut, Ellie thought, looking at the white gauze. 'According to his daughter, Symanski panicked. The plan sounded fine in theory, but when we showed up at his house, the thought of living his last months in prison got to him. He figured that as long as we found the earring, Jake would get sprung even if he got away. And once I had him cornered in the alley, he decided he'd rather die right then and there. Suicide by cop.'

'So where are we?' Knight asked. 'We start from scratch?'

'We've got more than you think. We know we've got someone who started killing in the late nineties, almost ten years ago.'

Knight furrowed his brow. 'Why are you so sure Lucy Feeney was his first kill?'

'There's no way to be sure until we find the asshole, but it does fit a pattern. What ties the girls together is the collection of their hair. The victims are all grabbed after going out to the clubs, but my guess is that's not part of anything special to him. It's opportunistic. It allows him to find girls when they're vulnerable. It allows him to hide himself by preying upon that vulnerability in a city where a lot of girls have bad things happen to them at four in the morning. So it's really about the killing and the hair. Lucy Feeney was strangled and also stabbed. She also had her hair blatantly hacked off, like Chelsea Hart.'

'A total release,' Knight said.

'Exactly. No restraint. No fear yet that his MO will be detected. With Robbie Harrington, he strangles her, but does not couple it with stabbing. He's more discreet about the hair, limiting himself to the bangs. He doesn't want police to see the pattern. With Alice Butler, he switches things up again. He stabs her eighteen times. There's some slight bruising on her neck, but he doesn't strangle her. Something about the fact that she got her hair cut short set him off, but my guess is that he still took a souvenir, either by somehow collecting some of the clippings from the salon when she had it cut, or snipping off some small pieces after he killed her – so subtly that no one noticed.'

361

'Then we have a six-year break before Chelsea Hart,' Rogan said.

'Exactly, and six years is a long time. By now, he's no longer worried about law enforcement detecting a pattern. He does what he truly wants. And after six years of controlling himself, he's got a lot of pent-up violence. He strangles her, cuts her up, and hacks off all her hair.'

'Just like Lucy Feeney,' Donovan said.

Ellie nodded. 'That's why I'm fairly confident that we're going to find out that Lucy Feeney was his first. Or if he did kill before, it was in another series preceded by another long break, or it was outside the New York City area.'

'So why the hiatus?' Simon Knight leaned back in his office chair and steepled his fingers beneath his chiseled chin.

She shrugged. 'He could have been in prison for something else. He could have been in some kind of long-term relationship that somehow satisfied his urges. His life could have changed in a way where he no longer needed to kill to feel satisfied.'

William Summer had stopped murdering women in Wichita around the same time he earned a promotion at his job working private security at a gated community in the suburbs. After his arrest, the residents reported a pattern of abuses of Summer's power, such as it was. Armchair psychologists had concluded that the new responsibilities in his job had satisfied his egotistical need for control in a way that only murder previously could.

'But now he's back,' Rogan said, 'and that apparently has something to do with you. He dumps Chelsea Hart where you'll find her, setting her cell phone alarm for added assurances. And he dumps Rachel Peck outside Vibrations, knowing you'll get wind of it from your brother.'

It felt good to hear her partner articulate the theory aloud. No cynicism. No sarcasm.

'And he messes with Rachel's hair to send a message to me. This is where we're way past starting from scratch.'

'Because, as lovable as you are, only so many people can be jonesing to fuck with you this hard.'

'Or one would hope,' Ellie said. 'I've only been on the job five years, and until a couple of months ago, I was working fraud cases. I only got major time on a handful of creeps, and most of those are still in the pen.'

Simon Knight followed the implications. 'So we need to look at your old cases and look for enemies who went to prison after the Alice Butler murder, who recently got sprung.'

'There's a shot. I've been thinking about this, though, and there's another possibility.'

Ellie paused, making sure she had their complete attention.

'Our guy could be a cop.' She watched the surprise register on all three faces, particularly Rogan's. With him, it was more than hearing the unexpected. It was the shock of a slap to the face. 'I don't like this theory. At all. But I keep coming back to the timing. I got my assignment to the homicide unit a month ago. I was actually working in the squad for only a week before Chelsea Hart turned up on my running path. He wants to engage us. He wants us to know that after hiding his pattern for so long, he's coming out to play. And it seems like the person he really wants to play with is me – and I was warned going in that other cops would resent my assignment to homicide.'

'The coming out to play is what's been tripping me up,' Rogan said. 'He bobs and weaves, denying himself the cutting that seems to define his MO. But now he drops a billboard in your front yard.'

'So the question is, why is he upping the ante after getting away with it for so long? One possibility is, it's a bad guy I put away in the past. But it's awfully coincidental that when they get sprung from custody, I just happen to be in the homicide unit, where I can catch the new cases. Another possibility is that we've got a cop who stopped for some reason but has now decided to kill again as a way to challenge me.'

'He *was* clean as a whistle with Chelsea Hart,' Rogan said.

'Right. The only physical evidence we found on her pointed us to Jake Myers. One of the lead detectives on Rachel Peck's case tells me there's no physical evidence with her, at least so far. And I've seen the files on Feeney, Harrington, and Butler – no blood, no semen, no hairs. This guy is good. And he knows the pattern of city homicides. He knows he can obscure the serial nature of his murders by committing them at night, against drunken party girls, who go down in the books as unsolveds – lessons to be learned by others.'

'Any suggestions on where to look in the NYPD for a person like this?' Knight asked.

'Don't look at me,' Rogan said. 'Hatcher can attest that I was home at bed with my woman when Chelsea Hart was killed. She woke my ass up.'

'Well, we can apparently exclude Rogan and myself. That leaves approximately thirty-nine thousand, nine hundred and ninety-eight cops.'

'Do I look like I'm in the mood for jokes right now?' Knight asked. He certainly did not.

Ellie adopted a more somber tone. 'I suppose we start by looking at anyone who's been trying to get into homicide and feels passed over. I think we've also got to look at the current homicide squad. They've got reason to resent me, plus it's possible they got wind of Flann snooping around a few years ago, and that would explain why the murders stopped until after his death.'

'So now what?' Donovan asked.

She was about to set out a process for going forward, but Simon Knight interrupted her.

'You all go home for a break, and I call the commisioner. We take a new look at everything tomorrow with an expanded task force, most likely with the assistance of the FBI.'

'Wait a second —' Ellie's words cut into Rogan's louder statement of 'Absolutely not.'

'We can do this, sir,' she said.

'And we don't need a break to regroup tomorrow,' Rogan added. 'This is our case, and we want to work it.'

'You *will* work it, but the question of how and with what other personnel is a decision well above your pay grade, and well outside the boundaries of this office. The Chelsea Hart case was being worked out of this office's Homicide Investigation Unit, with you in my command, because an arrest had been made and we were doing everything with an eye toward the prosecution of Jake Myers. Now that we're all agreed that we have no murder case against Myers, the two of you go back to police command, where they can figure out what to do with this – I think it's safe to say – clusterfuck.'

Ellie could see precisely where Knight was headed. He would tell the mayor and the police commissioner that his office had done everything it could with the case that had been given to them so hastily, but had no choice but to dismiss the charges once they had exonerated Jake Myers. Without a suspect, Knight was free to extract himself from the mayhem. Just as Rogan had warned, Knight cared more about himself than he ever would about them.

'No offense, sir, but I hope you'll point out to police command that Rogan and I deserve to run this. I'm the one the killer wants to engage. The more he's getting what he wants on that front, the more likely he's going to do something that will lead us to him.'

'The counterargument, Detective, is that the more he gets to push your buttons, the more dangerous he becomes. We know for a fact that the *Daily Post*'s break of this story is imminent. Who knows what kind of reaction that could trigger from him.'

'We need to warn people,' she said. She did not want to look at herself in the mirror tomorrow morning if the killer claimed another victim while she was taking Simon Knight's mandated 'break.'

'I don't want to do anything that validates the *Daily Post*'s story,' Knight said. 'It's premature.'

'We don't need to validate the story. Any casual news watcher is going to at least wonder if there's a connection between the deaths of Chelsea Hart and Rachel Peck. Even without confirming that we're looking at a single killer, we can contact the clubs and bars. Make sure they're watching girls, warning them about wandering off alone.'

'They're not the only ones who need a warning,' Knight said. 'I'm sure you're smart enough to have figured out where this game might be taking this man.'

The thought had more than crossed her mind. A killer who came out of the shadows to announce his existence was taking a risk of getting caught. And if he was willing to get caught, there had to be a payoff. Maybe besting her at a cat-and-mouse game would be enough for him, but she suspected that this was all just a warm-up.

'I can take care of myself.' The words didn't come out as confidently as she'd intended.

'I'm sure that's true,' Knight said. 'But if I were you, I'd stay away from dance clubs for the time being.'

An hour later, she and Rogan had drafted a press release that passed muster with both Knight and the department's Public Information Office, and had forwarded it to every precinct in Manhattan to hand-distribute to the city's hot spots. Ellie was impressed that Donovan had stuck it out with them, even going so far as to take a stack of the announcements with him to post around his NoLIta neighborhood.

By the time they finally called it a night, it was eight o'clock. She hadn't eaten anything since the Danish she'd bought from Manny that morning. She felt guilty thinking about food, but she couldn't help it. As if pushing her over the edge, her stomach let out a little rumble in the courthouse elevator.

Donovan placed his hand flat on his stomach. 'Was that me or you?'

'Nice of you to try to take the blame, but that was all me.'

'I could use something to eat myself. Are you guys up for a bite?'

Ellie looked to Rogan.

'The man said take a break. I'm taking a break and going home for a serious sleep session. I'll see you tomorrow.' He walked away, leaving Ellie the privacy to accept or reject Donovan's invitation on her own.

'Food sounds good.'

'Five Deaths, Ten Years,' read the headline on the *Daily Post*'s home page. The photograph accompanying the teaser was a shot of Rachel Peck. She looked more glamorous in the picture than the man had ever seen her – even more than the night he'd taken her off the streets of the Meatpacking District. His guess was that it was a publicity shot taken for a literary agent. From what he could tell, publishers cared about those kinds of things these days.

He clicked on the headline and read the full text of the article at the jump. All of the basics were covered: Lucy Feeney, Robbie Harrington, Alice Butler, Chelsea Hart, and Rachel Peck. All wild. All drunk. All dead, snippets of their hair stolen as souvenirs.

The reporting was remarkably thorough, given that Rachel's body had just been discovered that morning. It was quite a scoop for the paper. Posting the story on the Web site gave them credit for breaking the news first, but they'd sell a lot of papers in the morning with a more detailed version.

He moved from the sofa onto the floor, slid the ottoman away, and pulled up the wooden tiles, followed by the piece of particleboard. He removed five plastic bags – two new, three discolored with age. Lucy's and Chelsea's bags contained the most hair. Robbie's and Rachel's were less full. Alice's held just a few snips. How tempted he had been to retrieve all of those beautiful locks she'd chopped off. He'd caught sight of her walking into the salon and had watched while the hairdresser clipped away. But he hadn't dared to walk in, let alone attempt to pilfer the piles of hair on the salon floor.

Lucy, Robbie, Alice, Chelsea, and Rachel. Thanks to the *Daily Post*, he was no longer the only one to know that their stories belonged together.

Now just one last victim remained.

Chapter Forty-Three

Max directed the cab to the Flatiron district, and then led the way to Sala One Nine, a Spanish restaurant on Nineteenth Street.

'I hope you like tapas,' he said, opening the heavy wooden door to a red restaurant with exposed brick and stone, lit by small tea candles scattered throughout the room.

'I love anything that involves getting to eat seven different kinds of food in a single sitting.'

The restaurant was already filled with hungry customers. Rather than cope with a forty-five minute wait, they accepted the host's invitation to eat at the bar, where Max ordered a pitcher of sangria and some *queso* and *croquetas* to get them started.

This was their first chance to be alone since their coffee that wasn't quite a coffee had ended the previous night. The transition from their official roles to what was presumably a date was not an easy one for either of them. Ellie found herself wanting to talk about the case, and apparently Max had questions of his own.

'So, tell me if this is none of my business, but I picked up on a kind of secret language between you and Rogan today.'

'Nothing secret. We're still getting into the groove of being partners.'

'From an outsider's perspective, you seem to have found the rhythm pretty quickly. I could tell he was the one who was resistant to let Knight and me in, but the two of you seemed to work it out without even exchanging words.'

'We exchanged words,' Ellie said, flashing back to the scene in the car while they'd been waiting for Donovan. 'You just weren't there to hear them.'

'I've got to tell you, I've been doing this a few years now, and you're not like most of the cops I've met.'

'Being a girl type person is still enough to stand out in the NYPD.'

'It's more than that. I don't know. You were pre-law at some point, right? Do you ever regret not seeing it through?'

Ellie had come across this reaction before. Cops were supposed to be simple-minded, blue-collar traditionalists. She'd gone to college. She lived in Manhattan. Her last boyfriend was an investment banker. She even used big words on occasion.

When people said she didn't *seem* like a cop, it often said more about their stereotypes of police than anything having to do with Ellie. The investment banker, for example, had continually asked her when she was going to 'get over' being a cop. Bill's refusal to accept that she wasn't too good for her job was one of the reasons she lived on her own now. She hoped she wasn't going to have the same problem with Max.

'When you grow up around here, people are doctors and lawyers and corporate executives. But my father was a cop, and my mother's a bookkeeper. The neighbor to our left was a plumber. The one on the right worked graveyards at Boeing. Being from Wichita, it never dawned on me that I would need to apologize to anyone for being a cop.'

Donovan set his sangria down and braced his palms against the bar. 'Okay, let's clear up a couple of things. One, I grew up around here, but it was in Kew Gardens, where my father's still a shoe salesman, and my mother was a dental hygienist. When I told my dad I was turning down a six-digit salary so I could be a prosecutor, he acted more like I was on the other side of an indictment, begging for bail money. So as far as I'm concerned, no one who loves their job ever has to apologize to anyone.'

'I'm so sorry. I just get so used to –'

'No explanation necessary. I should have been more clear about what I meant.'

'You mean you *weren't* challenging me to an I-grew-up-poorer-than-you-did contest?' Ellie could still feel the red in her cheeks.

'You're not like most of the cops I know because you don't seem to have the same kind of us-versus-them mentality.'

'Ah, well, that's an easy one,' she said, relieved by the shift in the conversation. 'I don't see the point in any of that. All I care about is getting the work done.'

'And when you were pre-law, did you ever think about being a prosecutor?'

'I like being a cop. I like the directness of it. You're there from the very beginning. You get to talk firsthand to witnesses and victims and suspects. Your instincts shape the investigation from day one. If I'm going to do law enforcement, I want to do it as a cop. When I thought about being a lawyer, I was in it so I wouldn't have to deal with the dark, dreary, and depressing shit my father thought about day in and day out. I was in it for the money.'

'So you're saying I've got the worst of both worlds.'

'No offense.'

The truth was, Ellie had wondered a few times in the last two days whether perhaps she was better suited to the district attorney's office. Where Eckels saw her youth and enthusiasm as hurdles to be surmounted, Knight had seen a dream witness. Dan Eckels and people like him were always going to run police departments, and she would always be butting heads with them. But with Simon Knight, it had seemed like it was all about cutting through the bullshit and getting the work done. She could nail down murder cases for trial without being front and center, on the news, and in books written by ex-boyfriends.

But tonight, when the case against Jake Myers had collapsed, Knight had shown his true colors. He did what he needed to cover his ass with the police commissioner and the mayor's office. He was talking about a possible task force. Even FBI involvement.

And she had responded just as Rogan had. Possessive.

Territorial. Knight had shown his true colors, but so had she. And hers were bluer than she liked to acknowledge.

Her true colors also made her the kind of cop who couldn't stop talking about work.

'So do you think Myers was right?' she asked.

'To hire some guy at death's door to take the rap for him? Uh, no, I'm pretty sure in any version of morality, that wouldn't count as right.'

'No, I mean about us having tunnel vision. We all wanted it to be him. It gave us an arrest. A suspect. A trial. The mayor's office was happy.'

'I've known you three days, and I can already tell you're a good cop. If he'd told you the truth, you would have fought like hell against everyone to make sure we did the right thing.'

'Maybe,' she said, popping another *croqueta* in her mouth. 'Maybe if he'd come clean Monday night. If he'd told the truth when we first questioned him at Pulse. But once he lied about everything –'

'No jury would've believed him,' Donovan said, 'that's for sure.'

'I don't think I would have either.'

They had just ordered another four little plates to share when the television above the bar cut from a break in the Knicks game to a teaser for the night's local news.

'*Tonight at eleven.*' At the top of the telecast was a scaffolding collapse on the Upper West Side. A window washer had plummeted thirty-six floors and survived.

Plus, a local newspaper drops an Internet bombshell. Is a serial killer targeting Manhattan's elite nightclubs? And why isn't the NYPD telling you about this killer and his shocking MO? The paper promises more details tomorrow morning, but we'll have the scoop for you tonight, at eleven.

The screen changed to an AT&T ad.

'Jesus,' Max said. 'Those kinds of stories piss me off to no end.'

'Did you notice how they phrased it? "A local newspaper drops a bombshell." That way the story is about the story.'

'That's what irritates me. One of the tabloid newspapers prints some wild speculation, and then the rest of the bottom feeders pile on, repeating the same crap without having to do any kind of verification like a real journalist.'

'Ah, except this time, the *same crap* happens to have a wee bit of truth to it,' she said, leaning in so others at the bar would not overhear.

'Well, shit. *They* don't know that, and they don't really care. They scare people and shock them to get better ratings. And if they screw up an investigation, or put people at risk, or make it harder for us to get a conviction – they don't care about any of that either. Sorry, I get a little riled up.'

'Don't apologize,' she said. 'It's nice to talk to someone who gets it. My ex-boyfriend – sorry, I know exes are taboo first-date talk, but this was forever ago – he would always ask me why I had to dwell on such depressing topics.'

Like most people, Bill got through each day by refusing to think about the horrible things that people did to each other on a regular basis. With Peter, she had been grateful that he at least shared her inability to blissfully ignore the realities of the world. But they would never see those realities through the same lens. Peter got worked up over crime because a body found in the right location, and abused in just the right way, could make for great copy. His commitment to his book was just a sign that he would never really get her.

'Well, do you know how many women I've gotten even semi-serious with before they start asking me when I'm going to cash in on my law degree?'

'Did you go straight from law school to the DA's office?'

'Nah. I did the big-firm thing for a couple of years to pay down my loans, but I can't imagine ever going back. Eighty hours a week, all for some multimillion-dollar commercial lawsuit and squabbling over who would get the biggest bonus or who'd make partner first. Once you've seen the kind of cases I've worked on, you just don't look at things the same way. What everyone else considers the real world seems like a complete fantasyland. It's like you get a new definition of normal. Do you know what I mean, or should I stop babbling?'

'Please, you're not babbling, and I know exactly what you mean.'

Donovan, like her, had seen the aftermath of the

crimes of people who were inhabited by pure, untarnished evil – men who inflicted sexual torture, who casually took the lives of others, who could bury a child alive and then make themselves a bologna sandwich.

Ellie had spent her entire adult life chasing the normalcy that came to others as naturally and effortlessly as breathing. Since the day her father's body was found, Ellie had been convinced that her darkest thoughts would someday be put to rest, once she finally uncovered the true circumstances surrounding his death. But she had returned from Kansas with a new acceptance of the possibility that serenity would never be a part of her makeup. She would always wake up with nightmares. She would never learn to turn off the job.

A new definition of normal. Maybe that was what she needed to get past the feeling that she was never going to be like other people.

The vibration of her cell phone startled her. It was Peter, yet again. She felt the phone buzz in her hand seconds later, indicating a new message.

She did her best to ignore it. She was having a delicious dinner with a smart, sweet, over-the-top-good-looking guy who might actually share her same ridiculous sickness. She had every reason to ignore her stupid phone. She made it through four more bites of chorizo before excusing herself to the ladies' room.

'Hey. It's me. I swear, I'm not a fucking stalker. Well, okay, maybe a little bit of a fucking stalker, since I am calling from outside your apartment.'

Ellie shook her head. '*I shouldn't have come, I know, but I hate the idea of you hating me. I don't want things to end this way.*' Jess had been right about Peter. The ending itself wasn't the problem for him. He just couldn't stand the idea of being the bad guy.

'*So I'm sitting on the stoop of your building, being semi-stalkerish, and I noticed a car circle around the block a few times, then park out front. By the time the driver got out, I had gone into the coffee shop to warm up. Anyway, it was your lieutenant. I couldn't tell if he rang up to your apartment or not, and I just saw him drive away, but I thought I'd let you know. Either you're having a secret affair with your nemesis, or it's something important. And, no, I won't try to figure out what it is so I can write about it.*'

She found herself smiling sadly.

'*Sorry for rambling. I won't bother you anymore. The ball's in your court. Bye, Ellie.*'

Ellie knew she'd eventually go to Peter's apartment to end things with him on a better note, but at that moment all she could think about was the image of Dan Eckels outside her building.

No DNA. Clean crime scenes. A knowledge of city crime patterns. The stakeout abilities to nail down her running routine.

Simon Knight had asked her earlier in the day where they might begin looking for a killer among forty thousand officers in the NYPD. One of them had just jumped to the top of the list.

Chapter Forty-Four

J. J. Rogan and Max Donovan seemed out of place on Ellie's familiar brown couch. A few weeks ago, she hadn't met either one of them, and now they sat side by side on her living room sofa, hips nearly touching, surrounded by piles of magazines, clothing, and empty beer bottles, all of which she made a point of blaming entirely on Jess.

As soon as she'd heard Peter's voice mail, she'd known she had to head straight home. If Eckels was looking for her, she wanted to be here. She wanted to be found. She wanted to look him in the eye and figure out how he'd fooled so many people for so long.

Max had insisted on coming with her. And when she'd called Rogan from the cab, he'd insisted on driving in from Brooklyn. And so now here they sat on her sofa in a room that was usually restricted to her, Jess, and restaurant deliverymen.

'Let's not get ahead of ourselves,' Rogan was saying. 'Lieutenant Dan Fuckin' Eckels? Strangling chicks and cutting them up and hacking off all their hair? I mean, Jesus H. We need to think through this shit.'

'I *have* thought it through,' Ellie said. 'He was the lead detective on Alice Butler's case. He mentioned in the reports that Alice told her sister someone was following her shortly before her murder, but he left out the fact that she picked up on the guy after she left a hair salon.'

'And you're so sure that's a detail that you would have included in a report?'

'Would *I* have included it? Of course.'

'Okay, but you're fricking rain man. You're positive that *every* cop would've noted that?'

'Of course not. That's why I assumed Eckels had simply left it out. But after we caught the Chelsea Hart case, he never bothered to mention the possibility of a pattern. We know for a fact that McIlroy went to Eckels three years ago about the earlier cases. And one of those was Lucy Feeney's – and you can say that Robbie Harrington and Alice Butler and Rachel Peck don't look like the Chelsea Hart case, but you can't deny the similarities between Chelsea and Lucy. Both strangled. Both stabbed. And the hair – give me a break, that's not something you miss. Why didn't he mention it? He pressured McIlroy three years ago not to pursue a connection, then did the same thing with me yesterday morning in his office.'

Donovan cleared his throat before interjecting. 'And McIlroy's snooping around three years ago could explain the gap in the killings. Eckels may have been ready to kill again, but got scared off when McIlroy picked up the pattern.'

'And with McIlroy gone,' she said, 'the coast is clear.

Eckels also knew that the photograph in the *Sun* – taken that night at the restaurant – came from Jordan McLaughlin. And as a cop, he could have easily come into contact with a guy like Darrell Washington. The neighbors said he had a way of talking to the cops too much.'

'Shit,' Rogan said. 'You said Washington lived in the LaGuardia Houses?'

'Right off the Manhattan Bridge. With his grand-mother.'

'Eckels used to work out of the Seventh back in the day. He would've been in and out of those projects all the time when Washington was a kid. Now I'm getting sucked into this whack idea.'

'And Eckels isn't exactly my biggest fan,' she reminded them.

'He thinks you're a pain in the ass,' Rogan said. 'That's not the same as wanting to carve your initials into some girl's forehead.'

'Then do you want to tell me why Dan Eckels suddenly showed up at my apartment tonight, circling the block and coming to my front door?'

'Maybe Peter made that shit up just to have an excuse to see you.'

'He wouldn't do that,' Ellie said. 'If he says Eckels was here, then he was here.' She hadn't bothered filling Donovan in on the specifics of her relationship to Peter Morse, and he'd been polite enough not to pry.

'Hopefully we'll get an explanation soon enough,' Donovan said. He had called Simon Knight, who had covered his butt once again by pointing them to Deputy Chief Al Kaplan for guidance. As the head of Manhattan

South Detective Borough, Kaplan had been the one to pull the strings necessary to move Ellie into homicide, and now here she was on his radar again already. Kaplan was unnerved enough to hear that the DA's office would be dismissing the murder charges against Myers in the morning. He wasn't about to ignore the possibility – however remote – that one of his own had something to do with this.

The Deputy Chief had been the one to make the call. As the three of them sat waiting in her pigsty of a living room, investigators from the DA's Homicide Investigation Unit, accompanied by Internal Affairs, were on their way to Eckels's house in Forest Hills.

Donovan was placing his fourth call to the HIU investigator. 'Any sign of him? . . . I know you said you'd call. That doesn't mean I'm not going to call you every thirty minutes for an update . . . Good. Thanks for staying on it.'

He flipped his phone shut and looked at his watch. 'Almost one in the morning. Is Dan Eckels the kind of guy who stays out until one in the morning, even on a Friday night?'

Ellie had that discomforting, racing feeling caused by a combination of sleep deprivation and an overdose of adrenaline. 'I don't know anything about the man.'

She remembered Flann McIlroy's description of a lecture from Lieutenant Eckels: *Just imagine the mean, gruff boss in any cop movie you've ever seen.*

She had come to assume in the short time she'd known her lieutenant that he behaved that way to compensate for his own insecurities. Now she wondered if the adoption of a well-worn and familiar persona wasn't the perfect cover for a much darker secret.

'I'd feel a lot better if we'd found him by now,' Donovan said.

'Me too.'

She had finally convinced Rogan to go home shortly after midnight, with a promise that she'd call with any news. The more time that passed without any sign of Eckels, the less implausible of a suspect he seemed.

'If he weren't a cop, you'd be yelling at me to wake up the most conservative judge I could find to sign a search warrant for his house.'

'I wouldn't yell.'

'Beg?'

'In your dreams.' Ellie sat in her off-white armchair with her knees pulled up tight in front of her, wondering why she wasn't pushing harder. If they were right, Eckels had already killed at least five women, two on her watch. If they were right, he could at that moment be selecting his next victim, or planning to come after Ellie directly.

But maybe they were wrong.

If they were wrong, and she led the charge to execute a search warrant at Dan Eckels's house, her career would be over. Tomorrow it would be good-bye homicide unit. Within a year, she'd be chased out of the department altogether. Another cop could go gypsy, relocating to another city to start anew, but not her. She was Ellie Hatcher, that chick on *Dateline* and in *People* magazine whose whack job of a father offed himself with his service weapon.

Ellie trusted her gut. She trusted it so much that she'd kick down the door on Eckels's house personally if her gut told her it was the right thing to do, damn the consequences.

But it wasn't the devastating consequences of a mistake that had her tucked into a ball in her armchair. Her gut was telling her she was missing something. Her head knew the facts, but her instincts were telling her that there was another way of looking at them. Like a child's blocks that could be formed into an infinite number of completed shapes, the facts would tell a different story if she could somehow rotate and rearrange them until they fell into the correct combination.

She just wasn't ready to pull the trigger on Eckels. They had people watching his house. They had investigators quietly calling Eckels's friends in the department to see where he might be – a girlfriend's, a late-night poker game, some explanation for his disappearance after the mysterious drop-in at Ellie's apartment.

Another hour, she thought. Ninety minutes. Two-thirty in the morning would be the tipping point. Two-thirty was late enough to confirm her suspicions. She still had ninety minutes to see what she was missing.

'Don't you have an apartment of your own that you need to get to?' she said.

'I do in fact have an apartment, but I have absolutely no desire to go there right now. I'm staying here until you kick me out.'

'I appreciate the sentiment, but I don't need you to

protect me. Look, big gun,' she said, pointing to the holster she'd tossed on her kitchen counter.

'If you think I want to be here so *I* can protect *you*, you have seriously overestimated my manliness. I'm a pencil-neck lawyer. You're doing all the protecting tonight.'

'You can't stay all night.' Somehow the words came out in a voice that suggested precisely the opposite. Max heard it, too.

'Don't think of it as all night. Just until you kick me out. If morning stumbles along before then, so be it.'

'I've known you for all of three days.'

'Yeah, but think of how much time we've spent together.' He looked at his watch. 'Like, fourteen hours, today alone. That pretty much makes this our third or fourth date.'

'A date administering polygraphs and figuring out if my lieutenant is trying to kill me.'

He rose from the couch and walked toward her. 'Well, that's just how I roll. A date with Max Donovan is always an adventure.'

She could tell he was at least as exhausted as she was, and he was forcing himself not to look worried. And in that moment, Ellie – who so often preferred to be alone – found herself happy he was there. Here was a man who might – maybe, possibly, one day – actually understand her.

When he knelt against her chair, she did not stop him. And when he leaned in to kiss her, she decided to stop thinking and to let things simply happen.

Chapter Forty-Five

Lieutenant Dan Eckels buttoned his trench coat as he walked through the marble-floored lobby of the Trump Place apartment complex, then climbed into his black Dodge Charger. He pulled onto the West Side Highway, feeling slightly less stressed than he had a few hours earlier. Marlene had that effect on him.

It had been four years since he'd met Marlene, and if someone had predicted then the odd relationship he shared with her today, he would have called the paramedics for a straitjacket.

He had busted the sleazeball who paid the rent on Marlene's high-rise apartment right before he'd earned his white-shirt promotion. Precisely where Vinnie fell in the hierarchy of his crime family was still unclear in Eckels's mind, but on that particular day, Eckels popped someone under Vinnie's supervision for scalping counterfeit concert tickets.

When Eckels caught up with Vinnie at Elaine's, his bleached-blond, fake-tittied goomah was on his arm. When Eckels pulled out the cuffs, Marlene offered to blow him in exchange for cutting Vinnie loose. Eckels was only one year divorced at the time, and he knew guys like Vinnie always managed to beat the rap anyway. Given his own stereotypes of men like Vinnie, Eckels would have expected him to give Marlene a good jab in the temple and to take him down just to save face. Instead, he'd remained at the table to finish his veal piccata while Marlene and Eckels took a little walk to the car.

Four years later, Vinnie didn't seem to have a problem if Eckels occasionally dropped in on Marlene, as long as Eckels did him the occasional harmless favor in return: fixing tickets, running off a competitor, tracking down a plate – nothing that would get anyone hurt. The two men had an understanding.

Why Marlene put up with any of it remained a mystery. Vinnie took care of her, but she was in a 500-square-foot studio on a low floor just above the elevated portion of the West Side Highway. As far as Eckels could figure, all that mattered to Marlene was that she lived in a building bearing the Trump name.

He was careful not to take advantage of the arrangement. He dropped by Marlene's maybe four times a year, and only on days when he really needed the escape. She had a way of calming him down.

Being with her tonight had helped, as he knew it would, but he was still anxious. The *Daily Post* was running a story tomorrow morning tying the Chelsea Hart murder to four others. The department would be going into full-on task-force mode.

He had been so relieved when Jake Myers had come along. The asshole looked good for it, and the possibility of a connection between Chelsea Hart and those other girls floated away. But then Hatcher had marched into his office, ragging about those same old names again.

He didn't have much time before his captain, or maybe even the assistant chief, started asking him the hard questions. He'd caught the Alice Butler case, the third case in the series, and had failed to see the pattern. That alone would only render him a mediocre detective. No one would have a hard time believing that. He knew he wasn't the best cop. He'd gotten the promotion based almost entirely on his test scores, but he'd never commanded the respect of the men who worked for him, or above him, for that matter.

But when the department got around to its postmortem analysis, they'd be looking at more than shoddy police work. When Flann McIlroy had come to him three years ago with his wacky theory, Eckels had shut him down and ordered him to stop investigating the cold cases. Not that McIlroy would have ever obeyed an order, but others wouldn't look at it that way. His biggest mistake by far, though, was failing to speak up when his own detectives caught the Chelsea Hart case.

The department would come after him. He needed to cover his bases. He needed to find Hatcher. She was a pain in the butt, and he had no doubt that she'd gotten where she was based on her sex and her looks, but he had to admit that she was smart. She was also reasonable and, in the end, a decent person. He would find a way to turn those characteristics to his advantage.

He took the Forty-second Street turnoff and made his way east to Fifth Avenue, then hung a left on Thirty-eighth. He planned on parking in front of the same hydrant he'd blocked earlier tonight, but some asshole in a Ford Taurus was already there.

Eckels rolled down his window and gestured for the Taurus's driver to do the same. 'Hey buddy, no standing.'

The streetlamp was shining on Eckels's car, so he could not see inside the Taurus. He honked his horn and signaled again for the driver to roll down his window, this time flashing the department parking permit he kept on his dash.

'Get a move on.'

The driver's-side door of the Taurus opened, and Eckels saw the back of a man's head and a tan coat in the dome light.

'Small world, Lieutenant.'

It took Eckels a moment to recognize the man walking toward his car. This was a prime example of Dan Eckels's unique brand of bad luck. Eight and a half million people in this city. He gives one of them a hard time, and they just happen to recognize him. On top of all his other problems, all he needed was this loser telling people he was a jerk to boot.

The man removed a gloved right hand from his coat pocket. Eckels extended his own hand to return the shake through his open window.

He saw a quick flash of movement in his periphery. 'What the fuck?' Trying to pull away from the damp cloth pressed against his face, he reached for his Glock. His seat belt restricted his movement. His coat was buttoned tight around his body. He could not get to his weapon. In fact, he could not feel it at his side.

Maybe he should have listened. Maybe he shouldn't

have been so wedded to the case against Jake Myers. But with the mayor's office hounding him at every turn, it had been what he'd wanted to believe. He wasn't the first cop to get a case of tunnel vision. If he'd mentioned those old files the minute they'd caught the Hart case, he wouldn't have been in this position. All he'd wanted was to protect his job. If he made things right with Hatcher, she'd cover his ass.

He was getting dizzy. Just before passing out, he realized his gun was on Marlene's nightstand. If he'd been a better cop, he would have realized that coming here would be dangerous.

The driver of the Taurus opened Dan Eckels's door and took a quick look up and down Thirty-eighth Street. A couple was crossing Park Avenue, but they didn't seem to be paying him any attention. He saw no obvious snoopers peering from the windows of the adjacent apartment buildings.

'You're in no shape to drive, man,' he said, just to be safe. He unbelted Eckels from his seat, reached in and moved his legs to the passenger side, and then pushed his body over in one full shove.

He removed the parking permit from the dash, tossed it into his own car, and locked up the Taurus before taking a seat at the wheel of the Charger.

He had himself an NYPD lieutenant, and he was willing to bet he could trade him for a young blond detective.

Chapter Forty-Six

'Fuck. My eyes, my eyes. Someone please hand me a spear so I might gouge out my eyes. Cover yourselves, people.'

Ellie sprung from what felt like the deepest sleep of her lifetime. She saw light creeping through the living room blinds and her brother standing at her apartment entrance, keys in hand and grin on face.

'Shit. *Shit.* What time is it?'

'Five forty-five.'

'Damn it. Ninety minutes. I was only going to wait ninety minutes.'

Max Donovan was coming to on the living room floor next to her. He grabbed a corner of the fleece throw Ellie was clutching to her chest, then settled for a blue pillow instead.

'Shit, we fell asleep,' he said.

'Master of the fucking obvious.'

'My brother, Jess,' Ellie said by way of explanation, scrambling to her feet and wrapping herself in the throw.

'Hey.' Max offered Jess his free hand. 'Max Donovan. Uh, sorry about the circumstances.'

'You'll understand if I don't return the gesture. I really don't need to think about where that hand's been at six in the morning.'

'Jesus, Jess.'

Jess dropped a newspaper on the coffee table. 'I thought you'd want to see this. Hot off the presses.'

It was a copy of the *Daily Post*. A glamor shot of Rachel Peck occupied the entire front page.

With no further pleasantries, Max was simultaneously pulling on his pants and pushing buttons on his cell phone.

'Why the fuck haven't you called me? . . . You've just been sitting there? . . . Nothing? . . . Damn it . . . No, don't leave. You stay there until we tell you to leave.'

Ellie had pulled on a blue terry-cloth robe by the time Donovan hung up.

'He never got home. Eckels is in the wind.' He was struggling to get his arms into the sleeves of yesterday's shirt. 'We need to get a warrant. I need to call Knight.'

He was fumbling with the buttons of his cell again when Ellie caught sight of the newspaper headline blaring above Rachel Peck's photograph: 'The Barber of Manhattan: A Serial Killer Strikes Again?' On the bottom of the page in smaller print: 'Creep Collects Hair as Souvenirs.'

'That Peter sure does work for a class act,' Jess said.

Ellie found herself reading the words again. Then a third time. Then she picked up the paper and rifled through the pages until she found the cover story.

The nagging feeling that she'd had in her gut before

she'd fallen asleep was returning. That feeling that they'd been missing something. The facts unstacked into a jumble of individual blocks, floating in random rotations in her mind – flipping, rearranging, and then settling back down into a new and entirely different pattern.

And then the tumblers clicked. Same victims. Same pattern. Same facts. Different man.

'Stop. Hang up, Max. It's not Eckels. Hang up.'

She was already hitting a button on her own phone. It rang three times before she got an answer.

'Peter, I need you to tell me about George Kittrie.'

They were inside Kittrie's apartment within an hour. Three minutes to make the call to the Twenty-third Precinct to post officers outside the building. Fifteen minutes in the cab on the way to the Upper East Side, while Donovan persuaded Judge Capers to authorize a telephonic no-knock warrant. Five minutes to track down the super and his master keys. Another two minutes to figure out that Kittrie had installed an unauthorized security lock that the super could not bypass. Eighteen minutes to call in the old-fashioned battering ram.

Now Ellie, Donovan, and four backup officers were inside the apartment, and Rogan was on the way. She led a protective sweep through the apartment. As she'd expected, it was unoccupied.

'Damn it. He got to Eckels. I just know it. I should have figured this out yesterday. We could've stopped him.'

There was no legitimate way that Kittrie could know about the common link between the murders. When she had called him about the three cold cases, she had kept the fact about the hair to herself. And the killer had been so careful to hide his MO that Ellie herself had been unsure of the connection, even after speaking to Robbie's father and Alice's sister. Only after seeing Rachel Peck with her own eyes was she certain.

She'd thought through all of the possible leaks, but there were none. Rogan was solid. And even if Knight or Donovan might have been the type to talk, there hadn't been time. Kittrie had sent Peter to get a quote from her before she told either of them about the cold cases.

She had assumed that Capra had been the source for the story about Chelsea Hart's hair, but in fact there had been no leak at all. Kittrie had even covered his tracks by getting the information slightly wrong – asking her whether Chelsea's head was *shaved*. And there had been no contact with Flann McIlroy three years earlier. She had assumed that Peter was lying when he said Kittrie had a quick trigger on running the presses, but it had been Kittrie who lied about his contacts with Flann.

George Kittrie knew that a killer was collecting his victims' hair because he had committed the murders.

When she had met Kittrie with Peter at Plug Uglies, he had looked familiar. Kittrie played it smart, convincing her she could have seen him at the bar during one of his investigative happy hours. But now she knew where she'd spotted him before. He had been caught in the background of the photograph Jordan McLaughlin had given her of the three girls at the Little Italy restaurant.

They had an APB out on Kittrie's 2004 Ford Taurus and an emergency service unit on its way to his East Hampton cottage. In the meantime, there was nothing to do but begin a search of the apartment.

She snapped on a pair of latex gloves and started with the desk. She found what she was looking for in the file drawer, inside a folder labeled 'Medical Records.' She couldn't make out the terminology on the stack of papers from Sloan Kettering, but she didn't need an M.D. to understand that repeated references to glioblastoma multiforme in the cerebral hemisphere were not good.

Those rumors Peter had heard about his boss's condition were true: George Kittrie had an inoperable brain tumor.

'When we found out about Symanski's meso-thelioma, we were talking about the desperate things people do when they know they're dying. Symanski wanted to go out a hero. Kittrie wants to take others with him. Or maybe he wants to get caught. If this thing goes to trial, we might even hear some expert argue that it was the brain tumor causing his violent tendencies all along.'

'And why is he so focused on you?' Donovan asked.

'I've gotten a lot of media attention, and that's probably important to him. It could have been those things I said in the *Dateline* interview about William Summer being a loser. A man like Kittrie could empathize with someone like Summer. Both share the same desires. Both men stopped acting on those desires for long periods of time, which is probably seen by them as a sign of power and control. Summer was just given a life sentence, and now Kittrie finds himself at the end of his life. I can see how his desire to kill again could get transferred onto me.'

She scanned the wide array of titles shelved above Kittrie's desk. Mostly nonfiction: civil war histories, biographies of the robber barons, a few contemporary memoirs. She spotted three consecutive copies of the same book, *9/11: Scoundrels and Profiteers*, by George Kittrie, and pulled one from the shelf. Kittrie smiled at her from a black-and-white photograph on the inside cover. She checked the copyright date. Five years ago.

When she replaced the volume on the shelf, a thick black-leather-bound book caught her eye among the colorful dust jackets. She opened it to find a collection of feature articles authored by George Kittrie, arranged in chronological order. She noticed that the prominence of the stories increased after the publication of his book.

'It could have been the book deal that made him stop after Alice Butler,' she said. 'William Summer stopped because he got a promotion at his job. Maybe being a published author gave Kittrie the satisfaction he needed to gain control over his urges. Until I set him off, of course.'

'Hey,' Donovan said. 'This is *not* your fault. He knows he's dying. He would have killed those girls anyway.'

Ellie nodded, even though she was not convinced. 'He must have had this bound after he got his diagnosis.

The articles go all the way up to a few months ago,' she said, flipping through the pages. She was about to replace the tome on the shelf when she backtracked a few pages. 'Unbelievable. Take a look at this.'

Donovan peered over her shoulder.

'This article from last April is about gangs in the city projects.' The story was accompanied by a large photograph of a man's back, covered with gang tattoos, as well as smaller photographs depicting life in the projects. 'And that picture right there,' Ellie said, pointing to one of the smaller images, 'was taken outside the LaGuardia Houses. Kittrie knew Darrell Washington.'

Rogan charged through Kittrie's front door like a racehorse out of the gate.

'I'm on the phone with Pier 76 impound.' He covered the mouthpiece of his cell phone. 'Kittrie's Taurus got towed two hours ago for blocking a hydrant. He had a city parking permit on the dash that didn't match the registration.'

'It has to belong to Eckels,' Ellie said.

Rogan removed his hand from the mouthpiece. 'Where was the car? . . . Thirty-eighth and Madison?'

'That's half a block from my apartment,' Ellie said as Rogan flipped his phone shut. 'He must have taken Eckels on the street when he came to see me, which hopefully means Eckels is still alive. We're going to find them at Kittrie's cottage.'

'We've got Emergency Service Unit officers on the way with a truck and tactical weapons,' Donovan said.

'They're almost to the end of the Long Island Expressway. They will take him down.'

'That's still an hour away from East Hampton, and we're another hour behind them. If we have any chance to save Eckels, Kittrie is going to want to see me there. I need to be there.'

Rogan was dialing again. 'We can be in a chopper in fifteen minutes.'

Chapter Forty-Seven

In her brief time as Rogan's partner, Ellie had never felt a sophistication gap between them. That all changed, however, when they pulled up to the helipad at Thirtieth Street and the West Side Highway.

She wasn't even sure whether it would have ever dawned on her to request a department helicopter, but the idea certainly hadn't come to her as quickly and as effortlessly as it had for Rogan. He had immediately called the borough commander, who approved the request and gave the necessary orders. Given her partner's familiarity with the process at the Westside heliport, Ellie got the impression that Rogan had prior experience with helicopter travel, and she wondered if perhaps her partner hadn't seriously understated the extent of his outside money.

Rogan badged the officer waiting for them at the gate. 'We're heading out to East Hampton.'

'The Bell 412 just arrived from Floyd Bennett Field.'

'The ten-million-dollar beast, all for us?'

'Nine-point-eight,' the officer corrected. 'They weren't sure how big of a team you'd have. The 412 holds the crew plus seven men. Excuse me, ma'am, seven people.'

Rogan pulled the car to the edge of the concrete, and they scurried across the pad. Rogan helped hoist Ellie into the cabin, and then climbed in himself. He reached behind him to give Donovan a hand.

'You sure you want to come? This isn't part of your job description.'

'I'm going,' he said, joining Ellie on a bench seat running the length of the chopper. Rogan began distributing Kevlar vests that had already been piled into the back for their use, while Ellie unwrapped the gauze from her hand.

Wasting no time on introductions, the pilot asked if they were going to the East Hampton Airport.

'Suffolk County police will be waiting for us,' Rogan confirmed. 'We've got what? A forty-minute ride?'

The helicopter's entire body shook from the power building in the four-blade rotor.

'More like thirty in this bad boy,' the pilot said. 'Whatever you've got planned out there, I'd start getting yourself ready for it.'

George Kittrie's cottage was on a narrow strip of road called Gerard Drive, surrounded on both sides by water – Accabonac Harbor to the west, and Gardiner's Bay to the east. By the time their Suffolk County cruiser pulled onto Gerard Drive, the road was lined with police vehicles – a black NYPD Emergency Service truck, three other Suffolk County patrol cars, two ambulances, and

400

four cars that were probably the entirety of the East Hampton Police Department's fleet.

They had decided on the way to the helipad that there was no point in trying to conduct a stealth takedown of Kittrie. Eckels hadn't reported to work, and neither had Kittrie. He would know they were coming for him. A massive show of their presence was warranted.

Rogan pointed to the ESU truck at the side of the road, and the Suffolk County officer pulled his cruiser behind it. Rogan was out of the car first and homed in on a man dressed in all-black tactical gear. 'J. J. Rogan. My partner, Ellie Hatcher. ADA Max Donovan.'

'Jim Foreman,' the officer said with a nod.

'How are we doing on evacuation?'

'I've got officers knocking on doors at every house along this inlet. We've got about fifty percent of them confirmed clear.'

'And the others?' Ellie asked.

'The local PD says this road's popular for vacation houses. They could be empty. On the other hand, they tell me nine a.m.'s considered pretty early around here.'

'So we don't know how much exposure we have,' Rogan said.

'My men know to make as much noise as necessary.'

The houses on the water were packed closely together. The last thing they needed was to have neighbors hurt in a shootout or for Kittrie to take the battle onto someone else's property.

'You ready?' Rogan asked.

'Ready to do what?' Ellie said. 'If we storm the house, he kills Eckels.'

'I'll tell him later that you cared.'

'If there's a later,' she said. 'I say we call Kittrie. He obviously knows we're here.'

Her cell buzzed at her waist. She checked the screen. 'That fucker. He's calling from Eckels's phone.' She flipped her phone open. 'We're here.'

'I noticed.' Kittrie's tone was breezy, almost singsongy in its inflection, as if he were a kindergarten teacher feigning artificial patience with an antsy child. 'And I assume you know this isn't your lieutenant.'

'Send out Eckels, or we'll have twenty police officers storming that little shed of yours within two minutes.'

'Nice try, Detective, but if you're anywhere near as good as I think you are, then you know that death threats won't go too far with me. I can't say the same about Lieutenant Eckels. I think that means I get to set the rules. Since you like the sound of two minutes so much, let's say you have exactly two minutes to come to my front door. Alone. Unarmed.'

'Absolutely not.'

'Two minutes, Detective. And get rid of the vest. If they take a shot at me, they need to know they might kill you instead.'

The line went dead.

He had known about the vest. He was watching them. She pulled off her Kevlar and threw it to the ground.

'What the fuck are you doing, Hatcher?'

'This is what he wants. Me at the front door in two

402

minutes. No weapons. No vest. Otherwise, he'll kill Eckels.'

'No way,' Donovan said.

'You don't get to have an opinion on this.'

'He's bluffing,' Rogan said. 'Shit. We should have brought a fucking hostage negotiator.'

'I don't need a negotiator. We know enough about this guy to know he's got nothing to lose.'

'Except his leverage. If he kills Eckels, this is over.'

'And if he doesn't kill Eckels, it's over because we'll know he's a bluffer. I'm going in.'

Officer Foreman interrupted. 'I can't let you go in there, Detective, as much as you want to. You don't even know he'll let his hostage go. His hostage could be dead by now.'

'"His hostage" is one of us, and he's our lieutenant.'

Foreman tried to block her way. She dodged him. Rogan grabbed her arm, but she pulled it away. 'Damn it, J. J. If either of you tries to fucking stop me one more time, I am going to physically hurt you.'

She ducked behind the ESU van, and Rogan followed her. 'Give me your weapon,' she said, holding out her right hand.

'What are you doing?'

'I don't have time to explain. Just give me your Glock.'

He unholstered his gun and handed it to her. 'You can't do this.'

'I *have* to do this. Don't you see that? *I* did this. *I* found Chelsea Hart. Those were *my* initials carved into Rachel Peck's forehead with a knife. *I* was the one who had all the information we needed – his cancer, the timing of that book, the knowledge he had about the cases, his fucking *picture*, for Christ's sake, before I went and cropped it into the ether. It should be me in there, and I swear to God, I am not going to let you stop me.'

As she spoke, she ejected the magazine and let it fall to the ground, then slid out the chambered round and tossed it aside as well.

'He will kill you.'

'He'll kill Eckels faster. Me, he wants to brainfuck first. Take any shot you get.' She tucked Rogan's unloaded weapon in her waistband beneath her coat. 'Do you hear me?'

Donovan was next to her now with his hand on her elbow, but Rogan pulled him away. 'We're going to get you out of there, Hatcher. You're not alone in there, you understand?'

She swallowed and nodded, hoping that he was right, and stepped out from behind the van. She rushed toward the house, stopping in the middle of Kittrie's yard to unholster her own service weapon and toss it onto the grass.

Chapter Forty-Eight

Ellie stood on the porch for thirty seconds before Kittrie's front door opened, a tiny gap at first, then another few inches, until she could see the terrified eyes of Dan Eckels peering out at her. His mouth was wrapped with silver duct tape. His hands were taped in front of him, and his legs were bound together at the ankles.

'It's okay, sir. Come on out.'

She pushed open the door slowly until she heard a voice from farther inside the house. 'That's far enough. I saw your SWAT bus.'

Eckels turned sideways to slip through the crack in the door. He looked into her eyes intensely and gave her a slight shake of his head. He was trying to tell her something. He was telling her not to go inside.

Is . . . this . . . a . . . trap? She mouthed the words silently. Eckels responded with the same intense stare and a harder shake of his head.

'This is a trade, remember. You get in here before he gets out.'

405

Ellie turned sideways as well and pressed herself past Eckels. As the two exchanged places, she saw him blink back tears.

'Go,' she whispered. He looked at her one more time before hopping down the porch steps. She saw Foreman running to meet Eckels on the front lawn before she heard the voice behind her again.

'Shut that door.'

She closed the door, only to be slammed immediately against it. She could feel George Kittrie's body pressed against hers, his hands groping beneath her jacket. The weight of Rogan's Glock left the small of her back.

'That was quite a show when you dropped your weapon in the yard, Detective. I'm not that stupid.'

He yanked off her coat and threw it to the floor. He stepped away from her and moved farther into the house. Ellie turned and took in the layout.

At the front of the house, the living room shades were drawn. The vertical blinds that covered a set of sliding doors off the dining area in the back were pulled shut. He had positioned a wood-framed dining chair in the entry to a small hallway that broke away from the living area. He was smart. The entry to the hallway gave him cover from any incoming bullets.

'On the couch.' He gestured toward a beige sofa against the living room wall as he took his own protected seat in the hall, placing the gun in his left hand on the floor beside him. She tried to keep her eyes on his, but they automatically leapt to the glint of the silver blade on the knife in his right hand.

On another day, in a different context, the image

should have scared her. But instead Ellie felt emboldened. He had been holding a police lieutenant hostage. Now he had a new captive, exchanging one source of unpredictability for another. If he was at all comfortable with guns, she would be looking down the barrel of one – either his own or the one he'd just taken from her.

Her instincts had been right. Only one of Kittrie's victim had been shot – Darrell Washington – and, as Ken Garcia had said, whoever killed Washington had been a lousy marksman. He also used the same weapon Washington had wielded to rob Jordan and Stefanie, then left that gun at the scene. Kittrie's current location in the hallway ruled out immediate access to any place where another gun might be hidden.

She knew now what Eckels had been trying to tell her – Kittrie didn't have a gun. Kittrie had apparently managed to restrain her lieutenant before Eckels had established that critical fact. She wasn't going to let the same thing happen to her. She was a good, strong fighter. If the only advantage Kittrie had on her was a knife and Rogan's unloaded gun, she might just walk out of here alive.

She took a seat on the sofa as instructed and saw for the first time a pair of orange-handled sewing shears on a glass end table. Kittrie must have noted the movement of her glance, because he said, 'Unh-unh. Not yet. Later. I want to look at you here. Left hand into the cuffs.'

Only then did she notice a pair of handcuffs dangling from the same glass table where the scissors rested. One end was hooked through the table's wrought iron base. The other hung open. Ellie slid across the sofa, crossing her left leg in front of her, and closed the cuffs around her left wrist.

'So I would ask you to tell me about your father, but I know how you feel about men who've watched *Silence of the Lambs* too many times. I don't want to be a cliché.'

He was reciting from her *Dateline* interview. Ellie stared at him as if he were a lizard on display behind glass.

'Tell me about William Summer instead.'

'What about him?' she said.

'Why are you so convinced you would have found him earlier?'

'I found you, didn't I?'

'I was waiting to be found.'

'So was William Summer,' Ellie said. 'It's another thing you two have in common.'

'Tell me more about that.'

'You both have an ability to control the pace of your killings more than most profilers believe is common. You both stopped when something else in your lives brought you satisfaction, a feeling of accomplishment. You both resurfaced when your lives started to feel weak again – him because a newspaper article made him sound like an irrelevant relic, and you because there's cancer metastasized in your brain.'

'So would you say that I, like Summer, have an "insatiable ego"?'

'I don't purport to know you, Mr. Kittrie.'

'Neither did Rachel Peck or Chelsea Hart. Go ahead and pick up those scissors.'

Ellie wiggled her restrained left arm.

'Cute, Detective, but I'm sure you can manage.'

She raised the scissors with her right hand.

'Your hair, Detective. Is it naturally blond?'

'Yes.'

'I thought so. And is that the length you usually wear it?'

Ellie's hair was well past her shoulders, longer than it had ever been since she became a cop five years ago. There had been no time for a haircut in the past two months. 'No,' she said. 'I cut it this short a few months ago.'

For reasons she would never be able to explain, she took comfort in the small lie.

'Please go ahead and cut the rest of it off for me now.'

'Excuse me?'

'You saw Chelsea Hart, I believe. Go ahead. Not too quickly,' he said, unbuttoning his pants. Ellie suppressed a gag reflex.

She tilted her head and held the scissors up to the lock of hair that fell forward, but could not force herself to bring the blades together.

'Would you like to put the scissors down and find another way to do this, Detective?'

She clenched her jaw and clamped the scissors shut. Six inches of her hair fell to the floor. She reached forward to pick it up, but he stopped her.

'Leave it wherever it falls. It looks good that way.'

He was beginning to slowly pleasure himself. Ellie desperately wanted to avert her gaze, but knew that would disrupt the choreography. She opened the shears around another section and snipped again. Then a third section, and a fourth. She tried to stop thinking of the movement of his hand against himself.

She picked up the pace of her cutting and willed herself to look at Kittrie's pinched face, starting to color. She told herself she had to do this. She had to do this for five girls who had suffered far worse.

She saw the muscles in Kittrie's body begin to tense and she knew she would have only seconds to respond. She cut away another two clumps, feeling stronger with each lock that fell to the floor.

When Kittrie lurched forward, she was ready. She dropped the scissors and reached for the top of the left ankle boot crossed in front of her. She unsnapped her Kahr K9 and pulled the trigger softly to disengage the striker block and cock the weapon.

Kittrie opened his eyes and spun from his chair, dropping the knife as he reached for the Glock on the floor. She continued to press against the trigger, locking her elbow and tightening her forearm muscles to absorb the recoil.

She heard the blast of the pistol as her arm jerked against her will and searing pain tore through the wound in the back of her hand. A magenta stain slowly blossomed across the left sleeve of Kittrie's white shirt. She had clipped him in the shoulder.

Kittrie winced as he moved his left hand to support the Glock. Even through the pain of the gunshot wound, he managed a slight smile as he looked down at Ellie, handcuffed on the sofa, and pulled the trigger. Realizing his mistake, his smug expression changed to one of confusion, then anger. He threw the gun at her and lunged for the knife he'd discarded next to his chair.

Ellie fired again, this time a pair of quick shots, compensation for the lack of control that came with one-handed shooting. One bullet through the screen of Kittrie's television, one in his left side. Kittrie barreled toward her, the handle of his knife clenched in his fist.

She threw her body to the floor and drop-rolled in the direction of the end table. Using the leverage of her cuffed wrist against the wrought iron, she pulled herself up to a forty-five-degree angle. She leveled the butt of the K9 on her left forearm for support, and popped off three rapid-fire rounds.

All three shots landed in center mass. Kittrie's mouth formed a large O as he stumbled backward, then collapsed to the floor. Ellie allowed her own muscles to relax as the convulsions in his body subsided.

The sound of a thousand cars crashing at once broke the silence. A helmeted ESU officer emerged from the shattered sliding glass door just as Rogan burst through the front door at the head of a battering ram. They must have coordinated the simultaneous entries with the first shot fired. What had felt like an eternity to her had taken place in just seconds.

Ellie then saw the scene in the living room through their eyes. Kittrie dead, shot five times with his pants around his knees. Ellie handcuffed to a table, lying on the floor in a pile of her own hair. She looked at Rogan and began to laugh, hysterically and uncontrollably, until she found herself sobbing harder than she had in years.

Chapter Forty-Nine

'No one told me it was prom night.'

John Shannon set his roast beef sandwich on his napkin and used the back of his hand to wipe a smear of mustard from the corner of his mouth. Given Rogan's usual appearance, his black suit and gray silk tie would never have drawn Shannon's attention. But Ellie's wardrobe change in the locker room was apparently another story.

Thanks to their squad neighbor, all eyes in the room were on her. Shannon's partner let out a wolf whistle. Someone else asked if she was already trying on outfits for this year's Medal Day Ceremony, a reference to the broad speculation that she would be receiving the Police Combat Cross for her role in what the media were now calling the Manhattan Barber case. Apparently the press didn't see the irony in retaining the sensationalist nickname originally conjured by George Kittrie for his own byline.

Ellie looked down at her black wool A-line dress and slingback pumps, and touched the fringe of her new, very short hairdo. The fact that this stood out as a special effort had her rethinking her everyday attire.

Dan Eckels emerged from his office and placed his hands on his hips. 'Quiet down out here. So Hatcher cleans up all right. Leave the woman alone.'

She sucked in her cheeks and faked a model's awkward pose, and a few more detectives broke into laughter. It had been four days since she killed George Kittrie, and she'd noticed the ongoing efforts to make her smile. It was too soon to know whether the new thaw in the ice was a sign that she had passed some kind of litmus test with the squad, or just a temporary warm front.

'Great. See what happens when I try to stick up for you? You're encouraging these assclowns.'

She looked at her lieutenant for some kind of confirmation of the rumor she'd heard the previous night at Plug Uglies. Apparently questions regarding the whereabouts of Eckels's gun when he was abducted had led to some kind of investigation into his extracurricular activities. If the rumors were true, Eckels seemed surprisingly untroubled. Perhaps surviving his night with Kittrie had given him a new perspective on life. Or maybe the rumors were just rumors.

'I believe the two of you have somewhere to be?' Eckels asked pointedly.

'Oh, they need to be somewhere all right,' Shannon said. ' "*Going to the chapel, and we're gonna get married.*" '

Ellie held her palms against her ears until Rogan handed her her coat. They could still hear the squad's off-tune singing when they hit the staircase.

* * *

Rogan parked half a block away from their destination on Bleecker Street.

'This was really generous of you, J. J.'

'Stop thanking me.'

They made their way inside and were directed to a room off the main entrance hall. Powder blue velvet curtains hung from ceiling to floor. Mauve upholstered chairs were lined up neatly in four rows. About a third of the seats were already occupied.

Ellie recognized a bulky man in the front row. Detective Hank Dodge gave her a nod of acknowledgment, and she returned the gesture.

At the front of the room, a blowup of Rachel Peck's author photo, the one that never had the chance to grace the back of a book jacket, rested on an easel next to a simple wreath of pastel roses and a closed casket.

Ellie had phoned Rachel's father three days earlier, pleading with him to claim his daughter's body so she would not be buried in a cardboard box on Hart Island, where prison inmates stacked the coffins five high. By the time Ellie hung up on the man, she'd called him several names she was pretty sure weren't supposed to be directed at a man of God.

She would never have asked Rogan to pay for a funeral, but he had caught her side of the conversation. An hour after she hung up on the Reverend Elijah Peck, Rogan had already set a time and a place. All she had to do was notify Rachel's friend Gina.

Ellie felt a lump in her throat when she saw a familiar face in the back of the room. Her brother had even worn a sports coat for the occasion.

'Where'd you get this?' she whispered, tugging at his sleeve.

'Don't ask, at least not without Miranda warnings.'

As they took three seats in the back row, Jess and Rogan muttered their hellos in the whispery tones that came automatically in these settings.

'You are such a softie,' she said, giving her brother's shoulder a little squeeze.

'It's no big deal.'

She had told him that morning that she was worried no one would show up at the funeral home. As she looked around the room, she realized her concerns had been misplaced. Rachel may not have had a family, but she had been a woman with friends.

One of those friends took her place now at a lectern beside Rachel's photograph. She introduced herself as Gina DaCosta. She told the guests that she didn't know what she was supposed to say at her best friend's funeral. The nice man who ran the home had suggested a few prayers that would be appropriate, but they all knew that Rachel would come back and haunt her ass for allowing any such thing. So instead she talked about Rachel's generosity. Her talent. The night she'd given herself a concussion trying to leapfrog a parking meter on Jones Street. She invited others to share their memories as well. No sad talk allowed, she warned.

Ellie recognized the latecomer slipping quietly into the room. Finding a seat, he spotted her in the back and gave her a sad smile. She raised a hand for a quick wave. She had known he was the kind of man who would be here today.

As people took their turns at the front of the room, she clasped her hands in her lap, closed her eyes, and silently delivered her own testimonial: *I had three days to save Rachel after I found Chelsea on Monday morning. It wasn't enough. I wasted thirty-six hours going through the motions while I had three cold cases in my backpack telling me something was wrong. Thirty-six hours would have made the difference. I had three days, and I failed. I second-guessed my own instincts. I wasn't confident enough. Next time, I won't hesitate. Next time, I will picture Rachel and Chelsea, and I'll be better.*

When Ellie opened her eyes, she felt her guilt begin to wash away. She felt at peace. She felt like she belonged here, in this room, at that moment. She felt normal.

Tonight, after Jess left for work, and from the solitude of her living room, she would do one last thing before turning the page on the case. She would call Bill Harrington and thank him for phoning the tip line. She would thank him for listening to Robbie.

Author's note

I've often heard it said that writers conjure up plots by starting with an initial observation and then asking themselves over and over again: *What if?*

On February 25, 2006, New York City graduate student Imette St. Guillen was barhopping in SoHo with a girlfriend. The friend called it quits, but St. Guillen stayed behind for one last drink. Her nearly unrecognizable body was found the next day. Five months later, eighteen-year-old Jennifer Moore was drinking in a Chelsea nightclub with a girlfriend when city authorities towed her car. Denied access to her vehicle at the impound lot, she wandered off alone along the West Side Highway. Her body was discovered in a New Jersey trashbin. In the fall of 2007, reports were filed by two separate women who claimed that they had been kidnapped and then raped after leaving the Box, one of Manhattan's hottest nightclubs, on their own.

I began to ask myself, *What if Ellie Hatcher caught cases like these and saw a connection where no one else did?*

The inspiration for *City of Fear* lies in none of the above-mentioned cases, and yet in all of them. For many of us – especially women – that alcohol-fueled argument at two in the morning is familiar. Someone wants to go home. Someone wants to stay behind for one last drink. I have been both of those women, and I have been lucky. But I know from the cases I saw as a prosecutor, and from the string of tragic cases reported in New York City, that sometimes the luck runs out. *City of Fear* is fiction, but the danger that made me ask *What if?* is real and universal.

My hope is that the policing depicted in *City of Fear* is also portrayed authentically. Having learned most of what I know about cops as a prosecutor in Oregon and as a law professor in New York, I have been assisted in my depiction of Ellie Hatcher's professional life by the generosity and knowledge of others. For helping me transition from the prosecutorial viewpoint to the police perspective, and from the localized norms of Portland to the culture of the NYPD, I am grateful to Assistant District Attorney Matthew Connolly, Nassau County; Retired Desk Sergeant Edward Devlin, NYPD; George Q. Fong, Unit Chief, National Gang Targeting Enforcement and Coordination Center, Deputy Program Director, National Gang Intelligence Center, FBI Headquarters (phew); Chief Carla Piluso, Gresham Police Department (who confirms that female detectives do in fact carry purses); and the anonymous desk sergeant at the Thirteenth Precinct who served as my impromptu tour guide. I especially appreciate the input of Retired Lieutenant Al Kaplan, NYPD, who didn't know me from a hole in the ground but helped me out anyway.

I was also helped by my agent, Philip Spitzer, Lukas Ortiz, Fauzia Burke at FSB Associates, my family, and the incredible team at Harper. Special thanks to my friend and editor Jennifer Barth.

Read on for a look at Ellie Hatcher's profile . . .

PROFILE

CONFIDENTIAL

Name: Ellie Hatcher, short for Elsa May.

Occupation: NYPD Detective, Homicide Squad.

Age: 31.

Location: Manhattan.

Place of Birth: Wichita, Kansas.

Marital Status: Serial monogamist.

Children: Does the older brother who crashes on my sofa count?

Smoke: Quit (usually).

Drink: Johnnie Walker Black, cold beer.

Exercise Habits: Kick boxing, but I promise not to hurt you.

Father: Jerry Hatcher, Wichita homicide detective. Lead detective on famous College Hill Strangler case. Deceased. I'd prefer not talking about the circumstances.

Mother: Roberta Hatcher. Retired book-keeper in Wichita. Talk to her every night, whether I want to or not.

Education: Started with some pre-law classes at Wichita State University, then followed my brother Jess to New York so someone could keep an eye on him. Decided I wanted to be a cop, and then earned my degree at John Jay College while waiting tables.

Appearance: Blond hair, blue eyes. The next person who tells me I look like a Midwestern beauty queen is risking a roundhouse kick to the chest.

Do for fun: Hang out with the afore-mentioned sofa-crashing brother, usually in the West Village, sometimes watching his band (Dog Park) play, and almost always keeping him out of trouble. Take-out and TV's OK too.

Politics: To be avoided.

Religious views: Don't be a jerk.

Music: The Clash, The Pretenders, Dog Park.

Best feature: Dogged curiosity.

Biggest Fear: Failure.

LIFE SENTENCES

Laura Lippman

What if you found out that the central story of your life was a lie?

Writer Cassandra Fellows has achieved remarkable success baring her soul in her bestselling memoirs. But returning to her hometown of Baltimore on the trail of new material she stumbles into the middle of a mystery which takes her back to her schooldays.

Growing up, Cassandra's best friends were elegant, privileged Donna, sharp, shrewd Tisha and the wild and worldly Fatima. But a fifth girl orbited their world – a shy, quiet child named Calliope Jenkins – who hit the headlines years later, accused of killing her infant son.

Yet the boy's body was never found and Calliope refused to give up the whereabouts of her missing child. Jailed for seven years, the court was finally forced to let her go. But why did she remain silent? And whatever happened to the little boy?

Cassandra believes this real-life mystery could be her next bestseller.

But her homecoming is not welcomed by everyone. And by delving too deeply into Calliope's dark secrets, Cassandra inadvertently unearths a few of her own – forcing her to re-examine the memories she holds most precious, as the stark light of truth illuminates the past . . .

ISBN: 978-1-84756-093-3

Out in March 2009

SHADOWS STILL REMAIN

Peter de Jonge

When a gifted student mysteriously disappears from a New York bar, Detective Darlene O'Hara unravels a chilling story of murder and deception.

Running from a troubled past, Francesca Pena's come to New York to reinvent herself, earning a scholarship and the admiration of her more privileged friends. But none of them knows the real Francesca.

Following a night of partying with three friends, she's reported missing. Detective Darlene O'Hara from New York's 7th Precinct and her partner Serge Karamanoukian – 'K' – investigate.

A week later, Francesca's body is discovered severely mangled in a toilet by the East River. The case quickly becomes a high-profile hunt that the Homicide Unit are quick to snatch away.

Covertly, O'Hara and K continue their own investigation in the city's seedy underbelly. And they could never have predicted what they would uncover.

From Peter de Jonge, who previously joined forces with the *New York Times* bestselling author James Patterson to write two No.1 bestsellers, comes a tense and electric thriller set in the rotten core of the Big Apple.

ISBN: 978-1-84756-056-8

Out in April 2009